RETURN

By
Don Hayward

© 2023

Acknowledgements

As always, my wife Diane and my beta-reader, Alex provided corrections, insight and encouragement.

Any errors are the author's responsibility.

Inspiration

Taken: Steven Spielberg Producer
Sci-Fi Channel from December 2 to 13, 2002.
Produced by DreamWorks Television
Paramount Worldwide Television
Created by Leslie Bohem
https://en.wikipedia.org/wiki/Taken_(miniseries)#Production

E.T. (Spielberg 1982 Written by Melissa Mathison)
Close Encounters of the Third Kind (Spielberg 1977)

Return is a sequel and homage to Steven Spielberg's mini-series Taken. It does not pretend to achieve the level of a Spielberg approved script, but it attempts to embrace his portrayal of aliens as a non-aggressive and perhaps a bit of a bumbling entity.

It would be helpful to the reader to have watched the ten-part mini-series, first aired in 2002 and to be familiar with E.T. and Close Encounters of the Third Kind to get a feel for Spielberg's portrayal of star visitors.

You will not find invading space monsters here.

Some of the character names from Taken, and general references to events from the series appear here to give continuity.

This is not an official sequel and no one connected with the television series has sanctioned it. The promised sequel did not appear, and after 18 years of waiting, I decided to write my version.

-D.H.

Also by Don Hayward

The collapse thread: Five book thread about economic collapse

Collapse

Under Shadows

The End of shadows

The Seventh Path

Journey's End

Other stories

Murder on the Goderich Local

Sherwood Green   A story of eco-resistance

Echo of the Whip-poor-will   Biographical story of Don's early life

High Falls - A pictorial history of High Falls on the Spanish River

---

Contact Don: haywardon@gmail.com

https://www.danddhayward.ca/

Chapter One

Happiness

Hello listeners, this is Quantz Nedmar of CBC Radio One coming to you this morning from a secret location in Goderich, Ontario. This is the first segment of many interviews I will have with Charlie Keys, the father of Ellie Keys. Because of the recent spectacular events, Ellie's name is likely on all of your minds. Most of you have seen lights in the sky and perhaps ships for yourselves. Otherwise, I am sure anyone with internet or television has seen the almost unbelievable video by my colleagues, Jimmy Smith and Bobby Briscoe. Both of my friends have spent much more time with the visitors than I have and Jimmy has travelled hundreds of millions of kilometres with them. I have spoken to Ellie, and she introduced me to her father, Charlie. The situation is still dangerous as I sit here in this cozy room with Charlie Keys opposite. We might have to move often to keep us both safe. Everyone, from governments to the mobs, wants a piece of Charlie Keys.

Please, go ahead Charlie; tell the listeners your story.

Why am I telling you all this, Quantz? I have no clue, but I know I need to tell someone. I have just lost someone I loved, murdered by the CIA. Now, I'm afraid we are going to lose my daughter once more. The pain and joy inside my heart must escape somehow. Quantz, you migrated to Canada. You know what it's like to be an alien.

It all began in 1947 in Texas over 20 years ago, when a starship disappeared with our daughter. The hole that the alien craft made in the Texas sky so long ago lingered as rifts in Lisa's heart and mine. I could never share Lisa's grief, a mother's grief, but my sorrow consumed me, at least until last September. We could not give each other the comfort we needed, and we drifted apart. Lisa returned to Seattle, played in her band and now teaches music at a state college. We both are trying to keep living our lives despite this furor that is all around us.

I fled to Canada, away from the sorrow and tragedy, to be somewhere that did not remind me of either. You can never run fast enough or far enough. Neither of us could be completely free of that old farmhouse in Texas. It stayed in Lisa's family, and when her uncle died, she inherited the title. Every year, on the anniversary of them taking Ellie, we return to the place, seeking comfort, but invariably only deepening the voids in our hearts. We could not stay away, as if it were a scab that we could not stop picking.

Somehow, despite the remembered pain, it also healed us and gave us another year of hope. We both hoped that on one of these anniversaries she would miraculously return as if the date would somehow be of the same significance to her and to them. Like everything about our daughter, she would surprise us, but Ill get to that.

What... yes, Ellie is our daughter, and she inherited some alien blood from Lisa. Neither of us ever married or had a new family. We would say that we had never met the right person, well; I thought I hadn't, but we both knew we were lying to each other and ourselves. Ellie lived somewhere up there, and she was the family we both longed for. The aliens had brought us together to make Ellie. It was not our doing, and that we care deeply for each other makes no difference. Lisa and I both know we were never to be a couple.

Okay, perhaps I am bigoted. Lisa, too, is part alien, and my treatment by the star visitors created a still-festering hatred that their reclaiming of our daughter only softened to anger.

The reason I did not waste my days plotting murderous revenge is I know Ellie did not want that, and she is more of them than she is of me.

I know, I know, get on with it. Here have some more coffee.

There were never any lights in the sky after they took her, at least nothing that I could consider the visitors. Everything went quiet and UFO sightings died down to the level of crackpot stories. Some might have been true, but most people made them up. Although some just wanted to believe, many knew the truth.

Even though the crowd was huge in Texas that day, with an entire battalion of soldiers too, along with television, the event gradually became a myth. The official government denials did not help, although they fuelled conspiracy theories. Sadly, those theories were mostly true. There were many bad people, both official and rogue operators. In one case, it was that family against ours. They were obsessed and nearly killed Ellie, but sceptics doubted and then derided them. Soon, it was back to true believers and adamant deniers. The moon landing hoax community led the charge. Everyone at the farm that day kept quiet. The old abductees had had enough; the reporters didn't want to ruin their careers by being labelled crackpots, and the military followed orders. When a few retired soldiers wrote books, no one took them seriously. I'll give you a reading list. Most of them are accurate.

This climate of disbelief pleased me. No one came looking for me, at least after the initial few months, but that was enough to force me to flee to Canada. Up here, even though probably some had heard of the incident in Texas, most were not interested in intruding into anyone's life, and no one ever recognized me. I kept a low profile and got a factory job in this little backwater in Ontario.

Do I feel safe with people knowing where I am?

Yes, they can't harm me now. Sure, some people might want to hurt me or use me to extort Ellie somehow. The CIA already tried, but she and the aliens have no worries about that. Even if they threatened me, her work will go on. I won't say how, but they protect me. We're meeting in this hotel for your safety. Some of these same people don't want the truth out there. They are afraid of the people and can't control them unless they keep them ignorant.

"So," you ask, "what's the story?"

Twenty years is a long time. I rose into management in our company. My job took me between our Goderich headquarters and another plant in Orangeville. I could schedule my holidays in April for the Texas trip, and it allowed me to own a country place just north of town. My place has a marvellous view out over the lake with open fields inland. That let me see much of the sky, and the nights were darker. Many nights I sat out in the dark, watching. Perhaps I expected that one night a big saucer would come down and Ellie would emerge in white robes or something. In these bad times, we all hope for a saviour.

Ellie is over 30 years old now, our time anyway. I do not know how they measure time, or age, out there.

Is she happy? We wanted to have her with us so badly. Perhaps Lisa and I would be together if Ellie had stayed. It was her choice not to hurt us, but to keep so many others from being hurt and perhaps dying. That last look on her face just before she went up, she suffered too; she didn't want to go; Ellie sacrificed all her happiness for our safety. I love her...

Oh sorry, did I space out again? I do that a lot. My mind wanders back. It's funny, despite recent events, I still daydream in the present tense; I had those thoughts so often over the years. Even now, even though I'm more content, even though Ellie's return has given me peace, I still sometimes travel back to those years.

Okay... back to it...

Even after 20 years, I would startle at a meteor, or a bright satellite passing over. I almost despise the space stations, and those regular launches of communication satellites and the ships preparing for the Mars transfers almost mimic an appearance from long ago. I became blasé about these things, so I was unprepared for the real thing.

Could you pass me one of those donuts, please? Pumpkin will do.

You look fidgety as if you don't believe me. You don't believe my daughter is part alien, or she went with them, or that her mother, my forced lover, is part alien. Well, that's okay, as long as you listen, but it all happened and is still happening. Several US government insiders risked their lives. The star people wanted them to remain quiet until they announced themselves. They didn't want these people in harm's way, but reporters like you put events out of control... oh, sorry... no harm meant.

... back to my story. For two years, we didn't get to go to Texas, with the pandemic and then the troubles down there. This year we went, and it was the usual refreshing disappointment, but with a difference. On the second night, we sat on the porch step, sipping beer and watching the sky. Lisa sobbed and said she felt sure that we would see Ellie soon. When I asked why, she looked far away and said, "It's just a feeling, but it has been growing for months. I'm sure."

She hadn't cried in a few years and I thought perhaps it was because of the two years gap, but she shook her head. "It's real," she said, "I've seen lights. They're looking for me."

I hugged her and made reassuring noises, but I dared not hope. The Texas sky teased me. I heard Lisa restless in her room. About 3 AM, I got up and took a beer to the porch. I sat enjoying the cool air and brilliant sky when the lights came. It took a minute to accept that they were different, moving in a perfect equilateral triangle, not like those Mars transfer ships in parallel lines. The formation passed over the house, so I ran into the yard. I don't know if they stopped, but they seemed to be too high in the sky by the time I could look over the roof. They moved off in formation. I watched the rest of the night and only saw human orbiters. I had seen nothing for 20 years that resembled a visitor ship, and I was still not sure what I saw.

They move a certain way, you know. That's why those damned comsat and Mars launches are so aggravating. They could fool you, but they always make a straight line.

I watched Lisa for the rest of the visit, hoping she wasn't cracking up. She has always been more stable than I have, but Ellie and Lisa had a mother-daughter bonding, and maybe that had worn on her. Lisa seemed to be fine, and we never talked about it again, not even in one of our regular e-mails.

I came home and spent another summer of sky watching, not knowing if Lisa still thought she saw lights. Hell, I wondered if I had seen something that night. I stay out of the UFO loop and did not hear of the new sightings all over, but especially around Texas and Seattle. In hindsight, it's logical I saw nothing. Without a tracking device, they had no way of knowing I was here, but they knew where Lisa lived.

Science fiction attracts many fanatics. People didn't expect how ordinary and unspectacular Ellie's return would be. Aside from the light show from alien ships, it might seem that nothing happened. You have heard governments say that the alien contact is a hoax. It took a big show to convince everyone. I don't think the aliens planned to appear the way it happened. Ellie told me that the Mars crisis surprised them.

Don't worry. I'll get to it all soon. I just like your company. I've been alone for too long.

Yes, yes, you can say loneliness drove me mad, and that's where this crazy story came from, but you don't believe that. You've seen the evidence, or you wouldn't even be here, so listen. You want the background. It will make your career.

The summer passed with nothing happening. My eagerness had gone long before, but Lisa and the Texas sky had stirred me, so I spent extra time outside, especially at night. Perhaps what we saw 20 years ago would reappear. It didn't occur to me they might have improved their techniques and could exploit our space efforts. The quiet skies lulled me back to my old resignation.

Then, I received an e-mail from Lisa.

"She's on the planet."

I replied with a dozen questions, but Lisa did not answer. I received the message early in the morning, before I drove to our plant in Orangeville. Lisa was silent all day. I cursed her for teasing me.

Anyway, our teamwork initiative had faltered in Orangeville, and I intended to motivate the managers to take it seriously. It would be a pleasant cheerleading day with a nice dinner before the drive back. The meetings went on longer than I expected and dinner ended at 11 PM, so I only got on the road a bit before midnight.

Charlie stared into the dark, sliding along County Road 34, and looked forward to bed. The day of meetings and then the too long excursion to the pub for dinner took their toll. He cranked up the Toronto jazz station to keep alert.

The car drove itself, a nice Martian X, the latest in the line and named in honour of the first crewed Xplorer landing on Mars a decade before. Charlie's unease with the technology kept him alert and was a long way from the banger pickup he had been driving.

The car sped along within its sensor zone. Charlie thought of the similar nights, long ago, when the stars might move and some alien surprise would snatch him from reality before dumping him disjointedly back on Earth. His resentment for that still smouldered, but he no longer feared. They had removed the tracking device and abandoned him after they bred him with Lisa. Charlie lived with the assurance that Ellie had enough importance that the aliens would honour her last promise to him and all abductees that they would never violate them again.

It's likely, he thought as he sped through the night, *that they won't do it to anyone else. Ellie's sacrifice accomplished so much, but the pain has been an enormous price for Lisa, me, and Ellie.*

The thought of Ellie reminded him of Lisa's cryptic message of the morning. Charlie pulled up his e-mail on the dash-pad display. The Starlink connection made it instantaneous.

Nothing...

Charlie dictated a quick e-mail, asking the same question he had sent in the morning, and added a plea for Lisa to answer him. It came almost immediately:

"Soon, you'll know everything. We will all be together soon." She included a silly, smiling face.

The car topped a small ridge, and a bright glow appeared just beyond the next rise. His heart raced. The light looked so familiar with a flickering yellow and blue reflecting from low clouds and dancing in the early fall mists.

No...!

The car sped on, oblivious to Charlie's emotions. The road dipped to cross Timm's Creek, and the glow grew stronger as they slid up the next rise. Mist produced cascading shafts of pink, blue, green, and flashing yellow. Flashbacks to horror and memories of sadness hit Charlie. He gripped the wheel but did not disengage the autopilot. They crested and suddenly, in all its miserable industrial glory, the yard of a large pork operation and grain depot glowed to the right under the glare of vapour lamps so strong they lit the sky.

Damn, why don't they use full cut-off lighting? Neanderthals...

Charlie calmed; fear, or was it hope, faded, and he concentrated on the music. The Martian X fled into darkness and soon cleared the roundabout at Wingham. It seemed instantly they were on Donnybrook Road and nearly home. Lightning flashed to the southeast.

I must have dozed off.

The radio spluttered as if passing out of range of the transmitter. He switched to the internet. The network was down. Starlink had never failed before. At the top of a hill, the farmyard light that marked the long descent to the Maitland River did not appear.

Strange...

Charlie's eyes grew heavy as the long day stubbornly overtook him. He drifted into a transition between thoughts and a strange dream. His quiet stupor ended. The car braked to a stop that threw him against his harness. Two figures stood in the headlight cone. He blinked at a doe and her fawn. Unhurriedly, it seemed, they blinked back. *Do deer have eyelids? Thank god for the car. The software is great, but...* he glanced at the time display. *It's after midnight, usually too late for deer... something spooked them.*

Charlie searched into the darkness, looking for the culprit, some hunter illegally jack lighting white tails out of season. He refocused on the road. The pair eased off into the opposite ditch, not acting spooked, and disappeared as if satisfied the car was harmless. They certainly did not seem to be afraid.

The autopilot had disengaged and patiently waited for orders. Charlie reached for the touch screen.

What... movement... to the left on the edge of the bush where the deer disappeared.

Through the half-light at the edge of the headlamps' field, two human forms emerged onto the road.

A young woman and a girl... what are they doing out here so late?

Charlie's mind raced, but his thoughts froze.

Both figures wore matching dresses that seemed too flimsy for the cool of a September night.

They slowly approached Charlie's Martian X. The driver's door window rolled down. He balanced between panic and hope.

"Hi, Dad," the woman said.

"Grandpa," the little girl said.

Chapter Two

Breakfast

"If we could all begin every day with an unanswerable question, we would have a day full of thoughtful wonder." -**Ellie Keys.**

Charlie had a dream, a kaleidoscope of light, dark, action, peace, happiness, then sorrow, and then happiness once more. It was a vivid rewind of that final night when aliens had taken Ellie — no, when Ellie had gone with her alien family. When the morning sun woke him, Charlie sat in his car in his driveway, alone, rested and somehow comforted by his dream.

Damn, that self-driving thing is good, he thought.

His e-mail demanded attention, Lisa's avatar.

"I said that you would find out soon enough."

"Find out what? I had a dream."

"No, you didn't, at least not in the normal sense. You relived that night at the farm in your head, didn't you?"

"But the dream ended happily. That night was so sad."

"The happiness is now, Charlie. You'll know that soon. Bye for now." Lisa sent another silly smiley icon.

Hunger gnawed. It seemed appropriate to make a breakfast of steak, eggs, and home fries. Lisa's uncle at the Texas farmhouse had always insisted on what he called "a Texas breakfast".

The steak neared done, along with the chopped and seasoned potatoes. He cracked two eggs and watched them sizzling in beef fat.

"I hope you have enough for three," the soft voice came from behind, "Mom only served health food, organic veggie stuff; Seattle, you know."

Charlie turned.

The moment, the reality suspended in twenty years of longing, those years folded into realization. Her face matured but her face, her smile and wide eyes, as they had been that last night in the Texas pasture.

Charlie dropped the eggshells. His eyes blurred with tears.

"I didn't mean to surprise you, Dad, but..."

"Yes you did, Mother," a youthful voice as soft as the woman's, teased. "You always tell the jack-in-the-box stories."

"No, I don't, Âطنلإ". Ellie, she was indeed Ellie, or perhaps Charlie's wishful hallucination of Ellie smiled down at the girl. Charlie could not make out the name, which seemed like an impossible string of ear-shattering alien sounds. The little girl, or at least what appeared to be a little girl, shot a string of sounds back at Ellie's apparition. Ellie giggled and turned to Charlie.

"Oh, I'm sorry, Dad. That's her star name, as I like to call it. Her Earth name is Roberta Heather. Mom and I, and of course RoH herself, decided on the contraction RoH to avoid confusion, and because no one can pronounce her star name without living there. It links to the stars. Names out there are honorifics of the parents' names but with some extra meaning, although conception is usually clinical now. What we call parents are simply contributors of the genetic material, another thing my star family has lost, but not in my case. I insisted I raise RoH." Ellie had a twinkle in her eye and RoH giggled out some alien gibberish.

"Naughty, Âطنلإ, I'm glad your grandfather didn't understand that, and yes, your great grandfather did eagerly adopt the Earthling ways. You don't need to be graphic."

Still laughing, she turned to Charlie. "To be serious, Mother understood the explanation. Roberta Heather is your second name, Robert, and her second, Heather, combined to meet local cultural norms. We decided, since your granddaughter is new ground, that she should have a gender-neutral name, and so RoH is the contraction."

"It's just because I'm short," RoH pouted.

"Shut up," Ellie giggled. "You'll be an ice moon stalagmite soon enough."

RoH brightened.

The steak popped, and the eggs threatened to burn. Charlie found the strength to take them off the heat.

"There isn't enough for us all." Charlie could say nothing but the mundane. He felt numb.

"You eat, Dad. I'll make more."

Ellie stepped around the table and wrapped her arms around her father. Charlie's arms embraced her for the first time in over 20 years. She had seemed so small and frail back then and easily fit onto his lap. His tears flowed. Loud, long sobs accompanied his trembling body, and he hung on for dear life.

"Just like Grandma," RoH giggled.

"I love you, baby," Charlie's mumbles sounded through the sobs.

"Be happy, Dad, be happy," Ellie kissed his neck. "We love you."

"I'm hungry," RoH suggested, tiring of the emotional scene, the same one she had witnessed in Seattle an Earth day before.

"Children never change," Ellie released Charlie.

"You have." Charlie stared into her eyes.

"I know," Ellie quietly said, "but for the better, Dad. I'm happy."

"Eat, Dad, get me the stuff for more."

Charlie fetched steak from the freezer along with eggs and potatoes.

"The steak's frozen. This will all take a half-hour." Charlie put the contents of the steel skillet onto his plate. "Use the microwave."

"Sit, Dad," Ellie gently supported the dazed Charlie to the table. She turned to the stove.

Charlie had barely splashed some ketchup onto his home fries when Ellie placed two perfectly done steak breakfasts onto the table.

"How...?" Charlie stammered.

"I used to watch Uncle Tom do breakfast," Ellie's smile teased.

This memory cleared Charlie's head.

"More like some alien magic," he smiled. RoH giggled.

"Not magic, Dad, but there's a more efficient way to direct energy."

"If your mind can do it," Charlie muttered.

"Yes, if your mind can do it, and Earth isn't ready for that." For the first time, Ellie had a serious expression. "It's not yet something Earthlings should know how to do. Maybe in the future, we hope."

Despite the alien speed that the food had cooked, breakfast quietly lingered. Ellie and Charlie savoured being together. RoH ate, but she seemed thoughtful, and Charlie watched her look around as if absorbing the kitchen. She then gazed at her grandfather with the same quiet, piercing eyes of her mother as a ten-year-old. Her smile washed over him.

It seemed as if a feather touched his mind. Charlie suddenly felt happiness, a completeness that he had never experienced before, and love.

Chapter Three

Safety and Doubt

Quantz, I hope you are patient. You won't be able to do this in one show, I'm sure. At least you can't do that and tell the entire story.

"I want to tell the complete story."

It'll be the story so far. We haven't seen the end, but hopefully, Earth will, or at least, the end of the beginning of something good, better.

"In some ways, it's already better."

Aliens came here because they sensed goodness on Earth; evil too, of course, but they hoped the good would win. They had lost any concept of that in their advanced state, and they felt that, somehow, human diversity, our capacity for good, for empathy is something worth having, if it can indeed vanquish evil. They think it is the next evolutionary step. Ellie is that step and the bridge with humans and all life.

"You're philosophical."

Ellie made me think about these things. Before they took me, before I met Lisa, before Ellie, I was brain dead. All that suffering woke me up. Now I'm happier than I could have imagined. Except...

Ellie and RoH are taking care of Lisa and me; they want to take care of everyone. They can't, you know. Humans have to do it ourselves.

There is something else, though, something Ellie isn't telling me. I felt a brief flash of fear from both of them. There is something in the background, something to upset even these powerful aliens. Oh, maybe I'm just making that up. It was a fleeting feeling, nothing I guess...

-from my conversations with Ellie's father and recorded before the Mars event.   (Quantz Nedmar–CBC News.)

"**D**ad," Ellie's voice pulled Charlie from his euphoria, "I have something serious to say, and hopefully do, right now. Mom said yes, but you can refuse, and that will be fine."

Charlie shuddered, and a sudden chill overtook his newfound contentment.

"What?" he feared the answer, expecting some more heartache, another loss.

"What I have to do on Earth might put you in danger and Mom, too. If we knew where you were at all times, we could keep you safe."

"We...?" Charlie trembled.

"My family there," Ellie glanced towards the ceiling. "Great Grandfather is near. Part of this effort since he started it all."

"My dad is with him," RoH said proudly.

"I want to do something so we can locate you. You can say no. The original experiments were so invasive and upsetting, but I hope you agree. This will be nothing like that, only a beacon that your mind will control. We all understand that the struggle between good and evil is human, and it will be a long time before that goes away. I came back to show that the path towards good is the only way to the stars, but there will be resistance and horrible efforts to stop me and..." Ellie's voice trailed off and she seemed to catch herself.

"And what...?" Charlie asked.

"I want to protect you. I love you."

Ellie wrapped her arms around Charlie. His feeling of love and contentment became real. Small arms wrapped around his waist and flooded him with the euphoria RoH's smile had raised at the table. He looked down to see his granddaughter smiling up. For that, he would agree to anything.

"Yes," Charlie whispered.

"I know it is hard for you, Dad. I know we... they inflicted so much pain on you using the old ways. That won't happen again. I promised when I left, and it still holds; however, if you are ever in danger, we will know. We will always know where you and Mom are."

"It's okay, sweetie," he looked at Ellie and then RoH, "I love you."

Ellie reached out to touch Charlie's forearm. Charlie felt strangeness, just for an instant, and then Ellie's lips soothed his arm.

"It's done, Dad, undetectable," she kissed again. "Just so you know, sometime you might think you are in danger. You might have to endure it and wonder where we might be. We will know when to let things develop before we do something. Never be afraid."

"How did you find me last night?" Charlie had puzzled over that since Ellie and RoH had appeared.

"Mom told me."

"How did you find Mom?"

"Mom told me." Ellie giggled.

"That's circular logic."

"Dad, remember Mom and I have a strong bond, feeling each other's presence, even during those horrible times that the government had me? Even when away, all these past years, I could feel her, and she told me she could always feel me. Remember, she is part star people."

"She told me she thought you were near just this year at the farm." Charlie thought back. "I thought she made it up in her mind."

"No, but she could never be sure."

"When you were at the farm this year, you saw our craft pass over. That was RoH's father. I asked him to watch over the place. It has terrible memories, and I always feared someone would find and harm you there. It reassured me."

"I was on the road last night, but you came to me out there. How did that happen?"

"That fancy car of yours talks to the sky all the time. Mom told me all about it and gave me your e-mail address. We intercepted your car's signal. The rest was easy. RoH wanted to do the doe and fawn trick. She remembered an Earth fable I used to tell her. As I say, she's an imp."

"Show us outside, Grandpa. Earth is different, not like anywhere I've been." RoH grabbed Charlie's hand and led him towards the door. "Please show me Earth."

"Dad, do you remember I once said that the universe was full of questions and maybe there were no answers? I'm not here with answers either, but there are questions. The main one is if humans can overcome their capacity for evil with a greater capacity for good. Can empathy triumph? The crowd that protected me the night I left had empathy."

"We saw it from you, especially in your deciding to leave." Charlie adjusted his position on the back step and Ellie snuggled closer. RoH lay on the grass examining a dandelion flower and seemed to sing to it.

"It was the hardest thing I ever did, so lonely at first, but I gradually discovered it was worth it. I already knew it was necessary to protect those I loved. You know I love everyone, don't you, Dad?"

"Yes," Charlie said, "we all need to be like you."

"I'm not complete, Father. I'm not the ultimate." Ellie gazed down at RoH, who had now shifted her attention to a healthy-looking plantain and gingerly massaged its leaves.

"Mimicking you would be a grand step for humans."

"I'm only the X version, Dad. There is a possibility, though, for both Earth and the stars, the Y version."

RoH sat up as a passing wasp caught her attention.

"Mom used to say that we find the biggest lessons in the smallest things. RoH learns those lessons all the time." Ellie smiled at RoH.

"They are beautiful, aren't they, RoH?" Ellie called out. The warmth in her face took Charlie back through the years to when Ellie might be in thrall to nature. It was a warm place in his memory.

"Mom is a wonderful musician," Ellie suddenly changed the topic and Charlie thought perhaps she had finished the line of thought.

"She showed me videos of her students. One young boy, about RoH's age, studies at the college and is her personal tutored student. She gives him that time because she says he's a genius. He is. Several videos are of him playing at a public piano downtown. He plays everything from classical to modern pop music to the traditional rock stuff Mom used to hate when she was a brash, know-it-all rocker. No matter what he plays at that piano, crowds gather, partly because he is young and so good, but also because the music draws them to him. No matter the music, you see the same happiness, joy and contentment on people's faces, many of whom come into view harassed and hurrying. He, his music, gives them peace."

"Dad," Ellie stared into her father's eyes, "I'm only the piano; RoH is the music."

"So you brought my granddaughter to save the world?" Charlie watched RoH sitting cross-legged in the sun, eyes closed and with a quiet peace on her face.

"No one is a saviour, Dad. This isn't a comic book or a silly movie. When I left, it seemed the ship was a hero rushing in to save me, but it wasn't like that. They made a path available. If I had decided not when standing beneath the ship, they would have left me. I made the choice."

Ellie hugged and trembled as if she knew hard times were coming.

"You're afraid, aren't you?" Charlie scowled, but watching RoH still brought peace.

"I'm not afraid for myself. No harm will come to me, or RoH, but I'm afraid our being here will make things worse. We don't know it all." She glanced skyward. "No one knows it all."

Mother, should we tell him of the other?

No, RoH, he isn't ready; Earth isn't ready. It may not be necessary.

Father and Grandfather are concerned, Mother.

I know.

"Dad, I was a scared little girl. I didn't know what was happening or why. RoH is in a better place. She has no fear, but is brave and smart. Remember, though, she is still a little girl."

"I almost wish we didn't have contact with them." Charlie glanced skyward. "I used to think it would have been better with no contact at all; I sometimes still think so, on those lonely nights staring at the sky."

"Dad," Ellie took his hand, "that's the question that they had to answer for real once they learned how to travel the galaxy. The answer was actually no contact, but humans, generations ago, on the cusp of either disaster or taking that step to the stars became too enticing to ignore. Humans will soon have to make the hard choice. I'm hoping, if I think the time is right, to present that hard choice. The people amongst the stars are not zoo keepers or gardeners. Humans will not survive by anything but their ability. We want to discover how to relearn the empathy and courage we find here, but if humans kill themselves off, it isn't the star people who will save them. That is an old rule. Not even my Methuselah family remembers when it developed. Long ago, some made mistakes in trying to intervene and accidentally killed off entire intelligent species or caused them to commit suicide. We won't do that."

"There are other species out there that can travel the stars, but many more failed when they reached the point Earth is at now. Planets with Earth technology commonly destroy all higher life with that technology. Those that didn't have the gift of fossil energy, like coal and oil, perhaps are the best outcomes. These eventually reached a low technology stasis with their planet's ecology and some have survived for much longer than the human species has existed. A few of these developed high-level mental capacity but no technology. It is that or reaching into the galaxy or death. There seems to be no fourth outcome. "

"Another inter-stellar species has reached the level of my family's species, and they have atrophied. The knowledge needed removes what you call humanity. That's ironic considering the evil side of humans, but there is agreement that the sum is for the good on Earth."

Ellie shuddered at the memory of her own experiences when RoH's age threatened by ruthless humans, but also the many others who fought to save her. Those had reason to hate aliens, but did not.

"They all think Earth is on the verge of success and about to make the next step to the stars without destroying itself and all life. Failures litter the galaxy, and we have hope here. Right now, with us here with you and Mom, and others in places all around the world, we are deciding if we should take the next step and try to make official contact and motivate a surer path to success. We are not sure. We know it's a risky idea."

"There are others like me and RoH, and none of them know yet that they are partly star people. Our alien agents spend energy just appearing to be locals. I hope there will be many more Ellies and RoHs, but voluntarily this time, or at least without the children being hounded into fleeing, as happened to me."

"We don't know how to reach the stars, Ellie."

"Yes, that's true, and we will never just share the technology. Besides, that development is more in the mind than technology, and it will take every mind on Earth being part of it to achieve it. Perhaps the ones to lead the breakthrough are already born, in Africa, South America, China or even right here. There are current human efforts to prolong the life of its species that focus too much on the technical and not on solving the fundamental problems. Billionaires building space ships and Mars settlements will not provide the answer. That effort will fail on its own, and humans, if they do not learn how to survive on Earth, will never make it a success. We saw that in ancient relics on countless planets."

"We are trying to decide if we can provide a path of peace and unity for humans to have time to make that climb. We may decide soon, but for now, we wait and watch."

"You will save us from ourselves," Charlie remembered old movies.

"No, we want you to save yourselves. Perhaps we can be a catalyst. RoH has decided she wants to wait here with you. She thinks her father and other star relatives are stuffed shirts. RoH teases them by asking them to learn music, and when they produce perfect harmonies and melodies just by thinking them out, she waves her hand backwards in disdain and tells them to learn the drums. Mom gave her that, I think. They don't know what to make of her, but they dote over her, and if they could spoil a star child, she would be the one. Her natural form is what you can see, but she looks like them too, sort of the reverse of great granddad. When she goes into the presence of the star side family, if she looks like them, they know she is there to learn. If she appears as herself, they know she is to teach them or at least question their bias. I can change too, but for me, it's lots of effort. RoH does it as if she is changing socks."

"She just told me they had never made a dandelion amongst the stars."

Ellie gazed at her daughter, and Charlie stared at his grown-up little girl. The power of her mind amazed and frightened him. It was a great power, fortunately, surrounded by a bodyguard of empathy.

Chapter Four

Sniffing Dandelions

I wonder if Ellie's empathy is all from humans, or did the aliens give her some as well? Family tradition says that Ellie's great-grandfather loved her great-grandmother. Lisa's uncle, Tom Clarke, wrote books and kept notes and files about the entire story, going back over 80 years. There is a lot in there, many incidents that seem to suggest that the aliens lack empathy. They understand they are missing things like that in their great intellectual ability. There are hints, though, that much of the suffering their interventions caused was because they were more ignorant than cruel, although my family suffered from their carelessness, and I find it hard to forgive. Only Ellie's existence softens my heart. I have decided their caring is merely intellectual and they need the emotional part to support being kind and empathetic. Aliens think they have reached the place where they need real empathy or they won't survive. They need to re-populate their fleets with Ellies and RoHs. They need love.

Quants, read all that material. Ill lend you my copies.

A large, electric pickup truck swept into the yard and braked hard behind the Martian-X. Charlie hurried to greet his boss, who was more his friend. They had a common understanding. Mike had lost his family in a bitter divorce, and so they both had shared deep loss.

"This is Mike, Ellie. Mike, this is my daughter, Ellie, and that's my granddaughter, RoH."

The adults stood together on the back porch. RoH remained firmly on the lawn, her feet apart and staring intently at Mike. She smiled.

"Hi," her soft voice came from below. RoH walked up the steps, looked deeply at Mike, and smiled more warmly.

"You are so sad," she said.

Mike stumbled backwards and sat hard on the wooden porch swing. Charlie thought he saw tears in his eyes. RoH eased to Mike, took his hand, and once more stared at him.

"It will be okay. You will be happy again." She grasped Mike's fingers. "Come, I want to show you my dandelion."

Charlie and Ellie stood together in the shade, not touching but feeling each other's warmth. RoH had Mike kneeling on the grass, gently fingering the yellow flower.

"Mike is obsessive about his lawn," Charlie said. "He sprays all weeds away. I think nothing is a weed, and people need to learn that. It has given RoH something to explain to Mike. That makes me happy, but I see that going through her to others."

Mike smiled at the bright yellow flower. RoH stared intently at her new acquaintance. Ellie took her father's hand.

Why does her touch always bring me peace? Charlie wondered.

"When we were about to leave the ship last night," Ellie began, "RoH's great-great-grandfather took her hand and said, Remember, one little girl can't change everyone. What she said was profound and had him shaking his head. She replied, You're so smart. You understand exponents, but you don't understand exponents."

"You see her with your friend? She is thinking of the multiple dandelion sniffers she will create through him, and then the ones they will teach through the power of the exponent. It's the same job I have here if we decide to go ahead. She will work her way, and I will do mine."

Mike had brought beer. He shared with Charlie, but Ellie demurred. As the men sat together chatting in the porch's shade, Ellie and RoH occupied the swing seat, scrutinizing the men socializing and silently discussing the scene, struggling to understand what conviviality might mean to their quest. They observed the oneness between Mike and Charlie, different from the life they had shared with everyone in the stars.

Mother, humans enjoy being with each other for no reason other than to be together. I know they can't talk in their minds as we do, but sometimes they sit silently too and communicate.

Look at their faces, my Sweet. Humans say a lot just with their faces. Your father and the others have lost that.

It is nice. RoH smiled. A deep feeling of love washed her mother.

Me too, Â طنلإ, me too. Ellie touched RoH's face.

I hope human bonding will do the work of our mission, Ellie thought. *If we can't bring them together, we will fail and withdraw. Humans must do it themselves.*

Why didn't great-grandfather and the others just come and tell everyone? Our need is so great; the thing is getting close.

Thousands of Earth years away, but yes, close.

These are the most dangerous times ever in human history. Their world is about to undergo a major change, and that will bring hardship and kill the majority in horrible ways, unless they can cooperate and make the right decisions, for themselves and all life here. We can't tell them what to do; they spook easily.

Despite everything in her history, Ellie shuddered at the memories of having to flee. She looked at RoH.

A young woman with a little daughter is less threatening to humans than some leader that doesn't take on a human form and arrives on a ship that is far beyond current Earth's capabilities.

People are preparing to come looking for us. We don't want them coming with guns. We don't want to use our power, at least not yet. Eventually, humans have to accept other species in the universe for what they are. It's discouraging that they can't all accept even their other native species. Maybe we can help them achieve that change. Maybe that's one way we can tell they are evolving.

They have weapons that would destroy most life, and we calculate that if they do, life on Earth will never recover enough to develop a new species that can think at the level humans can now.

They could take our route and let cold science govern things, but we are here because that way costs us so much and threatens us now. Our star family lost that conviviality and somehow empathy and the ability to love. We want humans to give that to us. That's why I, and especially you, my sweet Â طنلإ are so important. We have that empathy too, from our human part.

But Mother, if we fail, everyone may suffer; we may all die.

Not yet, dear, not yet... not for a long time...

In a gesture more human than alien, Ellie squeezed her daughter's hand. To RoH, thousands of years seemed like tomorrow.

It's important, they both concluded, *and weeds are the key.*

Mike is so sad. RoH looked along the porch. *He has a deep loss.*

"Your granddaughter is something else," Mike swigged the beer straight from the bottle. "How did RoH know I was sad? I miss my kids so much. It must have been amazing watching her grow. Why didn't you ever tell me before about your daughter and granddaughter?"

"I only just met RoH today," Charlie muttered. "And Ellie and I have been apart for a long time. It hurt a lot. I never got to watch her grow. That's why I never mentioned her, and I never even knew about RoH until today. Ellie returned."

"But you see her mother every year. You told me you go to Texas to the old farm or something."

"Lisa and I last saw Ellie at that farm years ago."

Mike stared at Ellie, and she suddenly looked his way, as if she knew he was watching. Mike jerked his head away.

"She was young. Did they take her from you? Sorry if I'm nosey."

"Yeah, ten years old when they took her. She's returned though."

Charlie brightened, unable to suppress his new happiness.

"Uncle Mike," RoH suddenly stood in front of the men, "call your kids today."

"I don't know where they are," Mike sobbed slightly as his newfound peace threatened to slip away. He did not notice Ellie's stare from down the porch, but he felt as if a feather had brushed his temple. Mike instinctively rubbed the non-existent object away, but it was such a fleeting feeling, a feeling of sudden contentment.

"Mother…?" RoH looked down the porch.

"It will take some time, my sweetie." Ellie smiled and RoH bound down the steps to investigate a tiger swallowtail butterfly flashing yellow in the sun.

"She called me uncle," Mike smiled. "I guess we are brothers."

The men laughed and swigged some beer.

"RoH has adopted you," Charlie said. "I suspect you have no choice."

The sun sank into the lake. After a meal of sausage and fries that Charlie insisted on preparing, fearing that Ellie might show off again, they escorted Mike to his truck.

"Take care, Uncle Mike." RoH hugged the man.

"Mike," Ellie leaned forward and pressed a slip of paper into Mike's hand. "Here is the phone number for your kids. I think they will want to talk with you."

Mike clutched his key fob and staggered against the cab door.

"How..." he began.

"Shhh, call them when you get home." Ellie flashed a mysterious smile. Its warmth soothed Mike. He had not seen her on the phone or on the internet. He could not recall her being out of sight for more than a minute.

A large aeroplane, a C-130 Canadian search and rescue craft, swooped overhead, shattering the peaceful scene and heading towards the sunset. RoH grabbed her mother's hand and trembled, but Ellie calmly watched the noisy intruder speed out over the lake and into a long sweeping turn, to come back about a kilometre north.

"That scared me, Mother. Are they looking for us?"

"No, RoH, they are looking for our ship."

"A ship?" Mike asked, "you have a ship?"

Charlie panicked, but Ellie calmly made up for her mistake.

"It's just a game RoH and I play when she's frightened."

Mike nodded without conviction.

These two are mysterious, Mike thought, *and Charlie has been no better. Why were they apart? What is this ship business? Why would RoH think anyone is looking for them, especially the military? There were helicopters around all day too, east of town near Belgrave.*

Mike drove down the laneway.

"Oh, I made a slip there. Will Mike be trustworthy if he finds out?"

"Your true identity is so unbelievable, he would never think of it. Besides, I think he bought your story."

"No, he didn't," Ellie frowned, "and where I got his kids' phone number puzzled him. He's smart. You might have to tell him, Dad."

The trio walked arm in arm to the bluff to enjoy the blazing sunset.

"It reminds me of great grandpa's home world," Ellie said.

"I must go to work tomorrow," Charlie said.

They sat in Charlie's favourite evening spot, where the eastern sky hung unobstructed and where he could see the northwest past the house. Sunset had given way to a clear, dark sky. The stars leapt out. The house hid most of the glow from a distant Goderich. Charlie had spent many long nights watching from this spot.

"Dad, I must leave too. I have to begin my work."

"What?" Charlie sat bolt upright. "You just got here, and I want to spend more time with you and that little rascal of ours."

RoH sat at the garden table with Charlie's laptop, logged onto the internet. She scrolled at what seemed to be an impossible speed. From his spot on the lounge, Charlie thought RoH had an overflow of open tabs.

"What are you looking for?" Charlie's curiosity ran deep.

"Dandelions, Grandpa. Mother and I must cultivate the weeds. I need more dandelions to smell."

"That's why I must go," Ellie smiled and touched Charlie's arm. He felt peace once more.

"Are you going to see the leaders? How will you get to them?"

It seemed a silly question. Charlie knew Ellie could engineer anything she wanted.

"Not at first," Ellie smiled, "we haven't decided yet if that should happen. Anyway, we won't meet individual leaders of nations, but only a grand summit of them, if they call one. If not, we abandon that project. Meeting with individual governments might just deepen hostilities most nations have towards rivals. We must work to end that rivalry. Of course, our thinking might change."

"The time seems right. The global economy is weak and most leaders are feeble because of it. There are dangerous forces and the good needs help before the evil gets a chance. My people don't want that to happen. Earth is too important to us to let it destroy itself."

Ellie looked at RoH, where the flickering light from the speeding computer screen flashed from the little girl's eyes.

"I'll be meeting dandelions first."

That frail little girl, who they took so long ago, now seems to be the key to human survival.

Amazement flooded over Charlie, who did not yet understand that RoH amazed the aliens as well. When they had accidentally started their genetic experiment years ago, they did not know the unintended consequences. If Charlie could have discussed it with anyone from the stars, he would have discovered that the wisdom gained over the eons did not involve fortune telling. He would later learn most of that from RoH, but for now, he had to accept and enjoy his granddaughter's eyes shining in the fading light.

"Look Grandpa, up there beside the star you call Vega." RoH pointed and Charlie stared. A faint point occupied a place beside the bright blue star, where Charlie knew there was no star. It moved ever so slowly and then slid sideways, passing in front of Vega. The bright star dimmed slightly, and after a few seconds, regained its glory.

That's big, Charlie thought.

"It's big, and a lot closer than it looks. Dad did that on purpose." RoH smiled. "He's letting us know they are near."

Charlie watched as the pinpoint remained motionless near Vega.

"Unless we are approaching the planet, which has been infrequent for years, we like to stay far enough out and near a bright object. It's less likely they will detect us. The sky is in daylight half the time and few large instruments ever point at known, boring objects like Vega. We pick the star by season. Vega and Sirius are the two best."

"We had to come close last night. Their electronic detectors saw us and probably anyone who had been outside within 50 kilometres of where we met you. That's why they are looking. The same thing happened in Seattle the day before yesterday."

"Once or twice, we have detected complaints that a communications satellite has ruined someone's astronomical photograph, always from amateurs, but it was likely us. Professionals know the orbits of Earth-made objects and avoid them."

"We mostly passively monitor. Earth's nuclear paranoia has made activity hard to hide. That's what caused a lot of trouble when they used primitive implants to track subjects. We have better technology now... untraceable."

Ellie patted her father's forearm.

"There is still an alien-hunting task force in the USA with a global network. They don't have implants to track since that night in Texas when we deactivated them all. I gave you a new system. Humans can't find you through it."

"Except for me, and Mom," RoH said. "We don't need gizmos for Dad to know where we are."

"Don't be full of you, my dear," Ellie scolded her daughter. "What we are, nature gives us to us. We can't take credit and shouldn't boast about it. Besides, there are the others."

Both giggled. Charlie frowned.

The exchange reminded him that Ellie, even with her amazing abilities, had been a frail child, growing in her wisdom, but still a child.

RoH seems different at the same age, Charlie thought.

"Yes, Dad," Ellie knew Charlie's thoughts. "If you remember, I was afraid on the night I left. I am from here. I didn't yet to know my alien home. RoH is from there, and she came here with me on a grand adventure. She can do that because she is with me and is part of me. RoH has known many worlds. She is more than capable of looking after herself and you, too."

"She will deny that she is the completion. There are other Earths in the galaxy with unique characteristics, but we have applied the lessons we learned on Earth elsewhere. They will have their RoHs without traumatizing some Ellies."

"How can you so easily discuss yourself as if you are a third party, detached, and neutral?"

"Because I am a third party, Father, and RoH is the fourth party. Years ago, people thought I was the ultimate, but evolution doesn't have a stop sign. We are hybrids, and therefore are more resilient than purer breeds, like humans or star people. The little imp is likely to decide we need a fifth party, but that won't involve Earth directly. DNA is common and similar throughout our galaxy. Some of our scientists have been vector-tracing DNA for thousands of years with little luck. The theory is that we all carry the original DNA from some ancient source, but no one has proved where that source was. Did it come spontaneously from life on a planet, did a super-nova somehow create it or did it come from another galaxy?"

"See, there are things even the all-powerful aliens don't know."

Ellie giggled, tousled RoH's hair, and muttered some alien gibberish, at which RoH seemed to glow in happiness.

It warmed Charlie, even though he did not know what those impossible alien sounds meant.

"You're a trooper, Dad." Ellie hugged her father tightly. "So is Mom. You could love her."

"I already do," Charlie whispered, "but we will never be a couple. We don't love that way."

"I know, Dad, but you will love someone one day now that your heart healed."

Ellie paused. The feeling that she also loved someone teased her brain, but the identity of that human seemed to hide in her memories. She thought it might be dreaming.

They lingered in the yard beneath the jewelled sky. Charlie watched Vega as it slid towards the west with its faint artificial companion.

Ellie said nothing, but the concentration on her face suggested that some serious thinking absorbed her.

This late in the season, there was little insect life at night, but RoH had found earthworms, and busied herself on the grass, enjoying the rapid damping from the dew.

"So," Ellie suddenly exclaimed, "I'm leaving in the morning. RoH is staying with you, if that's okay. I don't know how long I'll be gone."

"Of course it's okay," Charlie replied, "but I'll be away at work. How are you going? I can drive you."

"There is a bus leaving at eight in the morning for Stratford. I must find someone there. I'm taking that bus, but where I go after that will depend upon that person."

"RoH is fine on her own. You will never need to worry about her, and despite her impishness, she's responsible. I'll be in touch; I promise."

"Why would you come to a backwater like Canada and not the more powerful places like the States?"

"You mean other than to be with you," Ellie smirked. "We have examined all that. There are two main reasons. The USA is becoming chaotic, along with all the large countries. We think it will fragment. There is a huge amount of historical resentment towards the USA, for obvious reasons. The same applies to China and Russia. It would be better to have secondary states lead any change. We think the marginalized ones would be best, but they have brutal leadership. We aren't in the business of starting revolutions in those places, so changing global conditions is better. It will eventually make those places change too, even the USA. Sadly, we have to sell it as meeting their self-interest. I hope that global unity will develop faster than any attempts to exploit it. Ending these nation-states altogether seems necessary and inevitable. They have little time left before the climate does that job."

"If you want to unite humanity, why don't you make us fear you?"

"If they see us as a military threat, it will give evil humans all the power to defend the Earth. Their people will have us to hate. We want to have humans feel they have a friend amongst the stars, and a hand, not a fist, is the way to greet that friend. Good must be in charge."

Chapter Five

Strangeness

Quantz, putting Ellie on the Stratford bus that morning was a damn sight less traumatic than Texas. Maybe one day you can talk with both Ellie and RoH to get the details of what happened to them next.

Charlie and RoH saw Ellie on the bus. They lingered in the town square until the big vehicle turned up Kingston Street, heading for Highway 8. Charlie frowned at the cloud of diesel smoke and hoped the new batteries might soon make inter-urban travel, electric.

"I'll drive you home." Charlie turned towards the car.

"No, Grandpa, I would like to stay and explore."

Charlie's objection died on his lips.

RoH is fine on her own. Ellie's words defeated his fears.

"Here's lunch money." Charlie extracted a twenty-dollar bill. "I doubt they bankrolled you on the ship."

"We never thought of it." RoH smiled. "We don't use money. I have a new lesson to share up there on how to invade a planet."

Their laughter attracted a few glances, and Charlie sped off to work. RoH crossed the street and wandered along, examining storefronts and the faces of every passerby. Nothing looked that much different from Seattle, except Goderich had clean streets.

RoH reached the halfway point of her exploring the square when she came across an older woman sitting on the bench in front of a bank. The word "bag lady" from her mother's memories came to her, but this person seemed frail and thoughtful, not a product of poverty or insanity. RoH sat beside her and stayed silent. The woman finally turned to her.

"Whose little girl are you?" The voice seemed firmer than one might expect, and the woman smiled. "I'm Emily."

"My name is RoH. You haven't seen your grandchildren recently." RoH smiled in return.

"No," Emily sighed. "It's the way it is."

"Why?" RoH asked.

"It just is," the older looked sad.

RoH reached out and touched the back of her new friend's hand. "They love you."

"I know," Emily smiled again and dug into the cloth bag on her lap.

"Here they are." Several wrinkled, coloured photographs appeared showing smiling children, four of them ranging from a toddler to a pre-teen about RoH's age.

"They are older now, in high school or college. Everyone is too busy to send me new pictures." The sad look returned.

"Why do humans separate like that?" RoH asked. Emily gazed at her.

"You sound like you aren't... human, I mean."

"Oh, I'm human, at least a bit, but..."

Emily smiled, and for the first time, her eyes came alive. This little girl seemed too strange to be real.

"Are you from up there?" She pointed to the sky above the courthouse. Her tone suggested a mixture of teasing and seriousness, as if Emily hoped RoH would say yes. "I see lights in the sky sometimes. I saw them last night."

"Yes," RoH said, "but I'm from here too."

The woman squeezed her hand and smiled. "I expected little green men, not little girls."

"They are grey, and not so little."

"I always wanted to go, you know, I mean, to be an astronaut or something and fly into space. I used to fly aeroplanes."

For a brief instant, her face became wistful and her eyes closed. Then they snapped open.

"Only for fun, and when I had the money, but I dreamed."

Suddenly, Emily felt light and in the air, her young self, with her dark hair flowing in the slipstream and laughing her old laugh of joy, hands on the stick, speeding over the fields and the town, kicking the bi-plane into a bank towards the lake and watching the white of waves breaking on the beach. It seemed to be real. Then she was in space, seeing the curve of the

Earth, the white clouds against the impossible blue of the oceans, and suddenly circling the moon with its craters stark in the slanting sunlight and zooming over the moon base that had grown large. It looked identical to the pictures she had seen on television only last night. Then she was back on the steel bench on the Goderich town square as people hustled into the bank. The seat beside her was empty. She had not felt the light touch on her arm as she soared into space.

Emily smiled and cried tears of joy.

Thank you, star child.

Emily did not hear or consciously think of an answer, but she felt *"you're welcome"* in her head.

RoH found herself attracted to a used bookstore, Hobo Books. She wandered inside. The door tripped a bell. She stared up at the brass device, absorbing the lingering resonance.

Roslyn, the older proprietor, watched her from her comfortable stool behind the sales counter.

That kid should be in school, she thought.

RoH wandered around, mesmerized at the variety, colourful spines and strange titles, all random but each making sense on its own.

"Can I help you?" Roslyn came to her side.

"Do you think they have used all the combinations of words yet?" RoH fingered a volume with the obscure title of "The Strange Life of a Pygmy Pansy."

"No one ever asked that question before," the woman laughed. "What's a little girl thinking about that for, and shouldn't you be in school?"

"I am in school, Roslyn." RoH looked up at the woman's shocked expression. "What does that title mean?"

"It's called a nonsense title, but the story is for youngsters, or maybe for all of us, about a pansy plant in a nursery that is too small to sell so they throw it into the compost heap where it meets some weeds and they become friends. How did you know my name?" Roslyn gasped.

"That's an important story," RoH quietly replied. "I am a pygmy pansy looking for weeds."

Roslyn froze in shock. Little girls like this only existed in stories.

"You sound like a character from science fiction."

"Science, not fiction..." RoH replied, and wandered deeper into the store.

Roslyn had spread local history books carefully on a table in the centre of the room. RoH fingered several and picked up one with a deep blue cover and the picture of a sailing ship.

"That's about the boats that used to come here," the woman said.

"I come from a ship," RoH said as she turned each page, one after another, quickly, and in five minutes had leafed through the book, absorbing each page.

"They repeated themselves three different times, but that's interesting. My ship doesn't have to hide from storms."

"I've heard of speed reading, but I've never heard of it like that."

"You want money for the book? How much is it?"

"Twenty dollars, but you don't need to buy it."

"You live by selling books." RoH handed over the lunch money Charlie had given her. She would walk home for lunch. "Grandfather says that's the way it works here."

"That's the way it works everywhere. Who's your grandfather?" the shop owner somehow wanted more of this strange girl.

"Yes, I meant all over Earth," RoH said Earth as if it were an object she viewed from a distance, a foreign place. "His name is Charlie Keys."

Strange, Roslyn thought.

"Oh, that Yankee alien guy in charge of the woodworks out Bayfield Road. He even buys books." The woman smiled. "He's a nice guy, strange, but a nice person."

"So are you," RoH smiled. "People like it. You make them happy."

RoH touched Roslyn's arm, just above the elbow. Roslyn felt a fleeting, almost imperceptible faintness.

RoH abruptly turned and disappeared out the door.

The woman stood, holding the twenty and staring at the door. The bell seemed to tingle longer than normal.

Charlie never hinted at a family. I want to know that little one better. You will.

"What?" Roslyn exclaimed, but there was no one to hear. *Did I answer myself?*

Chapter Six

Escaping jails with no locks

There is nothing more confining than a door with no lock; such is the state of humanity.
-Tom Clarke in his memoir, *A Clarke is a Key*.

Ellie waved from the bus window at the rapidly diminishing figures of two of her loves. The bus was a cumbersome option, and Ellie had access to more efficient ways, but she preferred to meet people. As her mother used to say, "It's the journey, not the destination". Her great-grandfather said the same thing. Here, the journey formed a key part of her strategy and was the only course open until they decided whether to contact Earth. Perhaps that decision pivoted on her results; perhaps they balanced on this one bus ride. One never knew.

The bus had barely reached the outskirts when one of the other passengers, a woman in her fifties, stood and scurried to sit beside Ellie. The vehicle had few travellers and most seats remained empty.

"It's nice to talk with someone, don't you think? I'm Mary." She extended her hand. Ellie felt the sadness.

"My name's Ellie. You are grieving."

"Mother died about a month ago. We had planned to see, As You Like It, Shakespeare, you know, so I'm going by myself and have a rose for Mom's seat."

"Ah, wandering in the forest, searching," Ellie smiled, "that seems to be my life now."

"Isn't it for all of us?" Mary's eyes teared.

"She will always be with you in memories," Ellie took Mary's hand and the woman suddenly sat with her mother watching the play, but it was years ago, the last time it came to town with that Canadian actor starring. They had picnicked in the park because her mother thought that fit the play, and they had sat on a bench watching the swans. Mary smiled.

"Oh, I'm sorry," exclaimed Mary. "I must have blacked out."

"Keep those memories," Ellie whispered.

"Mother is in heaven. Are you an angel?" She asked.

"I'm not from that far. I'm from Seattle," Ellie smiled gently.

"You don't sound like a Yankee, oh!" Mary panicked and drew away. "Are you with that cult in Clinton?"

"I don't know of any cult. At least I didn't, but no, I'm not a member. You might say I'm only from the universe."

"Oh, the Unitarians then," Mary smiled, thinking she had finally found firm ground with the enigmatic woman who seemed to exude peace.

"Tee hee, you might say, I'm more of a star person."

Mary suddenly found even more mysterious but solid footing.

"There was a UFO near Belgrave two nights ago. Was that you? Are you," she paused as if saying it might change her world forever and whispered, "an alien?"

"Only partly," Ellie smiled again, "but I'm as human as you."

Ellie took Mary's hand. Both became quiet. Mary closed her eyes. As the bus sped towards Stratford, she relived the happiness she had shared with her mother, even some minor details that had not come to her in many years.

"I still think you are an angel. Thank you, I love you." Mary hugged Ellie as they stood on the Stratford sidewalk.

"One day," Ellie squeezed Mary's hand, "I will need your love to help me and the love of many more like you."

Mary closed her eyes, happy. When she opened them, Ellie had disappeared. It mattered not. Ellie left happiness. Mary clutched a picnic basket and a red rose, headed to the theatre and her mother's favourite play.

Ellie hurried along a quaint, tree-lined street. The leaves had turned into the glorious autumn she had missed among the stars and now promised to reinforce her long-remembered humanity.

Her aim appeared, an old age home, now quaintly called a Long Term Care facility as if its inmates might live forever. In this one, Cedar Haven, an old man slept. She could feel his life force and although he languished in semi-wakefulness, Ellie knew his heart remained strong and he had many more years to go, but the man's past drew Ellie. They had taken him, as a child, and he remembered.

"You're here," Peter smiled from his bed. Ellie stood quietly, examining him. He had awakened as she had entered.

He knew I was here.

"They saw a light and a UFO a bit from here," Peter sat up. "The abductee network says there are lights all over the planet. I have been expecting you, at least hoping."

"Hello, Peter," Ellie reached out to take his hand.

"They took you." Peter swung his legs over the edge of the bed. "I can't read your mind. Who are you?"

"Ellie," she said. "I need you."

"You will not probe my nose, will you?"

"No, Peter, I convinced them years ago to stop that. Besides, we don't need that anymore."

"Good," Peter relaxed. "When they shoved that stick up my nose for the virus test two years ago, I freaked. They couldn't figure out why. Fortunately, I calmed down. They didn't throw me into a rubber room."

Both laughed.

"This is a fine room," Ellie glanced about at the pleasant decor.

"It's a jail," Peter said, "a damned cell. The whole place is a jail with no locks, but we inmates don't think about leaving, so they trap us. Cedar Haven is a library of the dying."

"There's a lot of knowledge in this library," Ellie frowned. "They are wasting it."

"No one cares about the old. We have become obsolete and not relevant in the young world. We don't buy enough junk. It has always been that way."

"Not up there," Ellie glanced at the ceiling, "not up there."

"Can I go?"

"Is that your fee for helping?" Ellie knew Peter would not refuse anyway, but her reply implied she could arrange it.

"No, damn you," Peter hugged her. "Years ago, the network of us crazy abductees told me about the night you left. You have grown."

"Yes," Ellie sat in the wing chair near the television. "I'm on a mission."

"How can I help?"

"Come with me. You have friends I must meet."

"Who do I know whom you might need?"

"Other abductees like you, at least the ones who don't hate aliens."

"There are some who hate, for sure. I know a few who helped the Yankee government hunt you."

"You don't hate me, do you, Peter?"

"Why would I? I hated what they did to me. All my life, I worried they would take me again. Five times was enough. When someone told me you had made us untraceable, I felt better, hoping the aliens might have changed their minds, that they would listen to a ten-year-old girl and she would convince them to stop doing it."

"That's close to what happened, Peter, although they had figured it out on their own. My great-grandfather, after he had conceived my grandfather, realized that there was a better way to approach Earth and humans. Eventually, I became part of that better way, and my daughter is the ultimate or nearly so."

"You have a daughter?" The news stunned Peter. "You're so young. Is her father...?" Peter's voice trailed off.

"He's all alien," Ellie smiled, "but it wasn't an Earth romance, in vitro, as human doctors say, although I carried her to term. She's me and much more than me." Ellie smiled once more.

"I don't hate you, and I won't take you to any who do," Peter said.

"Will haters be a threat? You are intellectual and saw the possibilities, even in your abuse. Others likely don't."

"I'm not an intellectual. I taught high school and ran one."

"A high school teacher is close enough to an intellectual."

"You don't know many high school teachers," Peter laughed. "You left too young."

"The home won't like me going off. They think I'm demented, and I'm not allowed to leave."

"Can you walk?" Ellie stared at the wheelchair near the door.

"Oh that," Peter followed her gaze. "I had given up, waiting to die and made them push me around. I could walk, but had no reason. Now I do."

Peter dressed without embarrassment in front of Ellie. He knew that aliens, even a young female part alien, did not suffer from titillation.

"Good morning," Peter greeted the woman, a PSW in blue scrubs just outside his door.

The middle-aged PSW gaped at the unlikely pair before her. The young woman was a stranger. She had never seen Peter walking. Her eyes lingered as the pair headed towards the lobby.

Oh well, strange, but he's not my inmate to worry about. She hurried off to change "old lady Jenkin's" diaper.

Peter had afforded a room on the ground floor, even though a debate had raged between the home and Peter's daughter over when they should move him to the nursing wing. Luckily, Peter still occupied the comfortable location. It helped in his escape.

"Shhh," Peter held up a hand and peered around the corner, searching the common space and lobby. "Damn, the duty nurse is alone at the desk. Too bad she wasn't gossiping."

"Okay, walk beside me, away from her. She might not notice."

The unfamiliar sight of Peter walking got them past the front desk before the duty nurse recognized him. Her nursing training quickly overcame her confusion.

"Mr. Williams, STOP," she hurried around the desk.

Ellie and Peter rushed to the door, which slid open in front of them, and snapped shut behind. The automatic contraption would not budge for the nurse. She banged in frustration on the thick glass and watched with a gathering crowd as Peter and a strange young woman disappeared down the street.

Ellie could have used her abilities to pass unseen from the residence, but it suited her purpose to cause commotion. Humanity had to become used to strange happenings. Ellie thought her manipulation would pass as a malfunction and not that of an alien witch, but it would raise questions.

The door suddenly opened, but the crowd that stampeded to the sidewalk could see no trace of the escapee and the woman everyone became convinced was his abductor.

"So you can control matter," Peter gasped as they hurried.

"Not this time," Ellie slowed for the old man. "I made them think the door wouldn't work. I withdrew when we turned the corner."

The police scratched their heads in puzzlement at the kidnap report that an old man, formerly senile and confined to a wheelchair, had raced out the front door in the company of a beautiful snatcher. If a half-dozen people had not told identical stories, they would have believed that the nurse had been watching too many movies.

Chapter Seven

But she be mighty fierce

Quantz, you know of the American government's efforts. That whistle-blower told that story and since then they have made it official.

I know nothing from my involvement, but Ellie has verified it all. Their efforts to find her and get her to set up a meeting with the aliens are not public knowledge. I'm telling you for the first time. The aliens rejected that idea, and so we are in the international disruption we see now, of the big three powers trying to cooperate for a bit to gang up on the rest of the world to take over control of alien contact.

I can tell you this: if they succeed, the aliens will just withdraw and leave us on our own.

At the National Agency for Aerial Phenomena, NAAP headquarters in Virginia, USA, Siglinde Hilfreich, agency head, entered the room in her usual understated way. The serious faces around the table nodded.

Too many men in suits, Siglinde frowned.

These careerists shared a unified outlook on science and society. They were a skilled but handicapped bunch.

"Good morning," Siglinde nodded at the other woman here, a black woman, Liz, with degrees in anthropology and communication.

Two women against these stuffed shirts *except for Ted*, Siglinde took her place and opened her laptop at the summary of what she called "our pathetic knowledge so far".

Liz kept a notebook beside her computer. Even though electronics recorded the meeting, Liz liked to write ideas without waiting for the official record. At the beginning of this effort, she had quickly grown weary of the hours of babble that hid the few relevant bits.

Siglinde relished after-meeting debriefs with Liz, and lately, Ted, who stood as a renegade in the cloister of establishment thinking. He never wore a tie unless they were meeting political big shots.

"We need to think outside the box," became Siglinde's favourite cliché, but except for the three, the rest, while good at data, technical stuff and contacts in the government seemed to be the dead cat part of Schrodinger's experiment and forever trapped in their boxes.

Siglinde owned a doctorate in quantum theory, and they had picked her to head the project because of that, and her ability to organize and get things done. She considered herself a good herder of cats, even dead ones.

With her background bias, Siglinde believed that, if they ever discovered how these aliens did what they did, defying Einstein and other rules of physics, she would find that quantum process, ones she could not dream of, underlay everything. Siglinde also thought why the aliens did things as the more important question. Aliens existed and visited Earth. They possessed un-opposable power. The facts from the past 80 years proved it.

Damn, we need more data. The thought always haunted her.

"Is there anything new?" Siglinde brought the meeting to order with her usual lack of formality.

"We have two sightings since our meeting last week," Ted analyzed data for the group. His specialty in astrophysics meant he had skill in analysis and computer modelling. He had written powerful search algorithms for the irrelevant SETI project, but the government kept supporting that fiction to convince the majority that they still had not discovered aliens. Money laundered through the SETI budget paid for NAAP.

"The first one appeared in the north-west, Washington State, Seattle, to be exact. We detected two, on successive nights, lasting only about twenty minutes each, but they generated radar targets and disappeared almost instantly, so they fit the model. The second occurred the night before last, only a few minutes after the last Seattle contact and east of Michigan over south-western Ontario, Canada. There has not been a second contact at that location."

"False alarms," a few comments huffed from around the table.

"I don't think so," Ted frowned at the lack of imagination.

"So what does it mean?" Siglinde had a bias towards alien explanations, a partiality she fought.

"I don't know," Ted's frown deepened. "I would be happier if they were identical, and we had had another Ontario event last night."

"Why do you want two events in Ontario?" Liz asked.

"It would verify the Seattle contacts as meaningful." Ted tapped a key on his laptop.

"All the data is in the top-line folder on the network." Everyone opened the screens. "The radar contacts show that the thing paused right over downtown Seattle, both nights. The video is a compilation of dash-cam and security cameras that we stitched together. There are probably hundreds out there, but we didn't want to spook the public. These are from police cars and public buildings. On the third one, we get a hint of a disc."

Sounds of satisfaction and scepticism broke the silence.

"The Ontario incident has no visual record except for a few statements of seeing lights. The NORAD data pinpoints the stationary spot at just west of a place called Belgrave, near to Lake Huron and, more important, Goderich, Ontario."

"Why is that important?" someone asked. Liz made a note.

"It fits something that we have known for a long time. Document 1675-06 details the girl Ellie's departure on a saucer. Her mother lives in Seattle, and her father, for some unknown reason, exiled himself to Canada, to Goderich Ontario, to be exact. Tracking of his car's WiFi signature showed that Keys travelled between Orangeville and Goderich last night within five kilometres of Belgrave just after the detection ceased. This might connect the two incidents, but we don't know why."

"In most modern Earth cultures, we often take vacations to visit relatives," Liz said. "Since, especially in English North America, we usually have family living back home. We visit one and then others nearby, making several stops before returning home. That habit made the pandemic worse. Maybe Ellie has come for a family visit."

"She had closer ties to her mother than her father. Why would she only have a night with mom and then go to dad?"

"And stay," Ted said. "There's no other sighting; she's in Goderich."

"We already have a team on the ground. When we didn't get a second event, Ted let me know his estimation. They landed this morning and last reported from Goderich." Siglinde glanced at her screen. "There have been no updates, but I'll ask for one before we're done here."

"Are they working with the Canadians?"

"Are you kidding? The Canadians still think flying saucers are a hoax. We've always kept them in the dark. It gives the USA an advantage."

"I hope all that doesn't blow up in our faces one day. It would end any cooperation we might get from Canada, and probably most other countries. They might cozy up to the aliens."

"Okay, so far we think Ellie might be on a family visit and she likes the fishing in Lake Huron better than the weather in Seattle." Siglinde smiled, but no one laughed.

"That's the first blush," Liz added, "but would they do all that to have one person, or whatever we call them, just come for a family visit?"

No one would hazard a guess, not even Ted.

"We need more data," Ted growled, "but there is some new analysis from my tank."

Ted had a team with him, a collection of number crunchers and free thinkers who only allowed their less-fanciful ideas to escape outside what they called their tank.

"If they can travel a significant fraction of the speed of light, but less than c, then this gives a clue about the distance to their star system, or at least their closest base outside the solar system. It would put them between a Base type and a type 3 Kardasheve species. They seem to appear in twenty-year cycles of maximum sightings, so that would put them at somewhat less than twenty light-years away. If they travel faster than light, they are a full type 3 civilization."

"Or perhaps a civilization that is qualitatively above that scale, one that can integrate so completely and efficiently into the galaxy that they are invisible at a distance. They could approach us, and we would never know unless they revealed themselves."

"Are you saying that everything we see, like that incident in Canada the other night, is a deliberate calculation on their part to let us know they are here? Does that mean they could be here when we don't know about it? That would blow the 20-year cycle out of the water."

"Perhaps..." the conversation paused, as smart people tried to process all possibilities.

"It may have nothing to do with distance, no matter where they are on the development scale. Let's say they are conducting biological experiments, and people's stories seem to suggest that is so. 20 years is about one human generation. Is this a breeding experiment?"

"We know there was breeding before. Ellie proves it. Maybe they are doing more. Maybe she's here to get pregnant or have a baby."

"So," Liz laughed, "we might look for a night-clubbing alien trying to pick up a one-night stand to get knocked up, or we need to find a midwife involved in a strange home birth."

Several people laughed at Liz's joke.

"What portions of the electromagnetic spectrum do they appear in?" Siglinde wanted to turn from speculation to concrete information.

"Not enough data, but the whole visible, microwave and radio fringes. No one has any high-energy measurements, but there has been no residual radioactivity. They don't emit ionizing radiation within the atmosphere."

"We could interpret that they reveal themselves where they know we would look, but they make sure they leave nothing harmful."

"They harmed many humans over the last 80 years."

"Damned right they did. I think they are a threat."

"Lock and load, eh, Danny?" Siglinde smiled at the one uniformed man in the room.

"I'm saying we shouldn't expect flowers and music."

"Considering their power, a deeper bunker here might be good." Danny said.

"Danny, put your six-gun away and shut up."

"This can't get to the President," Siglinde said. "He can't keep his mouth shut if he thinks something makes him look smart."

"Maybe we can get him to add money, anyway. Ask the Controller to tell him Project X is an X-ray laser we are developing for the Space Force."

"Aren't we?" Everyone laughed in surprise that Danny made a joke.

"Okay, here's an update from Goderich. The team has located the father and where he lives."

"I'll tell the team to lie low. We need information, not a confrontation that might spook the aliens."

"They are going to install surveillance devices and stake out the house. They say it's quiet right now."

"Well, we meet again tomorrow. Let's hope for more info from up north." Siglinde stood, ending the meeting.

"Elliana," Siglinde paused at the desk of the young woman administrator for Project X. "The team up in that hick town in Canada, watching the father of that alien kid, is going to bug his house right now.

We think the kid might be back, and if we're lucky, we'll nab her. Please set up a firm link for me. I want to know all their moves."

"I'll have their Starlink connection in a minute."

"Good, and have a Lear on standby at Anderson. If they find the kid, I want to get up there and lead any interrogation." Siglinde hurried away.

Elliana stared at the wall for an instant and then reached for her phone.

***

RoH sat at the kitchen table, munching a sandwich and examining the blue history book with the picture of a ship under sail.

Books are inefficient, she thought, *but it feels good to hold.*

The barely audible sound of a vehicle stopping in front of the house did not bother RoH. She had followed it after it had turned into her grandfather's lane. Besides, the warning from her father had prepared her. Dangerous men rode in the van, but they were not the ones from the American agency. She laid the book aside and contemplated how to turn the developing threat into an opportunity to fertilize a dandelion.

The black van crunched to a stop on the gravel driveway. The three occupants had no fear. They had cased this place. The owner would not return until dinnertime but scanned Charlie's WiFi for signs of activity before heading to the front door. Their dress was a disjointed array of denim fashion. The door yielded to the expert lock picking.

RoH waited at the kitchen table. She hoped the intruders would damage nothing before they found her.

"I wonder if this guy has any beer," a voice came from the hall.

"Try the kitchen."

When a stubble-faced young man rounded the corner into the kitchen, he froze in surprise. RoH stared at him with calm eyes and smiled.

"What? Hey you guys, I found a kid here." His face clouded. He brushed his tumbling bangs away from his eyes. He realized they had a bigger problem, a witness. The others hurried into the kitchen.

"Damn," one cried, "what do we do now?"

"You're here to steal my grandpa's stuff." RoH sounded matter-of-fact. "I don't think you should."

"Oh, she's a cute little thing, ain't she?" The third man stepped forward. He was tall and fit and the leader of this little gang of thieves. The other two feared him. He was the only one of the trio ever to be violent.

"I'll have some fun." He grinned. "This will only take a minute."

"You can't kill her," one man gasped.

"Not right away; not before I have some nookie."

RoH showed no emotion, as she looked right into the threatening man's face. He pulled a revolver from his pocket and levelled it at RoH. His eyes caught RoH's, and he paused.

"Why aren't you scared, little girl? You are going to suffer and die."

"Boss, you can't do that," the others cried out.

"Yes, I can. You two shut up if you know what's good for you."

"Don't worry," RoH looked at the others. "He won't hurt me."

"I damned well will."

"I don't think so. You can't do it."

"You smart ass, no little girl calls me out," he snarled. "I'm the boss. We'll just go to step two. We don't like witnesses."

The gun pointed directly at RoH's head. He pulled the trigger.

It is unlikely any of the three would ever understand exactly what happened. The bullet left the gun barrel and rattled harmlessly to the floor. The handgun immediately joined it and slid into the corner of the room.

The two accomplices thought they saw the sweet little girl at the table turn into a horrible space monster. They screamed and disappeared into the hallway and headed to the van. The monster looked exactly like the one they had watched on television the night before.

The tough leader froze in place. Later, he would wonder if the little girl had somehow held him there. RoH had remained a weak little girl in his eyes, but she sat at the table as if in command.

"Come and sit." RoH pointed to a chair opposite her.

Outside, someone vainly tried to start the van engine.

"Why are you like this, Richard?" RoH's eyes bore deeply. Her tone did not sound scolding but curious.

"Call me Rick, not Richard, or Dick." Rick clenched his fist.

I can take this little bitch, he thought.

"Your mother called you Richard and your father Dick. You hate them, except they are both dead."

"What?" The blood drained from Rick's face and his fist unclenched into a shaking hand that vibrated on the tabletop. "How do you know?"

"I know because you know, Rick. They abused you. Strangers took you when you were 14 years old."

"Yeah, that was the best thing that ever happened to me, but it didn't last. The CAS threw me out at 18 and I had nothing." Rick regained strength and slammed the table.

"That's why you steal, but why do you want to rape and murder?"

"You're so smart, you tell me."

"Rick, if you don't tell yourself, you'll always want to do it. If you confront it yourself, you will have hope; you will change. You have killed no one yet. What is that horrible thing they did that makes you want to hurt and kill?"

Rick's face went blank and then contorted into fear and anger, but his eyes locked onto RoH's face.

Rick was little, cringing in horror as his father beat his mother. Her begging screams pierced the night. His father was not drunk; he was never drunk but went wild without warning. Rick's mother was always drunk. Rick did not know which incident this was. They happened every week. He would hide in the closet if he could.

Rick is in bed. Suddenly his mother is on him, touching him, doing those things. *No, Mom, stop... please stop... Mom... please.*

There was no mercy, and then his father took his turn... *NO! NO! oh god... please... Mom help. Mommy...it hurts.*

The cops are at the door. They are taking away that piece of shit. Mother is in the corner, drunk and bleeding. There she goes too. No, don't take me. I'm under the bed and dragged out by my ankles. I'm scared. Where's this house? A woman smiling, not drunk, with a toothbrush and pyjamas... peace.

"Rick, go. You're 18 now and they say you can take care of yourself. Goodbye, Rick, stay in touch."

"I tried to stay in touch." Rick seemed to talk to himself. "When I needed help, they brushed me off and told me to go to welfare. I thought they loved me, but they were just doing their job."

Rick sobbed.

"Women or a little girl aren't your mother, and other men aren't your father. Hating everyone will not help now." RoH stared at Rick.

"I know, but I just lose it, can't help it, get so mad that I go nuts."

"You forgot those nights, the suffering, and you hid the memory of the night they took you away."

"I had to. It hurts."

"It'll hurt less now, Rick." He felt her hand on his as she reached across the table. "It hurts less now."

"I'm sorry," Rick sobbed harder, "I'm so sorry."

Rick became faint and dizzy, and he thought he would pass out, but the feeling passed almost instantly.

"Do your friends have guns?" RoH released his hand.

"No."

"Find something good to do with your life, and take your friends with you. They look up to you."

"They do just because I'm a tough-guy punk."

"You don't need to be a tough punk to lead, Rick. They will follow you. Choose your path."

Rick reached into his pocket and took out a dozen handgun cartridges.

"I won't need these anymore." He smiled.

The van started instantly and hurried back to the county road. RoH took the gun and threw it and the bullets into the lake. She hoped her grandfather would not notice the hole in the wall above the stove where Rick's bullet actually had slammed home.

The second van arrived while RoH sat in the backyard with her yellow-flowered friends. RoH mused about how others might see her and her mother's visit as a mere biological expedition examining all forms of alien species, including the humans who had contributed to her DNA. Of course, they had done all the basic evaluations many Earth years before, but seeing, feeling, touching and talking with humans took her far beyond her virtual education on the ship. She looked around.

I have two homes.

As RoH occupied herself with these thoughts, part of her mind tracked the progress of the invading vehicle. It was a rental van with the words, New Times Leasing, on the side panels.

A man and a woman walked around the corner and mounted the porch. RoH knew two others had already entered the front door. In contrast to Rick and his gang, these were well-dressed professionals. RoH kept herself invisible as they swept their eyes over the yard and the scrub trees lining the bluff above the lake.

Making sure of their ground, RoH understood.

The unlocked door upset them. Being Americans, they hesitated. Back home, no one left any door unlocked. They had no guns, but the pair did a duck and cover.

RoH smiled and admired their efficiency inside the building as she curiously examined the Earthly limitations. They could do remote sensing, but humans had nothing to emulate the mental power of herself, her mother, and her star family.

The intruders swiftly concealed high-resolution mini-cameras, sensitive microphones and infrared detectors. A spy bot found a hideout deep inside her grandfather's home computer. The intruders said little, but as the work ended, they became more talkative.

"When do we do his office?"

"We have to case the place. We might have to figure out how to defeat the alarms."

"Piece of cake," the woman said. "Let's get going. I'm starving."

RoH watched them leave through the front door and tracked the van to town. They checked into the Comfort Inn and RoH lost interest. Grandfather would soon be home.

Mother, how do we handle this?

This way, Â.طنلإ

"Grandfather," RoH intercepted Charlie at his car, "I'll explain later, but go into the house and make a phone call to this number." RoH gave a number that would direct the inevitable snoops to a house in London. Any follow-up would lead to an old woman on Richmond Street who would say that Charlie had postponed their visit.

"Tell them you'll be away until further notice and you'll see them as soon as you can. Call some cleaners or a fumigator, whatever sounds good, and book them to come tomorrow and do this house. Then, go upstairs, throw some clothes into a suitcase and come to the door. After that, I'll take care of the problem and fill you in."

Charlie eventually appeared at the door. RoH swept her eyes over the building and stepped inside.

"It's okay now, but I'm not sure for how long. It'll depend on how smart they are."

RoH explained what happened with the Project X agents. She did not mention Rick and the threatening gang, but in the grand scheme of things, that had little importance. The human part of RoH thought she might meet Rick again.

"They are bugging your office tonight, and I can't neutralize that. Just don't refer to Mom or me, especially to Mike. These aren't dangerous people. There is a far worse bunch that even this group doesn't know about, but they are from the American government. We would rather avoid them. The Americans want to control the agenda. That's against what we want to accomplish, if we decide to do anything at all. Mom is working on that. Reports from other countries are mixed. We need to have more input."

"Tonight, we'll check into a motel. Book it for a week and I'll stay there. Tomorrow night, you come home, so I can stop holding them off and it will seem normal. Just don't talk about me or Mom in your sleep." RoH giggled. "Don't call the motel from here or the office. We just can't be in touch until we see what they are doing. They'll probably come to see you in your office. They have no proof we are here, so other than telling them that, say whatever you want."

Charlie said, "I would normally resent a kid telling me what to do, but you are RoH, way beyond me and someone I love."

They both felt the warmth of their hug.

"Who was that I talked to on the phone?"

"It might have been the lady who lives there, but I think it was Mother, although she's not in London right now."

Chapter Eight

Like men in black

Things were getting complicated, Quantz, and I wished I could leave on that star ship. You remember, a lot of old movies showed people running around with powerful ray guns, knocking off ugly alien monsters. My favourite fun ones were those "Men in Black" movies. Anyway, in real life, aliens aren't like that. My daughter and granddaughter look like us, although RoH can take on her alien appearance, and she can make us think she's an ugly monster. Both of them can play with our minds.

"Charlie, isn't it scary that aliens manipulate our minds?"

No, Quantz, why would it? Our government and marketing do it all the time. Aliens, at least my family, are more responsible and deliberate. RoH only used it for protection, and Ellie the same thing. When those agents poked, I wished I had those powers, but then, I might have hurt them. Anyway, they now had my home and office bugged.

"**H**i, Charlie," Mike sauntered into Charlie's office. He had not asked Kerri to announce him. No one saw Kerri as a secretary. Charlie and Kerri collaborated on estimates and training. She wished they worked even more closely, but Charlie had never shown interest.

"I'm intrigued by your daughter and granddaughter." Mike said.

Charlie jumped up and hurried from behind the desk.

"Let's go get a coffee." Charlie tried not to look around for a camera.

In the parking lot, inside the rental van, the snippet registered on the solid-state recorder and with the woman wearing the headphones. It frustrated her that the target had left the range of the microphones, but it seemed important. She played the snippet back for her partner.

"I'll call Siglinde," he reached for his cell.

"Mike," Charlie began, "I don't want to discuss Ellie and RoH in the office. I'm recovering from the shock. Kerri might have overheard."

Charlie hoped Mike would believe his excuse. They sat in the shade at a picnic table near the rear receiving dock, sipping the excellent coffee that the shipping and receiving department always had ready. Charlie found the previous night in the motel comfortable, but the pace of events and the lingering shock of Ellie's return had made it fitful. He yawned.

"Okay, I understand," Mike sounded none the wiser, "but they have me hooked. The number Ellie gave me worked, and after a bit of awkwardness, my son warmed up. He gave me my Tracy's number, and she sounded interested. We are getting together for Thanksgiving."

Mike's smile warmed Charlie.

"Ellie found that number with little effort. The last time I tried to trace them, I hit a dead end. Ellie seems to have magic and RoH, too. RoH made me feel so peaceful. They are special. I want to know more."

Charlie stared at his coffee, deciding how much to say. If he told the truth, Mike would think he was crazy, and it would put everything in danger. Ellie said he would never be in personal peril, but if the alien's purpose was to help humanity and to gain the empathy they needed from the human psyche, spreading too much knowledge might ruin it all. Charlie had no inkling of what Ellie had planned.

"Mike," Charlie began, "the complete story is too unbelievable. If things go the way we hope, I'll fill you in later. Right now, I can't. Is it good enough that they like you and always keep you safe?"

"That sounds ominous," Mike frowned, "as if something big is going on that might make trouble."

"Yes," Charlie agreed, "it's something big that might make trouble."

Charlie glanced to the far side of the parking lot and noticed a woman standing by a rental van and holding binoculars.

RoH called that one, he thought. *I'm sure they bugged the office.*

"What happens might be spectacular, out of this world, you might say, but it either won't happen, or it will be for the good."

Charlie hoped that the reference might soften Mike up to learning about the alien reality sometime soon. Most humans remained ignorant, sceptical, and hostile. There had been too many alien monster invasion movies.

"That sounds even worse," Mike smiled. "I'll take your word for it since Ellie and RoH don't appear to be monsters or aliens or whatever."

"You can't call them monsters, that's for sure." Charlie wondered if Mike noticed he did not deny they were aliens.

A man talking into a cell stood beside the woman. Charlie sipped his coffee and tried not to look towards the van.

"Mike, people may come asking about me and my family," Charlie glanced across the parking lot from where the pair of strangers watched. "Don't get yourself in any trouble, but telling them less instead of more might be good. You could tell them you met a woman and a little girl at the house. You'll have to play it by ear."

"That sounds bad. Is your ex trying to cause trouble?"

"Maybe worse." Charlie did not seem eager to say more.

"Well, I would love to meet them again, and when my kids visit, I would like them all to meet." Mike swallowed the last of his coffee.

"You will meet them again, I'm sure, but I don't know what will happen by Thanksgiving, but maybe we can all do turkey at my place."

"Sounds good, hey we need to talk about the Harmsworth order. We lost it, they went bankrupt, never recovered from the pandemic, so we need to reschedule, and now there's some surplus inventory to deal with."

"I see our famous parking lot sale coming up." Charlie laughed.

The men went inside. The watchers disappeared into the van.

***

"Two of them," Siglinde Hilfreich stared at her cell in Virginia, and addressed no one in particular, although she, Liz and Ted were in Elliana's workspace. "This is more complicated than we thought. He said, 'your daughter and granddaughter'."

"Siglinde," Liz began, "it looks like the aliens have a bigger operation. The little girl, Ellie, has come back, but they sent an older companion."

"Ellie might have grown up by now," Ted said. "The daughter and granddaughter phrase makes me sure it's adult Ellie with a kid of her own. More alien, unless they bred her on Earth..."

"Don't get crude, Ted." Liz's indifference to men could almost stray to the hostile, even towards men she liked.

"... sorry, conceived with a human, the little one must be more alien. Ellie showed some great mental powers. The little one may be stronger."

"We have seen some returnees who didn't age over many years being away," Liz replied while examining her text copy of the report from the field in Goderich. "It is possible, even likely, that Ellie is in the same situation. If she has grown, who's the girl and would they send a child?"

"I agree with Liz," Siglinde said. "We have no reason to think the visitors have changed their way of doing things. The little girl is Ellie."

Ted shrugged, unconvinced but lacking facts to argue.

"Elliana," Siglinde sat beside her assistant, "please call the airfield and tell them I'll be there at 10:30 am and to file a flight plan to Canada, the nearest international entry point to Goderich Ontario."

"That's London," Elliana reached for her phone. The woman paused and briefly stared into space. Siglinde had noticed her peculiar habit several times and guessed that Elliana had a dislike for the telephone.

"Please book a room for me wherever the team is staying."

Outside the plain low-rise office building in Arlington, Virginia, Danny, Major General Daniel Ringwald, eased into his limousine.

"Fort Belvoir, George."

Danny sank into the comfortable cushions and watched the nondescript low-rise brick headquarters of the National Agency for Aerial Phenomena, the home of Project X, disappear as the car turned sharply into traffic. It would be a brief run down the 95 from Arlington.

"How was the drive, Danny?" The civilian, Greg, in a designer suit and immaculate tie, stood and waved at the empty chair to the side of the rosewood desk. The desktop supported a clutter of folders in a rainbow of colours, along with two large computer screens. A third enormous screen hung on the wall beside the door, displaying an aerial view of a few urban blocks from somewhere.

"Coffee…?"

"Daisy, get the General a regular and a big sticky bun…"

The receptionist had paused after ushering Danny in and had stared at the screens on the wall. She hurried away.

A quick handshake and the pair sat. The lack of formality suggested that the men shared equal authority; however, Danny coming to Greg's office signalled subtle deference. Beneath all of that, Ringwald was the third of the family to hold the rank of General. He carried some influence inside the Pentagon and political circles. Greg had to treat him with care, even while cynically intending to use him for what he considered the greater purpose.

"It's a quick ride, Greg," Danny handed a tablet device to Greg, "but I had enough time to consider this new information. We have two aliens on the ground, up in Canada. The group suspects it was the girl and an escort. We think they stopped in Seattle first to visit the girl's mother."

The receptionist placed two coffees and a plate of pastries in front of the men and absorbed the conversation.

"That's all, Daisy," her presence annoyed Greg. Although she had high-security, Daisy, Daphne DuMaurier, was not privy to secrets.

"That's our reading." Greg shifted to examine Danny's tablet, but frequently glanced at the big screen by the door. "They visited mommy, but she didn't leave with them."

Daphne quietly closed the door behind her. Greg locked the door.

The image zoomed in on a small street. The lighting suggested that the location was morning on the west coast. Long-range cameras distorted the image.

"We've watched her since the second sighting. We have a plan."

"What?" Danny flared. "I'm supposed to be in the loop."

"You are in it now, Dan... Relax... there was no time for a formal discussion, and the operation has begun." Greg nodded towards the big screen. Black SUVs and police cars with lights flashing filled the street.

"We don't need the military here. Hopefully, we won't need it at all."

Danny recognized the street. "Does Lisa have Ellie's abilities?"

"There is no evidence she does," Greg pointed at the thick file dating back 20 years. "The little girl seemed to be the only one."

Danny tapped the file. "Here are the details of what happened when they had the grandfather the first time. They took him right through a concrete wall. I hope you know what you are playing with."

Several figures hurried from the SUVs into a storefront walk-up apartment. They led a middle-aged woman out, handcuffed but not resisting. The camera zoomed in. Lisa seemed to have heard the camera drone. She looked directly at the camera and mouthed words.

"I wish I knew what she said." Danny frowned.

"She said, I'm okay, sweetie."

"How..." Danny began.

"Lip-reading is part of agency training. Until now, it only made baseball games more fun. It's as if she knows Ellie will see this. This is a top-secret, secure circuit. No one will see this that isn't supposed to." Greg frowned and involuntarily glanced at the ceiling. It would have been closer if he had looked at the door to reception.

"Well, that seals it," Danny smiled. "So, what's the plan now?"

Greg handed a file to the general. Danny glanced at the first-page summary. Greg would take this directly to the White House, but the President's man would only skim that first page that said nothing.

"The Canadians are going to be pissed."

"They don't matter," Greg snarled, "but they won't know about it. We have been on the ground there for months, and in Seattle, waiting for some alien contact with the mother and father. Now we have it."

"Canadians aren't stupid," Danny offered.

Greg shrugged. "They are a bunch of colonials. They would go along with us even if they knew."

"When will they arrive in Canada?"

"She and you will fly into the Goderich airstrip about 3 AM on a C-130 TACAMO, which is resistant to alien interference. A team will meet you at the Goderich Airport. Working out of the country is better."

"You are leaving for Selfridge AFB in Michigan in," Greg glanced at his wristwatch, "two hours. Hilfreich and her people are already on the ground in Canada. She would be more pissed than the Canadians."

"She won't find out either. None of that bunch knows of our team, but we know everything Hilfreich is doing." "We go for the father tomorrow. Once we have him, his daughter and the chaperone will have to come for them."

"What's my role? Who's the boss?"

"There's a tactical commander on the ground, but you are the strategic decision-maker. If you and TAC disagree, then you contact me. I know you, Danny. You understand the issues and have a level head."

"This could blow up in our faces."

"Nothing will go wrong."

***

In Goderich, Charlie left for the day at his normal time and was halfway home as Siglinde parked her rental car beside the van at the plant.

I wish I could talk to RoH, Charlie thought, *but she seems to be sure.*

Charlie resigned to being alone and fretting every minute. It had only taken a day to want more company in the house. When he looked about, he happily noted that the cleaning contractor had made the place spotless. Charlie could never have kept it in that condition.

Why haven't I thought to do that before? Charlie thought with a bachelor's bewilderment. *Kerri once offered to do it said she needed the money, so I gave her that raise. She seemed upset at not doing the job. Maybe I should take Kerri to lunch to make up for it.*

A car crept to a stop on the road shoulder, just out of sight of the house. A laptop displayed Charlie's progress to the kitchen and the watcher heard pouring lemonade. The cameras switched as Charlie made his way to the back porch to relax with the lake filling his horizon. Although everything went via Starlink to headquarters in Washington, the local team had to keep a sharp watch.

"We would like to talk to Mr. Hammersmith."

A few kilometres from where Charlie enjoyed the lake view, Siglinde's smile embraced the woman occupying the open cubicle on the second floor. "I'm sorry, we don't have an appointment, but we have a deadline quoting a job in north Huron and need a supplier price."

"Oh, that must be that new resort at Port Albert," Kerri normally did estimates and had already seen the schematics for the Port Albert job. "I'm sure we can quote. Mike, Mr. Hammersmith, knows the specs."

Soon Siglinde and her team member were sitting at Mike's desk.

"You aren't here to talk about Port Albert."

Mike jumped to the point as soon as the introductions ended. He had quoted Port Albert to two general contractors, both with connections to organized crime, and as far as he knew, they had awarded the contract. The job up there was an insider thing for a government favourite. These two did not appear to have ever put up a pup tent. They looked like government people of some type, and they both had American accents.

"You aren't here to talk about a quote," Mike wore his best poker face. "Why are you here?"

The sudden appearance of this pair puzzled Mike, but seemed another part of the recent events that had disturbed his life. Ellie and RoH's mysterious appearance led to his chance of restoring his family. He hoped this might go the same way. Charlie had warned that Mike should expect a visit from strangers.

"You are right," the woman seemed in charge. "We would like to talk about your employee, Charlie Keys."

Mike, people may come asking about me and my family. Mike tensed.

"Are you a cop? Do you have I.D.? You don't sound Canadian."

"We aren't Canadian, nor cops," Siglinde amicably replied, "but we represent the American government, researching things that interest the planet."

The woman spoke better English than Mike did. He guessed she had an education. Perhaps that excluded them from being crackpots.

"I.D." Mike insisted.

Siglinde wore a practical, professional-looking dress jacket and produced her wallet from the inner breast pocket. Her partner extracted a cardholder from his shirt.

"What's this ' National Agency for Aerial Phenomena?'" Mike examined plastic cards that displayed their photos, the formal title of Project X, and the signature of some anonymous bureaucrat beneath the embossed seal of the United States of America.

"NAAP is an American governmental agency researching reports of strange occurrences," Siglinde replied.

"Hot damn, flying saucers," Mike exclaimed in glee. "I knew it."

Siglinde winced at the accurate description but caught the last statement.

"Knew what?" She smiled.

"You aren't Canadian. Why should I tell you anything?"

"We have no official standing here, and we'll leave if you want us to go, but you have something you want to be explained, don't you?" Siglinde had the expression of a cat that had cornered a mouse. She also had some experience with students' unfocused questions.

"How is this going to be used?" The woman was right. He badly wanted to know. He wanted his suspicions of Ellie and RoH confirmed, although that both were aliens and claimed Charlie as a relative perplexed him. It seemed too much like fiction.

"We simply want to talk to his family," Siglinde tried to make it sound homey and safe. "We think they might have seen something."

Mike hesitated, sitting silently for some time. Siglinde and her partner waited. Mike had to resolve a struggle between loyalty and curiosity.

"So, Siglinde Hilfreich, what do you want to know?"

"Did you meet a woman and a little girl?"

"Yes, at Charlie's house."

"Are they still there?"

"I don't know. They didn't have any plans to leave as far as I know. Charlie said he hadn't seen her in a long time. I assume they stayed."

Even though he was eager to find out what the actual story of Charlie, Ellie, and RoH might be, he would not reveal too much. Strangers did not deserve the courtesy, at least not until they earned trust.

"So, it is his daughter," Siglinde sounded excited.

"That's all I know," Mike sighed, "You're right, I want to know it all. Will you keep me in the loop?"

"Yes," Siglinde sounded sincere, "I promise you."

"Yes, it is his daughter." Mike decided not to bother to detail which of Charlie's visitors was which.

"Why don't you talk to Charlie?" Mike wanted to end the discussion before he said too much.

"That's our next step," Siglinde stood. "Can we chat again?"

"For sure," Mike said as they all stepped out of his office. "Call ahead next time, though."

As the pair walked past Kerri's cubicle between Mike and Charlie's offices, she looked the visitors over closely. Kerri scratched off the possibility that Mike had a new girlfriend. This chick, in her sophisticated suit jacket and dress slacks, did not seem the type interested in small-town hicks, as she described herself and her community.

"What's up, Mr. Hammersmith?" The visitors were still in earshot.

"Mike, it's Mike, you goof." Mike leaned on Kerri's cubical partition. "They were asking about Charlie's family."

"Mr. Keys has a family?" Kerrie feigned surprise. Charlie had given her approximately the same message that Mike had received in the parking lot. Charlie had told her his long-lost daughter had surprised him and they all wanted privacy and not to tell. She would not have given the visitors the time of day, but she thought, *Mike knows what he's doing.*

"He has a daughter," Mike returned to his office, not wanting to expand the circle who knew the story.

Kerri reached for her cell and hit the speed dial to Charlie.

The NAAP log recorded Kerrie's call warning him that strangers were interested in his family. Charlie had urgently reminded the woman not to discuss it with anyone, but then suggested that soon he and Kerri would do a pub night. Then he would give her the whole story.

"A pub... night," Kerri emphasized night, "would be perfect."

The watcher would notify Siglinde.

Charlie's evening deteriorated into boredom, climaxed by the excitement of going to bed. The infrared watch seemed pointless.

What should I do, Mother? Should we call Father in?

No, Âإنْطِ, this is an opportunity. Even though we want to encourage the small countries, we can't ignore the three major powers. We have a rule not to lie to humans, but we don't have to tell everyone everything. That woman is an intellectual, and although there are many ugly people similar to years ago, she is not one. Discuss the basics with her. She likes to have things to think about. She and a couple of others are a potential positive influence on our work. It might be necessary that they act as if they are betraying their country. If things work out and humans survive, Siglinde Hilfreich will be part of the key solution to star travel.

By the way, another group from the US government has kidnapped your grandmother, but she's okay.

How do you know?

Âﻹنط, my dear, they have that group trying to monitor us. We have had a way to watch them and an advantage since they don't have anyone inside our ships

RoH received a mental picture of how they spied and a clear image of the key.

I don't think you need to worry about that until later.

Mother?

Yes?

Please call me RoH. It makes me feel at home on Earth.

How do I meet her, Mother?

Chapter Nine

Sprouting exotic flowers

Well, Quantz, things were moving along nicely, although I saw more danger than hope and couldn't see any progress. I'm glad I didn't know about them taking Lisa then. I would have done something stupid.

By the time we knew of the Project X people in Goderich, Ellie had started what we humans call a grassroots organization. It looked like a collection of useless old folks, but they had a powerful motivator. They knew the truth.

She didn't intend them to be a guerilla army but to argue the alien case at the street level. As events have shown, the street has been as important as the halls of power. Ordinary people must oppose the crazies. Even tin-pot governments like Canada try to behave as the big three did. You say, did.
Recent events end that way of governing the world.

"**M**ost of my contacts, at least the ones who aren't in old-fogy jail, live in London. I don't suppose you have an Earth car waiting," Peter smiled, sipping his coffee and looking out the coffee shop window into Stratford's Albert Street. "Can you magic carpet us there?"

"That wouldn't be a good idea," Ellie giggled. "How do we do it?"

Peter drew a small plastic folder from his pocket.

"I couldn't keep cash at the home. There are too many light fingers, both staff and inmates, but I have my bank cards, and my library card," he laughed. "I ordered E-books online; didn't think a pile of paper to clean out when I kicked the bucket made any sense. Let's find a bank machine."

Ellie wanted to get out of town quickly. It might take a few hours or days for the local police to notify the provincial force, but they would have Peter's picture on the evening television news.

Peter made his first cash withdrawal at the ATM in the coffee shop. Banks all had security cameras on the machines.

"Let's go to that Shell on the corner," Peter headed down the street. "If I use local machines, they will waste time looking in the neighbourhood."

Once he had hit his withdrawal limit on one card, he used a second. Then a cash-back on the purchase of a baseball cap gave them over a thousand dollars.

Peter found a store that sold knock-off cell phones and soon held a basic unit with a pay-as-you-go monthly account.

"I had to use a credit card to get the account. If they trace it, at least it will still be in Stratford. That might slow them down a day or two." Peter handed Ellie a chocolate bar. "How do we get to London?"

"You're the expert," Ellie laughed. "I didn't grow up around here."

Peter hailed a taxi.

"Is this your car?" He asked the driver. Peter cast an admiring glance at the neat Chevy Spark electric sedan.

"Yes sir," if Peter had been young, the driver would have sped away, but this old man did not look like a carjacker.

"I'll give you 300 to take me and my daughter to London, off meter."

The cabbie gave Peter another look. He did not look like a high roller gangster, and Ellie did not look like a captive or a hooker.

"Hop in, buddy. I'll take half now and the rest in London."

The taxi driver drove them a hundred kilometres to London Fairground and returned home with 300 dollars for a few hours of work and ten dollars' worth of electricity. It would be some time before he told the cops about the strange "old guy and a young chick".

"The cops will eventually find out about this," Peter punched in the number for a friend in the local alien abductee community. "They may not even try for a nobody like me, although the home will probably push them. They'll be afraid my daughter will sue their asses off." Peter's laugh turned a few heads. "She will, you know. She's a feisty one."

"Jim and I used to get together, swig beer and watch the sky, wondering if we would ever again meet aliens, or have to endure being taken again." He frowned and Ellie touched his arm.

"There will be no more ordeals, Peter. I promise. Once they connect you with me, you will be somebody. They'll spend a lot of resources and likely track you down, but don't worry, they can't harm you."

Jim owned a little Honda and had a two-bedroom condominium that he shared with a cat and a talkative cockatoo.

"I married several times," he told Ellie, "but they couldn't endure my nightmares and never stayed long."

"Crazy Jim, crazy Jim," said the cockatoo.

"That damned bird belonged to my last wife. She called me crazy." Jim glared at the snow-white creature and winked. "Her new boyfriend didn't like it, so now we are in a relationship."

"Love Jim, love Jim," the bird fluttered on its perch.

"One wife even asked if I was a war vet. What we went through caused similar PTSD."

Ellie repeated the promise that she had made to Peter.

Jim's and Peter's eagerness to be involved and "get the show on the road" led to a small gathering that evening in Jim's living room. Ellie had to reassure everyone they would not suffer more alien bumbling. She then had to deal with the opposite problem of everyone wanting to be involved in something important and eager to rush into the streets with the news.

Ellie's deprecating description stimulated a discussion of how everyone had felt hopeless in the face of the all-knowing, all-powerful visitors. They had to adjust their thinking to understand that a part alien had a more pragmatic opinion of the alien and her own abilities.

Ellie explained her mission, at least as much as she could divulge. She emphasized the aliens wanted to win the support of the ordinary people to influence governments to unify in a common cause of saving life on the planet. The aliens had been watching Earthlings long enough to know that the masses needed things kept in small bits of digestible understanding and goals. They had developed an informal scale of rating various human societies by the sophistication in the content of the commercial and political advertising aimed at the masses. They had taken the rather practical approach that opportunistic humans would have found the best ways to motivate people to their purpose. The star people also knew that humans functioned best in small, convivial groups.

"If you ever end up on a ship again, it will be because you asked to go. We would welcome you as a visitor or to stay."

Ellie, as the unthreatening and charismatic face of the alien cause, calmed her audience. Almost everyone had read her great uncle's books. The group eagerly discussed action.

"I can get you near the MP, Liz Dafoe. She's only a backbencher."

"I can set you up with my MPP, Lucan Highbury," another said.

The pair glared at each other and suddenly burst into laughter. They both realized, with no interference from Ellie, that their partisan politics would have to go to fulfill Ellie's quest and the needs of humanity. Several had an anti-authoritarian attitude. Anything that disrupted the powerful was good for them. The group had differences that would have kept them separated in the normal flow of life, but they found solid unity in the common task of saving humanity and all life on the planet. It made their lives, dislocated by the aliens, worthwhile and for a purpose. A part alien had appeared as their healer.

"I'll leave it to you all to decide how much effort you will give to this, but I hope you will start spreading the message. Tell people the facts about your own experiences and the details of the alien flap twenty years ago. Using my great uncle's books would be a help. I'll do E-book versions and put them on a free book website. It'll be under my uncle's name but with a foreword by Ellie Keys."

"Peter," Ellie smiled, "I'll set it up so you will be the online contact, but make up a name. We don't want them rounding you up because of this. The book will be free, so it should find many readers you don't know. Track all of them and make contact. You were an English teacher; put your stories on the site as a free book? All this would be a start."

"People will think we're crazy," a woman piped up.

"They do anyway whenever we try to talk about this." Jim seemed at ease with people.

"Crazy Jim, crazy Jim," the cockatoo cried.

Ellie frowned, "Don't get discouraged. Speak to as many as you can. If we reveal our presence, those people will remember and will talk to the media. If we decide not to do anything, I'll offer you some options."

The historic possibility that they could help make humanity a star-travelling species added to the excitement of people who only hours earlier had thought they were of no use, waiting to die. Ellie felt renewed hope. This group was a good start. She needed a few billion more.

The next evening, Ellie's accomplice ushered her into a small auditorium where the meeting would confirm the local MP to represent the party in the soon-to-be-called election.

"It's nice to see some young blood here." The mostly older folks shook Ellie's hand, thinking her a recent convert to the partisan cause. Younger people grouped around the candidate, opportunists eyeing the woman with eager anticipation of when she might retire, giving them a shot at the fat pension. All were eager to work hard to earn the opportunity. While they eyed Liz with anticipation, they circled each other with the caution of male wolves seeking the chance to castrate the other. The circling pack included two women.

Liz Dafoe had the instincts of a successful politician and noticed Ellie almost instantly. The newcomer was by far the youngest, best-looking audience member, and Liz saw her as a potential supporter, and perhaps more. Such a fine woman would look good on the campaign trail and elsewhere. The MP contrived to be standing next to Ellie.

"Hello, I'm Liz Dafoe," Liz took Ellie's hand without asking.

"I'm Ellie," she pressed Liz's hand and then withdrew.

"Just... Ellie?" Liz smiled.

"Oh," Ellie had not thought of her last name, "Ellie Keys."

"Ellie is just in from..." Ellie's escort gushed.

"Goderich," Ellie intervened, "I just arrived from Goderich."

Several people demanded Liz's attention, but she did not want to leave it there. Fortunately, Ellie gave her an opening.

"I want to talk with you."

"I tell you what," Liz tried to deflect several of the demanding opportunists, "I have a suite upstairs in this hotel. I want to chat with you, so come up after the meeting. It might be late."

"That would be fine." Ellie wanted a private chat, away from the ears of the eager mob. "I'll wait."

Liz disappeared and Ellie wandered about with her escort close by. While the evening proved mostly uneventful, Ellie overheard two interesting snippets of conversation.

"Liz the lez..." drifted in a whisper between two of the younger ambitious types.

The most intriguing bit came from a gathering of several veterans.

"There were lights up in Huron. I think it was a flying saucer."

The laughs did not discourage the speaker. Several others added their own beliefs in alien visitation. Ellie's escort joined the group. Ellie hoped she would not betray her "prize alien". It would be awkward if this crowd found out, but it encouraged Ellie that there seemed to be people ready to believe. Unfortunately, believers could be friends or enemies. The American agencies trying to trap her and RoH were dangerous believers.

Ellie had no more interesting encounters and although she did not drink alcohol, she found it useful to hold the provided full glass of Champaign to discourage refills.

The gathering ended after Liz's thank you speech and a cheer.

The suite had a touch of luxury. Liz travelled in style. This entitled, excessive living disappointed Ellie. It would be hard to get those used to extravagance to accept a life of only enough to fill their needs and allow for noble sharing. Every race in the galaxy that had become sustainable, and that meant all that had avoided their suicide, had embraced life with enough to meet each individual's physical needs and comfort, avoiding competitive destruction. No failed technical species had survived to die in a natural occurrence, like an asteroid impact. Some internal flaws always destroy them first and often the ability of the planet to sustain life.

"Have a seat," Liz ushered Ellie to the overstuffed leather couch. "Would you like a drink?"

"Just water." Ellie settled comfortably and realized the seductiveness of excess. Liz poured a wine, retrieved a bottle of cold water from the bar, and came to sit close to Ellie on the couch. Their knees touched. She examined the younger woman she considered desirable and vulnerable to the power and charm of a politician.

"Thank you," Ellie accepted the water, and examined Liz, who had targeted her for other reasons. The obvious situation did not worry Ellie.

"What did you want to discuss?" Liz leaned closer.

"Saving the world," Ellie smiled.

Liz sat bolt upright. In her fantasies, she had hoped Ellie had the same lust as hers, but this took her by surprise.

"What do you mean?" Liz hoped Ellie was not a wacko. Her hand rested on Ellie's knee.

In a brief flash, Liz saw Ellie's story and the brilliance of her mission.

"Who are you?" Liz gasped and recoiled in fright, her game forgotten.

Liz bolted for the door, and away from what she felt was this monstrous threat. Her frantic yanking on the door handle had no effect.

Trapped...

Liz Dafoe crumbled against the door, whimpering in fright. Ellie had lured her into an inhuman trap. Liz's legs weakened.

"I am an explorer and, hopefully, a messenger. You just saw my autobiography, and now know my mission. I need your help."

Ellie moved swiftly to the door. Liz prepared for death and flinched. Ellie reached out to support the crumbling woman. Her touch calmed. Liz's sobs lessened.

"You're..." the words trailed off, but death no longer seemed near.

"No, I'm not an alien, not a total one. I care about the Earth as much as you do. We want to give guidance and hope humanity can save itself."

Ellie eased Liz to the couch, so it supported her trembling body. Ellie's finger gently cleared Liz's dripping tears.

The gentleness of the touching, not Ellie's ability to manipulate, comforted. Liz's mind cleared.

"And you think a lowly MP from London, Ontario, can save the world?" Liz laughed sardonically. "I have no power, none, and as you just saw, no courage." To Liz, her statement seemed a pathetic admission to her role as a minion in a political party. It also seemed an admission that whatever happened in this room had passed beyond her control. Liz knew she had to submit to the mercy of this... *creature*.

Liz shuddered.

"Despite what you think of yourself, you are courageous and people respect you. You are not a minion, as you seem to think, and if I'm a creature, it's a human creature."

Ellie, knowing her thoughts, jarred Liz even more. She no longer doubted Ellie's rationality, and it emphasized her frightening power.

"You don't need to be afraid," Ellie said. "No harm will come to you, or Earth, even if this doesn't succeed. Of course, if it fails, humans will probably destroy Earth. Our calculations give intelligent life on this planet a 10% chance of survival, if nothing changes and zero probability of maintaining any sophisticated technology."

Liz sat in a numbed stupor, her breathing shallow. Ellie touched her and the woman jerked to awareness.

"You are real?"

"Yes, and now that my star family has stopped our bumbling interference, we aren't an accidental threat. We need something from humans, though."

"Water, oxygen, resources," Liz listed off things she had seen in several old space-invader movies, "sex, and I thought I was going to seduce you, how ironic."

Ellie giggled. "You wanted sex from this alien a few minutes ago, and our DNA is similar. We want genetic material." Ellie winked.

Liz blushed.

"No, we need nothing physical. There are many dead planets with those things, and even on its airless bodies, this solar system has much more of those resources than Earth. We normally don't do personal physical gratification, what you think of as recreational sex," Ellie sighed as if remembering. "We understand the importance of the pleasure aspect of reproduction in almost all species that reproduce sexually and in most the need for that emotional bonding you call love, but we reproduce in a more prosaic way. Maybe we need to change that too. We store our reproductive material in several places in the event of a local catastrophe. It's infrequently used as necessary to replace attrition. Although most times, fertilization and gestation happen in vitro, I had the privilege of carrying my daughter inside my body for nine months."

"My existence, and now that of my daughter, has motivated extra reproduction for the Earth project. We could produce many copies of my daughter if that became necessary. Fortunately, it hasn't. I love the uniqueness of my little girl and hope newer, different ones will eventually occur. The female parent raises the hybrid child, and we develop strong bonds. As you would say, I love my daughter and she loves me. It is new. Rearing a child on a starship is a novel activity."

"Sexual pleasure and love bond is another thing star-people have lost."

Ellie paused. Her last statement triggered an old, deep feeling of love for someone other than her family.

"What *do* you want with Earth?" Liz still thought about the horrifying answers from fiction. She found it hard to accept the other goals.

"Star people have lost their empathy and ability to interact on less than an intellectual level, at least my pure star family has. I'm mostly human and have those. They somehow think repopulating themselves with more of me, and my daughter especially, would be an improvement. That will take many thousands of your years, considering how long the aliens, as you insist on calling us, live. In the meantime, they hope that empathy, the thing you all call humanity, can save all life on this planet. Earth genes will let those of us who have learned to travel the stars achieve a higher level of existence."

"Small order," Liz murmured, "I don't think humans can do it."

"It's your last hope, and our next hope. There is an opinion amongst the people that we should just entice good human breeding stock to come with us and carry on the project on a suitable planet with no suicide weapons."

"And you don't agree?" Liz moved closer.

"I'm part human," Ellie put her hand on Liz's, "and as you say, I have skin in the game of human survival. My parents are both human and I love them; I am them, except for a little stellar genetic material. My daughter is almost half-human and I think the ideal. We would like more of her."

"I guess I'm not good breeding stock," Liz managed a chuckle. Ellie joined in the laughter.

Ellie touched Liz in a way that if she had been an Earth woman, Liz would have thought to be an invitation to intimacy. She resisted drawing that conclusion with Ellie.

"No, I know your sexual make-up and you would not be happy, although perhaps we could use zygotes from your ova, but you will be happy here, including that love."

Liz looked doubtful. Another image jolted her.

"No, she hates me."

"She can't express herself." Ellie took Liz's hand. "You must lead."

"I need to learn about political leaders so I can decide if we bother with them. You are returning the day after tomorrow. Can I come with you and have you teach me about some of those? And you can build your relationship with her."

Liz smiled, doubtful of Ellie's confidence in the future of her love life. That Ellie knew her agenda without Liz telling her led to the simple conclusion that she could not lie to this being.

"Is this a dream?"

"No, and you will remember everything. I could make you forget, but I need you to act from knowledge. You may, one day, have to verify that I exist, that the star people exist."

"I'm not sure I am that brave."

Liz had already changed what she had hoped to accomplish with the local politicians. Ellie's aim seemed so rational. She could not tell them about an alien, but she could talk about improving the world without opportunistic self-interest. They would have to learn about aliens from someone else. Liz was not that stupid.

"I'm couch-surfing. I'll sleep right here." Ellie patted the cushion.

"Are you sure I can't offer you the bed?" Liz smiled.

"No, thank you," Ellie smiled in return, "wait for your love." Again, an image flashed through Liz's mind. One day, when necessary, you will be brave.

"I need tomorrow to make two other visits. It's a matter of language."

"I would like one thing, though. If you let me, I want to make it so I can be in touch with you quickly. You might come into danger, and I can help you with that. I will need your help again. You can say no. It won't hurt, and it is no danger. Will you let me?"

Liz, still somewhat dazed, nodded.

Ellie's hand touched Liz's forearm, a faint dizziness, and then everything returned to normal.

As Ellie drifted off on the comfortable couch, she thought about what she needed, what her life lacked in intimacy. It was not physical pleasure, although that certainly would be acceptable, but the need for companionship, the conviviality that her people recognized as a human strength. Perhaps she could find some companionship with Liz, a need much more important than gratification. Ellie longed for her mother, and now, strangely, she longed for another. That longing seemed to come from when she was RoH's age.

Chapter Ten

RoH and Siglinde

Quantz, you have not met RoH yet. She says she wants to talk with you sometime. Believe me, for all the questions you have now, once you talk with RoH, you'll have a thousand more.

The demanding buzz from her cell interrupted Siglinde's breakfast.

"Charlie Keys left for work about ten minutes ago. Then, a little girl appeared on the road, walked up to Keys', and went into the house."

"Thanks, Roberto, we'll be there in ten minutes; don't lose her."

"Let's finish and get moving." Siglinde said to the man and the woman with her. "Roberto just saw a little girl go into Keys' place. She's alone."

That the OPP was thin on the ground around Goderich probably prevented Siglinde from getting a speeding ticket.

"She's still there," Roberto leaned into the window of the SUV.

"I'm going in alone," Siglinde said. "Ellie is not a threat."

Siglinde had memorized the file, and Ellie had showed great mental power years ago. The girl had hurt no one, but her cerebral gymnastics could be devastating. Siglinde hope she did not appear as a threat and receive a mental blow that would overwhelm her.

She is here, Mother.

Siglinde found RoH in the kitchen.

"Hello," the little girl said as Siglinde stepped through the doorway. "I hoped we would meet."

"Why would an alien want to meet me?" Siglinde arranged herself at the table across from RoH without invitation.

"Why do you think there are aliens? Doesn't the Drake equation show it's likely impossible?"

"Mathematics is beautiful and useful, but it's also elegantly stupid. That analysis lacked knowledge of the key factors, and besides, we know you exist. I head up Project X, which took over from the shambles you made of the army effort. Fortunately, they kept everything but the actual artefacts. Yes, we know you exist and you know we know."

"There you go, assuming things about me," RoH smiled. "Maybe you're in an asylum and imagining this conversation. Maybe I don't exist."

"Don't gaslight me, young lady, we are both real, and since you look to be about ten, I'll assume that you being able to talk and think like this makes you into something much more than a little girl, something alien."

Siglinde did not sound horrified or judgemental, but merely curious.

"I'm still a little girl here to visit family." RoH frowned. Despite her intellectual ability, she had succumbed to a youngster's desire to impress and betrayed too much intellectual capacity. On Earth, ten-year-old children normally could not hold such a sophisticated conversation with an adult. She quickly shifted to another subject.

"What do you think about the state of humans on the planet?"

"What do you mean?"

"Humans don't seem to be advanced but ignorant and most do not use their thinking capacity."

"Well, everyone is different," Siglinde shrugged. "We do not expect everyone to be an intellectual; some are just not intelligent enough and others detoured while maturing."

"Do they need to be intelligent, as you narrowly define it, or lost in their upbringing?" RoH pressed.

"Look," Siglinde flared, "some people are simply stupid."

RoH's pained look seemed to condemn. Siglinde felt she had flunked a test. RoH remained calm.

Why is this little girl getting to me?

"Yes, physically there are some brains that cannot process abstract thought; however, much of the problem is from crippled opportunity, not innate lack of intelligence. Many of your scientists in the field understand that, but your system has evolved tests that are simple and generate a nice number that sorts people with no context or nuance. Your world wastes many minds. Those with organic issues such as Down's syndrome or autism, as you label them and call it a condition are performing at a high level that is hidden by a communication barrier."

"I am young," RoH went on, "and struggle to understand and have almost everything to learn, but everyone always encourages me, especially the harder I find things and the more wrong answers I give. That is part of the difference. On Earth, it is too often a crime to be wrong. They mark you down for wrong answers on a test simply for administrative convenience. The crime is not getting the answer wrong, but not struggling for the correct one. It's a bigger crime to judge people for their errors."

"You have an immense problem with ignorant, lazy, unhappy, hostile people. We can teach away ignorance, but most laziness comes from never being praised for trying and always being made to feel pain at failing. After a while, individuals give up. It's easier not to try than to be condemned for errors. Most of those are intelligent, but they become depressed and hostile. They kill themselves, become murderers or join cults; some latch onto the craziest things; what you call conspiracies because believing in them makes them feel smart without having to struggle for the truth."

"Everyone can learn to dance," RoH suggested in an unexpected parallel, "but there are so many kinds of music, so many dances."

"What does that mean?"

"Everyone has their place on the floor, intelligent or not, but there are many spaces, many tasks that need doing for the success of everyone. The right music makes people dance the best they can no matter where they are. It would be wise to bring out the best in each person; we need to play the right music for each one to thrive and contribute. Everyone is glad when we dance to the right music, and happiness is essential for all species to thrive, including yours."

"Most of Earth's human advancement comes from many individuals, working at their capacity contributing something to that learning. Some may only dig ditches, but those of us who benefit from that ditch must respect and honour the digger."

"Occasionally there appears what you call a genius. They are rare and the genius is in the masses, but these individuals function well beyond the 20% that some think is a barrier. It's probably unscientific and useless to even give a percentage. The greatest human mind hit almost 30%."

"Einstein?" Siglinde narrowly thought of science.

"No, Mozart..." RoH smiled, "he made music. If he had known how to do it, he could have made the piano play without touching the keys."

"You play guitar and sing like Einstein talking to Mozart through music. You get some decent quantum ideas while singing."

"I still do not understand what you are getting at."

"There are too many humans on Earth, but only about 40% are using their thinking capacity and maybe 20% are excelling at whatever they apply that ability to do. It's such a waste. The rest live a little better than animals, even those who have wealth, material success, and what you call intelligence and formal education. They are dancing to music that isn't theirs, making them unhappy, and they give up and become self-destructive or angry and destructive to others, or just accumulating stuff and greedily destroying the planet looking for happiness."

"So, what does it mean? That's the way it is and nothing can change."

"You didn't believe that as an undergrad at MIT."

"You're right. I thought I could change the world. How do you know I went to MIT?"

RoH smiled. It no longer mattered if Siglinde knew who she was. At the end of this conversation, RoH would do what she must do. For the short term, the woman was not a threat, and in the future, Siglinde's old idealism would motivate her to do some good, perhaps with an alien nudge. She might help save life on Earth and take a step toward the stars.

"I know all about you, Siglinde. You are a good person, and smart. Your specialty in what Earth calls quantum physics is the path to the stars. In a few years, you will do what you most desire and be involved in its theoretical development. You will be happy."

Siglinde again felt that warm glow.

The feeling that mumbo-jumbo Reiki people claim to create, Siglinde thought.

"Those Reiki people are sort of on a good track," RoH said as if she was inside Siglinde's head, "but they don't know what they are doing, invoking all that supposed channelling of energy and things, as you say, mumbo-jumbo. That warm feeling you had comes from within. Your mind just went where you could feel it, where you are happy. Those Reiki practitioners, the good ones, relax you enough to go there. It's not magic or the focusing of external energy, but a cure for a disquieted mind. You can find it yourself; you would if you walk in the forest and sing."

Once more, the little girl stunned Siglinde. The Ricki thought had been so fleeting. Siglinde felt naked.

"How did you know I like the forest and deeply miss nature?"

"I told you, Siglinde, I know all about you."

Siglinde knew RoH had examined her mind. A fearful admiration settled on her. The reports from 20 years before held a warning about the power of this girl. She tried to close off her thoughts, to hide her mind.

That's useless. Is that my thought or...?

RoH contemplate Siglinde with an enigmatic expression that was a combination of laughter and empathy. Siglinde felt peace once again.

"You don't need to fear me probing your mind, Siglinde. I am only doing it now because I need to be clear on what is important to you. I promise I won't invade your privacy to manipulate you."

"You know, Siglinde, your present circumstance of being trapped in a bureaucratic backwater, away from the things that make you who you are, your science, your music and your forest, resembles the situation my star family has experienced for millennia of Earth years. They have experienced an environment of controlled, high-tech sterility. It is rich in intellectual activity and engineering, but no more. We live in a bubble in the cosmos. Our planetary communities are similar. None resembles Earth."

"Earth is unlike any place we have, although there are many thousands of near-Earths in the galaxy. Yes, I have learned about it from the records of centuries of observation, but it is different and much richer actually to talk with the dandelions."

"You talk with dandelions?" Siglinde sounded confused.

"It's a metaphor, although I feel the plants' life vibrations. I would not call it communicating, more like empathizing. The plants are all of life on Earth, including you. Previously, because of disconnect from natural processes, the star people did not have that empathy, that feeling of oneness with all life. Mother was a lucky accident. Great great-grandfather accidentally fathered her great-grandfather. The star people would not have approved it if proposed beforehand, but his ship crash marooned him and put him out of communication for a long time. He succumbed and learned love from a Texas farm woman."

"It stimulated a few deliberate attempts to interbreed with humans, but some were disasters. You have seen the records from Alaska and elsewhere, but scientifically, those horrors created a new understanding.

The important factor was in great-great-grandfather loving great-great-grandmother. She knew he was an alien before they conceived great-grandfather. It broke both their hearts when he had to leave. When that understanding appeared, all efforts to inter-breed ended, until my grandmother and grandfather conceived my mother. They chose Grandmother because she was a direct descendant of my great-great-grandfather, and grandfather came from generations that we took many times and were suitable because they showed courage and fought back."

"Not very romantic, is it?" RoH smiled towards a wide-eyed Siglinde. "They focused on avoiding horror like the old mistakes. Happily, Mother is not a horror, and please don't think I am. Each step, starting with great-great-grandma, has concentrated human empathy higher in each generation and combined it with star abilities. I have no choice but to care about you and all the dandelions on your beautiful planet. Because of this, I am already grieving the possibility that this will come to nothing."

"If humans are to reach the stars, no..., if humans are even to survive," RoH jumped back to her earlier metaphor, "you have to play music for everyone, each person, develop the best in everyone and provide what they need. That requires a change deeper than you will admit to right now, and it will help you humanely reduce your population and exploitation of the planet to a level Earth can handle. When people use their minds to their potential, and flow their feelings honestly, they will find enough physically and seek only enough. Over consumption to satisfy emotional emptiness will go away with no other trick required. Humans already use automation to do drudge work. As you extended that, it would free people and provide surplus resources to create art and starships. Because of your bonus of fossil energy, humans have a temporary glut of technology and material. You have squandered it."

"I think that's impossible," Siglinde slumped in her chair.

"Maybe we can help." RoH gave her new friend a lead into the truth.

"We?" Siglinde smiled. "I knew you were Ellie from the stars, the Ellie who fled so long ago. I know your mother is partly alien, but she's a nice music teacher in Seattle."

It was time for the big bomb.

"Ellie is my mother," RoH focused on Siglinde, watching for the slightest sign of instability. "Lisa is her mother, my grandmother."

Siglinde laughed.

"I had a hunch when I heard there were two of you. Ted, my co-worker, is sure of it."

"He's right. He's right on many things, Siglinde. Ted is more than he appears. Listen to him. He's in love with you, you know."

"I know," Siglinde sighed.

"You love him." RoH showed no expression. "You need that love soon. You and Liz will need strength."

Siglinde did not bother to ask how RoH knew of Liz or how she knew of Ted and her feelings. They had never expressed them to each other, let alone to anyone else.

"You sound like you know the future. Are you alien time travellers?"

"Not in the fictional way you might be thinking. Time is not a real thing, independent of energy transformations, and entropy is a cruel master. You can't go back in time, but my people live for a long time. Longevity is a sort of time travel into the future, although we can only return to the past in memory. We can examine human minds, and project a probability of your future, and we find some organic issues that let us predict things like someone in their life having a heart attack or stroke. We are about 99.9% accurate in that. I don't like that they used it as a weapon several times against dangerous humans. You know the story from back then. The file is on your desk."

Siglinde could not hide her surprise. It seemed as if the aliens had a spy watching Project X, *but then*, Siglinde decided, *nothing this 10-year-old ancient said should be a surprise.*

"My knowledge is old. I am young," RoH responded to the thought and laughed. "I'm not ancient."

"What happened in Texas years ago tells you what might happen. Your government, the way your people think and want control, makes them still behave in the same way, trying to use power and control for their profit. They have convinced themselves that if they could make us visitors allies, it would give them power. Project X is just trying to learn and make contact. A group that is spying on you is working to exploit our presence. If they subvert our intention, everything fails and humans will die out. Most life on Earth will die out, and this is Earth's last chance. Every one of the major world powers thinks that way. It's the people who control those political structures that think that way, with petty greed in place of the well-being of humanity and the Earth. The only hope is for the smaller countries and ordinary people to lead and give the big ones and their masters no choice but to follow, and for all countries to disappear. You are one species and your artificial separations cause all of your disasters."

"We calculate, given the rate of your depletion of the natural resources of the planet, and the growing mental fragility of your cultural and economic system, Earth has about two years before the chaos. That will quickly lead to horrible collapse and losing all of your sophisticated technical ability. This is your last chance."

Siglinde sat dumbfounded, but then nodded. "There are many here who have made the same calculation."

"Most of the galaxy is desolate in terms of life. In the places like Earth, rich in life, nature has cycles of verdant paradise and desolation. Intellectual species always interfere with the natural cycles, but the trick is to do that without destroying the essential living base. Most have failed. Earth has strayed from that. You must restore it or die."

"You will need to go against your government sometime. It won't be easy, and we won't make that decision for you. They will probably force you. All humans must freely decide to take the path to survival, or they will die out. That will make mother and me sad, of course. We are part human."

"If we decide this, can you star-people help us? What about this other group I never heard of?"

"They are a threat." RoH frowned. "They are about to act, and that may cause us to move sooner than we planned. If that happens, there will be more chaos than we had hoped. The best option is slowly to prepare the population for our public appearance."

"You won't have any influence on your government or stop this other plot," RoH laid a hand flat upon the table, making a final judgement.

"I know," said Siglinde, "I'm not in this thinking I'll make a difference; I'm here because I want to understand. Maybe I can help."

"You know you want to make a difference, Siglinde, but they won't let you." RoH frowned. "They will kill you first."

"I know that too," Siglinde seemed resigned, "but it's worth the risk. I wouldn't be the first to die because of you aliens."

"We can't help you decide or do the right thing. I can take steps to keep you personally safe, and Ted and Liz too, but you must allow me. Will you let me do a little thing so we can know where you are, and if you are in physical danger? I can't decide for you. It won't hurt or be a risk, but you have to trust this little girl in front of you who you are only half-convinced isn't a monstrous body snatcher."

RoH smiled gently.

Siglinde trembled, poised on the high cliff of a monumental decision, fearful of the fall, and yet the wind of freedom caressed her face. She tried hard to envisage RoH as a monster. Siglinde only hesitated for an instant.

"Yes," she whispered.

"Give me your arm," RoH reached across the table and her fingers touched the offered forearm. Siglinde felt a brief faintness.

"There will be a time when you feel you must pass on secrets of your government, not to the star people, but other humans. That might be vital, and if it is, you will be in grave danger. Be brave, and count on our help. There are no guarantees in anything. You may still fail, or die, or both, but I think now, the odds of you surviving will be in your favour."

Siglinde felt peace and certainty wash through her.

"Thank you," her voice was barely audible.

"Try to get Liz to make the same decision you just made. If she agrees, someone will take care of it, but not me."

"You won't remember this conversation except for a strange feeling of understanding, snippets of thought and needing to know more, and you will for some strange reason want Liz to shake hands with Elliana." RoH smiled. "I hope, one day, we will meet again, continue from here, and reminisce about the great thing we all did. If we can't do that, it will mean we failed. Then you may have to make the same decision my mother made years ago. We might have that conversation among the stars."

"My name is, Â لإنط

The sound assaulted Siglinde's ears.

"It's not exactly Earth music, is it?" RoH smiled mischievously. "Our language is another reason we need some Earth influence. One Earthly linguistic theory is that language changes how an individual sees the universe, or at least his or her place in it. Several Earth centuries ago, my ancestors, most of whom are still alive, realized that their language seemed to be a prison that kept them from understanding other species. Since then, there have been many efforts to overcome this, mostly by trying to decipher other planetary languages from afar. The same accidental biology experiment that has led to me changed that effort. They now realize that the only way to understand the interplay of language is to experience it, to use it. Mother was the first to help. I am the mommy-plus version, and I am learning so much here on Earth. Mom and I used to play language tricks and tease our star family. It is serious work; however, and mother is connecting with some Earth linguists to have, from her soccer playing days, more eyes on the ball. The flip side of that," RoH enjoyed using local expressions, "is that you will all expand your viewpoints by being exposed to star language."

"Siglinde," a stream of alien sound followed, "I just said you have a beautiful mind. It's a garden in the universe."

"My grandfather and grandmother call me RoH, and that means Roberta Heather. I thought you would want to hear what our language sounds like. If I tried to translate my real name, it would approximate New Dust That Spreads New Life. The word is the same one, except for a minor inflection that describes the material that exploding stars inject into the galaxy, and where everything new comes from. My name has some metaphorical importance to my father and the others," she rolled her eyes towards the stars, "like they understand a metaphor." RoH giggled. "I'm a little girl. I like RoH."

"Thank you," Siglinde said. "I feel honoured, RoH. Can I... could you...?"

Suddenly Siglinde saw an unclothed alien form sitting at the table, somewhat smaller and *more energy-efficient than I imagined*, Siglinde thought. The creature's colour wavered between a grey and a blue, sometimes iridescent, then opaque and with a bipedal shape near to human. The alien smile seemed skewed, but a smile beneath proportioned dark eyes and an attractive nose, all topped by a hairless head. Siglinde thought female, although there were no apparent secondary sexual characteristics and perhaps because she knew it was RoH. The hands were smoother with longer fingers than earthly digits and an opposable thumb, and then RoH appeared once more. Siglinde felt as if, somehow, this alien, or at least this part alien, this ancient wisdom as a little girl, had accepted her as an equal.

"You are part of the universe," RoH said, once more wandering Siglinde's mind, "and we are not gatekeepers deciding who belongs in the universe. You are already one of us, one of the life forces in the universe, part of the great cry against entropy. Of course, entropy doesn't exist with Base energy, just with type 1, which is merely mass."

"Base energy?" Siglinde, the physicist, pounced on the casual phrase.

"Type 1 is what we see in the universe, mass-energy. The Base is the energy of the continuum, or perhaps we can say it is the continuum. Its entropy is constant, everywhere, so the universe has no time; it is eternal."

Siglinde's perplexed expression caught RoH's attention.

"Normal mass-energy is obvious, and you human scientists have been struggling with trying to describe everything in its terms. Since you came up with the equivalence, Einstein's equation $E=m$ you have stalled out."

"The equation is $E=mc^2$," Siglinde smiled. She had caught the little girl out. Maybe Earthlings could keep up.

"Well, the c is simply the ratio between baryonic mass and electromagnetic momentum of massless particles. Light has no mass but momentum. It is of little consequence unless you want to use that conversion to create technology, to blow up a star, or to destroy Earth." RoH frowned. "It's all mass, so $E=m$ is a good enough approximation although the scale of the ratio, c squared, is important in describing how Type 1 and Base interact. When you convert mass to photons, the mass may seem to disappear. It becomes massless momentum, preserving Type 1 energy, and the photon imparts momentum to any mass particle it hits. You on Earth observe this in nuclear effects, fission, and fusion, but that is just the mass equivalence of the nuclear-bonding energy."

"So what's this Base energy?" Siglinde ignored RoH's first year physics lecture, but felt she was on the verge of a great scientific breakthrough, albeit second-hand.

"Einstein nearly had it when he invented the continuum. Base energy is the continuum, but not exactly. Einstein's field equations require the continuum to expand. They require the continuum to have entropy. It does not expand; it's flat so that description of the continuum is wrong and your observations only see the effect of Base energy on type 1 energy."

"The continuum is just a mathematical abstraction," Siglinde said.

"Well, no, it exists and without it, nothing would exist. General Relativity is too simple. The math dealing with it is a complicated mess, and that's fitting, since it's more a boiling quantum soup than anything; it's the energy of the universe. Some of you call it vacuum energy. Understanding the continuum is like a word you can't remember, but it's on the tip of your tongue. You humans almost get it."

"So how can we see it, or at least know it's there?" Siglinde was sceptical. The whole of her training did not allow acceptance of this, and a physics lecture from a little girl seemed preposterous until she remembered who this little girl might be.

"Yes, it seems ridiculous, a little girl teaching, and I am a little girl," RoH grinned broadly. She enjoyed revisiting what had been her early, much-simplified lessons in physics. "I know as much about this as you knew about math in Grade 3. Gravity manifests the interaction between Type 1 energy and Base energy. What you would call space itself. You suspect it's there with your rather contrived and inadequate terms of dark mass and dark energy and general vacuum energy."

"What we see as the force of gravity isn't a force at all, and you have all been barking up the wrong tree, as your metaphor would put it. You won't find a graviton. Gravity is simply Type 1 baryonic mass displacing Base energy, putting it into a higher energy state, and the observed effect of gravity is Base energy merely trying to flow back into the void that the Type 1 mass has created because Base wants to be smooth and uniform in its lowest energy state. It drags everything along with it, including baryonic mass and so things fall, as you would say, towards the geometric centre of the displacing mass. I know Earth scientists have a narrow use of the word baryon, but I use it as a general term for all Type 1 mass-energy."

"It's all wild. When Type 1 displaces the Base, the resulting flow to fill all those voids is chaotic. It does weird things, some of which you have discovered in your field of work, quantum effects. Photons interact with Base, actually are more like a ripple in the base by either gaining or losing momentum or energy, or by curving in the flow and changing direction. The Base does not slow down photons but simply reduces or adds to their energy, gaining or losing its momentum. Electro-magnetic energy behaves in what you call a quantum effect, like your quantum tunnelling. Photons always lose energy in a flat continuum, but they lose more if they are going in the opposite direction to the Base energy flow, and gain energy if the Base carries them in the same direction. Einstein's equations are accurate enough to describe it."

Imagine ripples on the surface of a fast-moving river caused by throwing a stone into the water. The disturbance flows with the river and if you marked a point on any little wave, it would seem to gain speed and therefore energy flowing downstream and the opposite against the flow. Points rippling sideways would follow curved paths. Just like photons passing a centre of baryonic mass. It's only a simple analogy. Water has mass and photons do not.

"Locally, a lot of this cancels out, but over cosmic distances, it has a noticeable effect, such as the cosmic red shift that you observe. Local perturbations cancel, but over a long time, a photon loses noticeable momentum to the Base. Electro-magnetic energy loses energy but no apparent velocity, but baryonic mass in motion dumps its momentum or adds to it by changing relative velocity. Inertial mass is the ideal of a motionless baryonic particle. Base energy presses against it evenly so it resists motion. Of course, all Type 1 energy is in motion, so inertial mass is ideal. That is a whole other discussion."

"Once we learn to work with Base energy on the quantum level, we can use it to manipulate Type 1 baryonic reality. Every mind, including yours, Siglinde, is a quantum generator. That understanding unlocks the way to travel the universe and other things like being able to sense someone's thoughts."

"Our propulsion systems mimic Type 1 energy in the direction we want to go, you might say we create a hole in the continuum and then the flow of Base energy trying to fill into what seems to it to be a vacuum pushes our vessels in that direction. The hole always travels in front of the ship, so the light-speed limit disappears because it is travelling into a place where the continuum does not exist. It creates no radiation and leaves nothing for you to detect when you have been able to measure an encounter with a ship. It also lets us manipulate Type 1."

The book RoH had been reading suddenly lifted from the table and then gently returned to its starting point. "But it's easier for me to just make you think that happened." The book repeated its flight. "You can't tell the difference, but I didn't just trick you. I tricked the baryons of the book as well. I made a hole in Base energy above the book."

"To know what you are thinking, or make you think you saw and heard things, I tune my quantum brain to your quantum frequency. I have never done it with more than a handful of people, and usually, it's just one. You remember in the Dakotas when Mother was my age, she did it to hundreds of minds for several hours. It nearly killed her. I am much stronger than she ever was, but I have to be careful. I'm just learning."

Siglinde lifted above her chair, hovered about 30 centimetres, and then slowly sank back onto the seat.

"Whoa, I felt that. It was real."

"Was it?" RoH giggled. "I can do these little tricks on this small scale, maybe influence a few kilometres, but to move a ship and travel the stars, it requires several minds and an amplifier. You might say our ships are amplifiers, but that is a child's simplification."

"You have most of the facts about alien encounters over the past decades memorized, including the crash at Roswell. We know that one constant question about it all from sceptics is, 'Why did a ship from a super-advanced civilization crash in the New Mexico desert?' Some people even embellish it by claiming it hit a weather balloon, simply incorporating the US air force's laughable cover story. Remember, it takes the coordinated mental activity of several individuals. With that ship, it was five. In an incident so rare that we measure its frequency in millennia, one pilot died while they were underway. It was too close to the surface and the remaining four, including my great-great-grandfather, could not stabilize the ship before it hit the ground. It was sad but simple. I wouldn't be here if that hadn't happened. They have made changes since then and will phase out that technology over the next thousand Earth years. There are resource constraints, even amongst the stars."

"Wow," Siglinde flushed, "I knew quantum mechanics was the key to understanding how your abilities and technology work," Siglinde became excited as it confirmed her instincts. Siglinde wished she had a tablet to record notes. She felt the same as she had as an undergraduate, even as a first-year student full of her success as a secondary school student, full of ideas, but humbled by the intellects that taught her and even those, smarter than herself, who shared her classes; humbled by this alien child whose incomplete education dwarfed her pinnacle of earthly understanding. Still, from Siglinde's understanding, RoH's explanations seemed like non-science gobble gook.

It would fulfill my dream of interstellar travel. Siglinde's thoughts raced.

"It is a bit like what you call Alcubierre Drive, but that is an incomplete and wrong understanding, close but incomplete and requires infinite type-1 energy. You and Earth aren't ready for interstellar ships," RoH smiled in the kind way a wise master might tolerate a novice. "Your minds must develop, and you have the rather important job of saving life on Earth first. Not that you have to earn the right as if it were a moral test, but if you don't make Earth livable, you won't develop the ability to explore the stars."

"Mars settlement and similar plans will fail unless you heal the Earth."

"I should have studied biology," Siglinde hid her disappointment with a joke, and both laughed with RoH knowing, and Siglinde suspecting, that she had the right training and emotional tools to help heal the Earth.

"But there's more," RoH mischievously smiled. We still haven't solved the problem of why the universe exists at all. Why is there type 1 energy? The fundamental law of conservation of energy and its adjunct rule, no process creates nor destroys energy, seems to say that the universe, from a type 1 energy perspective, cannot exist. Where did it come from? Are Base and type 1 energies just variations of the same thing? The most common theoretical position is that type 1 is Base energy spun up to the limit. Even then, we make the scientifically unsatisfying assumption that Base energy just exists and has always been. However, we understand that what we call the universe must interact with a non-universe, as some star scientists are calling it. Adding both would be net-zero energy.

"They propose something they call Base non-energy. It is sort of like your idea of a multiverse with one difference; their hypothesis suggests that the non-energy is an overlay with Base energy, a sandwich if you will with Type 1 energy the meat. Base energy and Base non-energy surround us always. They even suggest that perhaps when we thought we were tricking Base energy to drive our ships, and make anti-gravity, what we are doing is making holes in our reality that expose the non-energy. The effect we see is Base energy rushing into those holes. It explains why relatively low-power, organic mental processes can have the effects we have learned to control. It's as different from General Relativity as Einstein was from Newton."

"Our level of understanding is like yours. Even though relativity and quantum physics are incomplete, you can make technology that works based on that partial knowledge. Star people make technology, like our ships, that works based on our current knowledge. We know we need to learn more."

"You and a smart friend of ours will chat about that one too, I hope. My mentors have not included me in those discussions, and I have much to learn. Some argue that there is no scientific basis for an answer. Purists say science explains everything. Those thinkers embrace the non-energy idea. These may be the last significant questions, the last markers of universal knowledge and understanding. Where did it all come from? Maybe humans will answer that. Maybe no one can."

"Another question: why is life so similar everywhere in the galaxy? Sentient beings vary in morphology, but all use DNA. Why is that?"

"We have not travelled to the nearest galaxy, what you call Andromeda, although there is a plan to see if life there is similar. So far, no beings from there have come to our galaxy. We don't know if they might be DNA-based or not."

Suddenly, RoH's face darkened at her thought of the Andromeda system.

What is that? Siglinde startled. *Is that fear in RoH, or anguish?*

"There is a concern about Andromeda," RoH frowned again, having read Siglinde's thoughts. "But nothing to worry about in your lifetime, we don't think, and maybe not even in my lifetime."

Siglinde caught a fleeting look from RoH that suggested she might hide the complete story about Andromeda. The star people believed sentient beings in Andromeda had sent a craft into intergalactic space towards the Milky Way, or "The Great Organism," as the star people called it. The uncertainty about such an expedition worried the star people who had become used to certainty.

"I wish I could take notes. This is fascinating and I want to study it more."

"You won't remember it until we meet again." RoH calmly gazed into Siglinde's face. "I can't let you have it that easily. It isn't my decision to share it, but I think you and I will get to chat again with less constraint. Maybe Mom will join in if they allow me to let you recall this. It will depend if we decide humans can save life on Earth and thus be worth our effort. That will involve making our existence known to everyone on Earth, not just the government insiders in the major powers. In that case, you'll get your chance to study it."

RoH looked at Siglinde. She gently inserted a trigger in Siglinde's brain that would unlock these memories. It was not a thing done lightly. Allowing Siglinde to know would come from discussions involving RoH, Ellie and the project collective. They hoped to set humanity successfully on its path to the stars. Failure was a possibility and a personal danger for Siglinde. If all failed, Siglinde would face the same decision that Ellie had made years before in that Texas pasture.

Siglinde stared at RoH. The little girl had presented something that tantalized her and begged her to examine it, to either verify the truth or debunk nonsense. Her disappointment dripped from her face.

"In the meantime, you will now think your job is not to represent a government or simply learn about aliens, but it will be to save life on Earth. To convince everyone that it is the most important job."

"I don't want to forget this conversation." Siglinde frowned. "Please..."

RoH scooted around the table and hugged Siglinde.

"Goodbye, for now, Siglinde."

Siglinde emerged from the house.

"I thought you saw the girl here," she shot an accusation at the team leader. "I just wasted my time looking under beds."

"I watched her go in." Roberto glanced around, as if expecting to see a little girl fleeing across the field. "It took an hour to look under beds?"

"Well, she isn't there. You wasted my time," Siglinde yanked the car door open, "let's go."

Even though Siglinde led the team, two others hurried inside and spent a fruitless fifteen minutes searching anywhere a little girl could hide. They found no trace that she had been in the building. RoH, with impish amusement, had watched from her chair at the kitchen table.

"I'm sorry, Roberto," Siglinde turned to the team leader, "I didn't mean to snap at you. This is the biggest thing that has happened on our watch. I'm stressed. We need to find those aliens. I'll buy lunch."

Strangely, Siglinde resting in the comfortable rear seat of the SUV had faint whispers passing through her mind.

Type 1 and Base energy... the universe does not exist... the last great question... save Earth first... and Andromeda, a little girl... an alien but a little girl... not Ellie... Ted is right... Ted...

She could not relate the thoughts to anything and did not know where they came from. The need to do pure physics work suddenly had seized her, but the need to save life on Earth dominated. The bureaucratic tangle of Project X had let her forget the big questions that had made her a scientist.

Siglinde had thought that the alien visits were the biggest problem on the scientific table, but now that seemed to have turned into a door opening onto larger questions. She would have to fit searching those issues in with her duty to NAAP. She had the nagging belief that her duty to all life on the planet Earth exceeded her obligation to science, Project X or the American government. Along with the swirl of confusing thoughts, another threatened to raise paranoia. *The government is watching me… us.*

She sank deeper into the soft seat as they sped into town. It seemed the first promising lead from Mike Hammersmith had turned into a blind alley. Maybe the tail on Charlie would yield something.

"Roberto," Siglinde leaned forward, "tomorrow we'll try to flush the grandfather out so we can meet this little alien. Here's what we do…"

Chapter Eleven

Mr. Jorgensen, come here. I want you.

Ellie climbed the stairs to the old mansion located deep on the campus of Western University. Vines covered the brown sandstone outer walls. The pointing and window frames cried for much-needed maintenance. This corner of the university hosted several of the less popular, meagrely patronized disciplines and seemed a quiet backwater to the hustle in the arts, science and professional faculties' main campus.

The new, aluminum-framed door easily opened to her touch, and she stepped into the cool gloom of the linguistics department.

A young woman, perhaps 25 years old, sat behind a modern desk that would have fit in the foyer of any major corporation. The polished redwood supported a fancy curved fake-marble top. The person looked up, somewhat startled, as she sensed Ellie's presence. She removed the ear buds and smiled.

"I would like to see Steven Jorgensen," Ellie said. She could not help pronouncing Jorgensen in its original Scandinavian way, although the man represented the most recent of several generations of descendants from the original desperate farmers who had initially emigrated.

"Oh, you mean Dr. Jorgensen," the young woman's accent drew her words into an almost musical drawl, translating the department chair's name into American phonetics. She stared, wondering if this was a nutcase or a foreigner. *Both,* she thought, *would be interesting.*

"You're an American," Ellie returned the smile, "from their state of Georgia, I think."

"Yes," another smile and no puzzlement. Canadians had always found Rachel's native accent to be transparent. "I'm Rachel Cisse, from Atlanta."

"My name is Ellie. I particularly like the diversity of American accents," Ellie said in an accent that told of her early life in the American north-west. "I find the one in Seattle endearing. Your last name does not sound like a traditional southern one."

"No, I had my last name changed from our old family name of the slave-owner who owned them. Cisse is in honour of my slave ancestors, who came from Senegal. I don't know what family name my original slave ancestor might have had, so I picked one I liked from a list on the internet."

"You got your undergraduate degree and your masters from the University of Georgia, and are here because Steven Jorgensen is an expert in obscure colonial native languages, and you want to study the languages of your kidnapped ancestors. How is your doctoral thesis coming along?"

"Fine," the woman said, startled that the stranger seemed to have read her non-existent biography, or perhaps she had access to the university records. The motivation of Dr. Jorgensen's specialty had never appeared on any record, and Rachel had seldom told anyone about her motives.

How does this woman know that?

It suddenly reminded Rachel that Ellie had distracted her from finalizing what she thought was a clever sentence she had been composing for the summation. "I'm nearly done, and it will be ready for Steve... uh, Dr. Jorgensen's review before my submission and defence." That fact reminded her of Ellie's original request.

"Do you have an appointment?"

Rachel drew a book across the desk and frowned at the blank space opposite today's calendar.

"He's a busy man," Rachel said, "so perhaps I can make you an appointment. You can't just barge in on him. He's the Chair of the department, you know."

Ellie ignored the hint of self-importance, a trait all too common with the secretaries of departmental chairs. Here, it reflected Rachel's protective custody of her mentor. Ellie replied with a grating but almost singsong string of sounds, her stellar language at its poetic best.

Ellie never knew if she was being ironic or sarcastic in assigning any poetic qualities to the language of an intellectual, technical species capable of travelling the stars. The phrase she had uttered sounded like a combination of a train wreck and a thundering waterfall. Others would use harsher metaphors. She considered poetry to be guerrilla warfare that she and RoH conducted against the scientific juggernaut in their small corner of the galactic diaspora. She also understood that even in their clinical efficiency, those minds knew they needed tempering to continue to thrive and take the next steps into the greater universe. Of all the developing sentient species on countless planets, humans represented one of the better chances of retrieving some of that needed primitive emotion, empathy, togetherness, and a different perspective. Often, when she and RoH had sat together, they discussed what their existence represented, and how they were the vanguard of what would be a completely new galactic race of intelligent empaths. It appeared to be an impossible task.

"I think he would like to hear that, and more." Ellie smiled at the young woman, who wore an expression that flickered between revulsion and curiosity. Rachel picked up the handset and punched in four digits.

"Dr. Jorgensen, there is someone here I think you will want to meet." she paused, listening. "I can't repeat her introduction in a dialect I have never heard before."

"No, she's not some Trekkie speaking Klingon," Rachel giggled. "I'm fluent in Klingon."

"Come with me. You'll like Dr. Jorgensen."

"I more than like Dr. Jorgensen. I met him once, over 20 years ago."

Rachel paused and eyed Ellie, both because her statement had reminded Rachel of the age gap between her and her mentor, why her admiration had not turned to infatuation, and because Ellie had referred to a time that left an inexplicable gap in Jorgensen's CV; a black hole Steven Jorgensen would never discuss.

Jorgensen's office was a suitable example of intellectual chaos. Shelves jammed with books, CDs, DVDs and folders could not contain all the piles of material that littered the floor and most free space. A battered old teacher's desk from many decades before shared a load that gave grudging space to a new desktop computer. Two bunches of writing implements reached skyward from old coffee mugs, one with the name Steven in black letters above a bright yellow beach umbrella and the word "Bahamas" beneath. The other, brown glazed, represented the back end of a Canadian moose with the handle where the head should have been.

"Hello, Steven, it's nice to meet you again." Ellie removed a folder labelled "miscellaneous" and sat, without invitation, in a chair that seemed to have escaped from a funeral parlour. Her matter-of-fact action hid her intense emotion at reuniting with someone she loved.

Steven Jorgensen burst into a smile. He paused, lost in memory. The overwhelming image was of his mother. She always called him Steven when everyone else, including him, had moved on to Steve. She loved him, and her formal name always reflected her caring. In his memory, his mother's love also translated to what he had felt from Ellie so long ago.

"You grew up," he said as if he had just met a long-lost child. "I never thought we would meet again."

"We never lost track of you. You were on my list." Ellie smiled. "My feelings for you were real, then and are now."

Steve blushed. It had not been that kind of love, then at least.

Rachel stood in mystified silence, torn between finishing her summation and wanting to know *what the hell was going on.*

"Rachel," Ellie turned to the confused woman, "Steven and I met in the Dakotas when I was ten years old and about to leave on a grand adventure. Steven belonged to the team that tried to stop me."

"I had a small part in that stupidity, as a newly minted post-doctoral fellow who this university contributed on loan, in the spirit of international cooperation to neutralize the alien menace." Jorgensen laughed. "I mostly held the boss' pencils."

"We hardly talked." Ellie returned to Jorgensen. "Your boss did most of it and not nicely either, but she's dead now, and you were there because you are brilliant. Our conversations comprised you trying to reassure me and to get a clue to 'alien speak', as I heard your boss call it, and my trying to fend you off. I did not know the star language then."

"I'm afraid you got yourself marked by my people for your efforts and at my insistence. I like you," Ellie fought to keep a poker face, "and have kept an eye on you."

"This doesn't help," Rachel blurted out, suspecting the reference to Klingon might have been closer to the mark than she had thought. She had never supposed that one day she might be an extra in a Star Trek episode. "What the hell is going on?"

"Sit down," Rachel sat without question on a folding chair that Steve had found beside the road.

"I'm part alien, from Earth and up there." Ellie pointed at the ceiling.

"You're nuts." Rachel glanced at the door as if planning an escape.

"No," Jorgensen said, "she is."

Rachel considered the possibility her mentor was a cuckoo.

"You don't need to be afraid or plan to run," Ellie smiled. "Neither of us is crazy. Dr. Jorgensen can tell you, although I can scare the stuffing from you, I never will hurt any human."

"True," Steven said and wondered why Ellie had returned to find him. "I tried to forget it when you left. I thought it was all over, forever."

"Perhaps not over; ... perhaps for forever." Ellie smiled.

"You knew I thought you were nuts, and you know my history." Rachel joined the lengthening line of humans, startled by Ellie's mental power. "Can you read minds?"

"Yes," Ellie said. "Low-level quantum-based electromagnetic processes are straightforward as long as there is no interference from electric fields or other shields."

"I guess I should make a tinfoil hat then," Rachel appeared to be serious. Steven cast a disapproving look.

"For you or me?" Ellie laughed. "They did that to me once, scared the hell out of me."

"Steven," Ellie asked, "you spent twenty years trying to forget?"

"No," Jorgensen leaned back in his chair and closed his eyes. Other than the computer, his chair was the one piece of modern technology in the room, an ergonomic device that the university had insisted that all staff use. Jorgensen had never been sure if concern for their comfort or fear of lawsuits motivated them. He appeared to have fallen asleep. Ellie waited.

"No, I have never had a more exciting six months in my life, perhaps frustrating but exciting. I regretted not being in Texas the night that you left, but they sent me back here after the Dakotas. Up to that point, they had applied more science; after that, they pursued you because of obsession. I've spent twenty years hoping, not forgetting. Now, here you are. Should I have wanted this?"

"Yes," Ellie frowned at a mixture of happy and fearful times. "And true, they forced me to leave to avoid tragedy."

"Has it worked out?" Steve flashed a smile of genuine concern. He had cared for Ellie, then a little girl, over the few months he had been involved.

"I'm not sure," Ellie thought of how deeply she missed her mother and her father, although Charlie had been a minor player if one can describe the person who contributed half of the genetic makeup as a bit player. He had been out of her life for ten years but was instrumental in safely getting her to Texas where she had to be. Ellie had grown to love

Charlie then and often wished he and Lisa had fallen in love instead of leaving her conception to an alien experiment. Her great grandfather, the last pure alien in her lineage, had eased her through the years on the starship, displaying empathy that most aliens lacked.

"I'm here to see if we can make it succeed. I think you and Rachel," Ellie emphasized, "will be central to relations with my star people."

"You want me to help?" Steve brightened.

Rachel leaned towards the conversation. Her brilliant thesis summary faded in importance. Steve made a slight nod towards Rachel.

"Of course she can stay. You'll need all the help you can get with this one, mister hot-shot language guy." Ellie echoed the self-deprecating self-description Steve had given to the ten-year-old Ellie so long ago. "Rachel is brilliant, Steven, just like you. She is a happy accident for us."

"You can't tell Rachel she's smart until she gets her degree," Steve pretended to frown. "She might argue more than she does now."

"Oh, that's good," Rachel looked at Steve, "and I get equal billing on any papers along with 40% of speaking fees, bobble head dolls and so on."

"Watch it, kid. You don't have your Fud yet. You'll need that Ph.D."

Even though she longed to linger with Steve, time was not Ellie's friend, and she dove into her need.

"Humans must develop the capability of understanding our language. It is essential that humanity trusts us. Earth will need independent translators. Our bumbling in the past gave aliens a bad name, and I don't expect to be trusted. Those nonsense, alien monster movies do not help."

"Learning to do that is a problem." Steven leaned on his desk.

"We have determined," Ellie giggled, contemplating the irony, "that your theory of language determinism is essentially correct, although it's a two-way street. Our language has grown from our experience of the universe, but it limits our perception of the universe. Your Earth languages are the same. You have observed that mixing languages and learning several languages changes your perception of reality, and for the better."

"A long time ago, star people decided they needed to do that, but they took a technical approach. I am an accidental discovery in that process, an entity that lives in both star language and English, although now all Earth languages are important. We still need to learn, and you need to embrace our language to take a step in your learning, to meld the detailed love of Earth with the love, not fear of the universal."

Ellie shot a string of alien sounds in his direction. It sounded less poetic than the easy snippet she had unleashed on Rachel. Steven and Rachel grimaced.

"It hurts your ears, at first." Ellie laughed. "Our scientists and negotiators speak like that sample when they can't have mental contact or want to build trust." She turned to Rachel.

"The bit I said out there was the way I and my daughter speak. Let's say it's a human poetry contribution to star language."

"Daughter...?" Steven needed a diversion from the recent assault on his ears, but he somehow felt deflated.

"You'll meet her sometime. She's with my father right now, with her to-do list and much better prepared than I was at ten."

"... unbelievable..." Steve muttered, "so you are married."

"Not yet," Ellie looked at Steve.

"Where do we start?" Rachel picked up the thread from her temporarily distracted boss.

Ellie set a small book, a miniature electronic device bound in fake blue leather, onto the one open space on Jorgensen's desk. He picked the object up and swiped it. The unreadable small script somehow resembled the symbol library in a computer word processor.

"You need someone with better eyesight," he laughed, but clutched the little offering. "Try optometry on the other side of the campus."

"Set it on that table over there," Ellie pointed to a bit of uncluttered furniture. The three grouped around the table as Steve placed the book in the centre. Ellie touched a small starburst symbol on the spine. The small device suddenly expanded into some type of electronic tablet twenty centimetres square, displaying what looked like a title page. The script was alien to them; a joke Steven and Rachel would use when lecturing about alien language, but that would be in the future. For now, the tablet seemed to be a prop from a science-fiction movie.

"This is a dictionary, of sorts." Ellie swept a hand above the device, not touching it, and the display morphed into one, then to another and another page of lists. She then put a finger near the device and raised it quickly. The space towards a wall filled with slightly shimmering text expanded to a meter and hung in thin air.

"That might be easier to read," Ellie smiled.

"At least you use bold serif fonts and italics," Rachel said in a distracted tone that suggested she had gone into analysis mode.

"Lexicons are valuable," Steven muttered as he examined the display, "but we need more context, complete spoken and written passages."

"I can fix that," Ellie pointed, and the tablet spoke the word. "You'll at least know the sound associated with each word. Give me a book," Ellie stood back and swept her eyes over the confusing array of bound reading material; some resting in a dignified upright way on shelves, others more casually leaning in spaces too large or on cabinet tops and askew against a handy wall. Many more fought for floor space with piles of journals and other assorted folders and loose paper. The covers created a pleasing random display of size and colour.

Jorgensen handed Ellie a copy of Basil Johnston's "Ojibway Heritage". He felt it was perhaps appropriate under the circumstances.

"Do you have sound recording software on that old machine?" Ellie pointed at Steve's state-of-the-art desktop computer.

"A language guy always needs recording and editing capability, just in case random aliens drop by."

Steve set up the machine and sat. Rachel half-sat on the table. Ellie opened the Johnston book, scanned the first few pages, and assaulted their ears for five minutes as she verbally translated the book into the machine.

"That's enough of that," Ellie ended in English, but then translated even that into stellar cacophony.

"Buen toque," said Rachel.

"El gusto es Mio," Ellie smiled.

"Do you have any fiction?" Ellie searched in vain.

Steven looked perplexed. The only fiction on the shelves was in several languages other than English. Rachel slipped from the room and returned with a trashy romance novel. The square-jawed Adonis on the cover seemed to need a shirt. The title was, "A Stranger's Heart".

"That seems appropriate," Ellie giggled.

"Is that in your thesis bibliography?" Steven deadpanned.

Rachel felt no shame. Romance novels were about the only thing she could read without analyzing the language, and considering the weight of her academic work, they made up the whole of her current love life.

Ellie skimmed through the flimsy volume and delivered the whole thing in alien dialect into Steve's computer. She glanced at Steve several times, as if reading the romance novel to him.

"Rachel," Steve intoned, "you know this book will be in the bibliography of our first paper, right?"

"That will shake up the old beards," she laughed.

"I hope that's enough to get you started," Ellie glanced at the wall clock. She needed to talk with Peter Williams.

"Not likely," Steve decided, "but we will see. Is your language agglutinative? I couldn't tell from your wildfire dictation."

"Huh?" Ellie exclaimed.

"Do you use prefixes and suffixes?" Rachel asked.

"Oh," Ellie pondered, "on page 36 of the fiction, there is the word 'advantage'. In our speech, it is a different word from the one for vantage." She made a sound that Steven took for the translation of vantage.

"We don't use a lot of modifiers and usually have different words for degrees of something or subtle differences in various things. Mom once told me the Earth's Inuit people have many names for different snow types. We use many words like that."

"Some think that kind of word usage is primitive," Steve leafed through A Stranger's Heart.

"We consider it more precise." Ellie did not sound insulted. "We have a few thousand words for stars; there are that many variations. In some ways, powerful memory replaces structure."

"I gave you materials that reflect our language in the way our ambassadors would use it, less stilted but still precise. We use different syntax and structures for technical things, just like Earth scientists. In casual conversation, the situational meaning is important and our chatter might sound like code compared to the way humans say things."

Ellie fell into deep concentration. They could not hear or feel her exchange with a nearby, but in human terms, distant spacecraft.

"Here." Ellie took one of Steve's notepads and wrote out a string of digits. "When you want more input, punch this code into your cell. When someone answers, just ask for Bob in plain English. You'll get all the extra material you need."

Steve examined the string of numbers. It looked like an extended international telephone number. In reality, it reprogrammed his device to connect directly with an otherworldly receiver.

"Do you have an alphabet?" Rachel had been puzzling over that problem.

"It isn't really necessary," Ellie said. "We do everything verbally or mostly mentally. We record everything important and our technology hasn't failed in many millennia. Anything written or engraved is graphic and only serves us as memory joggers or references for a data search. Pitman shorthand or your eastern written languages are the best comparisons I can make for written material. The tablet and other things present phonetic material in alphanumeric symbols."

"You know we can't just suddenly go to our colleagues and say, 'hey we have this neat E.T. language you should be excited about.'"

"Talk about a career-ending move." Rachel frowned. "What are we supposed to do with this? Is it a waste of time?"

"It might be," Ellie sounded all too agreeable, "but if we decide conditions are right, if we think it's worthwhile staying with Earth, we will make a huge worldwide public introduction of ourselves. If you two start now, we will shine a spotlight on you and you will be the translators of record for all interactions, at least the ones in English. I hope you work on learning the language."

Ellie did not mention that her star family hoped to appreciate humans better by learning from Steve and Rachel. They wanted to strengthen their understanding of humanity's emotional relationship with Earth. Steve and Rachel would unknowingly add to that as they interacted with the star team behind the name "Bob".

"Steve, I like you. You made a scared little girl feel safer in the Dakotas. I trust you and hope I'm giving you a reward. If it doesn't work out, I'll buy you both dinner and offer you a free trip around the galaxy."

"I have to run. If anyone comes asking about me, likely someone from the American government, you don't need to lie. They are the child of the group you worked for and already know a big part of the story, but none of the key stuff. They know I'm on Earth, and they are desperate to talk to me. Those are the good ones. The bad ones, well, you will know if they come to call. Even if they scare you, you both will be okay. You can just tell them I was here and went that-a-way."

Ellie giggled and then disappeared out the door as if she had never been.

"Was that a dream?" Rachel slumped into the still warm funeral parlour chair Ellie had vacated.

"I hope not," Steve Jorgensen looked at the two thin books on his desk and then at the open door. "I hope not. We may need to recruit more help."

"I need to recruit a six-litre glass of wine," Rachel sighed. "I've never met an alien before."

"I'm buying," Steve opened the office door. "Only part of her is alien. Most of her is as human as you are. I'm coming back later to work on it."

"I want to help." Rachel retrieved her wallet from the reception desk.

"Finish your thesis first." Steve did not mean to be cruel. "This alien thing might never be more than a fascinating secret that neither of us can share until our deathbed memoirs."

"I think they emphasize subject and object, or at least nouns before verbs." Rachel ignored her orders to work on the thesis.

"We have done no analysis, and how could you even guess at that?" Steve fumbled for the keys to his SUV.

"The romance novel, when she finished, I reread the first sentence. It says, 'Rogue landed with a thud in Elisha's life.' It sounded to me that Ellie said, inferring spacing that I found hard to discern, Rogue, Elisha, life, thud, landed.' The whole sound seemed to flow together, so the spaces might be my imagination. The tablet contains what seems like individual words. Silences between words are important."

"Either they are there, or it will make our job harder," Steve triumphantly rattled his keys. "We heard nothing, twenty years ago, only one artefact with graphics, and it disappeared with Ellie, so I have only what you have; however, I'm thinking that everything about the aliens involves efficiency, including language that has evolved over an extremely long time. The lexicon Ellie left gives hope for discreet words, but the spaces between might be some assumed context or similar. If that's the case, I'll be calling that Bob guy a lot."

Rachel paused beside the white vehicle.

"I'm suddenly feeling we might live in Pratt's contact zone, and not in the role of the powerful invader."

"That would be a first for us old white guys."

"Hey, masa, us slaves are used to it." The laughter rippled across Rachel's dark face and created a light show of highlight and shadow.

"A lot of humans are going to need your uppity, young lady. I think we need to talk with that guy who worked with Chomsky."

"What for...? We have a future language problem, not how speech developed."

"No, not those guys, but the one who picked up Chomsky's political speaking about history and imperialism after he died."

"Because you think the aliens want to colonize us." Rachel finished his thought, or so she thought.

"No," Steven climbed into the driver's seat, "I think I understand what Ellie said their strategy is. They want the weaker part of the world to oppose the big three empires, perhaps in some sort of popular uprising, and lead the charge to the stars by first saving life on the planet. We humans must invade ourselves first, and we need to understand the enemy. Knowing and loving Ellie, she won't want violence."

"Working with us is Ellie's strategy to worm into the intellectual world. Once their presence becomes public knowledge, we step forward with an already partly-constructed understanding of their language. That will intrigue the academic world and reassure many others. Perhaps we are part of an alien marketing campaign."

"Oh great, they have to convert the masses and tin-pot dictators to socialist anarchy and the big three have nukes," Rachel snapped her seatbelt shut. "And I don't like the idea that I am an actress in a commercial selling alien alphabet soup."

Rachel's lips expressed something between a pout and a smirk.

"I know." Steven did not look happy. "But you have a role whether you like it. From my history with her and them, twenty years ago, I understand their aims. They don't want to conquer, but they want to both learn and teach. Ellie mentioned the bad guys. I have a feeling that we are going to be famous, or dead."

Chapter Twelve

Do not go gentle into that good night

Quantz, I heard your interview with Peter Williams, and with the others in his group in London. You inadvertently became part of Ellie's grand plan for raising awareness and acceptance. Despite the spectacle that has happened, there are still disbelievers, hostile governments and condemning religious entities.

Ellie is sad that the negative is happening, but they had calculated the probability of that development. Once the world knows of alien visitors, they have predicted the appearance of a large movement of bigoted hostility based on fear and self-interest. The star people put a much higher probability on that and understand the risk to you, Peter Williams and other tellers of facts. For Lisa and me, life on Earth might be too dangerous to accept.

"**P**eter," Ellie touched his hand across the patio table where Peter sipped a strong whisky mix and Ellie her standard water, "your role in this is important. It will be dangerous or at least scary since we can protect you, but I hope you take it on. I'm leaving town for a bit, for Ottawa with Liz Dafoe. By the way, the police or reporters will probably ask you about me. You can tell them everything that happened, including that I left for Ottawa. It will be a rough ride."

Peter stared down the street, watching the descending gloom of the late September evening embrace London.

"I taught English at one time in my career." Peter sipped and paused. "Thomas is one of my favourite poets. Why would I go gently into the night? Bring on the rough."

He smiled at Ellie's puzzled look.

"What, they don't have Earth's classics in your interstellar bathtub?"

"We don't even have interstellar poetry," Ellie giggled. "My daughter and I have been working on that. I need to take time here to read."

"That will make you even more alien on this planet." Peter's loud laugh raised a scowl from a nearby patron who was listening to a talking-dog video on their smart phone.

Ellie leaned closer. "You will need to convince folks that aliens and hybrids like me and my daughter are real and peaceful. I know the evidence over the past century makes that harder. Abductions, probing and fatal errors were the norms."

"I will tell them my evolution from being angry at aliens, then wanting to convince people aliens actually took us and then we laid low to not have people see us as nut jobs. I'll do all that before I mention you are back. Everyone in the group will follow. They want to do something, and you eased their minds. Still..."

"Still…?" Ellie asked. She knew Peter's worry, but waited.

"I have a lingering idea that even you are a wolf in sheep's clothing."

"I will have to work to earn trust, Peter, but future events will ease your mind. I promise I am legitimate and not a wolf."

"Good. I never liked those alien monsters-in-disguise movies. Even in my greatest anger, I thought they were more like Spielberg's aliens."

"Me too," Ellie squeezed Peter's hand.

"Human monsters were Spielberg's thing, not werewolves."

Impish RoH would have howled like a wolf, and Ellie was happy that other things occupied her youngster.

Chapter Thirteen

The rats, cat, mouse and dandelions

The large aeroplane, its turbines throttled back to near silence, rushed out of the darkness over Lake Huron. With no landing or ground lights, the craft effortlessly swooped down onto concrete runway 14 of the Goderich Municipal Airport. The latest infrared and LIDAR systems gave the pilots a clear view. The autopilot landed the plane without a human hand.

It should have arrived unseen in the 3 AM darkness after its wave-hopping flight from Selfridge AFB in Michigan, but a small plane owner spending the night working on his kit plane had just stepped out from the hanger for a smoke. He felt the vibrations from the unseen aircraft and then heard the skid as its large tires touched. A slight whine faded to the far end of the runway and remained there with a faint moan of turbines. The curious man walked towards the apron to look. Landing without activating the lights violated regulations.

Two vehicles shot into view from the terminal parking lot and sped to the far end of the runway in a blaze of red taillights.

Perhaps it's an emergency.

500 meters of darkness obscured everything but the lights of the vehicles. The gangway of the large plane opened in a burst of light. Ground vehicle headlights illuminated part of the dark-grey monster.

Four turbos and military...

Several people climbed down a drop gangway. Five of them hurried to the vehicles. Four of the figures surrounded the fifth who, the amateur mechanic concluded, was a VIP or a prisoner. That person, much shorter than the others, paused, looked north beyond the nose of the plane and waved before being placed into an SUV.

Who's sneaking in this time of night? Only rats sneak around in the dark. No resistance, a VIP, who were they waving at, not the pilot?

As the vehicles turned and raced back to the main road gate, the mechanic decided it would be better not to have witnessed anything and ducked into the shadows. The SUVs sped down Airport Road towards the highway. They turned north as the plane roared down the airstrip and lifted off. It impressed him. Even his kit plane needed a longer runway.

RoH watched from a spot in the trees beyond the airport's northern fence-line. Her return wave to Grandma Lisa remained unseen but felt.

Mother, should I warn Papa?

No, he is okay, and they won't do anything to hurt anyone. Let this develop. We need to change the plan, but we will wait.

Ellie pulled the blanket back over her body and curled up on the hotel suite's couch and went back to sleep. RoH, with no thought of the September damp and chill, slumbered on the leaf-littered forest floor with some of her new night friends.

I must be patient.

The thought turned into a dream. Tomorrow would be interesting.

The amateur flyer closed up and headed home. From the size of the aircraft and the ground effort, he knew this had to be a government operation and best be none of his business. He now had stories to tell his friends. The tale about the most puzzling thing that had happened in his ten years of retirement should be worth some free beer.

Two kilometres from the airport, Siglinde stretched like a cat, slow to move after the wake-up call. Today they would finally get to Charlie Keys. Nothing could happen until after breakfast.

Charlie lingered over his eggs. Sunlight filled the front of the house, but the kitchen window revealed a dark weather front over the lake, leaving the Michigan shore. It promised to be a day of autumn wildness.

RoH stirred, and in sitting up startled a curious grouse who had wandered too close. The sudden wing beat made a pleasant end to RoH's night beneath the still green oak tree. She decided that hunger was the least of her immediate concerns and wandered through the bush to where she could watch events at grandpa's house. It would be some time before anything happened. RoH, after checking her mother, contented herself with examining the intricacies of a burst milkweed seedpod.

"Wake up," Liz touched Ellie's shoulder. "We'll have some breakfast and get going."

Ellie had been awake for some time, thinking through options in the plan and scanning London for any threat. All was quiet. The search for Peter remained focused in Stratford. It had received some shallow coverage on the local television news. Descriptions of Ellie from the breathless nurse would have people looking for a movie femme fatale. The official police report accurately described a blond 30-year-old woman of average height, but fortunately, that did not narrow the search. The police had not discovered the cab ride to London. They were still beating the bushes and scaring the swans in Stratford.

As a final bit of morning chores, Ellie did what she had done once every Earth day for over 20 years and sent a thought of love to her mother, who now slept in an old farmhouse near Goderich.

At the farm, Lisa had not slept well after the plane ride but felt remarkably fresh and alert, a feeling reinforced by the sudden feeling of love for her daughter and granddaughter. The feeling had grown each day since Ellie's return, but here it seemed stronger than in Seattle. Lisa insisted she had felt it every day of Ellie's absence, but Ellie said her feelings could not have crossed the many light years she had travelled since that terrible night in Texas. Lisa thought it ironic that her next abduction would be into the belly of ugly military transport. The greetings from RoH in the darkness had comforted.

The stronger feeling might mean they have brought me near Ellie and RoH, near Charlie too. But why did Ellie's people allow my kidnapping?

Lisa searched for a potential escape through the window of her comfortable second-floor room. Strangely, she did not feel the need to flee. Ellie had told her whatever happened, it would be part of a plan. Lisa remembered always telling Ellie as a little girl that things happened for a reason. This all seemed like some strange completion.

We are always together, even when alone. That was almost the last entry in Ellie's notebook, the night in Texas when she had left for the stars.

Lisa watched as two men in lightweight, black jackets chatted beside the decorative cedar-rail fence. A weedy pasture rose to a treed hillside and cloud softened blue sky. The landscape certainly was not in the mountains.

Sounds of rattling of dishes came from below, beyond the locked door. From the pleasant aroma, she imagined her dead uncle making one of his Texas breakfasts.

The situation did not threaten. Lisa had every confidence in Ellie's assurance that she would always be safe. Lisa had felt that forever, it seemed, ever since her childhood, but with her daughter's touch, a few days ago, the feeling became complete. Now, at this unknown hideout, she could sense Ellie's presence and protection.

The sound of vehicle doors slamming and the roar of an engine receding out the gate preceded a light rap, the rattle of a key, and the word "breakfast" as the door swung open. A tray of eggs, bacon, and thick toast ended up on a small table. It seemed as wonderful as a five-star hotel room service with a crisp white napkin and a carafe of coffee. She thought of her Uncle Thomas. Her hunger kept her from asking for a meatless offering.

***

"Okay," Siglinde spoke over her coffee mug, "we will ask him politely to come with us. We don't want to make a scene, but if we must, so be it. I doubt he will complain afterwards. Who would believe him? He won't risk his job. Just remember," her eyes swept her team seated around the table in the hotel pub, "no one must get hurt."

Above the bar, a television muttered, tuned to the London news. The video switched to a view of downtown Goderich, and then to a large old farmhouse on the edge of town. The peppy newsreader enthused.

"We go now to Huron County with a story that's literally out of this world. Bobby Briscoe has the report."

"Thanks, Tanya, we are speaking with David Alawa, a well-known local amateur astronomer and comet hunter. Dave, what's the excitement?"

"Hi, Bobby, it might not be that exciting to non-sky-nuts, but people like me always want to see something unusual. Two nights ago, I was calibrating my new 20-inch Celestron and video system, getting ready to stream next month's lunar eclipse on the internet. I use a handy bright star for that stuff. This time it was Vega."

"Is that the goddess of the vegans?" Bobby's snicker annoyed Dave.

"It's only 26 light-years away, a bright blue-white star we see high up this time of year." David casually pointed towards the zenith. "Anyway, I shot about a half-hour of video. When I looked at it later, about halfway in, Vega suddenly dimmed for about ten seconds and then brightened."

"Is that all?" Bobby sounded disappointed.

"No," David had his turn to laugh. "That could have been a glitch, but then a new, faint object had appeared near Vega. The video showed it there before the eclipse, but after the event, it was on the other side of the star. That freaked me out. It was there the next night, too. I used another scope to check visually. Even freakier, the thing disappeared last night."

Bobby appeared on camera.

"If you or I reported something like this, the professionals would laugh at us, but David Alawa is a respected comet hunter. He has found one comet, Alawa-1. So David, what was the response?"

"No one else saw the dimming," David frowned, "but several amateurs verified the object after I spread the word. Vega is a long way off the ecliptic so asteroid surveys aren't looking there, but an accidental field survey, the Sky Survey (CSS) and Spacewatch near Tucson Arizona doing some calibration, saw the new object. Everyone thinks it was real. No one has any idea what it was."

"Aliens," Bobby interjected, adding drama for his viewers.

"Who knows?" David did not appear to discount the idea. "It might be something in the solar system, but it would be a strange orbit and have to be big, or close. Perhaps a stray asteroid that was coming right at us and then veered off, but no one can find it anywhere in that direction and it seemed bright magnitude 4. The asteroid-impact people are excited. If it's a rogue asteroid, they want to know where it's going, but asteroids just don't veer sideways either. If it's as far away as Vega, or further, it would have to be a dwarf star, but that's still weird. It may have nothing directly to do with Vega but is simply in its line of sight. Whatever it was, I think it was real. It could be another Tabby's Star."

"A cat's star," Bobby giggled. David remained serious.

"No, no, Tabby's Star, Tyco number KIC 8462852 they named after astronomer Tabitha 'Tabby' Boyajian, is a distant star but not too far line of sight from Vega that we have observed strangely changing its brightness. One theory, discredited now, was that it was an alien-built Dyson sphere blocking the light."

"There you have it," Bobby intoned into the camera. "We have a mystery. Is it a stray, perhaps dangerous asteroid on the loose, or is it little green men on a flying saucer... aliens? Back to the desk..."

At the breakfast table, the word, "aliens", grabbed Siglinde's attention.

"Contact Elliana," Siglinde looked at Nancy. "Get her to find all the reports on this object, and especially the technical data. Things just don't pop up, hang around for 48 hours and disappear, at least, nothing natural."

The group trooped out to the three vehicles in the hotel parking lot and sped off to intercept Charlie Keys.

Charlie rinsed his plate, smoothed his hair, and headed to the door, grabbing his laptop from a chair.

RoH watched the black SUV glide quietly down her grandfather's lane, arriving at the turnabout just as Charlie stepped off the porch. It did not matter that she could not hear. She saw everything and felt even more. The menacing handgun that one intruder pointed at Charlie did not bother her. She knew they did not intend to hurt Grandpa, at least right away. The American government's reputation for torture might come later. They pushed Charlie into the SUV and it sped away.

Mother, they have taken grandfather.

Ellie barely looked up from the light breakfast she shared with Liz.

Siglinde does not know of this other operation, so we will give her a hint. Plans may change, so keep in touch with your father or me. We will find out what they intend. Here's what we do...

Ellie finished buttering a croissant and smiled. "Liz, we don't eat like this among the stars. My mother says that a good start makes a good day."

"Ellie," Liz's trembling hand rattled her cup into its saucer, "you still make me nervous. If you didn't remind me, I would never know you aren't just an Earthling."

"I hope you get used to me," Ellie sipped, "but I can only say I am genuine and star people intend no harm to Earth, neither on a large or small scale. If our hopes here vanish, we will withdraw and only document the sad future of life in this system."

"Liz," the depth of Ellie's look of concern startled Liz, "if we have to withdraw, I will offer anyone we have worked with the chance to leave with us. We won't force, but the future, out there, will be better than what will happen here if we fail."

"I... uh..."

"Don't worry, Liz. You don't need to decide yet. When do we leave for Ottawa?"

***

Siglinde sat in the third of the brightly coloured rental vehicles that waited in the factory parking lot. Charlie Keys liked to stretch his legs and always parked some distance from the main entrance. Right on time, Charlie's Martin X rolled silently to a stop in its pre-programmed place. Charlie emerged and stretched. He glanced to the west, where dark clouds with the faint rumbling of thunder preceded a cold front. Three vehicles sped across the asphalt. Several individuals jumped out.

"Charlie, Charlie Keys, I'm Siglinde Hilfreich. Could we please talk? Would you come with us?"

***

"Where are you taking me?" Charlie fidgeted in the back seat, flanked by two large men. Silence...

The SUV turned off a rough, narrow gravel concession road well down the priority list of township maintenance turned into a farm lane. The overgrown track ended in a neatly groomed yard enclosed by old cedar rails. It surrounded the yellow-brick century farmhouse that looked like a modern incongruity with its upgrades. A new steel-clad structure intruded behind the old residence with a Starlink dish on the roof and a larger parabolic device on a sturdy tripod beside the house. A self-propelled RV dominated the space between the outbuilding and the old house.

His kidnappers had not bothered to hide the route from him, suggesting that they felt he was no threat.

I could be cooperative or dead.

The flashbacks of the times the aliens had taken him years before no longer left him sweating and trembling, but this ride came close. The memory of Ellie promising he would never be in danger lessened the fear.

A middle-aged man approached.

"I'm Danny Ringwald," he offered a hand. "Thank you for coming."

Charlie saw no benefit in hostility and shook hands. Danny had a sincere grip. Charlie, ever mindful of official trickery, took it as habitual or deliberate deception. Danny's square posture hinted that he was military, and the casual black windbreaker could not hide it. At least Ringwald did not wear military camo, like the ones who had grabbed Lisa and him in the Dakota hills over 20 years before.

Charlie followed Danny through the front doorway. From her second-floor room, Lisa heard the commotion downstairs and felt Charlie's presence. Charlie could not do the same, but he was not a one-quarter alien.

***

"Sure," Charlie smiled at Siglinde. "Do you have any identification?"

Â طنإلا

Father?

We are here, watching.

Did Mother alert you?

A slight feather's touch brushed RoHs' consciousness

Charlie's smile deepened as he accepted the small plastic photo-identification card from Siglinde, with her name and photo. It said, "National Agency for Aerial Phenomena".

"What do you want? I'm not a weatherman and know nothing of aerial phenomena."

"We want to have a private chat." Siglinde ignored the joke. They shared the rear seat in Siglinde's rental and went back to the hotel.

"Charlie, can I call you Charlie? Please sit."

Siglinde pointed to the chair at the head of the deal table. The Comfort Inn had a suitable conference room and the table seated a dozen. Siglinde's team sat on both sides. He noted Siglinde took second place to his left. She did not invoke her status as boss. This reinforced RoH's earlier estimation from their kitchen meeting that Siglinde was a good leader. Charlie's location at the head of the table emphasized that the meeting focused on him.

"I think you know why we are here." Siglinde saw no point in trickery. "Your daughter Ellie has returned. After how many years?"

"Over twenty," Charlie smiled, as if the separation no longer mattered.

Siglinde frowned. Charlie Keys did not seem surprised or worried that she knew of Ellie.

"Where is Ellie?"

"She left town the morning after she arrived."

"She has a travelling companion. Did they travel together?"

"She is travelling with a woman now."

"Where is she going?"

Siglinde made a note. Charlie's claim that Ellie left town did not match her team's evidence that she was at the house a day later. She set that issue aside for the moment.

Why does that upset me? If he is telling the truth, then what is bothering me?

"I'm not sure where she's going. She took the bus to Stratford."

Siglinde noted it. They had their first lead.

Nancy had been on the ground in Goderich since the first sighting and slipped from the room. She would have Elliana in Virginia gather interesting news for the last three days in Stratford, Ontario. Nancy checked her digital map. She needed to know where she would be going.

Charlie smiled again. It suited the plan to have the pursuers follow Ellie's path. Giving Siglinde busy work would keep them occupied and help set the conditions for public action if that ever happened. Nothing would motivate the small group centred on Peter in London more than the US government asking questions.

For now, no one, including the star visitors, knew of a black swan, which would change alien plans, flexing its wings beyond the asteroid belt.

"I would love to talk with her and her companion." Siglinde said.

"I think," Charlie paused, "she wants to talk, eventually."

"She doesn't know I exist."

"We have known of your group for a long time."

"You mean 'they' don't you?" Charlie's slip made Siglinde uncertain.

"We're all connected, Siglinde."

The rest of the investigators had paid close attention, and the nuanced exchange drew their full interest. The team had highly honed investigative skills, and they sensed Charlie had deliberately led them down a path of his choosing, a line they did not understand. It upset them.

"So you are in touch with the aliens?"

"I have been my whole life. I have a message from Ellie. She would have liked to tell you personally, but she is with someone."

"We'll eventually catch up," Siglinde was less certain than she sounded and glanced at the door where Nancy talked with Elliana.

Siglinde spent a few seconds in self-recrimination. Apparently, they had known of Charlie Key's whereabouts for years, but they had not suspected or thought of talking to him.

He must have been in contact with the aliens all along, but it's too late for regrets, Siglinde thought.

"All I know, I have learned relatively recently." Charlie sipped some water. "I would have been of no use to you before now."

Siglinde stiffened. Could Charlie Keys read her thoughts? *What memory has this triggered?*

"How did you know what I was thinking?"

Charlie ignored the question.

"Ellie wants me to tell you that there is another, an ultra-secret agency focused on aliens. Your government considers it the important one, and they have someone inside Project X."

I have started it, Mom.

Good RoH, and that probably decides when we have to move.

"How does she know that?" Siglinde thought it a silly question as soon as she asked. How do the aliens know anything? Was Charlie Keys an actual alien? The record said he was human. Siglinde seized the idea that there might be an agent other than an alien spy inside her agency.

Everyone is spying on us.

"Yes, Siglinde, but the spies are not all bad. Ellie wants you to go back to Washington and discuss it with Liz, Ted and Elliana, but remember, they bugged your headquarters. You will find evidence, but don't act. Keep it quiet and gather more. It will soon be useful. Elliana is superb at ferreting out information. Siglinde Hilfreich, you are a good person. You have no reason to fear. You are safe, but the plan depends on timing."

"What plan is that?"

"The star people deciding if we disappear from Earth, or we stay to help you succeed. It is up to how humans respond. If we must go, then humans and a lot of high order life here will soon follow, but not by choice."

"You and we", he said. Is Charlie one of them, after all?

"We have no hope then. Who will lead? Who will follow?"

"There is already a global movement that humans consider an environmental one. Although that view is too narrow, it is unifying many countries' populations into a demand for basic change."

"That's led by that European woman. She began that when she was a strange, autistic teenager." Siglinde frowned.

"Ellie is autistic too," Charlie smiled.

Siglinde immediately saw the connection.

"You mean that European woman is..."

"Let's just say she is using over 20% of her brain. Her ideas come from her understanding and wisdom, not from the sky."

"Siglinde," one agent spoke, "I'm going for coffee. Does Mr. Keys want some?" He nodded to Charlie.

"I prefer hot chocolate," Charlie smiled at him. No one but Siglinde had heard the last conversation. Siglinde noted this as another puzzle. The reality of who sat at the table with her would come much later.

What the rest of the team heard was a long statement by Charlie Keys describing his abductions and the final one over thirty years before, when he and Lisa had conceived Ellie.

"That other dangerous agency spying on NAAP represents the problem with your government and those of China and Russia. We cannot let those three have control. With them, self-interest through brutality and opportunism is always their way. Instead, it must include everyone, and that woman's global movement is part of it. You must be part of it, too."

"Siglinde, I must do other things. Have your team follow the Stratford lead. That is necessary to build awareness and prepare people for the alien appearance. It will also give you something to report to your bosses. At some point, events will force you to go public, putting you in danger. Please be patient and brave."

Siglinde stared, dumbfounded, in deep thought. Even though the evidence accumulated since 1947 had convinced her, she now felt certain the aliens were real. She longed for the day she would talk with one.

The drinks materialized and led to another half hour of questions that included the whole team. Siglinde showed patience.

"Okay," Nancy reappeared, "Elliana has found a news report about a mysterious woman helping an old man run for it from an old age home. The description sounds like the being accompanying Ellie, and the way it happened is out of this world." Nancy giggled at her joke. "About 42 years ago, this guy, Peter Williams, claimed aliens had abducted him."

"Stratford is our starting point," Siglinde sounded sure. "I'm returning to H.Q., but you follow that up. Someone stay here to monitor Mr. Keys. I'll drive him back to his car."

If the team thought it strange that Siglinde had mentioned their surveillance in front of Charlie, no one mentioned it. Charlie stared at Nancy, making the woman uncomfortable. She hoped he was not a pervert.

"Siglinde, Nancy's work will get you closer to your goal." Charlie shifted in the passenger seat.

Siglinde nodded and did not ask. She accepted that these aliens, at least Ellie, knew and somehow had her interest at heart. She did not know where that feeling of trust had come from. Charlie Keys seemed to be a line of communication with the stars.

"Make sure Liz shakes hands with Elliana." Charlie's comment came from nowhere, but Siglinde, in response to the forgotten suggestion from yesterday, suddenly felt she must have that handshake happen.

Siglinde left Charlie beside his car and sped away towards the London airport. She anticipated seeing Ted more than making progress on the project. It escaped her notice that Charlie had not mentioned Ted touching Elliana. Siglinde only remembered the parts of the interview that Charlie wanted her to remember.

Charlie got into his car. The next step required cultivating more dandelions.

"Kerri," Mike balanced a coffee and a file folder and leaned on the privacy partition, "tell Charlie I need to see him as soon as he arrives."

"He's late," Kerri put aside the layout diagram that gave her a temporary geometry issue. *Damned architect...*

"He's usually here by now." Kerri frowned. Charlie was never late. "Maybe we can chat later, too. Yesterday's visitors upset me."

Mike frowned at the memory and at the newly hatched idea that Kerri knew more than he thought. Or at least she suspected something strange. Even more disconcerting, perhaps Kerri might know more than he knew.

"Let Charlie know," Mike ignored Kerri's request and hurried away.

Mike's not getting off that easy, she thought. Kerri hit the speed dial for Charlie's cell.

Charlie sat in a large stuffed chair in the farmhouse parlour. He sipped a coffee he would normally not have so soon after breakfast, but Danny had offered and Charlie played the game. A big man in a dark windbreaker sat opposite. The musical tones of Charlie's cell in the agent's jacket pocket broke the silence.

"I should answer that." Charlie sat straight in hope.

"Leave it, buddy," the man in the jacket snapped, "I have no orders."

"For the time being, we prefer you don't talk to anyone." Danny did not like the agent's curtness. Greg's men were not military. He disliked their superior attitude. Ringwald also knew he was not really in charge of this operation and the agent's attitude proved it. Greg had brought in the army to be a scapegoat if the thing went south. While Danny and Project

X were a secret, Gregg's group was as dark as anything could be. Danny thought he had more to fear from Greg than from any alien.

"Charlie, please come with me." Danny smiled, but gave Charlie no choice. They escorted him out the front door and towards the RV and its open door. Charlie hesitated, suspicious of the dark interior. Another flashback, years ago, but then a bright light had threatened him, not darkness. A man in a white smock smiled from the doorway.

"It's okay. We would like to do some X-rays; that's all."

***

Kerri left her third message for Charlie. *Maybe his phone is off.*

She went into Charlie's office and found the normal messiness. From his window, she saw the Martin X in its normal spot.

Good, he's here.

A half-hour later, Charlie had not appeared and Kerri went for another look. The car had disappeared.

"Mike," Kerri stood at her boss's door, "something strange is going on with Charlie."

Mike stood in alarm, more worried about what Kerri might know.

"His car was there, and now it's gone. Does this have something to do with your strange visitors?"

"Come and sit down," Mike closed his door, "I'm confused too, but here's what I know."

The Martian X pulled up in front of Hobo Books and Charlie slipped inside. He relished the tinkling doorbell. Roslyn looked up from her usual spot behind the sales counter and smiled. Charlie set a well-thumbed book on the counter. The title, over a garish but accurate image of a flying saucer, was "Taken by Aliens: Ellie's Story by Tom Clarke."

Ros glanced at the volume. "I have several of his books. He's popular and they come and go a lot... good for my business. The UFO nut crowd is a constant. Too bad Clarke is dead."

"Have you read any of them?"

"Not my brand of coffee. I like murder stories."

"You saw strange lights one night you were on the lake in that fancy sailboat of yours."

How does he know about that? Ros paused. *Maybe I forgot I told him.*

"Oh, yes, but that was the Yankee air farce spending more billions."

"You weren't sure when you first saw it."

"Well, since no little green men showed up looking for a map book, I figured it had to have an actual explanation." Ros' frown told another story. She had not convinced herself. Charlie Keys knowing about it upset her.

"Maybe they did, and you didn't recognize them. Maybe they bought a book other than maps." Charlie Smiled. "Did you know they saw lights in the sky the other night, over by Brussels?"

"Oh yes, I have a friend in Belgrave. They said the light passed above their house heading towards Auburn." Ros had to admit that since that night on the lake, she had paid attention to any reports of strange things.

"Hey, your granddaughter was in here the other day. She's a strange girl. You never told me you had a family."

"Read this, please. I have a granddaughter and a daughter, Ellie. This book is about her. Tom Clarke is her great uncle, and when you have finished, call me. We'll talk. You might get to meet her."

Oh well, it's a slow day, so I guess I can read.

Charlie eased out the door. The bell rang much longer than it should have. Ros stared at the door and fingered the book as the tinkling faded.

"Hi, Kerri, any messages?" Charlie placed one hand on his collaborator's desk.

"Where the hell have you been? You're late, but you came and went. I saw your car in the lot." Kerri's deeper feelings and her concern for him came through in her voice. She still hoped.

"Come into my office. I have a lot to tell you." Charlie disappeared.

Kerri followed. Charlie sat behind his desk, looking serious.

"Please shut the door."

When Kerri turned back from the door, RoH sat, looking somewhat small in Charlie's place.

"What..."

"Please sit, Kerri. I have a lot to tell you."

Kerri stumbled through a confusing fog and sat. RoH picked up the phone and punched a button.

"Mike, can you come over for a minute?" Charlie's voice did not match the girl holding the phone.

Kerri swept her eyes around the room, desperate to find Charlie. He was not there and the room only had one door.

"Mike told you all he knows, but he has not figured it out yet. We decided you two need to know. Kerri, I want you to know all about grandfather. I hope it helps you pursue your love for him."

"How..."

"Shhh, Kerri, he needs you."

The door opened.

"Where's your grandpa?" RoH in the chair did not surprise Mike.

"Where's Charlie?" Kerri echoed. "How can you assume I love him?"

RoH flashed a mischievous smile. Mike chuckled and muttered, "Obvious."

"The American government has kidnapped him."

"What?" Kerri sobbed. Mike nodded.

To an outsider, the statement would sound like preposterous fantasy, the dreams of a little girl. Mike took it as a fact.

"Was it that Siglinde person who talked to me?" Mike barked.

"No, she's an ally. It's a more dangerous bunch."

RoH began the story, going back to Roswell in 1947, her great-great-grandparents and through the generations. She ended with the morning's incident in the parking lot with Siglinde.

"Is Charlie in danger?" Kerrie choked on the words.

"Don't worry; grandfather will be okay in the end. Those people do not know what they are dealing with. They're the same as the last bunch who hounded my mother off the planet."

"Now I can't tell what is real," Kerry said. "How do I know what I am seeing and hearing isn't you playing with me?"

"I promise, Kerri, that the next time you see Grandpa, he'll be real. Of course, you might see me when others see Grandpa, but you will know, and you too, Mr. Hammersmith."

This powerful alien had just reminded them she was just a child.

"What do we do now?" Mike felt helpless.

"Nothing," RoH said. "Mother did not want you to worry, and she felt telling you the entire story would be the best way. Just try to carry on as normal, but at least it won't surprise you when things go public. Then you can tell everyone about it all. If Siglinde comes back here, you can tell her as much as you like. She doesn't know that grandfather is a prisoner, but she will find out at the right time."

"I have to go to give grandpa's kidnappers a scare. They don't know what they are dealing with, and they assigned me to give them a hint.

Mother is off on another tactic. That may be where publicity begins, and that will be your signal to go public."

***

Liz stood beside her luggage as she checked out of the hotel. Ellie waited by the door. She had gained a shoulder bag, barely larger than a purse. Liz wondered if alien females had the same needs as her, but then remembered that Ellie was mostly human. Perhaps she had ways to deal with these issues.

That might be an advantage of knowing aliens, Liz thought.

"I usually fly, but I wanted to spend some time chatting, and you get a look at the countryside, especially the fall colours towards Ottawa. I booked us on the 10:57 train to Ottawa via Toronto."

The women had to settle for coach class going to Toronto. Liz seemed miffed, but Ellie enjoyed observing ordinary people. Even in this comfortable environment, she sensed disquiet.

Perhaps it's a lingering effect of the recent pandemic, or that everyone is uneasy about the declining economies and the constant small-scale warfare around the globe.

Ellie speculated, but resisted invading people's privacy too deeply. This fragile mental state of humans could lead to either progress or disaster. As the train pulled into Toronto, the passengers' feelings of anticipation smothered this underlying anxiety.

Once through the confusion of Union Station, they sat comfortably in business class. Liz checked her electronic messages and relaxed.

"My family is the first stable line of star-Earth hybrids. Other attempts were horrific failures until they figured out why my line worked."

"You are the first," Liz asked, "are there more?"

"Once we realized that the factor to success was an actual emotional connection between both suppliers of genetic material, we tried a fresh approach. My great grandfather loved my great grandmother, and she loved him. That made my line stable. My great-granddad possesses emotional characteristics that are rare in the stars. He has lines in Africa and Australia."

"So other Ellies are running around the world."

"Well, one female named Adimu in Kenya and a male in Australia named Mike. Neither is yet aware of their status, although Adimu suspects it. Her mother is about to tell her who her father is. That is necessary for the plan. Mike's mates are wondering why he never falls off a surfboard, so he is questioning. Again, his mother will soon tell him the story of his grandmother and grandfather. These things must evolve. Awareness brings fear and the need for support. I know from my experience. We have sent tutors to help them avoid my trauma."

"There are others in Europe, South America and Asia, but from different star genes. These, so far, seem to be stable. There is great hope."

"The European one is younger than me and is a famous leader. I won't mention her name, but her movement is global and important if Earth is to keep high-order life. She is not aware of her origins. That will change when the time comes. If we are successful, she will need to know, as it's an important part of that success. If we fail, she needs to have the option of leaving the Earth. We will see."

"I don't think I could leave." Liz looked out the window and frowned. The landscape slid past in a blur. Liz wondered what it must be like living in one of those hamlets, vanishing behind the speeding train.

I suppose it would seem as bad as fleeing to the stars for many from these small places to have this train take them to Ottawa.

"Canada is home. I would feel dislocated among the stars."

"I lived that." Ellie took Liz's hand. "Seattle, where I spent my first ten years, was home. I had friends, went to school and played soccer." Liz saw a longing in Ellie's eyes. She took Ellie's hand.

"Even there, I felt disconnected. When I went to the stars, it was worse. If it hadn't been for my great-grandfather, I might have gone mad, but he was my familiar. We had met before I left, and in that short week, before I went, he removed my fear and gave me understanding. Even as a hybrid, I know how great a decision it would be."

"How can you talk about yourself as if you are a lab sample?"

"It's just a fact," Ellie squeezed Liz's hand, "and if nothing else, we must be honest and hang onto the facts."

"So what's my role? I have little influence."

"You aren't part star people either, but you and people like you are the genuine hope. You are one of what my daughter calls 'dandelions'."

"Dandelions…?"

"Prolific, deep-rooted, stubborn, spreading your seeds, beautiful…"

Liz blushed at the compliment and squeezed Ellie's hand, giving the metaphor more sexual innuendo than it deserved.

"You will see her soon," Ellie whispered.

Chapter Fourteen

The mouse becomes the cheese

"Hello, Lisa," Danny Ringwald waved the guard from Lisa's room and found a seat. Lisa lounged against the window frame. "We want to do a few X-rays."

"To see if I have an implant. You won't find one."

"I know," Danny said.

"Because you already did, Charlie, and he doesn't have one."

Ringwald flashed a surprised look. "How do you know?"

"You have Charlie here too, somewhere."

"How do you know that? Does he know you are here?"

"He doesn't know. I do because I have the right genes."

"Of course, you're a quarter alien." Danny had forgotten Lisa's story. Lisa's face flashed annoyance. "I don't like the word, alien."

Lisa followed Danny to the RV.

"Why don't you let Charlie and me meet?" Lisa and Danny were back in her room. "I don't see how it makes any difference. You're in a hopeless dead-end cause."

Ringwald fidgeted. Her subtle inflection on the word dead sounded ominous. Lisa highlighted his lack of authority in this operation. Greg issued the orders, and so far, they were to keep the two prisoners separated. Danny knew Lisa and Charlie were the cheese in a trap that Greg hoped would capture the alien girl. Greg saw a plot lurking in every corner. Having the two captives separated made it safer.

"Our plan is going to work."

"You don't know what you are dealing with." Lisa remembered the night the star people had protected her from the punks in the street.

"What's for lunch, something fresh from a local farmer?"

"There are no local farmers," Danny sniped.

An ancient diesel tractor clacked and sputtered down the overgrown driveway towards Charlie and Lisa's prison. The machine appeared to have escaped from the county museum and gasped to a stop beside the two guards opposite the front door of the house. An old man dressed in a red-checked jacket and battered baseball cap dismounted and limped forward. If any of the men in black jackets had watched old movies, they might have seen the grizzled apparition as a cartoon of a backwoods farmer, Pa Kettle, complete with ripped and stained bib-overalls and unkempt beard.

"G'day gents, I thought I'd welcome you to the neighbourhood." The old man extended a work-hardened hand. The men noted the stains from god knew what on the offered palm and kept hands in their jacket pockets, touching the reassuring cold of Glock 9 millimetres.

The old farmer ignored the slight and looked around. His gaze lingered, too long for the guards' liking, on the second-floor window above the main entrance. Lisa, watching the scene from her jail-cell bedroom, was visible through the glass. One man spoke into his cuff and moments later, Lisa disappeared.

The visitor glanced once more at the window and turned to the men.

"We ain't seen nothin' happenin' here before." He scratched the drooping denim covering his bum. We thought the old place was abandoned and fallin' in. You sure done a nice job fixin' her up. If yur plannin' to farm, I'd be glad to help you out, free for the conversation."

Guard One snarled something about it being a vacation property and glanced at the house as if appealing for directions.

Once more, the visitor ignored being ignored and gave the property a slow once-over, ending at that second-floor window.

"Old man Withers died up there," he said, at last, nodding at the window. "He was the last of the old bachelor farmers down this way. I gotta admit, this land looks pretty," he glanced up the steep, weed-filled pasture that ran up the hill beyond the rail fence, "but it sure ain't easy to farm. No one got rich farmin' these parts, includin' me and the missus.

"Some say the house is haunted," he whispered.

Loud thumping suddenly came from the house, from the second-floor window, as someone frantically nailed a heavy blanket as a makeshift curtain to block the view. The guards and the old man stared at the space as a pair of hands gripped both sides of the newly fixed cloth and pulled hard to verify it was firm. The eyes in the yard lingered on the window.

A few seconds after the hands disappeared, the blanket fell. A second frantic nailing effort seemed to be successful.

"As I was sayin', haunted..." he glanced back at the window. "So whatcha doin' over there?" He walked towards the new steel-clad building. "Yes siree, coulda used one of them fancy buildin's back when we thought farmin' was a good idea."

He picked up his pace.

The guards escaped their indecision and hurried to block his way.

"This is private, old man. Just move along, and don't come back."

The speaker shoved his hand deeper into his pocket, displaying an ominous pointed bulge. He appeared to be an oversized version of James Cagney as a gangster, but then he never watched old movies.

The old man chuckled.

"Guess yur right... none of my business. Sorry to have bothered yuh."

The tractor backed into a sloppy turnaround, almost hitting the rail fence, and sauntered off at a pace marginally faster than the old man could have managed on his limp. Danny emerged from the house.

"What was that about?"

"Some nosy old geezer..." They watched the machine make a sharp turn down the unkempt concession road towards what they had believed to be a dead-end at the river.

"No one lives down there, I don't think. Did he see anything?"

"He seemed to be interested in the woman's window."

"Damn," Danny frowned. He knew what Greg would do.

"Go after him and take care of the problem," Danny growled. "We don't want loose ends or nosy neighbours. Do what you have to do. We can't have visitors disrupting things."

The men in black checked their hand weapons. Their SUV followed the tractor by five minutes.

"General, we might have a problem." A woman in casual clothes, the sign of a technician who all refused to wear the black jackets, leaned over the back of the farm-parlour couch. Danny Ringwald had been in a deep funk, contemplating the order to kill he had issued twenty minutes before. A cold half-cup of coffee rested in his hand.

"What...?" Danny startled.

"We lost touch with the unit that went after the old farmer. Their locators stopped transmitting about ten minutes ago. It is rare one would fail, but not two at the same time."

"Ten minutes and you're just telling me now?"

"That's the protocol, unless we are in a hot situation." She glanced at her electronic pad, "and it's now about eleven minutes."

The same protocol that had resulted in a ten-minute delay now required Danny to order a firm response. Agents missing always became a serious matter. The CIA did not believe the romantic "no one left behind"; it did not want agents captured and betraying operations.

"Okay, eight agents in two vehicles using the standard approach in unfamiliar territory. Who's our best sniper?"

"Ripley... she's good."

"Send her in so I can brief her."

"Ripley," Danny eyed the somewhat diminutive woman dressed in camouflage and holding a long-barrelled weapon with a large sighting scope. "We don't know what we are dealing with. Remember, no one can take an agent alive. If it looks like we can't liberate them, well..."

Ripley nodded and headed for the door. She had done this before, in Mexico. Then, an agent suffered horrible torture, and she ended the suffering from a distance. Two of his cartel torturers went with him.

Ringwald now felt worse than he had after ordering the farmer's death. He only did what he thought duty required, but the third-generation officer now had growing doubts about what duty meant.

Danny sought Lisa. Strangely, he felt peace when in the woman's presence.

SUVs sped through the gate and turned right, but soon slowed as the unkempt surface gave way to a grass-filled ribbon of lightly worn wheel tracks. The road stretched through a tunnel of trees that created a deeper gloom. They topped a slight rise and braked so quickly that the second vehicle narrowly avoided rear-ending the lead.

Standing in the middle of the track beside a black SUV and an old tractor, not 25 meters away, a little girl confronted them, feet apart and hands-on-hips as if disapproving. The two members of the first pursuit team leaned on their vehicle and stared unblinking and grinning at the rescuers.

Ripley raised her weapon and froze. A shaft of sunlight penetrated an opening in the tree cover and bathed RoH in a golden glow. She raised an arm and pointed at the intruding vehicles. For a fleeting second, Ripley thought the girl looked like a witch casting a spell.

"You seem to be calm and unconcerned," Danny Ringwald had summoned Lisa to the living room.

"Why should I worry?" Lisa asked.

"You are captive, and you don't know the people you are dealing with. They will do anything to succeed."

"Oh, I know them, General, better than you think. None of you know who you are dealing with."

"You," Danny sputtered the scorn, "a powerless woman like you?"

"It isn't me you have to worry about. Charlie and I are sideshows."

"General Ringwald," a young man burst through the front door. "We have lost the signal from the SUVs. The GPS followed them down the road and suddenly, nothing. Their coms aren't working either."

Danny glanced at Lisa and frowned. She smiled back, at perfect peace.

"Send the APC after them. Tell them to take some firepower."

Ringwald followed the man out the door and hurried towards the steel-clad building. He dodged an armoured personnel carrier as it raced out of the large doorway with a helmeted figure poking out the top hatch, clutching the mount of a 50-calibre gun pointed dead to the front. Danny entered the darkened communication centre.

"Get Fort Belvoir on the line."

"Can't, Sir, the link is down. Everything went off at the same time we lost the go team."

"Keep trying." An icy feeling grew in Ringwald's gut.

Is this it?

Danny looked around the gloomy space. Twenty double-stacked bunks stretched along the far wall. He knew six more for the women lay walled off to the rear. A quarter of his force had gone down the road in pursuit of an old farmer. He rushed out to deploy the rest. As a former combat commander, he knew how to set up a defensive perimeter. The people were professional and took up positions where they could cover each other and the boundary with fire.

"Lock the captives in." Danny strapped on his 9 mm handgun and put extra clips into his pocket. He returned to the com centre.

The communicators remained silent and the digital network displayed "loss of signal" warnings. The operator pushed buttons and ran diagnostics. Everything seemed fine, but it remained out of contact.

An hour of silent worry ended as the sound of engines drew Danny outside. The three SUVs and the APC rushed down the lane. Danny stepped forward, expecting an explanation, but the original occupants of the SUVs were not there, just the rescue party.

"We found the SUVs abandoned, engines running where the road ends at the river, no sign of tractor tracks or a farmhouse. It looked like no one had been there in decades. They all just disappeared."

Danny did not like the look of fear on the tough agent's face. Worse, the TAC commander had vanished with the others. Now, Danny owned the problem.

"General," the shout came from the command building, "we have communications back."

Great, what do I say to Greg?

Danny had experienced the loss of people under his command, but a quarter of his force had simply vanished.

One concession road over, beside an old tractor and a happy farmer, a Martin X came to life and made a U-turn towards Goderich.

***

The train squealed to a stop at the Ottawa train station. Liz and Ellie soon found themselves in the main concourse. Ottawa station displayed all the dismal functionality of modern commercial structures with no adornments, save for meaningless art displays and advertising banners. Girders and other structural elements remained exposed, giving the place a factory feel empty of cultural meaning. This cut-rate shell testified to the low importance of the railways and the lack of concern for the people who lived at the lower end of the economy.

That they had located the place on the fringes of the city provided a last indignity. Liz looked for a taxi kiosk.

"This is dismal compared to the place in Toronto." Ellie frowned.

"Only the riffraff now take the train while the rich fly. There are two opposing forces in Ottawa: those who want to expand rail passenger service, as a service, and those who would like to kill VIA to balance the budget. Neither side will fight for their position. One thing you will not find in Ottawa is political courage. Everyone scrambles for the last fringe vote. Defending a principle loses those votes."

"You discourage me," Ellie said. "I think I'm wasting my time here."

"Probably, but I'm glad you came." Liz squeezed Ellie's hand.

"Liz," a shout came from across the vast cavern, "Liz, here..."

A short woman with long dark hair and dressed in business garb waved as she hurried from the entrance.

"I'm glad I got here in time. Your message caught me in a meeting."

Liz savoured the embrace of the woman she secretly loved.

"My message...?" Liz frowned. Ellie smiled and winked.

As a politician, Liz was quick on her feet. She would scold Ellie later.

"Oh yes," Liz said, "I realized this place is in the boonies and we would need a ride. I'm so happy you came." She released the woman and Ellie knew the other was equally reluctant to end the hug.

"Ellie, this is Dawn Waasnodae, MP for... never mind, the riding name is too long to mention. She's my pairing in the House for voting. If one of us is away, the other doesn't vote. Dawn, this is Ellie Keys, a constituent from Goderich."

"Anishinaabe territory, hello..." Dawn took Ellie's hand in a perfunctory shake.

Is Ellie my new competition?

"Liz and I are only friends." Ellie tried to reassure the woman.

Ellie had not and would do nothing alien to meddle with the women's emotions. They had to sort out their relationship on human terms; however, she would give it a nudge by doing small things like pretending to be Liz texting her love.

Liz knew why Ellie had reassured Dawn. It was no surprise to her that Ellie had explored Dawn's mind. She had come to an uneasy acceptance of having Ellie probing her thoughts. This minor incident reassured her that Ellie meant good in some obscure way.

Ellie wondered about Dawn's story and that of her people. She would have a conversation with the MP to explore and discover if Dawn shared Liz's cynicism about politics. Dawn soon had them in her compact car and headed towards the downtown core.

That evening, Ellie, Liz and Dawn climbed from the car in the visitor's parking space at the high-rise tower where Liz rented. They had dined at an upscale restaurant in the heart of Ottawa. Liz frequented the place, and they knew her there. It made for attentive service and Ellie found the food delightful. Since returning, she had had many new food experiences. While her great-grandfather had made sure the little girl who had chosen the stars had a familiar experience, including human food, he had learned a narrow knowledge of Texas cooking from her great-grandmother.

Ellie enjoyed the small talk and conviviality. She watched the two women interact, exchanging banter and gossip about Parliament.

The others did not notice Ellie's strange grin as they crossed the pavement.

It went well, Mother.

The cheese captured some mice. They are safe in the mouse hole.

That's fine, RoH. Your father let me know. I think you get a day off after today's work.

Thank you, Mother. I'll spend it in town.

RoH, how did you do it? Your father thinks you enjoyed it too much.

Getting some of them as guests was not my idea, but since they assigned a ten-year-old to the job, I had to make it fun. We ended up with ten. The first two would have been good enough, if you ask me.

Your father says you imitated an old farmer on a tractor. How did you get that idea?

I had Grandpa's car take me there. That self-driving stuff is great. I probably would have hurt a tree on my own. We were near the farm when we found an old farmer stopped at the side of the road trying to fix his tractor. Do you know they use some sort of power system based on explosions and high-velocity expanding gas? Neat...

The man couldn't seem to get it started. I pretended I was Grandpa and stopped to look. He had a crack in the metal chunk that holds the explosion, so it would likely never run, but he didn't know that.

I pointed at the thing and said, "just move that bit there. It's out of alignment."

When he did that, I made the crack go away and told him to try it. The power plant started right up. Then I got the idea to use the tractor, so I sent him for a nap in the ditch and took off on the machine. It was fun.

Mother...

Yes, RoH...

I think I'll stay on Earth and be a farmer. I love the wind in my hair.

Sigh.

So I looked like an old farmer from a movie. I was cheese for the rats. They followed me, to kill the old farmer. Mother, some humans are so cruel. Why do we want to learn from them?

They aren't all cruel, my love, and most can learn not to be. Remember, you and I are part human.

They caught up to me, looking like me, and thought they had their alien girl when, poof, as humans would say. They are now out there thinking they are having dinner with the old farmer and his wife.

How did your father get close enough to do that?

They brought the ship down fast. Then they left faster than the human radar systems can track. It was only for a few Earth minutes. Father dropped the tractor and me back beside the farmer. He enjoyed his nap. He's another dandelion.

Here's what I looked like.

Ellie experienced a high-speed replay of RoH's escapade.

RoH, stop laughing. What are you doing now?

I'm going to bed, and in the morning into Goderich to have a cheeseburger combo and chat with my friend on a bench.

RoH, stay out of trouble.

Yes, Mother, you too.

"Imp..."

"What," Liz stopped to stare at Ellie, "what did you say?"

"Oh, sorry, I was thinking out loud about my daughter."

"You have a daughter?" Dawn stared at the woman she thought was much too young to be a mother.

"Liz?" Ellie asked.

"Later, up in my condo. I'll let you know when."

It puzzled Dawn and angered that her love had secrets with a stranger.

Liz led them into the elevator.

Chapter Fifteen

Unwelcome guests

Interstellar space is a dark, inhospitable place and a rogue sphere of ice could live there for eternity, if it were lucky and did not fall into a star. For humans and aliens alike, the ones that fall into stars have little importance; a close encounter in a solar system could be another matter. The ones destined to almost fall made themselves annoying and dangerous. One such ball had been travelling through the Oort cloud, towards the sun for millions of Earth years, but now, having cleared the Kuiper Belt, it picked up the pace, accelerating to its doom. It would not remain nameless, first to be known as Clavette BBO2031-1621, a Bernardinelli–Bernstein Object and later, popularly as "Clavette".

The story in the media makes it into an exciting disaster movie with its intrepid scientist hero and all the heroics. The reality is more extraordinary and more interesting than that.
Quantz Nedmar-CBC Radio.

In a rather bizarre bit of irony, the actions that led to discovering the comet, Clavette, began with alien hunters having breakfast in a pub in Goderich. Initially, it had nothing to do with a natural interstellar intruder.

Siglinde Hilfreich's first action when she arrived back at headquarters was to call her overseer in the White House. This man had the President's ear. She told him they had detected what might be an alien spaceship and they needed the entire sky scanned immediately. The Commander-In-Chief appropriated Space Force funds and within hours, observatories around the world saw carefully orchestrated instrument schedules demolished as SETI experts confiscated viewing time through the strategic distribution of a billion dollars.

These searches, based on a sketchy amateur report and accidental professional data, ranged from the celestial equator to the poles. The Space Force told them to look for something within the inner solar system, so they programmed their searches for that distance. This bias delayed the discovery of the visitor.

Some disgruntled astronomers, displaced by the frenzy, combined their projects with the data from SETI instruments. A French astronomer at the Université de Strasbourg, Georges Clavette was one of these. This led to circumstances that mimicked the improbable scientific worth of a blaring television in a Goderich bar. The visitor emerged from Georges Clavette's opportunistic analysis of this data.

The LINEAR project at the site of the white sand in Socorro, New Mexico, had the honour of being the first to announce the comet. The observatory's location held irony since it was only 200 kilometres from Roswell, where the thread of circumstance and meddling that resulted in Ellie and RoH began in 1947.

Georges Clavette, who had piggybacked his project on the sky sweeps of the E.S.A. observatory in a polar orbit around Mars, had been interested in Kuiper Belt objects. He used a different computer algorithm to explore the torrent of data and images cascading from the orbiter's instruments and wide-field camera as it desperately searched for a nearby alien spaceship. The French professor alerted all observatories of a fast-moving Trans-Kuiper object his data had confirmed and they named it Clavette BBO2031-1621. LINEAR instruments had simply been in the best position to follow up with observations in that bit of space. Preliminary orbit calculation placed the object's path well away from Earth. The SETI astronomers returned to the search for aliens.

Similarly, a thousand individuals on the Martian surface, struggling to establish a settlement, knew nothing of the object that the instruments orbiting overhead had been so crucial in discovering. That would soon change, but in the short term, both Earth and Mars raced in their orbits, oblivious to the significance of the large, icy interloper.

In her second action, the evening of her return, Siglinde invited her most trusted and useful team members to her condominium for "a casual get-together". That group only included Ted, Liz and Elliana.

"This is a nice place," Elliana looked around, "much nicer than mine."

"I feel guilty," Siglinde laughed. "I don't even know where you live."

"I live in Springfield, a little apartment I share with a woman who works at Fort Belvoir. She does work like mine, but not as interesting, although we have the same security clearance. Daisy is more of a straight secretary. She even gets coffee for her boss."

"If I ever expect you to fetch coffee, shoot me. I would like to meet her someday."

"Oh, you will, one day." Elliana smiled. "But she has nothing to do with hunting aliens."

"Speaking of aliens," Siglinde said, "there are two visitors, Ellie, and an unknown appearing as a grown woman."

Siglinde stumbled over her words, as if she lied and the truth hid deep in her mind. She had the same feeling that had always hit her when one of her brilliant quantum ideas petered out in a meandering of mathematical gibberish.

"You were right, Ted. Nancy and a team are following up on the Stratford information you discovered." Siglinde nodded at Elliana. For the first time, Siglinde noticed her assistant's dark, fathomless eyes. The woman's return stare seemed both startling and warming.

"The older woman took that Williams guy from the old age home," Siglinde continued, "and we would like to know why. Maybe it is because he claimed a long time ago that aliens had taken him, or perhaps that's coincidental and there's another reason."

"Maybe he's an alien." Elliana laughed.

"Good thought," Siglinde said, and then on some impulse, she hugged Elliana, "I think we all should shake Elliana's hand for her good work."

Ted and Liz hugged their key assistant. Elliana grasped Liz's forearm. Liz took the tingling feeling as emotional bonding.

"I'll do my best to help you all and keep you safe, no matter what." Elliana sounded thankful.

Siglinde startled. Elliana's words seemed familiar.

"My only risk is too much of Siglinde's wine and making a fool of myself." Ted swallowed a pleasant sip.

"Siglinde, as much as I appreciate your hospitality, you have never brought your personal life into our work. What's up?" Liz sipped.

"I needed a private place, and I trust nothing at the office. We are being spied on and have an agent in our group."

"Who... what... why...?" Questions flew.

"I have been suspicious for some time." Again, Siglinde got the feeling that she was not telling the truth and the idea was much more recent. "I wasn't sure, but I checked after I got back. Have there been any reports about Ellie's mother recently from our people in Seattle?"

"No," Liz responded, "but I hadn't thought about it."

"The Seattle people send in a report every day," Elliana said, "but for the past few days they have not seen Lisa."

"Exactly," Siglinde said. "Elliana found a report of Seattle police assisting a federal operation on Lisa's street three days ago. I think some other federal agency, probably the CIA, has grabbed her."

"Who?... Why?"

"Our mission is to gather information about Ellie and her escort. This other group, whatever they are, must want to do something with that information, either to exploit or counter any aliens. It seems they have higher authorization than we do. We may not kidnap people."

"Now that we know about them, we can try to be the first to contact the visitors. We know the visitors exist and are here. That has been a fact for over 80 years. We have always thought we could establish friendly contact. Something going on behind our backs is sinister, and it frightens me. Maybe we can warn the aliens."

"That would be treason," Liz exclaimed, "but if we already have a knife in our back, why not?"

"It might build friendly relations instead of a fight," Elliana said, "especially if aliens don't want to talk to our government."

Siglinde stared at Elliana and suffered more discord.

"I think they want to use Lisa as bait to make the aliens do something. Maybe have Ellie and her escort surrender. I don't know why they haven't grabbed Charlie Keys," again Siglinde felt it was a lie, "and I can't imagine what plans they might have or think they have. From what we learned about the aliens over the past 80 years, I don't think the visitors would be worried. Remember, a move like that took Ellie into custody, but it led to the fiasco in the Dakotas, and long before that, the aliens snatched Ellie's grandfather through the walls of a concrete bunker."

"Do you have any evidence?" Ted tried not to sound sceptical.

"This microphone," Siglinde extracted a compact disc of metal and plastic and a wire from her pocket, "I found it under my desk. I figured my apartment would be more private."

"Then they already know about Ellie and the other one," Liz said, "and we had better get to them before these guys."

"So we are just useful idiots," Ted snarled. "I resent being used and lied to. Who's the rat?"

"My guess is Danny."

"The best place to hide something is to leave it in plain sight," Liz laughed, "and although they can buy anyone, the obvious one would be the best. Military people, even Generals, are cheap to control, just dangle promotion, or threaten court martial."

"So, what do we do?" Ted wanted to fight back.

"For now, nothing," Siglinde said. "But we want to keep actual information isolated and only share what we want with the team. That means, no more casual conversations at work, and everything needs to go to Elliana first, and you," Siglinde pointed to her assistant, "need to find a secure way to hide it."

"No problem, boss," Elliana always seemed un-fazed. "All the field stuff comes to me first. Say nothing on official channels. Here is where you can reach me, privately."

It seemed strange when Elliana wrote a number on a separate piece of paper for each of them instead of just telling everyone at once.

"Why didn't you..." Liz held her copy towards Elliana who put a finger to her lips, "Shhh" and glanced at the ceiling.

"The priority is to find Ellie and her keeper. I'll be going back to Canada as soon as Nancy gets a lead, but I want you to predict what moves the aliens might make."

"We have little to go on," Ted muttered. "They disappeared. Maybe it's time to let the Canadians know. We need their police to help."

"We have to do it below the radar for now," Siglinde said. "Our instructions are explicit, but if Nancy hits a wall, maybe then. I'm sure Danny's buddies don't want the Canadians to know about them."

***

The women relaxed in Liz Dafoe's living room. Liz and Dawn acted like two cats at a dog park. Ellie leaned back in a large, easy chair. She did not relish the others' nervousness, but saw it as a necessary part of their finding courage. It concerned Ellie that Dawn thought she was Liz' lover.

That made things tense. The two women acknowledging their feelings for each other would resolve things. Ellie could do nothing about that, except not being a third party. Ellie yawned.

"Oh, dear," Liz exclaimed, "You are tired. I'll show you the bed."

"Yes," said Ellie, "the past few days have been harder than I thought."

Dawn jumped to the wrong conclusion, but Liz showed Ellie the guest room, not the master bed. Ellie guessed, with her gone, these strong women would risk all and reveal their feelings. She fell into a profound sleep, and Ellie would not eavesdrop.

When she woke, Ellie discovered that the other women were asleep in Liz's bed. Ellie smiled and went to fetch a glass of water. She leaned against the balcony railing and watched the sun appear through the early morning mists. Liz and Dawn had found the courage and each other in the night. Ellie frowned. Sex or sexual attraction had not seemed important, but that closeness with a friend or lover seemed a good thing. She had never had that or thought about it until seeing Liz and Dawn. Her love for her parents, especially her mother, hinted at the power of such a bond. Her star family lacked this.

With love comes empathy, Ellie thought, *and it may be a prerequisite. Perhaps I should explore that with… no… I can't… yet. Great grandfather has it, or RoH and I would not exist. I must talk to him. RoH has something like empathy that far exceeds anything humans or star people possess. Damn it, I have been off-Earth too long and am too analytical. I just want to feel.*

An ongoing debate about the issue raged in the fleet. One faction felt that emotional and cultural effects were important, while others held that cold science had to reign.

On Earth, there is that fight between the sciences and humanities, Ellie thought. *At least star people share this split with humans.*

***

Greg re-read the report and punched a code into the red telephone.

"The Project X people know we are watching." Greg listened.

"They have guessed Ringwald… smart people," another pause.

"No, Danny isn't to blame. Hilfreich is a smart cookie, and she found a bug by accident." Another pause, "No, we don't need to do anything. Ringwald is in Canada at the site, and we will keep him there."

Greg listened once more.

"Need to know, my friend, need to know… don't ask. I'll fill you in once we know more. We're getting close."

Greg stared at the telephone. He did not feel guilty about not revealing that ten agents had disappeared into the woods in Canada. They might be alive and captured, or dead. He hoped they would never talk.

Maybe we are getting too close, he thought, and then picked up the handset once more, dialling Danny in Ontario.

"Dan, Hilfreich has figured out that you're spying on them. Call her and tell her the Space Force has sent you on a short-term assignment to sort out some problem at the Kodiak launch site in Alaska."

"By the way, it turns out my secretary, Daisy, is sharing a place with your secretary at Project X. What do you know about this Elliana chick?"

"Nothing," Danny replied, "She reports to Hilfreich."

"I'm looking into them both," Greg said. "It seems like a strange coincidence, and I hate those. Did you find our guys?" Greg waited.

"Damn it, keep looking. I'll send in replacements tonight, to the airport, same as when you arrived with the woman."

Greg did not mention that the team flying in that night was an elite group that usually took out drug lords who would not share the wealth or a Commie rebel in Central America. Ringwald had made the right move in asking his sniper to shoot the disappeared people if necessary, but now she was one of the missing, a potential risk along with the others.

Danny Ringwald rang off. Searchers had not found a footprint.

Greg doesn't know who we are dealing with. We're tickling the dragon's tail, and it's waking up...

Danny headed for bed, dead tired. He had dreamt last night about being on an alien spaceship, surrounded by cats. He hated cats. The dreams had woken him often. He hoped he would not dream tonight.

***

"Well, I'll be damned!" Ted re-ran the simulation.

"What?" Siglinde looked up from her laptop. She, Ted Kotwas, and Liz had been sitting around the conference table in Virginia in one of their common "silent" sessions. Each of them would go through all recent information trying to find anything useful. Silence occasionally gave way to a question or a comment. No serious discussion ever took place in the building. A week had passed with no new information. Ted had run out of ideas and turned to planetary simulations as a diversion. Siglinde walked around the table and leaned over, placing one hand on his left shoulder.

"What's this?"

"Did you hear about the new comet, Clavette? They detected it a couple of weeks ago, and preliminary orbital elements were only available today." Ted looked up into Siglinde's green eyes.

"I put the elements into our Earth impact programme running on the super-computer at MIT. The alien ghosts bored me, and I wanted to see where Clavette was going. What we see here is my downloaded result of that run. Watch this."

Ted hit the go icon. At first, nothing seemed to happen, but then a red dot sped across the screen as other bright spots, representing the planets in orbit, major moons, and a few larger asteroids, hurried around the yellow disc of the sun. A box of rapidly changing data remained fixed in the upper left corner of the screen. The red dot passed through the planetary orbit traces from above and dove beneath the sun. The view shifted to watch it emerge on the far side and shoot up to what one would expect to be a return trip to the icy expanse. It passed close to the fourth planet, an orange dot on the display, and for an instant, they seemed to merge. The path of red kinked into a new direction.

"Close enough to scratch the paint." Ted laughed.

"Wow," Siglinde reached around Ted and hit the go icon; she knew that a close encounter like that was critical. "Mars is a bull's eye. Are the elements accurate?"

"Within a few percent," Ted said. "I don't think anyone has run this sim before. We need observations to know if it will hit Mars."

"How big is this thing?"

"We don't know that either. If it's as big as the estimate, and it hit Earth at a high angle, it would be an ELE. Mars' atmosphere would be no protection, and as you saw, Clavette won't get close enough to Jupiter to be torn apart or diverted." Ted grabbed his cell and hit the speed dial to his associate at MIT. Before the end of the day, another set of eyes would review the data. Clavette would become the priority at the LINEAR observatory. Urgency would spread to other near-Earth observatories. Humans on Mars made an impact more than a scientific experiment.

"How did you get time on the Singh-Dashinsky machine at MIT? I had to wait almost two years to get 30 seconds to run a model."

"I helped design it," Ted smiled. "Singh still owes me a home-cooked curry meal for the bug I caught, and Mary Louise and I led the team that created the solar system impact programme. I have a gold pass to stick a run of that into the schedule whenever I want. Maybe I made you wait an extra minute in the two years, sorry," Ted touched Siglinde's hand that warmed his left shoulder.

"When is that Mars rendezvous?"

Ted touched the screen and slowed the graphic. In the upper left, numbers slowly changed. Ted focused on the second row, where a number with the accuracy of seven decimal places turned over and was slow enough to read. Above that, a similar number changed, with only the last five decimal places unreadable. The object approached Mars' orbit, and Ted slowed the display to jump frames, then hit pause. The dots merged.

"There," he pointed to the upper left display, "those Julian day numbers show," he quickly subtracted the upper number from the lower, "107 days from now, give or take a day and diminishing. That thing is a bullet. It's already inside the orbit of Jupiter, but its track is at a high angle to the ecliptic."

He looked further down the column of numbers.

"It would hit at over 50 kilometres per second, if it hit, likely near Mar's southern pole."

"How big is it?"

"Georges Clavette thinks it's huge, over 100 kilometres in diameter, and since it already has a BBO designation, others think it's minor planet size, maybe interstellar, but not a spaceship. Let me see..."

Ted searched through the original low-resolution Mars Observatory Clavette images and the better quality Earth-based sources.

"There's out-gassing, but only on recent photos. The brightness makes it large, and the spectrum hints it's mostly ice. There's an argument about that, so we won't know until the experts reach a consensus. That will happen when our visitor warms up a bit."

"100 kilometres times 50 kilometres per second," Siglinde muttered her mental math and reached a horrible conclusion.

"How many humans are on Mars right now?" Siglinde felt a chill.

Ted queried the internet.

"Between the IP-1 Base and the Russian-Chinese outpost, 1104..."

"We need to know how close it's going to get. We need that quickly." Siglinde's calm voice did not reflect the gut-wrenching turmoil beneath.

"It probably doesn't matter," Ted said. "Mars is in the mid-transfer phase. There's no Earth return orbit for a year, and they won't have enough fuel to get more than a handful of ships into Mars orbit. If that hits hard, they may need to be a lot further out than a low orbit. We could lose almost everything we have in orbit there as it is. The Chinese and Russians could do a return if the time was right, but in three months they still won't have a survivable Earth return option."

"I'll get them to hurry, but..."

Liz said, "I guess we have been interested in the wrong type of alien."

No one laughed.

Chapter Sixteen

Friends, ferrets and fogies

"This place is hopeless," Dawn nodded towards the parliament building. The stone facade glowed in the autumn sunshine, creating an illusion of grandeur. Dawn's long, dark hair swirled in the wind. "It is a racist, bigoted monstrosity. The security and other staff discount anyone of colour. In the Commons, if you aren't a white man, or a white woman acting like a white man, you don't count. You're an alien."

"You aren't encouraging me," Ellie sighed. "I guess actual aliens wouldn't go down well."

"What do you mean?" Dawn looked perplexed.

"Tell me about this fire we are sitting at." Ellie postponed the big revelation.

"This is the centennial flame. It marks the 100th anniversary of when the local settlers took over colonial control from the British. They acted the same way, or worse. Whatever it's supposed to celebrate, it reminds me of a traditional fire where, for thousands of years, my people sat to tell stories. Stories are the way we pass on knowledge and history. I like to sit here and think."

"In many old stories, the Ojibwe one that explains summer and winter, for instance, a bad dude is fighting a good dude. There is always a beautiful woman involved. Sometimes the bad guy wins, sometimes the good guy, or with the seasons, they divvy up the year. As most times, the disappointed woman dies. Either that or she tires of waiting for the damned outcome."

Dawn glanced at the massive building behind her.

"I think little has changed. I'm tired of waiting."

"It's appropriate that you and I are chatting here. I want to learn your stories." Ellie loved stories as a young girl, especially mother's stories.

"You know, I know nothing about you, Ellie. I like you, now that I have Liz," Dawn glowed, "but except that you have a daughter, you have said nothing."

Ellie glanced around the grassy expanse in front of Parliament. On an autumn weekday, a few people scurried about. She feared Dawn might overreact to the truth, and that was not a good thing in public.

"This location is open. I wanted to tell you privately."

"It seems fine here." Dawn swept the same sparsely populated landscape. "Why don't you tell me now?"

Dawn slid closer on the stone bench as if it increased privacy.

Ellie looked deep into Dawn's eyes. Instantly, Dawn knew Ellie's story, from birth to this bench, as if the memories had always been there. Dawn did not react in the way Ellie had feared.

Dawn simply nodded her head and took Ellie's hand.

"You have certainly reacted to that much more calmly than Liz did."

"Our forefathers and mothers have always told stories of bright lights in the sky, visitors of grey, and friendship. The stories become sad when they turn to the time these visitors no longer came. They gave hope and guidance, but never interfered in the doings of my people or other tribes. However, the stories talk about a great time of peace that ended when the visits stopped. Many of my people believe that the tribes all came from the stars and everyone is part star person. I am familiar with those beliefs. Liz warned me you were out of this world. She didn't say alien."

"I'm less alien than my mother, more of this world, but it became more refined in me, because of my father's genes." Ellie felt relieved.

"I am mainly human, but I can make you and others think they see me as another person or even in alien form, but it requires some effort."

Briefly, Dawn saw Ellie as an apparition from her people's legends, a silver-grey miigis beside her, then Ellie.

"That is not me," Ellie said. "I have a human body. My daughter is over half-alien and has both human and star form. RoH can appear as either, with no special effort. She chooses her human form on Earth, but she can appear as any form, human or alien, that she needs, or wants, the little rascal. She likes her human form better, I think. I'll tell you the Farmer Brown story sometime."

"Your ancestors met another race of star people, not mine. They stopped travelling the galaxy and retreated to a remote cluster to contemplate. That has lasted a thousand of your years. We leave them alone. Their power is great. We don't know what they are debating. Perhaps it is to do with those ancient contacts with your people."

"I would like to know more," Dawn said.

"I would like to know more from you," Ellie smiled. "I will explain what my star family is trying to achieve on Earth. Perhaps we will at least leave the entire planet mimicking your people's stories and acceptance. In addition, we would like to infuse human empathy, companionship, and, as I now think, humour into the star population. The people on the ships are a dour bunch, but my daughter and I have forced them to smile occasionally. My daughter is a regular comedian, and it drives the star family crazy. They do not understand that."

"There are humans like that," Dawn laughed. "Most are engineers or civil servants. I think school removed their funny bones. I would love to meet your daughter."

"RoH has much more potential than I have. As she matures, she will grow stronger. For now, I'm just happy the little scamp doesn't flaunt it."

"I am drawn to you," Dawn said, "as if you hold answers to my oldest questions. All the stories my mother and father told confused me between the scientific view of the universe taught in school and the deep echoes of my people. It has always unsettled me. You seem genuine; real… do you know what I mean?"

"Yes, and I'm drawn to you. Your stories of contact might complete what my star family knows. Tell me more stories about that time."

"The history of this land that is mostly taught in school begins with Europeans. The books have little about us original people. Our stories, passed down through the generations, fill in the thousands of years before that."

Dawn took Ellie's hand. "These stories are not gossip. The elders carefully guard their integrity. Only certain talkers can tell many, and after they have apprenticed for years with older oracles. It's a way to keep oral history accurate. Not just anyone can repeat them. Unqualified people, once hearing them, dare not repeat them. If they do, they might become pariahs in the community. Even worse, they won't get to hear any more stories."

"That sounds like our situation regarding the reclusive race. Whatever made those older visitors turn into reclusive people chilled their entire memory of them. It seems as if a rule forbids telling their story."

"My favourite story, just because it touches known scientific history of the ice age came from an older friend, ironically, an Iroquois who once lived in a community of my Ojibwe people on Manitoulin. He told of sitting with an elder at the edge of the water. According to the Iroquois, the old Ojibwe took his walking stick and planted it vertically in front of him, and using it as a guide pointed north at the top of his shaft. He said, 'That's where the top of the ice wall was when our people first came here.' From what we know, scientifically, that would place my ancestors on that spot at least 9000 years ago. It's supported by archeological evidence of the old Odawa quartz quarry. I love that story. It shows me a connection between modern science, the ancients and of the new generations too. That is not one of the sacred, guarded stories. They have honoured me to hear many of those. I will take you to the elders one day. They may honour you."

"That story fits with some of the ancient records on the starships." Ellie shifted uncomfortably on the curved granite bench. "I'll have that record translated into English and give it to you. The guardians of your knowledge might find it helpful. We have detailed maps of the last glaciation. We don't think any visitors came to Earth before then. They are the oldest interstellar species we know about. Maybe, one day, we will get to talk to the recluses in their cloister of star systems. Dawn, I like you. Liz has chosen well, and you have too in loving her."

Ellie glanced at parliament, now turning a dour grey in the late autumn light. Gusts whipped the flame into knots. They felt a sudden chill.

"I don't think there is any solution here for what we want to accomplish. You and Liz; however, might be part of the transition process for the planet. It will require bravery and wisdom. Both of you seem to have that strength and respect in your communities. If we star-people reveal ourselves, there will be confusion and hostility. Anyone with a stake in the old ways of Earth will want to exploit our presence, and some to destroy us. That will trap you in the middle. Your career here will end."

"My whole life, my people have always lived in the middle, between the people's way and the white man's way. We are used to it. Ever since the Europeans came, the nations confronted two choices: self-destruction and bravery. Lately, bravery has grown. My time as an MP is over. I will resign. There is no hope in white man's politics for my people. I guess that might make us natural allies of star people."

"I think it does," Ellie said, "but in the end, we want all of Earth's people to be united, not fractured by artificial things like colour and unhealed history. You are all one species."

"Our people have always believed that all humans are of one blood. Skin colour does not change that. I have always believed the solutions to our situation lay in the unity of ordinary people, natives, settlers and then globally. I love one of those settlers. That's my start, but I'll work amongst the people now."

"Things will develop quickly, maybe in only a year or two. The struggle will change if we reveal our presence. If we decide not to, you will have your battle and perhaps make progress. I hope we stay, but I know you and Liz will thrive in your work. There are American agents pursuing me."

Dawn looked concerned. "That's terrible."

"They are helping advance the plan. There are two separate entities of the US government trying to contact us. One is vicious and full of dangerous psychopaths. The other is positive, the contacts we would like to have, on our terms, of course. This better bunch will contact you and Liz once they connect me to you. They're getting closer. Please tell them everything, except perhaps that we are using them too. We want to keep this group open and friendly to star visitors. We won't let the dangerous ones near our friends. I would like to make you safer." Ellie took Dawn's arm. "You can say no, but it won't hurt or be a threat."

As with everyone drawn to trust Ellie, Dawn agreed. There was a faint feeling radiating from Ellie's touch, and then it was gone.

"I will always know where you are, and if I don't, others will. At some point, we will reveal the illegal American meddling in Canada, and that will cause uproar. We just haven't decided when." Ellie did not anticipate that stubborn human inquisitiveness would move events despite the well-considered star plans.

"Yes, can I help you?" The middle-aged nurse behind the Cedar Haven reception counter smiled at Nancy.

"I would like to ask about the abduction of Peter Williams. We are concerned." Nancy gave her best ingratiating smile and flashed a card that identified her as a member of the RCMP. She hoped her thin Californian accent would pass as Canadian.

"The Stratford cops already quizzed me. They treated me as if I was a looney." The nurse frowned. Her tone became hostile. "What do you guys want?"

"We don't think you are nuts," Nancy smiled. "That incident has serious national security issues. These town cops have no imagination. They don't have a clue what is going on."

"What's going on?" The nurse brightened. This had suddenly transformed her routine life into being part of something big.

"Tell me exactly how it happened."

"Dia saw them first, coming out of Peter's room. He was walking, and she had never seen that. Frankly, it surprised me when they passed here. I didn't realize at first that it was Peter."

"Who's Dia?" Nancy made a note on her electronic pad.

"She's a PSW on Peter's floor, but not his worker."

"When I called out, they bolted. It was two firsts for Peter, walking and then running. The door closed and then the damn thing wouldn't open. It worked once they disappeared."

"Tell me about the door." Nancy's fingers flew over her screen.

"The cops thought we made that up to cover our butts. There's nothing to tell about the door. It works fine now. The tech couldn't find anything wrong with it. Seven of us tried to open it."

"What about the woman?"

Nancy noted that the description perfectly matched Ellie's adult accomplice.

"The door and Mr. Williams walking are most important, and the woman. Thank you; call me if you remember more."

Nancy left her card, embossed with authentic Mountie symbols but with her cell number. She walked to the street and looked to the corner where Peter and Ellie had disappeared. It would be useless to follow the route. Perhaps the Stratford cops knew more.

"Thank you for seeing me on such short notice, Constable. The Service appreciates that. This is an urgent matter."

"Detective," the man at the desk said, ever jealous of his hard-won status. "I'm in charge of the Williams abduction case."

He re-examined Nancy's business card, identifying her as an agent of the Canadian Security and Intelligence Service. He also scrutinized a rather sketchy document from Ottawa asking for all local help. Black marker obscured several lines. He wanted to maintain control in his territory but wanted to know what this fiasco at the old age home had to do with CSIS.

"What is this all about?" Cooperation might be a feather in his cap.

"All I can tell you is that the woman is a foreign agent. I can't say for what country, but we want to get her."

"What does this Williams guy have to do with it?"

"We don't know," Nancy sounded honest, "perhaps the tip of some espionage iceberg. We must find out where they went."

The detective pulled out the case file and spent a tedious hour telling Nancy what she already knew, along with his opinion that "the goofs at the old age home made up the door story to cover their incompetent asses".

Nancy made encouraging sounds in response. After an hour, he gave valuable information.

"After the story played on the TV, a cabbie called us. He took an old man and a good-looking, light-haired woman to London that afternoon. They paid cash, but we couldn't lift prints because he had already spent it. We ran checks. Williams withdrew money from several bank accounts using ATMs. He covered his trail, but made more withdrawals in London. We are waiting for the London force to get him."

Nancy copied the list of machines Peter had used. One was at a café in London. There were several transactions there with one yesterday. Her team would find a pattern, a possible focal point to narrow the search. Nancy already knew where to start.

"Could I have a photo of Mr. Williams, please?"

A scan reached Nancy's cell in a few moments.

"Please keep me in the loop," the detective shook her hand. "Here's my card, so you can get my name right in the report."

"I'll let your superiors know how helpful you have been." Nancy, a veteran of the promotion game, understood the man's interest. She might need him again.

"Call me if you find anything else."

The logistics of setting up a secondary operation in London, Ontario, delayed Nancy for a day. Peter's habits made up for the frustration.

Nancy sipped a delicious coffee at a corner table on the café patio. It gave her a good view of the door and the street. Her cell displaying Peter's photograph lay on the table as she pondered the printed map of Williams' bank withdraws. The café operated near the physical focal point of the scattered transactions. Nancy did not wait long. Peter arrived and sat at a sunlit table not too far from Nancy. He took out a laptop and continued working on Ellie's suggested autobiography.

"Mr. Williams," Nancy sat without invitation, "could we please talk?"

Nancy was a smooth, experienced operator and knew how to set suspects at ease. Here, Peter was a clue, not a suspect. Peter startled and fought the urge to run.

Tell them all you know... Ellie had said that while sitting in the same chair that this stranger occupied. For some strange reason, Ellie wanted his bunch to follow her. He remained nervous, but resolved. The worst they could do was to return him to the home. Peter noticed Nancy's accent.

"You're American," he sipped his tea without shaking. "She said you would eventually get to me."

"Who is 'she'?"

Peter's surprising cooperation landed Nancy in Jim's apartment, surrounded by UFO nut bars and an even crazier cockatoo. Her backup sat in a van, recording the meeting. It excited the human participants that an official agency, even an American one, wanted to hear their stories. Peter, following Ellie's wishes, told all he knew after extracting a promise from Nancy that she would give his location to the home.

In the avalanche of sound coming from excited people eager to tell their story, and a cockatoo repeatedly calling Jim "crazy", useful information emerged. The most promising of all were the names Liz Dafoe and Steven Jorgensen.

Nancy did not judge these old fogies. Their stories paralleled and mostly matched the recorded testimony of hundreds of others gathered over the preceding 80 years. She promised she would keep them informed, although that would never be a priority for NAAP. Nancy left after a few hours of questions. Her report to Siglinde would be significant. The boss had to decide on the next steps.

***

"I would like to speak with Bobby Briscoe. Just tell him that Jim is calling. I have information on the alien spaceship he reported on."

Bobby Briscoe had hinted aliens might be involved in something seen in the sky. Bobby saw it as a joke. Crazy Jim saw him as a likely ally. Something resembling a circus would soon burst into the media.

Crazy Jim wanted vindication for his treatment as a "UFO nut". He now saw his opportunity. The visit of the American agent would be big enough news, but he knew aliens had landed in Huron County. Ellie, Peter, and now Nancy gave him actual information to prove he was not crazy. He would be famous and maybe get money too.

Jim's ambitions went against the interests of the Americans, not quite in keeping with the Ellie's wishes, and pushed events forward faster than planned.

For the Americans, their ability to operate was about to get complicated just as certainly as the inner solar system was about to be disrupted by a 200-kilometre diameter comet.

Chapter Seventeen

Fireflies, Fireworks and Sky-fires

When the big USAF transport touched down on its second late-night visit to the Goderich Airport, it carried replacements for the missing ten operatives and two large five-ton vans. It also carried the invisible cargo of optimism for Danny Ringwald and the remaining agents at the clandestine outpost. This optimism, as with the Lake Huron mists obscuring the departing plane, would soon evaporate.

The farmyard glowed like noon. Danny watched from the porch as the large black trucks struggled into the yard, one pulling the other. Danny reached the lead vehicle as it eased to a stop. The towed truck's front bumper banged into the rear step of its rescuer as the driver of that vehicle braked late.

"You're late," Danny said as the lead driver inspected for damage.

"We have the latest and best tech going in here," the driver thumbed at the vehicle and scowled as she noted a bent step, "but we can't keep a damned diesel motor running."

The trailing vehicle's engine then mocked her, as the driver tried the starter and the engine came to life, in a perfect diesel rattle.

"Well, I'll be damned," her annoyance deepened. Danny smiled, grasping for something positive.

With all that's going on, maybe I'm General Snafu.

"You can park over there by the ops building," Danny waved at the space, "and settle into the dorm. I'm going for a rest, but I'll be over later."

Mother Lisa woke with a start. *I'm here. We are never far away.*

Lisa saw Ellie, glowing and ephemeral beside her bed, but Lisa could not move. She desperately wanted to hug her daughter, but somehow her body became lead. She wanted to cry.

Don't fret, Mother, everything will be okay. Dad is there too, and you will see him later today. You two being here is part of the plan, and you will know when it has worked. Something is about to happen that we had not planned, but it may be better than what we might have done.

Tell General Ringwald everything you know. He may be a help later. Oh, and ask him for your vegan diet.

Lisa stared into sudden blackness and then fell into a quiet slumber. She awoke with a perfect memory of a comforting dream.

The team did not wait for General Ringwald's orders. When Danny emerged several hours later, after a brief nap and an excellent breakfast, a robotic dog greeted him. It wagged an articulated tail with a camera at its tip and looked up at the general with its metal head cocked to one side. The canine bot had run Danny's face through its artificial intelligence software and found him to be a friend. The thing resembled a dog. Its body was a military matt-grey plastic, the head a red-tinted sensor dome, and the tail more resembled a plumber's snake. The articulated spine allowed it to mimic a dog chasing its tail. One wanted to play fetch with the thing. The snout had no mouth, and the nostrils were chemical sensors. Four 9 mm guns with a six-clip hid behind sacrificial plastic plugs above the front and rear legs. A clone of the avatar dog pranced near the far end of the lane.

"We have established a security zone patrolled by Data and his buddies. There are four, Data here, Jordi, Scotty and Spock. There's a fifth one in the van, painted black, with two AP rockets and a short-burst flame-thrower. We call it, Vader."

The young man sat at a console with four large screens. They displayed forward-facing views from the robots, including the one who had trailed Danny into the van and was projecting an 5-G image of the general's pant-covered buttocks. A column of control icons ran down the left side of the screen and on the right, a miniature map displayed the probe's location with buttons below to give directional commands. Artificial intelligence allowed the things to function independently within the rules, but the operator could change these rules between stalk, threaten, and kill. The controller fingered a button, and the fourth robot hurried away from Danny to take up a circuit behind the house.

"Impressive." Danny knew that Greg's operators only gave him lip service and followed Greg's orders. While annoyed, he accepted his role.

"The critters are ready to go," a woman at the far end called out. Her screen covered the back wall with two dozen numbered rectangular boxes surrounding a blank central area labelled, "No contact".

The small rectangles filled with changing images. The primary display showed an above view of the van that quickly expanded to the inner farmyard as the camera gained height. Danny headed towards the display.

"The critters," the woman did not look up, "are flying robots the size of dragonflies and from a distance look like them. It's solar-powered."

"So, they don't work at night."

"Oh, they do. Aside from a home base recharge, they can drink electromagnetic energy. We set their receptors to resonate with our com transmissions. We also tune an energy transmitter to that same resonance, and their energy absorbers mostly depend on that. They are on guard, twenty-four seven. No one will notice these little bugs."

"Nothing will penetrate here," said the man handling the ersatz dogs.

Danny flinched at the agent's arrogance and ignorance. He had experienced the failure of that assumption on an old battlefield, and someone had poorly trained those infiltrators and humans, not aliens.

"Can we use these insects to go search for our missing teams?"

"That's the plan," the woman tossed over her shoulder and touched one of the small boxes. That view immediately filled her screen.

"I'm sending this one down the old road now." She touched a control, and the view moved quickly down the overgrown back road. A small map appeared at the bottom of the screen, showing the position. A red dot moved slowly down the map as the view shifted from side to side. Another touch and the display held an infrared version of the scene.

Greg probably has large holdings of Northeast Robotics stock.

Danny's progress up the military promotion chain had increased his cynicism and killed any idealism they might have had at West Point. He also owned stocks of many defence contractors.

"Looks like you have it all under control," Danny's shrug acknowledged his unimportance in the decision-making. "Please tell me if you find anything."

"Here," the man handed over a small cell-sized device. "This will beep the same alert we get from the probes. Hey, can we get rid of that tree over in the corner?" He waved at a large heritage oak that dominated the southeast corner of the fence. "We can't get a good view up that hill."

"Cut it," Danny sighed. He pocketed the buzzer. He did not know that the thing held enough C-4 to kill, and the command post could trigger it.

Danny headed into the house. He would have a chat with Lisa and Charlie. He felt he should bring them together in violation of Greg's orders to see if they revealed more in casual conversation. Danny enjoyed talking with them. As his mother might say, "they're nice folks". Danny did not consider the idea might not have been his.

***

Siglinde closed the door behind her. Ted smiled at her over his laptop.

"So, what do you have, Dr. Doom?"

"Singh at M.I.T. has been chasing the orbit data for our visitor. Clavette is going to hit Mars."

"...in 105 days?"

"The impact point is uncertain, but it will be about fifteen degrees off the Martian southern pole. We'll know more soon, but modelling suggests it will make Mars unapproachable for years. Just to make it worse, new observations give it a diameter of at least 200 kilometres."

Siglinde felt chilled. *A thousand lives...*

"What's being done?"

Ted flipped his screen to a timeline from M.I.T.

"Singh has already notified NASA. They have been in touch with Washington, and informed every observatory worldwide. All eyes are on this thing. NASA and the Martian Colonial Consortium have scheduled a press conference in Washington for this evening. I assume they told the Chinese and Russians."

"So, we aren't involved directly." Siglinde felt both helpless and relieved. Clavette would be others' nightmare.

"As long as it doesn't involve flying saucers and little green men," Ted tried to laugh.

"... little grey women," Siglinde said, "... shimmering little grey women, but the impact will make a lot of human corpses."

She seemed about to cry. Ted hugged her. He had never had the opportunity before. For a brief instant, Siglinde clung to him. Ted wanted to cry too, for the doomed Martian settlers. He had never experienced this emotion in his life. The embrace became more than a friend's comfort.

Siglinde backed away, conflicted between desire and decorum.

"I doubt the aliens will do anything. Even their power might have limits. If they lack empathy, they won't care. Fill Elliana in and ask her to monitor this for any hint that aliens have involved themselves."

"How do you know they're grey?" Ted asked. "No one has seen one."

"I just know. Maybe it's in the old records."

"I am returning to Canada. Nancy is in London and she has discovered some leads. One is a name from our files, from the old project. I didn't know any of the old abductees were still around. I'm meeting Nancy to follow up. It might be a few days. Call me tonight with updates."

Ted noticed the longing in Siglinde's voice. Having her fall in love with him had not been part of the plan, nor of him loving her.

Siglinde retreated, fearing her desire to hug Ted might overtake her. She had an hour to get to the airport.

Why did I think about alien empathy? Why are they grey? Was that body they had at Groom Lake grey?

A memory just beyond consciousness unsettled her.

She stared out the window at the lush parkland full of tall, proud oaks screening the Virginia countryside.

***

Lisa watched from her window as four people attacked the large oak with a chainsaw and ropes. Eventually, the thirty meters of the tree lay askew over what had once been a flower garden parallel to the rail fence. The chainsaw operator barely escaped the falling trunk as it kicked back.

Amateurs, thought Lisa, *Uncle Tom showed me how to fall a tree. Safety concerned him more than getting the firewood. It's a shame such a beautiful tree died because of their fear.*

RoH sat at the top of the hill overlooking the farmhouse. The mechanical dogs and insects had fascinated her, but she now watched in sadness as the old oak fell. It had been for a futile cause. She frowned and focused on the work party.

The chainsaw operator stooped to remove the first limb, but the saw died. A few minutes of progressively frantic tries failed to bring the machine to life.

"Damn, millions in tech, but a chainsaw is kaput." He stomped away.

Up the hill, RoH smiled and focused on her grandmother's window.

Lisa responded to a quiet rapping on the door. Danny Ringwald had decided that Lisa and Charlie should meet.

Chapter Eighteen

Poking the eagle

"What do you have for me?" Bobby Briscoe eyed his morning visitor. He laid a cell in the audio recording mode onto the table. Bobby had learned never to ignore a potential story, but for a probable UFO nut case, he would only meet in the security of the television studio's front lobby. The receptionist watched with curiosity. They had seen many offbeat characters sitting where Crazy Jim fidgeted.

"If I tell the story backwards, you might believe it better." Jim tried to smile. "I'm in touch with several people who the aliens took years ago. One is Peter Williams."

The reference straightened Bobby from his slouch. Williams' name had been on television, of course, but not in the past week. Even if Jim had stolen it from the news, Bobby wanted to check.

"Did you get that name from TV?"

"No, Peter and I go way back. We met because of the damned aliens. They took him too, you know. Here..."

Jim unfolded a yellowed newspaper clipping, a photo of him and Peter many years ago. Bobby recognized both.

"They took the photo at an abductee convention in Ohio, a long time ago. The paper made fun of us, but the picture is a keepsake."

"So, you have something more recent?"

"Last evening, an agent from the American UFO project, someone named Nancy, came to my place. She met with several of us, including Peter. They're in Canada because aliens landed in Goderich a few weeks ago. An alien got Peter out of that old age prison. She came to my place."

Bobby became interested. He knew a story when he found it, and even if this turned out to be a hoax, it had enough to last a few days on-air interest. The unofficial account of Williams fleeing the home had an air of magic or alien power. The news producer would love it.

"The woman...?" Scepticism still haunted Bobby. "The cops said she didn't look like an alien."

"Have you read much about aliens?"

Bobby admitted all he knew was from movies.

"Read the work of Tom Clarke. The woman's name is Ellie. Tom was her great uncle. She's part alien and went with the aliens over twenty years ago. She was ten then, now she's a woman. The aliens are up to something, but it's different. They aren't grabbing people at random."

"The Yanks want Ellie. They tried when she was a girl and failed. They think she will give them leverage with the visitors."

"They don't have a chance; we don't have a hope if we go toe to toe with the visitors. I've been there. The Yanks should know that. Once they had Ellie's grandfather locked up, and the aliens pulled him out of a bunker, right through the walls." Jim's laugh echoed through the atrium in a way that almost justified his cockatoo's insults. The receptionist eyed the phone, but Bobby remained calm.

"If the aliens decide to protect someone, or kill them, they can do it."

"You make them sound like my movie alien invaders."

"They aren't monsters or invaders. We met Ellie. She brought Peter here. Ellie said they were bumbling... too smart for their good, but they created her. That changed everything. She has had a big effect on them."

Bobby had made the alien joke at the end of the story about the amateur astronomer in Goderich. Now, it seemed ironic. Jim spoke well, and he would look good on camera. Bobby had an avalanche of questions.

"Can I meet Mr. Williams? That would corroborate your story."

"He doesn't know I've done this. I'll ask him tonight. I have something you can work on, though. Nancy gave us a contact number." Jim handed Nancy's business card to Bobby. "I want it back. It's the only evidence I have."

"What does Nancy look like?"

Jim described the woman.

"We don't know where Nancy is staying." Jim said.

Bobby had tracked down reluctant subjects before, and a Yankee agent operating illegally in Canada would spook at his first call. He had a friend in the police who could run the guest lists at the hotels. If he could locate the right place, stalking was part of a reporter's game.

"Can you list who was at the meeting with the Yank?"

"Tonight, if Peter agrees to meet you. One thing though," Jim leaned forward and frowned, "if you don't take this seriously, I'll be done with you. I'd like vindication, but no more ridicule."

"I won't make fun of you," Bobby was sincere. If he could convince the producers to air this, it would set off a fireworks display, maybe an international incident if he could prove that American agents were prowling about on the sly without Canadian handlers. It would not matter if Jim's alien story held up or not.

Bobby smiled at the thought. The story could mean a journalism award for him and the station.

"I want to make sure," Bobby added, "but if it breaks, you'll be a celebrity. Where's Ellie now?"

"Not sure, but I think she left with Liz Dafoe, the MP... probably to Ottawa."

"Does Liz know Ellie is an alien?"

"Part alien, part human," Jim frowned. "I don't know. Ellie talked to Peter alone before they left. Maybe he knows. She warned Peter about the agent looking for us. She told Peter to tell this Nancy person everything."

"So Nancy knows what you just told me?"

"More," said Jim. "I'm guessing they are hiding evidence."

"I'll wait to hear from you tonight, thank you." Bobby was eager to get on Nancy's tail and to discover what the alien planned in Ottawa.

The speed that his police friend provided the hotel guest lists surprised Bobby. The recent push to stop human trafficking hinged on an umbrella warrant requiring hotels and motels to provide guest lists and details twice daily. It had led to a dozen arrests and the freeing of twice that number of kidnapped, under-aged girls.

In the early afternoon, Bobby stood in front of the registration clerk at the Best Western, downtown. The top suspect in his search was an N. Deveraux from Virginia, USA. It listed the credit card under an American agency called the National Agency for Aerial Phenomena. He had the contact number for the agent and her office in Virginia and her cell number from Jim's card. NAAP had almost no public profile.

"I have a friend staying here, Nancy Deveraux... room 514. Is she in?"

"She's on her way down. That woman over there is waiting for her."

Bobby glanced across the lobby. A good-looking woman, perhaps in her late 30s, lounged in a stuffed chair, examining a copy of the Free Press. She seemed to scan it purposefully.

"Great, I'll just go check the car and be back."

Bobby hurried out the door and across the street. He waited in the driver's seat, expecting that whatever the women were up to, they would have to come out the hotel's front door.

Who's that other chick? Bobby wondered.

"Hi Siglinde."

"You've made progress," Siglinde said. "We may be closer to Ellie."

"So far," Nancy said, "it's just a tease. I think we'll get to her soon."

"How about lunch and we can talk it over?" Siglinde asked.

"Later, we have an appointment with Dr. Steven Jorgensen at the university in a half-hour."

"That name is a blast from the past. Did you know he was at the Dakota fiasco and junior support for the language guys?" Siglinde had memorized the names in the old files.

"Nope, but according to Peter Williams, Ellie went to see him. I figured he was the closest lead."

"He may be important in all this. Jorgensen was a whiz kid. He talked to Ellie back then. The file had a snarky note that he liked the little girl too much and hinted his being a Canadian made him untrustworthy. Maybe Ellie liked him, too. Does he know who we are?"

"Yes, he didn't want to meet. I mentioned NAAP, and he invited me right over. Let's go."

"I'll drive," Siglinde headed to the door. "I think Jorgensen is a key."

As chance had it, Bobby had parked right in front of Siglinde. He snapped a few photographs as the women crossed the street. Siglinde eased away from the curb. Bobby let a car get between them and followed.

Bobby photographed the women entering what a sign said was the Department of Linguistics, in an old mansion in a backwater of the Western campus. Except for a couple of lovers snuggling on a park bench and a worker clearing fallen leaves, the area was quiet. Bobby waited but pulled up the university website to see whom they might be visiting.

"Call me Steven," Dr. Jorgensen ushered his visitors into his motley array of seating. "Ellie told me to tell you all I know."

Rachel was away rehearsing the defence of her thesis, but Steven carefully closed his office door.

"We were going to ask questions, but please tell your story first."

Steven recounted Ellie's visit, but left out Rachel's involvement. It would not be fair to include her without her permission. He hoped these agents did not already know.

"Can you show us the artefact Ellie left here?" Siglinde had always been a patient listener, but now Jorgensen seemed to have finished.

"No," Steven stiffened. "I'll keep that for another time."

Jorgensen had decided that he needed some advantage with these people. They seemed to be the good ones Ellie had mentioned, but he did not want these Yanks to grab the device and then hire their linguists. However, he was certain that without the help of "Bob" in the spaceship, anyone else would try to discover how ancient Egyptians pronounced hieroglyphics. Ellie had not seemed to care what the Americans knew, but she, and likely the aliens, did not want to work with them, at least with their government. Considering how they had treated Ellie years ago, it did not surprise Steve. He waited, hoping the less friendly looking woman did not have a gun.

"I read the old files," Siglinde smiled. "They said they didn't trust you Canadians. They also said you liked Ellie. I agree. I don't even know her, and I like her."

"Has she played with your mind? She did that in the Dakotas."

"I haven't been near any aliens," Siglinde said, "Ellie or any other." She suddenly felt that she could not be sure.

... those elusive thoughts again... perhaps memories?

"It's hard to imagine a little girl with all that ability."

"She's a woman," Steven said. "She's over 30 now."

"What?" Nancy exclaimed and turned to Siglinde. "Then who's the little girl with her?"

"She didn't mention a girl," Steven said. "Maybe it's an alien dwarf."

"Hilarious, but just as viable as any other guess right now, I think."

Siglinde stared at the whiteboard on the wall behind Steve. Full of lines of phonetic groupings embellished with unfamiliar pronunciation marks.

"That's their language," Siglinde leaned forward. Steve leaned back and examined his and Rachael's handiwork. He spewed out a string of sounds so harsh and convoluted that they made the movie's Klingon dialect sound like nursery rhyming. He thought he said, "You are right".

His often-consulted alien mentor showed patience with the Earthling, but "Bob" made a sound that Steve had hoped was laughter.

Siglinde reacted with a white face and a rigid body, gripping the armrests of the funeral parlour chair. To Nancy and Steve, she seemed to have become catatonic. It only lasted a few seconds.

"I..." Siglinde stuttered, "I… it is."

In an instant, both of her conversations with RoH became clear memories. Steve's speaking alien triggered the mental trip that RoH had planted in their meeting in Charlie Keys' kitchen.

I know...

She also knew that she could not reveal to Nancy that she knew.

Good, now we will chat when you return to Goderich.

"What..." Siglinde exclaimed and looked around frantically for RoH. The voice in her head had seemed real.

"What?" Both Steve and Nancy said.

Siglinde caught herself.

"Nothing, I asked. What did you say?"

"I hope I said that you are right."

"Does anyone else know about this?" Nancy's professionalism filled in for Siglinde's momentary paralysis.

"No," Steve still would not draw Rachel into it.

"So, if we captured you now, no one would know."

"Nancy...," the aggression of her teammate shocked Siglinde. She had forgotten that her partner was a trained operative, not a scientist.

"Just checking," Nancy smiled. "From Mr. Jorgensen's reaction, I'd say there are others in the know. I wasn't suggesting we take him in. Unless you trust us, Steve, we will never know."

"Yes," Steve allowed his sudden tension to drain away, "you startled me, but I'm not afraid of you. If you read the reports from years ago, you would know why. You can't hold anyone if the aliens have decided you can't. Everyone Ellie has touched is in that group of protected ones. Letting you take me would be their plan. I do not know what the plan is."

Siglinde smiled. She had more understanding of their plan. RoH had set her on that path in Charlie Key's kitchen.

***

"I thought getting together in the kitchen would be friendlier," Danny Ringwald offered Lisa a chair. A guard ushered Charlie to the table.

The two had last seen each other in Texas. Lisa and Charlie badly wanted a private conversation, but knew that would not happen here.

"So, you have us both." Lisa showed no emotion, surprising Danny.

"None of this was my idea, General Ringwald began. The three of us are prisoners, although on paper I'm in charge."

"No one is in charge here," Lisa said. "The aliens are in charge."

"I think you're right." Danny thought of his missing team and mysteriously obstinate engines. "I wish I knew why they are letting this charade continue."

"We don't know either," Charlie glanced at Lisa for support. "We aren't exactly happy being here, but it seems to be part of a bigger plan. Ellie hinted at that when she and our granddaughter came to see us."

"Tell me about all that." Danny looked at both prisoners. "Don't worry, this isn't an interrogation. I would like to hear the story for my edification. They do not bug the kitchen."

An insect banged into the window behind Danny, making a loud tap. It then fell, stunned or dead, onto the outside sill. From her seat, Lisa had a clear view of the little black body.

"Maybe not bugged by your outfit, but I bet the aliens know everything happening here."

"I believe they do. It's like that internet joke about someone asking the FBI for a cookie recipe." Danny laughed. "I wish I knew their plan. My boss thinks we can control the aliens and exploit them. You would think we had learned in all the wars we have lost in the past few decades that we can't even do that with other humans."

"I didn't think Siglinde thought that." Charlie tried to remember how he knew that name.

"She isn't my boss. A guy named Greg at the CIA is the one."

Danny did not know why he had revealed that. His prisoners had learned more from him than he had from them.

"Tell me your story," Danny said, happy that he had betrayed Greg.

He glanced at the cook, who seemed preoccupied making lunch.

"We thought the little girl was your daughter."

"No," Lisa's face brightened, "she is Ellie's daughter, my granddaughter."

"You would love her," Charlie added, "but you wouldn't want to mess with her. You know from the record that Ellie has certain abilities. I'm not sure if Ellie's power would even appear on the scale of what RoH can do. We are lucky that both of them have love and empathy. They are only a threat to the status quo."

Danny pulled a folio from his pocket. "Here are my grand kids. They are around the same age as your granddaughter."

The innocent smiles of the young softened Lisa's heart, but they also sharpened the ache of her separation from Ellie and RoH.

"It is for these, and the billion like them, that we must solve our predicament on Earth." Charlie handed the case back to Danny.

"I began this job thinking of it as a military operation." Danny gazed at the photos for a moment. "We soldiers are best when we have a clear enemy. I thought we had one. Now, I'm not sure, but I have ten missing people, probably dead. That sounds like war."

"They aren't dead," said Lisa. "No matter what this Greg person might do, the aliens will not kill them. Look back to the Dakotas. Whom did they kill then, when Ellie suffered torture and feared she would die? They treated a ten-year-old girl like a criminal, and yet aliens killed no one." Lisa sobbed at the horrible memories.

"Besides," she recovered her smile, "if they were into killing people, you all would have been dead two days ago. Whoever that old farmer was, he could have killed you all right here."

Danny grimaced. Lisa only confirmed the fear that had gripped him from the time the team went missing. If the aliens could conjure up a hillbilly on an old tractor and take ten trained agents with no trace, they had the high ground on everything.

"They might be uncomfortable," Charlie had a flash-back to his long-ago ordeal, "or an old farmer and his wife might feed them fried chicken and potato salad."

"How did you think of that?" Danny asked.

"I don't know. It just came to me."

The guard burst through the back door.

"General, come see this." The tough ex-commando looked afraid.

They hurried around the corner of the house.

"It doesn't even look like a saw touched it."

On the far side of the farmyard, the large oak stood proudly, restored to its former glory; its bare branches cast a shadow over the yard and the crowd of agents.

Unseen in the bright sunshine, a swarm of fireflies flitted overhead.

Chapter Nineteen

Strange visitors and purple light

Bobby Briscoe captured 5-K video of Nancy and Siglinde leaving the university linguistics department. The rented car sped away in a flurry of fallen maple leaves.

What would American agents, UFO chasers, want with the university linguistics department?

Bobby sauntered across the street. The directory listed Dr. Jorgensen as chairman of the department. He passed into the reception area and found it deserted. An open door to the right revealed a middle-aged man in a dishevelled corduroy jacket, standing with his back to the doorway and staring at a scrawl-filled whiteboard. The nameplate beside the door said, Dr. Steven Jorgensen. Bobby retreated to investigate. The agents had visited Jorgensen. A reporter, like a talented lawyer, liked to know the answers before asking the questions.

Who is Jorgensen... and why him?

Bobby returned to his stakeout at the hotel. He begged off his producer's request that he attend the kick-off press event for the autumn pumpkin festival. Rita would have to cover that.

As he sat in the hotel parking lot, munching a tasty meatball sub, washed down with a Sprite, Bobby pursued the biography of Steve Jorgensen. The man had a solid reputation as a researcher and a teacher. Students gushed about him, and Bobby saved the university pages for later follow-up. He noted that on Jorgensen's CV, there was a gap between his achieving his doctorate and his appointment to a teaching job at an American university, NYU. Twenty years had been enough for him to progress through the academic nightmare to become a department chair, back in his hometown and his alma mater.

What happened in those missing months? Did he just goof off?

Goofing off did not seem like a credible activity for ambitious intellectuals, despite that image being the foundation of a long-defunct television series. Jorgenson's hiatus was six months and four days. He listed the dates with a question mark between them.

Somehow, Bobby surmised, *those six months are important.*

The NYU web page added a teaser of information. In its archived article welcoming Steven Jorgensen, Bobby found the line, "Steve comes to us after a brief time consulting for the military." Since Americans only referred to American things, it had to be the United States military. The line appeared in the caption of a photograph of the department head at NYU welcoming Steve. Bobby saved the page.

His cell chimed.

"Mr. Briscoe, it's Jim. Peter will talk to you, but on the patio of the Nutty Dough Coffee Shop, just down from here. 7 PM sharp."

Events conspired to arrange Bobby's schedule. Siglinde drove into the parking lot just as he talked with Jim. Bobby trailed the women into the lobby and took a seat with a view of the counter. Siglinde sat nearby and extracted her cell. Bobby pretended to text, but had activated an enhanced audio app, a handy tool for a reporter, and let it focus on the woman.

"Elliana," the agent said. "Nancy and I are flying to Ottawa early this evening. Please book rooms and a car rental at the airport. ... Yes, we are getting closer to Ellie. Call a Liz Dafoe, she's a member of their parliament, and set up an appointment, the sooner the better."

Damn, the station will never pay for a jaunt to Ottawa. Bobby wanted to go, but knew the lack of money held him to the London end of the story.

He followed the women to the airport and videoed them boarding a WestJet direct flight. Nancy had glanced his way and frowned. Her training made her remember faces in the crowd, but she could not recall where she had seen that man before. She felt for her weapon but realized she was in Canada and had not brought a gun. The PA called their flight.

"Thank you for meeting me, Mr. Williams." Bobby activated his cell and laid it on the table. The waiter arrived with their drinks and a sweet bun for Peter. Bobby gave the woman a ten and refused the change. He had built a career on information from waiters, valets and cabbies.

"Ellie said someone like you might come asking questions. Jim took a lot on himself, but no harm. We are the alien marketing department."

"Would you tell me about your dealings with the alien woman?"

"Ellie, I prefer to use her name. She's not so much alien as a human. Let me tell you about my abductions first. They happened a long time ago, but now seem real again." Peter sipped coffee, nibbled the bun, and sighed.

The story took half an hour from abduction, escaping Stratford, Peter and Ellie's conversation on this patio and finishing with Nancy's visit.

"Will you and Jim appear for an on-camera interview at the station?"

"Not live. If the cops knew I was there, they might send me back to the old age prison." Peter laughed. "My daughter is sure I'm dotty. I have too much to do to stay in that place. The aliens will make a move soon, I think."

"Soon…?" Bobby asked.

"Well, they either are going to stage a spectacular introduction to all of humanity, or leave and never return. That's what Ellie said."

Peter slapped the table. "I'm going with them. Ellie said I could."

"You trust them that much after your ordeals?"

"I trust Ellie. That billionaire might get his multi-planetary species thing after all, just not the way he hoped, with those settlers on Mars just scraping by."

Someone inside the café had turned up the volume on the television that carried news and sports.

"This is NASA television. Under the authority of the President of the United States, we have pre-empted time on all networks for a special news conference. Joining me," the announcer continued, "is the head of NASA, joined by the chairman of the Martian Colonial Consortium and Dr. Singh of MIT."

They found seats inside. NASA had never done this before.

The camera zoomed in over a room crowded with reporters. Two men and a woman sat at the table, grim-faced and nervous. A large screen displayed a representation of the inner solar system. The woman glanced at it, her eyes filled with concern.

The woman, introduced as the current head of NASA, took the podium. She looked straight into the camera.

"Excuse me if I ignore all the niceties," she ruffled some papers, "but we have a serious, and I fear potentially tragic situation developing involving over 1000 souls."

She glanced again at the screen behind.

"What you see on the display," she waved at the screen and the television feed filled with a graphic animation "represents the solar system, the inner planets, including Earth and Mars in real-time with lines to show orbits. Please note the red line and circle trending down from the upper right. This is as it appeared," she consulted her notes, 1245 hours, coordinated universal time, about twelve hours ago. That red object is our problem.

"Please speed up the animation." She looked off stage.

The circles representing the planets and the object moved quickly.

"This is what will happen over the next three months, compressed into two minutes. That red circle depicts newly discovered comet, Clavette *BBO2031-1621*. For convenience, we call it the visitor. French astronomer Georges Clavette discovered it using data from the Mars Orbiting Astronomical Observatory. Our scientists at Socorro, New Mexico, and MIT followed up and confirmed the orbit. It is 200 kilometres in diameter. MIT confirms the trajectory. Please watch the screen."

The red object disappeared below the sun and soon reappeared, rising on the opposite side. Even the untrained could see the object and the orbit of Mars converging. They met. The red object disappeared.

"The visitor is going to strike Mars in about 105 days, approximately 15 degrees from its southern pole. The good news is that it will never approach Earth. James Upton of the MCC will explain the rest. Then we will take questions. James..." She nodded and hurried to her seat.

James stood, staring at the now paused animation.

"Ladies and gentlemen," he nervously shifted his weight from foot to foot, "we have 1032 people in our enclave on the surface of Mars. The Russians and Chinese have about another 50. We gave both governments our data this morning."

He once more stared at the graphic.

"You see where the Earth and Mars are in three months. We face the reality that the planets are in the mid-point of a transfer cycle. They have no way to get enough delta-V, sorry, that is enough acceleration, enough fuel to return anyone from Mars to Earth. We must try to protect them in place. On Earth, this would be what we call an extinction-level event. Our team is trying to model what will happen in Mars's thin atmosphere. Clavette will hit at an angle above 60 degrees on the orbit-leading side of the pole. That means it will impact more directly, making the blast larger.

We hope that our sites, near the equator in Isidis Planitia and slightly off the actual trajectory of Clavette, will suffer a smaller direct blast."

To Bobby, unfamiliar with the physics, James seemed unconvinced.

"He's glossing it over," Bobby said to Peter.

"The size of the object is unprecedented. It appears to be at least 90 percent water ice, with the rest being carbon and solid methane. It is forming a tail as it approaches the sun. Spectra-analysis will confirm the make-up."

"Efforts are being made to save the souls in the settlements. NASA, MCC and a growing team of private industry are working on the problem. In some ways," he glanced to the NASA head, "it's like the Apollo 13 predicament in 1970. Solutions must be from resources currently on Mars."

"While this might seem symbolic to some people, Clavette will hit Mars at 11:17 EST, New Year's Eve, late in the solar afternoon at IP-1."

"Questions..." The moderator struggled to organize the onslaught of queries. Solid technical issues raised by informed journalists struggled through the avalanche of demands from ignorant reporters. The most important need seemed to be a list of the persons on Mars so that their networks could follow up with the intrusive harassment of relatives on Earth. Despairing and grieving families made for dramatic television footage.

"It's tragic," Bobby said, "but it sure will make people think about space, so maybe more will be interested in your story. Can you and Jim come about ten tomorrow morning?"

Siglinde and Nancy landed in Ottawa in time to check into their hotel and have dinner. Siglinde exchanged several calls with Ted, discussing the latest grim news about The Visitor. Back in Virginia, Elliana worked late, trying to contact Liz Dafoe. The woman did not answer her phone and the parliamentary offices had closed for the day.

Bobby Briscoe had more luck connecting with an old friend James from school, who had a lucrative business freelancing coverage of politicians' unofficial activities. He had revealed several scandals.

"You know I don't do sex scandals," James said to Bobby. "Liz Dafoe's orientation is her own business. She deserves privacy, and politically and ethically she's clean as a whistle."

"Don't think I'm nuts when I tell you what this is about, okay?"

"Okay..."

"She has a visitor whom UFO believers here claim is part alien, you know, from a flying saucer or something."

"Okay, you are nuts, but you always were," James laughed. "Glenda, in second-year thought you were crazy hot, in her words. Why are you into this stuff?"

"Don't remind me of Glenda." Bobby sounded wistful. "She's found a job in that god-forsaken outpost of Yellowknife, reporting on bears attacking garbage dumps and other important stuff. She loves it there but wants a bigger gig. Do you have any job openings?"

"You're still in touch?"

"Facebook..." Bobby avoided the bumpy road of his personal life.

"I normally wouldn't bother with these flying saucer folks. There are American agents chasing them, and they flew to Ottawa to visit Liz Dafoe. Would you watch Dafoe, see if the Yankees turn up, and get what you can? I don't know where the agents are staying."

"I know where Dafoe lives. It's late today, but I'll hang there a bit."

"I'm doing an on-camera tomorrow with two UFO types here. Call me with what you have. Try to get some footage of the agents. I can't pay for any video, but you'll get credit and pay for anything we use. This is likely nothing, but American agents wandering around on their own would be a good story no matter why they're here. That would embarrass the government. I want to confirm they're looking for an alien."

"If I catch them with Dafoe, I'll interview her after."

Liz Dafoe lived in a comfortable apartment near Dow's Lake. It was not the overblown accommodation of most MPs, but she preferred to be out of the way. The nearby parkland comforted her.

James backed into visitors' parking. Stakeouts usually called for hours of boredom and disappointment before something useful happened. By midnight, James figured he had finished for the night.

The Yanks will have a beauty sleep and likely Liz too.

James threw the dregs of a Timmy's regular out the window and the cup landed in the back seat, joining the pile he resolved to clean up when he got around to it. One last glance saw Liz Dafoe, Dawn Waasnodae, with a third unknown woman emerge from the front door. Liz and Dawn embraced the other woman. The hugs were of friends, not lovers. That killed any deviant thoughts James might have. The stranger glanced skyward and turned towards the street, passing by James. He concealed the cell recording the event and then captured Liz and Dawn exchanging a brief but intimate kiss as they disappeared into the building. James followed the third woman.

This woman must be Ellie, the one accused of being an alien.

...part alien...

Something made James correct his thought. Rumour claimed Liz and Dawn were lovers, but that was unimportant. Ellie was a bigger attraction.

Ellie crossed the street and into the park towards the lake. James hung back in what he thought was a discreet way. He could not see Ellie's smile.

James lurked behind a large maple. Ellie approached the lakeshore. Although Ottawa was a safe city, no one, male or female, would feel safe wandering around dark parks at midnight. She seemed unafraid.

Why is she here on her own? Why did she leave Dafoe's place at night to come here?

Clavette had caused as much disruption with the aliens as it was doing with humans. It had hit nothing yet, but the pending impact had forced desperate Earth planning and gave an unforeseen opportunity to the aliens. Agents were in Africa and Australia to awaken the latent equivalents of Ellie. There were only three Earth months to take advantage of the situation. Ellie hurried to Goderich.

Ellie stopped and seemed to wait. James recorded with his cell. His experience of stalking corrupt politicians had taught him to capture everything and edit later. Tonight, his foresight paid off.

Radar at the international airport detected a target before James saw a rapidly intensifying glow in the west. In an instant, the park stood in daylight. Dow's Lake glowed in an eerie purple. A large, brilliant-blue object dropped like a stone and hovered directly over Ellie. James had no reference for its size. He thought it hung just above the ground, but in reality, its size created that illusion. It stopped about a kilometre above the lake. Ellie rose in a brilliant purple-blue column. The ship shot up and disappeared in a fraction of a second. The airport recorded an elapsed time of ten seconds.

A police car shot to the edge of the grass. The two constables leaned against the front of the cruiser, staring into the gloom surrounding the lake. James slunk away in the opposite direction and hung behind The Man of Two Hats statue as a second patrol unit screamed past. He hurried over the street and back to his car. Jimmy had no desire to spend the night at the station.

Jimmy passed the night in his apartment, replaying his video. He trembled at the eerie episode and medicated himself with two large brandies. He calmed enough to edit the files and prepare a submission to his television contacts. Jimmy shared the raw videos with Bobby Briscoe.

"Don't use the Liz-Dawn kiss," James admonished in the e-mail. "I need sleep, but I'm going back to stake out Liz. Following her is the best way to find the Yankees."

Chapter Twenty

Light through the window

The craft slowed over Charlie Keys' house and hovered for an instant. At thirty-one minutes past midnight, few travelled the roads; however, a driver returning from having drinks with his buddies gawked at the bright light and rolled his car off the road. He was conscious enough to dial 911.

Ellie walked out of the pillar of light and went into her father's house. RoH slept peacefully. Unfettered by the orbital and rotational limits on a planet, rest cycles on a ship were flexible. She and RoH had adapted to Earth, and Ellie found a soft bed. The police activity on the nearby county road did not disturb her.

"I tell you, Sarge," the rescued car driver, cuffed in the rear of the scout car, sputtered, "I saw a flying saucer, big and so bright it blinded me. That's why I ditched it."

"Sure, buddy, that happens to me all the time. You blew point 09."

The constable squeezed the call button. "Huron 1420, dispatch, we have a 253, a single male, rolled it in the ditch. I'm 10-8 proceeding to Goderich Marine and then transport to Clinton."

The cruiser eased onto the county road, with the officer chuckling to himself. People blaming UFOs for their problems had become more common in the past few weeks.

People spooked because of those lights over Belgrave.

The young constable frowned into the mirror at his prisoner.

"Huron 1420," the radio spoke, "keep an eye open for reported lights in the sky near your 10-20 ... multiple citizens on nine eleven..."

Ellie had not overridden the NAAP bugs and an agent in a van had recorded her arrival. Light through the window had briefly brightened the interior before the camera recorded Ellie's entrance. Their call roused the remaining Goderich team from beds and by 3 a.m., a hurried conference began on the road just out of sight of Charlie Key's house.

"Apprehend them," Siglinde's sleepy voice came from a cell. "Nancy and I want to talk to the Dafoe woman before we return. Try to persuade them. We won't be high-handed on this. Let me know how it goes."

The opportunity no longer excited Siglinde. The return of her memories in Steven Jorgensen's office had given her a clearer picture of their powers. She knew they would not meet Ellie and RoH unless the aliens wanted to talk; unless it was part of the plan.

On the road in front of Charley Keys' house, they set the plan.

"We'll cover the back and go in the front at dawn."

"Mother," RoH roused Ellie at daybreak. "We have visitors."

"Is it time to talk with them, Mother?"

"No," Ellie stirred. "We want to talk with Siglinde when it is time. The visitor has changed the plan. It will be several months, and we need to build human interest before our appearance."

Ellie and RoH drove off in Charlie's car. The NAAP agents saw nothing and would soon make another fruitless search of Charlie's home. At least the video proved that Ellie had been there.

Events that Ellie did not know about would change the alien's planned gradual effort into an explosion of public interest.

James did not have to wait long. He finished his breakfast bagel and flung the wrapper over his right shoulder into the stash of paper cups as the two women arrived. He felt certain that these were the American agents. They looked too suave to fit the usual morning visitor mould, and they had arrived in a rental. He readied his camera and wished that he had a bug in Liz's apartment.

An hour into the wait, Liz and the visitors came out and shook hands. While there were no smiles, Liz did not appear to be upset. It struck James that the trio had looked skyward, towards Dow's Lake, as if expecting to see something.

... a hole in the sky, or perhaps something filling that hole. James smiled. The departure made for a good video and a witty voice-over.

James followed the rental car as it left the driveway. He always knew where Liz would be for an interview. He needed to learn more about the Yankee visitors. It was a short drive to the Hampton Suites hotel. The women took as much time as checkout demanded and rushed off once more. This drive ended at the Busy Bee car rental kiosk at the airport.

James paid for valet parking; he had no time and hurried after his prey. They already had booked tickets, and he watched them pass security. That was the end of the tail, but he examined the departures display. The 11:45 direct WestJet to London caught his eye.

James called Bobby at the London television studios.

Peter and Jim fidgeted in comfortable stuffed chairs under the glare of studio lighting. A young man in a colourful shirt dabbed makeup on their noses and foreheads. Bobby Briscoe reappeared.

"Are we taping?"

Bobby turned to the camera and opened with introductions

"Sorry to keep you waiting," Bobby took his seat, half turned to the pair but facing camera two. "I have some recent news about lights at Goderich last night, but we'll get to that. Peter, you escaping from Stratford started this whole thing. Would you tell your story from the beginning?"

"It began a long time ago," Peter's nervousness showed.

"Take your time and tell us everything," Bobby smiled. He would edit it all down into two versions, a one-minute snippet for the newscast and a longer one that the station might air later, and he hoped, attract network interest. Last night's light show might guarantee it.

When both Peter and Jim had finished their stories, Bobby explored their visits with Ellie. Both held steadfast to their belief that she was part alien and was the grown-up little girl who the aliens had taken over two decades before. Bobby would not find video from the Texas incident that the pair insisted news outlets in the USA had recorded.

"Please look at the monitor over there." Bobby pointed, and the producer switched to a clip that James had sent of Ellie leaving Liz Dafoe's apartment.

"Is that Ellie?"

"Yes..."

"A colleague recorded that last night in Ottawa. The other two women are MPs. why would she be visiting them?"

"Well," Peter began, "because the aliens would prefer humans to survive and reach the stars, but think we won't do it if we don't change how we treat each other and the planet. They believe, from evidence from other dead worlds in the galaxy, that we will commit suicide if we don't change. Ellie said that the aliens think we only have two years before the irreversible biosphere collapse. They want small countries like Canada to oppose the global control by the big three."

"Why do the aliens care about a technically immature species?"

"Ellie said," Peter fidgeted, "that they realized after the 1947 incident that began Ellie's genetic line they were missing human empathy and conviviality. They cooperate on an emotionless level with no conflict, but they decided that wasn't good enough to survive into the far future. She says they need to learn that from us."

Bobby had not heard that before. It seemed plausible and equally silly.

"You make these aliens look nice." Bobby sounded sceptical.

"You watch too many movies," Peter laughed. "Boring aliens don't make for exciting drama. Ellie feared that humans thinking aliens were monsters would be her biggest problem. She said the aliens made many bumbling mistakes and did some actual damage, but it is that flaw in themselves they want to fix."

Bobby had no retort.

"We have evidence that Ellie left Ottawa right after they made this video. Has there been a change in plans?"

"I don't know, Peter replied. I haven't heard from her since she left with Liz Dafoe a couple of days ago."

"Our evidence shows Ellie Keys leaving Ottawa by, shall we say, some unusual means." Bobby faced directly into the camera. "I can't share that now as a courtesy to the source who will introduce his video via other carriers. He has to make a living. Hopefully, I can show that later."

He turned back to his guests.

"We have some evidence that Ellie might have returned to Goderich. Here is a clip from a security camera, recorded about 12:30 this morning."

The screen shifted to a black-and-white image looking north from a service station on Victoria Street in Goderich. A bright, distant glow burst and faded quickly. Bobby faced the camera.

"Could that be Ellie returning, only minutes after we saw her leaving Dafoe's apartment?"

He turned to the guests. The camera captured their expressions of amazement and nods of agreement.

"It looks like when they took me." Peter's eyes closed.

"This fits with the time and manner in which we believe Ellie left Ottawa. I hope we get to share that soon. I also hope to share more on the

American UFO investigator that my guests have mentioned, but again, must allow the source to be the first."

Bobby rushed into the editing studio. By mid-afternoon, he had the short and long versions. The material impressed the producer of the six o'clock news. Bobby would have two minutes. He would be the follow-up of the newsreader's report of strange lights in Goderich and the story of a related DUI charge from the same area as the light. The developing story of the doomed Mars settlements would precede it all.

The local segment aired at the same time as Jimmy's coverage of strange happenings and secretive American agents in Ottawa. Main national networks refused the coverage, but a rival outlet opposing Liz Dafoe's and Dawn Waasnodae's political parties hoped that linking them to unauthorized foreign agents might further their agenda. The spectacular scene of Ellie's departure and the rush for the Americans to get to London defeated the broadcaster's opportunism. The viewers wanted to talk about aliens and Yankee agents, not petty Ottawa politics.

Those who Jimmy had exposed during his career quickly condemned the video as fake. The RCMP announced an investigation centred on possible foreign terrorists posing as American government agents and the links to the two MPs. Ottawa police launched an investigation into the illegal use of fireworks at Dow's Lake. The regulator for television in Canada started "an enquiry into fake news".

The Canadian and American governments issued simultaneous statements that there were no aliens and that no American security agents operated in Canada. The whitewashed releases did not reflect the heated exchange between the Canadian Prime Minister and the American President.

Chapter Twenty-one

Fitting puzzle pieces

In London, the following morning, Jimmy's episode, coupled with Bobby's presentation, touched off a flurry of activity. The station dispatched a reporter to Goderich to track down people who saw the lights and find the drunk driver and anyone who claimed to know Ellie Keys. It only took an hour to tie Ellie to Charlie Keys, and the hunt was on. The news producer lined up a slot for Bobby's longer piece and inserted the Dow's Lake video from Ottawa.

Bobby hurried in pursuit of Siglinde and Nancy, making a lucky guess that they had returned to the same London hotel. The small bribe of a clerk with the promise of an on-air interview about their guests had Bobby standing outside Siglinde's door at 9 AM the following morning.

About the same time in Ottawa, Liz allowed Jimmy to visit. The Mounties had grilled her the previous evening. The journalists gathered in the apartment's gloomy parking lot would have to wait. Liz agreed to an on-camera interview and arranged for Jimmy to talk with Dawn.

"Is it relevant that you and Dawn are lovers?" Jimmy recorded. He had no interest in souring his relationship with either woman.

"I don't think so," Liz was thoughtful. "We had planned to go public about us next week before you started this zoo." She laughed. "Ellie had an interest in Dawn to do with old tribal stories. Dawn will tell you more about that."

"I'll let you have an exclusive. We both intend to announce we won't be running in the next election."

Liz detailed the complete and accurate story of her relationship with Ellie, including her fear and horror. Jimmy left satisfied. He would interview Dawn and edit a video in the afternoon for the eager networks.

Three men in long coats surrounded Jimmy as he left Liz's building.

"Please come with us," one man grabbed his arm. He thought these CSIS thugs fit the movie concept of secret agents.

***

Charlie Keys' car eased to a stop, just out of sight of Hobo Books.

RoH savoured the mischief she had deployed against the annoying people who had kidnapped her grandmother and grandfather. The star side of her, along with her family and others in space, had integrated her playful toying with the American task group into a rapidly changing plan. Clavette, as unexpected for the aliens as it was for the panicking humans and their doomed Mars settlements, had disrupted a careful strategy, but it also introduced a new opportunity. Things would happen more quickly, within 105 days rather than the original year that they planned. The new strategy would introduce aliens to the world and divert human dreams about Mars into better priorities. The impact of Clavette would cast the aliens in a good light for humanity.

The bookshop bell tinkled. Ros watched Charlie pass between the table displaying the local history books and the shelves of crime novels.

"Did you read Clarke's book?" He asked. Ros nodded.

"If that story is real, then your granddaughter is... an alien?" Ros wanted to believe, but it all seemed like a mix of fiction and conspiracy.

"I read all of his books," Ros frowned. "It's quite a story from 1947. He is consistent, if nothing else."

"It's easy to be consistent when telling the truth." Charlie smiled. "She's only part alien."

"I'm too sceptical. I need an alien to appear. Do you have proof?"

"Wait there, I'll show you."

Charlie disappeared behind the shelves that divided the room. In an instant, RoH appeared around the far end of the stack. She moved swiftly to steady Ros and help her to her chair behind the sales counter.

"You... you're..."

"... an imp, as mother calls me." RoH giggled. "We need you, Ros."

"Where's your grandfather?"

"I am not all alien, part human, and Charlie is my grandfather. I love him. They have kidnapped him and my grandmother."

RoH's matter-of-fact attitude kept Ros from panicking.

"Can you come with me and Mom to the factory? We need to visit Kerri Grenier and Mike Hammersmith. Things are happening soon, and we need more humans to help."

Clutching Tom Clarke's book, Ros followed RoH outside. The bell tinkled sweetly. The lock clicked and the sign inside the door flipped to "closed". They hopped into the car with Ellie driving.

Reporters scurried about the town, all looking for Charlie Keys and his supposed alien descendants. Many of the press thought the taproom of the Bedford Hotel would yield the best information. They interviewed each other over drinks. As hapless locals wandered in looking for a quiet beer, a mystifying mob of outsiders swarmed around them. The smarter victims, once they realized what the reporters wanted and for a second free beer, spun sincere-sounding stories that had the aliens landing anywhere in the 60 kilometres between Lucknow and Grand Bend. The blizzard of fabrication would confuse the world. Bobby Briscoe had to convince his producer that he had not "missed the story" and that the events reported on rival networks had not happened.

The reporters had not yet linked Charlie Keys to the factory. Only the watchers from NAAP saw Ellie and an unidentified woman drive up and park near the front door. A large, floppy-eared dog was with them, running eagerly to the door and sitting, its tail wagging furiously and playfully cocking its head as if asking the adults what took them so long. Ellie wagged a finger and scratched the dog behind an ear.
Unable to reach Siglinde, the NAAP team called Elliana in Virginia.

Ellie and RoH gathered with Kerri, Mike, and Ros in Mike's office.

"Mother, you didn't need to rub my ear," RoH smirked. "Next time I'll play a mean dog."

Ellie patted RoH on the head.

"Just don't play a clown. They scare your grandpa."

Kerri and Ros had never met Ellie, and they watched, bemused. Mike had flash backed to Charlie's, the first time he had met the pair.

***

Charlie and Lisa shared the living room with Danny. General Ringwald was not having a good morning. Besides the restored tree, which his people insisted on calling Lazarus, all the flying robots, except one, had dropped to the ground, dead and not recoverable. The living probe behaved as if it were crazy, flying around in circles far down the road where the ten operatives had disappeared, and spontaneously cycling from camera to infrared and back. The technician had lost control.

"It's gone nuts. There must be a flaw in the design," the robot operator diagnosed without conviction. She had watched the Lazarus Tree jump back onto its stump, waving its limbs in the wind.

Morale had evaporated. The hardened operatives felt under siege.

To top off the awful morning, Greg lectured Danny over the phone.

"Ringwald, the press blew NAAP's cover and they are now useless. We called the Canadian CSIS outfit. They're trying to squelch the story. They grabbed the reporter before he can do more damage."

Because of either the strain or that he had had enough of the arrogant spy chief, Danny pushed back.

"How much time does that give us?" Danny mocked. "You don't know the power they have, and we have none. You CIA people live in a bubble. These aliens have us if they want. It's time to wave a white flag and asked them to talk. We won't win otherwise."

"Look, Ringwald, if you can't handle the situation, I'll find someone who can. Do your job. I'll do the thinking. I might go up there to help."

The line went dead.

Danny turned to his guests.

"I've had it with all this. We are weak. I just wish I knew what these damned aliens are after."

Lisa smiled. "Call Siglinde, she knows. Work with her, not the CIA. If you are lucky, you'll meet Ellie and RoH. They know the plan."

"Lisa and I are here for a purpose," Charlie added, "otherwise, you could never have taken us. I do not know what the plan is, but they want to learn from Earth, not to exploit or destroy us. Earth has nothing special to offer that they can find all over our solar system or the galaxy, except our humanity, the good part of it, anyway. We shouldn't be afraid, but we should be damned well curious and listen to them."

"I think our being here is to do with you, General Ringwald."

"You sound like Siglinde. I'm nothing here but the guy to blame if things go wrong. A general officer would be enough of a sacrifice for Greg to divert attention from his failure. What if he shows up here?"

"He would regret it." Lisa frowned.

Chapter Twenty-two

Jigsaw pieces

"**D**r. Hilfreich, I'm Bobby Briscoe from CKLN News. Please speak to me?"

Bobby had learned the women's full names from the clerk and had done internet research. Nancy seemed to be non-existent, but Siglinde Hilfreich was a Ph.D., a teacher at MIT and an expert in vacuum quantum effects. He did not know what that meant, but many had heaped praise on her. Recent news mentioned her being on a temporary contract with the National Agency for Aerial Phenomena, NAAP.

"Why should I talk to you? You have become a thorn in our side."

"The people Nancy talked to came to see me and gave that interview. I thought you might confirm or deny."

Siglinde cradled a cell against her cheek.

"Danny, I have to go. The press is at my door. Let me know what the CIA is doing."

Bobby tried to play Siglinde, and she knew it; however, Bobby had exposed the whole investigation. It probably could not survive this publicity. Danny's frantic call, confessing his role as an agent of the CIA, and his seemingly new role as a double agent, caused Siglinde even more confusion. This alien project had changed into something as complex as quantum physics. Bobby's ear perked up at the mention of the CIA.

"Come in, let me think about it."

Bobby set his camera on a coffee table. Siglinde's suite had more amenities than the simple motel rooms he could afford.

"I'll give an interview, because you and your Ottawa buddy have already destroyed the cautious approach we prefer. You can start."

Siglinde did not feel the imperious control she tried to project. She thought Bobby posed a serious threat.

Bobby set the camera on a tripod and did a quick light and sound check. He started with basic questions of whom, what, and why.

"I, and my colleagues, work for a US government group, the National Agency for Aerial Phenomena, NAAP, looking into reports of unexplained phenomena. We are not secret, but we wanted to keep a low profile."

"UFOs..." Bobby interrupted.

"Yes, we try to take the U out of the UFOs," Siglinde sighed, "but more than that. We examine the entire spectrum from landings, strange life forms walking about, and abductions. That's where the two gentlemen you interviewed fit in."

Bobby stopped the camera.

"Can I invite Jim and Peter here so we can have a discussion?"

"Yes, but make it off the record, unless they agree to go on camera."

Bobby punched in Jim's number and arranged for the men to visit within the hour. He then called his producer and explained he was interviewing a Yankee agent and might be all day.

"What is your background?"

Siglinde gave a short version of her academic history and position at MIT, finishing with why they chose her to head NAAP.

"They didn't want anyone with much political or spy savvy and no Washington baggage. They did want experts."

"You don't look or sound like a scientist or a spy." Bobby, like most journalists, was not immune from banality.

"What does a scientist look or sound like?" Siglinde flared. "There is a little girl, part alien, walking around nearby who is only beginning her education. She can hold her own or out-talk any scientist, including me. We imagine her dressing as a princess and going to a birthday party. My qualifications mean little in this situation."

"What is the situation?"

"Alien visitors are real, here now, and they won't attack Earth."

Bobby struggled to be professional. Siglinde had just handed him a bomb that would resonate worldwide.

"How do you know?"

"They told me, at least that little girl named RoH told me. I talked to her twice, and both times, she made me forget our conversations. I only remembered them a few days ago here in London. She arranged that too."

"Why did you remember them? Was it your visit to the university?"

"Stop the camera," Siglinde shouted. "I won't talk about that university visit on camera. It would violate a personal contact I don't have permission to reveal."

"I know you visited Steven Jorgensen at the linguistics department. What's his involvement?"

"Ask Jorgensen, since you already know about him. You can start again, but nothing about the university until Steven allows it. Giving this interview is likely ending my time at NAAP, perhaps my academic career, and it may land me in jail."

Bobby ignored Siglinde's anxiety. A journalist could not let concern for the subject ruin the story.

"So, NAAP has formal contact with the aliens?"

"No, RoH only met me because we were getting close to her grandfather and she intervened. The aliens have no interest in our organization, otherwise. We weren't part of the plan. Although RoH said we would be important later, something changed."

"What changed?" Bobby had slipped to the edge of his chair.

"I could just say you and your friend's interference," Siglinde said, "but there is something in the background that has had an enormous influence on what they had wanted to do, or how. It has something to do with the Martian impactor, Clavette, but that's a guess. NAAP's role now is just to argue that aliens are real and not a threat."

Bobby put the camera on pause once more.

"Have a rest while I make up more questions."

Jim and Peter hurried down the street. The hotel was not too far away. A police car pulled onto the sidewalk and cut them off. Another scout car stopped in the street. Constables jumped out.

"Peter Williams," a woman cop who looked like someone's Aunt Rambo approached, "would you come with us, please?" The word please softened Peter's Rambo judgement.

"Your daughter has asked us to detain you. You should be home."

In reality, the police did not respond to a mere citizen's request. Peter's daughter had gone before a court and a judge had issued an apprehension order under the mental health law. It had been a simple matter to trace Jim's residence. They assumed Peter would be there. Finding the men walking on the street simplified the capture. The cops pushed Jim aside. Peter did not resist as they put him into the back of a car.

At Siglinde's hotel suite, Jim's elation at the previous television appearance had given way to despair at Peter's arrest. He arrived as Siglinde turned on the television and tuned in to a Canadian national cable news channel. Bobby's producer had called him with a heads up that Dawn Waasnodae and Liz Dafoe were about to make statements.

Liz and Dawn stood at a makeshift podium set up in Liz's apartment parking lot in Ottawa. The weather threatened, but the publicity forced them to make the announcements a week early. The crowd of reporters and the television cameras far exceeded what might have been normal. These MPs had met possible foreign agents and a purported alien woman.

"Thank you for coming," Liz tried to tame her windblown hair. "I had planned to make a statement next week about my future as an MP, but events have changed that. To clear the air, I will not be seeking re-election. If my party expels me, I will continue to serve my constituents as an independent MP until the government calls an election."

"There are several more issues I must talk about. Yes, I met with two American women. Describing them as agents is an exaggeration. They are investigators for an American government agency looking into all aspects of alien contact, including what a movie once sensationalized as a close encounter of the third kind. My visitors asked about Ellie Keys. They didn't pretend to be official American government representatives."

"One of them is the head of their agency, the National Agency for Aerial Phenomena. She made it clear the clandestine nature of their work had the sole intention of avoiding alien knowledge of their activities, not to deceive the Canadian government, but it reflects the American government's desire to be the sole Earth entity talking to the aliens."

A murmur of doubt swept through the audience.

"I see you are sceptical despite the video broadcast last night. So be it. The Americans claimed they have evidence dating back to 1947 confirming the reality of aliens. I would have been as doubtful as most of you, except that I met Ellie Keys, and either I was on some sort of weird mushroom, which I am not, or she proved she has abilities far beyond anything we Earthlings would consider normal. I do not doubt that is the case."

"The Americans documented much of this over the years, including Ellie as a little girl. You need to talk to them. They left town as soon as they learned Ellie left. Everyone is now in south-western Ontario."

Producers for all the networks assembled teams to fly to London, Ontario, and begin the search. Bobby in London would label this effort as "the close encounters of the fourth estate".

"There is one more personal thing. I am a lesbian and have found my lifelong love." She smiled at Dawn. "No matter what happens, this has been worthwhile. Here is my love, Dawn, to make her statement."

Dawn stood at the microphone. Her lack of experience compared to Liz made her nervous.

"Thank you, Liz," Dawn flashed a loving smile.

"I too am resigning, but unlike Liz, I cannot see accomplishing much here. This place is for men, mainly white men, no matter how many nominal women and people of colour you see. I always felt marginalized and a token. Everything I ever proposed, especially concerning my people, received head nodding and hollow praise, but no action. My resignation letter will detail my experiences and frustration. The way of the people will not pass through here."

Dawn reverted to her native language and, since the television had no one to translate, her words went directly to the community. After a few sentences, Dawn reverted to English.

"I just told my people: I will resign soon and return to my home. I plan to tour the communities of our nations, and talk to the elders, but especially the storytellers. The stories pass on history and how to live. These life lessons are more important now than ever. There are old stories now seldom told amongst our nations about star people, miigis. They are key to prepare the people for what is coming."

"Thank you to all who voted for me and genuinely supported me, and those who will still struggle. I am of two spirits. I especially thank my love," she reached out and found Liz's hand, "for her love and strength."

Dawn backed away. An onslaught of questions swept over them.

"What is to come?" A fellow MP shouted.

"Our friend Ellie Keys must answer that," Dawn said. "She left Ottawa, spectacularly, as news reports showed. Her nature and what may develop is hers to share."

"Where is Ellie Keys?" The question came from every direction.

***

"In Goderich," Siglinde said from her perch on a sofa in a London hotel room. Bobby nodded.

"You are going to be hunted down here," Bobby said to Siglinde.

"I think I'll buy stock in Goderich motel rooms," Jim laughed.

Bobby frowned at the television. The camera had panned the crowd, but his friend Jimmy was not there.

Jimmy would never miss this, Bobby thought. He tried his friend's number. The message said, "… unavailable."

Rain fell in Ottawa, ending the open-air news conference. Much later in the day, Liz and Dawn appeared in interviews for all the outlets. Bobby turned back to his interview with Siglinde. He hoped that later he, Siglinde and Jim would have a long, off-camera chat, and perhaps include Nancy. He had not decided if he would follow up by talking to Steve Jorgensen or join the stampede to Goderich.

Ted called Siglinde just as Bobby and Jim were about to leave. Bobby pretended to have trouble stowing his gear. Eavesdropping came easily, although only hearing one side of a conversation frustrated him.

"Tell the director to calm down and call the Canadian minister for science, or whatever fancy name they have for it. Tell him to explain we are scientists, not spies, only unofficial investigators, and we'll share everything we know once we are certain."

Siglinde listened.

"I'll call the White House later. I'm following a lead."

Siglinde punched off and turned to Bobby.

"Can you please sit on that interview for a day? I would like to keep our project together if possible. You heard, our boss is upset. There's an argument in Washington about whether to deny or confirm we have evidence. I think it's too late for denials, thanks to you, Jim."

"My boss will ask why," Bobby frowned. "I want to remain in the mix before the network people steal it from me."

"If you do, I'll arrange for you to interview Steve Jorgensen. He knew Ellie over twenty years ago."

"Tomorrow…?"

"I'll try."

Bobby could not resist. Night had fallen. The interview had already taken him past the evening news deadline, so he would get nothing on air until the next day, anyway. He and Jim went to dinner. Bobby thought he owed Jim a meal. Sadly, Peter could not share it.

***

"Things are going to get wild around here," Ellie seemed thoughtful. "The three of you know my father, and the media will hound you. We did not plan this. That reporter in London did a good job of finding things out. Of course, my friends in London gave him a good start. I made a mistake not asking them to wait for the media to find them. I didn't realize how those years of people calling him crazy had hurt Jim and the depth of his need for vindication. It echoes the blundering that happened when they took people against their will."

"What can we do?" Mike and Kerri accepted the reality of these part aliens. Ros sat numb and quiet.

"First, Mike," Ellie said, "Father is going to miss having Thanksgiving with your family. That is the most important thing for you right now. Do not let any of this stop that. You deserve it."

"We could arrange Grandpa being there." RoH smiled.

"True," replied Ellie, "but that other group of Americans needs to be tormented. We must support Siglinde and paralyse that group with confusion and fear. They are dangerous. Now that the news of American agents in Canada has broken, we will use them to drive a wedge between the Canadian and American governments. Ottawa has already done something at the American request, and we need to rescue an innocent person before they can harm him. He's another unexpected player. We must decide how he can help."

"Why don't we let him have chicken dinners with those bad guys who kidnapped Grandfather and Grandmother?"

"That's an option, but not fair to him. We will decide soon."

"What are you two talking about?" Kerri asked.

"The Canadian security agency kidnapped the journalist who videoed me leaving Ottawa. Like the CIA, they are capable of torture. Although the man doesn't know more than they do, or what you saw on television, the police never believe that. They want to shut him up. We are watching."

"Where's Charlie?" Kerrie shuddered.

"Dad and Mom are at a farm on a dead-end road up the Maitland valley. Don't worry, Kerri, we'll make sure you get him in one piece." Ellie leaned over and touched her arm.

"Other than waiting, what is it we do?" Mike felt helpless.

"The press is after a story. They will find out my father works here. So far, they don't know about RoH. Siglinde and her group do. I would prefer it if you didn't mention RoH to anyone. Tell them you know about me and what you think I am, alien or imposter." Ellie glanced at Ros.

"I'm a believer," Ros laughed at RoH, "a shell-shocked believer, but a believer. Your little imp made sure of that."

"It would be nice if you can plant the seed for our presenting the other American group of spies. Tell them Charlie Keys is away, negotiating a deal with an ultra-deep group of American spies. They can't find out anything yet, but it will create the conditions when we reveal the truth. It will also upset those people when the press mentions that they exist. It won't be a lie. My father and mother are talking to one of them."

"Siglinde will come back to see you and maybe more of her associates as well. She will want friends by then. It seems everyone will come to Goderich soon."

A pack of a dozen reporters had finally gathered at the factory front. They took no notice of the company van leaving the back of the building. Ellie watched from the van as it headed to the street.

"I'm glad you're driving, Ros. Neither of us ever learned how to use these old-fashioned gasoline machines."

"You drove your father's car."

"It drove us. I know how to program a computer, and that car is just a computer with wheels."

"I know how to drive a farm tractor," RoH enthused.

"Don't brag dear. It makes you sound human."

They disappeared towards town. Ros had offered to put them up for the night, and since the press would also watch Charlie's house along with the NAAP bugs, it seemed like a good idea.

Ellie frowned and thought of Peter. He did not deserve one more day in that cotton-wool cell at Cedar Haven.

Mike opened the front door of his factory and held up his arms.

"Pick two of you to come in to talk to us; we will give you your story. Only two or nobody at all."

Peter would not suffer the cold imprisonment that Jimmy endured in Ottawa. He appeared briefly in front of a Justice of the Peace. An OPP cruiser whisked him back to Stratford and Cedar Haven to endure a scolding from his daughter and a nurse who resented Peter putting a smudge on her record. They did not place Peter under guard. That would reduce Cedar Haven's profits. Peter helped by refusing to walk.

Chapter Twenty-three

Upsetting apple carts

"Peter," Ellie's soft voice came from the darkness. He stirred... "Peter, it's Ellie..."

Peter rolled to look at the red LED clock face.

Almost 3 in the morning...

"Peter..."

He rolled the opposite way and could make out her form in the glow of street lighting. Peter sat up and his mind cleared.

"Not again..." his wit recovered first. "A big dude guards the front desk at night. Can we sneak out the back door?"

"We won't be sneaking out," Ellie said. "We are going to take a method you last suffered decades ago. This time, don't be afraid. Bring everything you want. You won't be coming back here ever again."

"Good enough for me." Peter climbed from the bed and flicked on the lamp. It glowed with a soft light. He had insisted the home change the glaring institutional lighting.

"I need to let my daughter know," Peter seemed sad, "can't let her worry, even though the ingrate had me arrested. I still love her. She thought she was doing the right thing for her doddering old dad."

He scribbled a quick note and left it on the nightstand.

"You will see her again," Ellie said, "but not right now."

Peter filled a satchel with his papers and a suitcase with a few clothes.

"That's it. I always travel light. I'm ready. This is going to upset someone's apple cart." Peter laughed.

Ellie led him out the back door without triggering the fire alarm.

Peter had the sensation of a rapidly rising elevator. He had no sense of time. It seemed he instantly stood in a strange living room. The house was small but neat, except for dozens of books on tables and shelves.

"Wonderful, you're hiding me in a library."

"Peter," Ellie said, "this is Ros' house in Goderich. She sells books."

Peter finished his sleep on a comfortable couch in Ros' living room.

"It seems all roads lead to Goderich." Ros laughed and sipped from her third mug of coffee of the morning, originally hot, but now at its usual tepidness. She eyed the microwave in her cubby behind the sales counter.

Peter busied himself rearranging Ros' bookstore into English-teacher order and laughed at her joke. RoH and Ellie occupied two of the soft customer chairs, watching Peter's efforts and Ros' apparent concern that Peter had upset the familiar order of her display shelves.

"It would look nice if you arranged them by colour." RoH contributed to Ros' pain and caused Peter to pause.

"Oh, that would help with those customers who say they don't know the title of the book, but it's red," Ros chortled at the stolen internet joke.

Living feral in Goderich gave RoH a taste for doughnuts and hot chocolate. She smirked mischievously over her mug.

Ros normally did not have the television on, but the news this morning was captivating. London had extensive coverage of the mysterious second disappearance of Peter Williams from Cedar Haven. He had not opened the emergency doors and had not appeared on any of the extensive security videos that covered every common space and entrance.

"He left a note for his daughter, but he's in the building," the administrator had first insisted. As the morning wore on, she admitted Peter had vanished. Already smarting from Peter's first disappearance, the home and the Stratford police called a hasty news conference.

"Did aliens abduct him again?" Bobby asked. His producer had roused Bobby Briscoe from sleep about six in the morning, and he had rushed to Stratford. His interview with Jorgensen would have to wait. It had been a fitful night for Bobby. He had desperately tried to contact Jimmy in Ottawa, but failed. Bobby worried.

"Who said anything about aliens?" The administrator scoffed. She felt uncomfortable in the sweatshirt and pants that she had thrown on when the call had come at 4 AM. The past two days of alien frenzy in the media opened up a bombardment of alien questions.

"What about the light someone saw this morning?" A reporter for The Star had been passing through on their way to Goderich and saw a bright glow near the downtown.

"Yes," the town cop admitted, "several citizens reported lights. Cedar Haven security video picked it up at," he consulted notes, "2:54 AM."

When the conference dissolved, every reporter filed a report: "aliens suspected of abducting Peter Williams". Most media ran it as a half-serious joke. Later in the day, when a video confirmed a light show in Goderich at 3:14 AM, the joking disappeared. The media then asked if aliens were visiting southwestern Ontario. As Jim had predicted, outsiders had booked every motel room within an hour of Goderich

At the bookshop, Ellie sat quietly. Ros thought she was in a trance or doing some alien thing, like sleeping with her eyes open. Ellie took part in a long-distance discussion amongst the star people about the next steps.

There were several short-term options, but all had to be considered in terms of the new plan involving the comet Clavette. They could free Lisa and Charlie in a way that disrupted the CIA operation, but, for now, they would be more useful by remaining near Danny Ringwald.

They decided they must cause some global political turmoil. This involved driving a wedge between Canadian public opinion and the interests of the Americans. The first step would exploit the media frenzy in Goderich by having ten CIA agents have their last chicken dinner with an old farmer and his wife.

"Okay," Ellie came to life, "Peter and Ros, you two lie low. Ros, your house is our safe house. No one knows you are involved. Mike Hammersmith will call a press conference at 2 PM in Courthouse Square."

***

"Siglinde, there is a fresh development with Clavette," Ted's image filled Siglinde's laptop screen. She and Nancy shared breakfast in her suite. "It has slowed down by one millimetre per second."

"Who gets that accuracy?"

"The global VLA gathered the data from thousands of observations and Singh's machine crunched it out. It's real. Preliminary radar data suggest its rotation axis is exactly 90 degrees to its direction of travel."

"What does it mean?"

"Singh's first run says that instead of smacking Mars on the leading edge, it will graze the South Pole. He's still trying to get the exact numbers and the atmospheric effects are important but hard to calculate.

There is a real buzz with the planetary folks right now. Mary McCormick in Australia says the drag and decreased airspeed from the retrograde spin on the planet side will make the thing hug the surface for a bit like a spinning cricket ball, not bounce off into space. It will super-heat and hit the surface much later than expected. Preliminary work suggests, Clavette will go to sub-orbital. It will hit near the equator after an orbit of about 270 degrees at a low angle and much-reduced velocity. It'll be a bit like sliding into home. Clavette will shed mass as water vapour and that phase change and drag will absorb a lot of the kinetic energy. Everyone is trying to confirm her opinion and the implications. The consensus is that it will make the Martian atmosphere dangerous for many years."

"We don't know why it changed velocity and rotation. The leading explanation is that it hit something on the far side of the sun big enough to cause the changes. Remember, years ago we showed with that NASA Dart mission that a small impact could have a significant effect. No one knows why it isn't wobbling like a spinning top."

"That seems reasonable," Siglinde said, "but it would have to have been big. Its unfortunate someone wasn't driving the thing. They would make it miss Mars completely."

"Unless they didn't want it to," Ted turned to his screen.

"When…?"

"It slightly delays the timing of contact. It's a worse situation for the settlers than we thought. I doubt they have any chance. The water vapour will be super-heated. McCormick's orbit has it passing west of IP-1. The Russians and Chinese are closer, but on the other side of Olympus Mons. If it's confirmed, NASA will have another news event."

"It's a zoo up here," Siglinde muttered.

"I know," Ted said, "it's all over the cable here. The movie channels are running every alien invasion flick they can find. Elliana stopped answering the phone."

"Sad," Siglinde said, "they aren't invaders, Ted. They just want to learn and help us."

"They need a new publicity agent," Nancy laughed across the table.

"Siglinde," Elliana's image replaced Ted. "You need to be in Goderich this afternoon. Mike Hammersmith is going to make an announcement, and you must take advantage of it. It will indirectly involve General Ringwald."

Siglinde did not question her assistant. They would be in Goderich.

"Tell Ted to keep me in the loop on Clavette."

"Bobby," Siglinde had finally connected with the reporter. "I can't set up Steve Jorgensen today. I have to be in Goderich."

"I may see you there," Bobby said. "I'm going too. Charlie Keys' boss has called a news conference in the town square. By the way, Peter Williams disappeared from his old age home again."

"I'm not surprised," Siglinde replied and punched off. She remembered some stories in the files when the aliens had intervened and rescued humans they valued, including Ellie.

I wonder what Mike Hammersmith has in mind. Why is Peter Williams important?

It didn't occur to Siglinde that Ellie simply cared for Peter and had promised to keep him safe. The aliens attempting to give him a future had been at Ellie's request.

Her unwanted celebrity status in the Canadian media made Siglinde hang back in the crowd. Word had spread through the small town, and it seemed half the population had flooded the space around the central courthouse. Mike had a solid reputation in Goderich as a supporter of kid's sports and charities from the women's shelter, homeless housing, and toy drives. That attracted a large crowd to any event that he sponsored, but the rumour that "it has something to do with aliens" attracted more.

Half an hour before the start time, the OPP gave up trying to clear gawkers from the ring road and blocked off all the streets that radiated away from it.

A mobile barbeque did a brisk business in smoked meat sandwiches. Journalists, accustomed to fast food, devoured the country fare.

How do these guys set up so fast? Siglinde wondered while she munched on thick pea meal bacon in a bun and sipped a can of Sprite. The scene was carnival time with little kids and mothers in the mix. Everyone expected the action to happen at the concrete stage and waited for Mike Hammersmith to appear. Shopkeepers and clerks stood against the fronts of their businesses on the square's outer rim. The journalists formed a tight mob at the front. News cameras and satellite trucks were everywhere, with a steady-cam filming the crowd from the stage. Internet media streamed the excitement.

Ellie walked onto the stage with Mike Hammersmith. The crowd quieted. Bright overcast hid an increasing glow from above until a bright circle of light came from the west and, hidden beyond the clouds, hovered above the stage. The crowd gasped and pushed forward. Mike looked up along with all the others, expecting something to appear. Ellie calmly stood and watched the centre of the stage. Siglinde watched Ellie.

"Ellie knows what's going to happen," Siglinde told Nancy.

A pillar of iridescence purple dropped through the clouds to the centre of the platform. It disappeared in an instant. Later, many would argue that it had not happened, or Mike had arranged a trick light show. The evidence remained on the stage. Ten figures dressed in the black forage caps and matching stealth uniforms of commandoes stood beside Mike and Ellie. One of them brandished a rifle with an oversized sighting scope.

Someone in the crowd screamed. Another cried out, "She has a gun."

To this point, the police contingent had been standing about, hoping the crowd would behave. Now they had a purpose.

"Drop the weapon," an officer shouted and brandished his Glock. It was not clear if the cop knew that although his weapon might have been the same 9 mm calibre as the woman's rifle, she had the advantage in throwing weight and clip load. A quick-thinking constable rushed to the side, gun drawn, and snuck towards the ten apparitions. Mike fidgeted, but Ellie approached the newcomers. The onlookers froze in shock. News camera operators who functioned in the reality of their image frames carried on calmly.

The woman vaguely waved her weapon.

"Drop it or I'll shoot," a voice commanded.

Ellie reached the woman sniper, gently relieved her of the rifle, and laid it on the platform. She certainly did not want anyone shot, especially this agent, but she wanted the Provincial Police to take the ten into custody. The public had to know that American agents were operating in Canada without invitation. The crowd needed to hear it first, before the authorities could suppress the facts.

"Who are you?" Ellie asked the sniper in a loud but gentle voice.

The disarmed shooter blinked, stared at Ellie, and she said, "We work for the United States of America, Defence Threat Reduction Agency. We are trying to capture aliens."

A dozen video cameras, including Bobby Briscoe, recorded the statement, confirming that American agents believed there were extra-terrestrials in Canada.

A frenzy of questions from the reporters accompanied the OPP as they zip-tied each of the strangers. In their stupefied condition, the arrivals did not resist and said nothing more. After they had confirmed that these were professional commandos, the police admitted that the ten, if they had been in control of their senses, could have easily outfought them.

The authorities, in desperate attempts to suppress the idea of aliens, could never admit to themselves that aliens had purposely deposited the agents in a confused, pliable state and that the visitors had pre-programmed the sniper's public confession. The best efforts of the government could not conceal the spectacular show and confession. It had occurred in front of live television, hundreds of citizens, and streamed globally on the internet. The government went to its backup claim Russian agents had kidnapped and drugged the Americans.

In the confusion, Mike and Ellie disappeared from the stage.

"Hello, Siglinde," Mike touched her arm. "Ellie has never met you."

"It's nice to meet you, Siglinde," Ellie looked at Nancy and frowned, "and you too, Nancy. Can we go somewhere quiet?"

"... back to my office," Mike glanced around at the tumultuous scene. "The reporters will stay here and chase the cops and prisoners to the Clinton lock-up. They won't follow us."

"Can that reporter, Bobby Briscoe, come too?" Siglinde asked Ellie.

Ellie clambered from Mike's truck into the deserted factory parking lot. Siglinde, Nancy and Bobby parked beside them. They hurried inside and hoped no reporter had followed. Kerri joined them in Mike's office. He secured the door.

"Who are those people that appeared in the square?" Mike had simply gone along with Ellie's lead.

"They are part of the team that has my mother Lisa and Charlie captive on a farm near to here. The ones we released today made the mistake of chasing my daughter down a road. More are going to meet her tonight."

"Is Charlie okay?" Kerri resisted a sob.

"He's fine," Ellie said. "I'm not sure when you'll see him, but soon I think, certainly by New Year's."

Ellie understood Kerri's double concern for her father. She had no lingering thoughts that her mother and father would be a couple. Ellie had listened to that discussion during the desperate flight to Texas over twenty years before. For some time, Ellie had thought of the relationship between her parents to be like the simple high school model of the water molecule. Lisa and Charlie only united in their unbreakable love bond with Ellie. Ellie was the oxygen in their relationship. Her father deserved happiness.

"Bobby, you caused all this turmoil and changed our plans."

"Hey, it fell into my lap. I am just doing my job," Bobby bristled.

"It's okay, Bobby. We had calculated a 50% chance things would not go according to our plans. You and Jim were that unplanned half. It's the comet, what you call a black swan event," Ellie looked at Siglinde, "we didn't even guess at that, but it has created a new opportunity. Clavette will lead to a spectacle on New Year's Eve. It will happen in China, Russia, Washington and here too."

"I hope we have nice weather for it," Bobby managed a smile.

"We can arrange that," Ellie said.

"By the way," Bobby said, "my friend Jimmy, the reporter in Ottawa who shot that video of you and the other women, well, I can't get a hold of him. I finally called Liz Dafoe, and she talked with him yesterday morning. He had an appointment to visit Dawn Waasnodae but never showed. I'm worried. I think the cops have him."

"Give me a minute," Ellie frowned and seemed to drift into a trance, looking for Daisy. A few seconds later, she turned to Bobby.

"Jimmy is okay for now, Bobby. The CIA had the Canadian security force arrest him. We should know in a little while where he is."

"You will tell us?" Bobby asked.

"Up there," Ellie glanced at the ceiling, "will keep Jimmy safe. They won't tell me until I need to know."

"How did you know they arrested him?" Nancy asked.

"Nancy, I guess it's time we discussed your role in all this." Ellie eyed the woman as a cat might contemplate a mouse. Nancy's eyes narrowed.

"What do you mean?"

"You knew all along about Danny Ringwald and his handler, Greg, because you are part of it."

Siglinde looked shocked. Bobby recorded a video.

Nancy wanted to lunge at Ellie, but something held her in her chair.

"Let me go," she screamed. Nancy could move everything from the waist up, but could not rise from the chair.

The others could not see the restraint. Her outcry startled them all.

"Relax, Nancy," Ellie said, "you are in no danger, but you threatened everyone else. You once worked with one of the ten agents who appeared downtown. I saw your look of recognition. No one will harm you, and I hope you decide to change. If not, we'll drop you in the middle of Fort Belvoir. You can explain to them how you got there."

A light knock, the locked door opened and Daisy walked in.

"The operation at Fort Belvoir is meaningless now. Greg is on his way and will arrive at the farm overnight." Daisy said to Nancy.

"My source," Ellie nodded at Daisy.

"You… you're..." Nancy sputtered.

"Yes, I met you when you visited Greg. You like your coffee black." Daisy added, and then for the benefit of the others, "I was the receptionist and assistant for a CIA operative named Greg at Fort Belvoir, Virginia. We discovered his setup after first inserting a source within the NAAP operation, which we have known about for years. Things are developing. Fort Belvoir is now useless. They just don't know it yet."

"The publicity has hampered NAAP," she smiled at Siglinde, "but we hope you will go public."

"You can't; that's treason," Nancy growled at Siglinde.

"It's okay," Ellie said. "It isn't time until after New Year's Eve. You can decide by then."

"It's still treason," Nancy muttered.

"Nancy, twenty years ago, when I had to leave to keep people from being hurt, you humans controlled the agenda on the ground. Today, the star people do and will serve humanity a cold dish of humility."

Bobby captured everything on video. Bobby had travelled from being the sceptic who interviewed Crazy Jim to knowing alien visitors were real. It was not a dream, but Ellie had convinced him it would be no nightmare.

"My star people have the power to finish humans," Ellie scowled, "but we won't. As I keep saying, if humans can't learn to save Earth, we will withdraw. Humans will commit suicide with no interference from the stars, and we won't step in to save you."

"That's not neighbourly," Bobby wanted to keep Ellie talking.

Ellie turned to Bobby and talked directly into the camera.

"My daughter and I are part human. I'm mostly human. We don't want humanity to fail, but millennia of observation and disasters elsewhere have shown the star people that interfering is unsuccessful and only prolongs horror on a planet. There is the concept of the great filter that Earth scientists have postulated. It exists and is necessary, although they think it involves asteroids and exploding stars and not sentient species committing suicide. That's far more common. Without it, species would gain too much power before they are ready, just as humans have developed nuclear bombs. It's too much power too soon. Such species would cause havoc in the galaxy, and there is a history of disaster when an interstellar species intervened. No one will ever again intervene, only reveal the possibility, and hope it stimulates humans to survive. Otherwise, you must die off."

"Your exploitation of fossil energy is perhaps even worse. It is already destroying life on the planet and you have little time left to fix that."

Kerrie gasped, and the others muttered. Siglinde nodded her head.

"There's no way I and my daughter could remain here if my star family withdrew. We might intervene because we care, but on our own, humans would kill us. It would be the second time I would leave those I love hoping humans learned. So far, we still have hope."

Nancy slumped into her chair. Ellie went and knelt in front of her.

"Nancy, I'm about to free you," Ellie touched her knee. "You will get to choose your future. I will not force you or stop you, whatever you choose. You are a stand-in for all of humanity and can choose to continue with the forces that wish to dominate and divide humans, or to work for the liberation of spirit and action required for your species to survive. Walk out the door and return to Greg and those who see violence and power as the way, or side with those who want a better way. Your governments will do anything to stop you."

Ellie found a place behind Mike and Kerri. Bobby panned his camera to capture the drama of the scene, and then framed Nancy.

"Bobby," Ellie said, "you can keep all this video, but you can't show it until after 11:30 PM on New Year's Eve."

"Okay," Bobby was happy he could hold on to it all.

Nancy flexed her legs and stood, looking about in confusion. She had never seen herself as the fulcrum upon which the future of humanity balanced. Years of loyalty, oaths, and belief struggled against the challenge. She walked towards the door. Dawn prepared to stand aside. As she passed Siglinde, Nancy burst into tears, leaned down and hugged her boss.

"Forgive me, Siglinde. I thought I was on the right side."
Nancy looked at Ellie.
"I will stay."

***

Danny Ringwald fixated on the spectacle on the big screen television.
Goderich looks like a pretty, little town... Danny had drifted into the only positive thought he could tease from the mesmerizing debacle. He had never been into town.

"At least you know where your people are." Lisa enjoyed the star family's carefully planned circus.

Danny's cell chimed. He glanced and laid it on the table. Talking to Greg was the last thing he wanted right now. He had to process this first.

"They look in one piece," Danny acknowledged.

... too late to keep them from talking too. Greg won't bother to take them out.

"That was my boss and my daughter on the stage." Charlie shared Lisa's satisfaction. "Ellie had to make sure there was no shooting and to get your person to confess in public. What are you going to do now?"

Danny glanced around to make sure no one on the team could hear.

"I'm doing nothing. I would let you go, but then those people outside would shoot us. Greg will probably arrive tonight from Michigan."

"I don't think he'll enjoy his stay," Lisa repeated her earlier warning.

"I hope he doesn't," Danny smiled. "He has no feelings, no morals, but a big ego. If your aliens knock him on his ass, it would work for me."

"I think I had better go talk to the troops," Danny looked out the window. "The team being safe will cheer them, but probably destroy any morale that they had left after the tree was reborn. They have given up. I hope we have enough white towels for them to wave. I wonder what bullshit Greg will use to get them back onside."

Danny's cell chimed again... Greg. He put it to his ear and wandered to the door, muttering.

RoH, you need to be near the airport tonight. Your father will give you the details.
He already has, Mother. It will be fun.
Don't hurt anyone.
They are dandelions, Mother. I never hurt dandelions. Greg has to meet Grandpa and Grandma. It will test him.

Love you, my little imp.

Love you, Mother. Maybe one day I can say that to Father, and he will feel it.

One day, dear, I hope. That's why we are here.

Chapter Twenty-four

Strange things done in the midnight moon.

RoH sat with Ros and Peter in Ros' car, discreetly parked behind a hangar at the Goderich Airport. In October morning darkness, the huge C-130 whined in off the lake and eased onto the concrete runway. As usual, it stopped and turned at the highway. Several darkened vehicles sped out from the terminal apron and formed a line beside the plane.

"Come on," RoH exclaimed, and jumped from the car. Ros and Peter hurried after her, over the short secondary runway and grassy verge. RoH stopped in the middle of the main runway, between the C-130 and the lake. She faced to where the darkened plane waited, with light pouring from its gangway. Several people hurried into the vehicles and sped away. The lighted doorway disappeared and the sound of the turbines drifted down the strip. The craft rolled towards the trio, gaining speed.

"Shouldn't we be running for it about now?" Peter's scared voice rasped. RoH stood firm.

The plane picked up speed, bearing down with the gap shrinking rapidly. Ros eased to the edge of the runway. RoH put her hands on her hips. The plane's turbines died, and the craft jerked to a stop. Its nose wheel collapsed.

Above the airport, a sudden glow appeared, burst into a blinding light, and instantly died. Everything plunged into darkness. The tinkling of falling Plexiglas from the exploded aircraft windscreen drifted to the watchers. The plane sat opposite the terminal, nose down, silent, empty.

"Those vehicles are going to where Grandmother and Grandfather are captive. Things are developing. It's only a little over two months now."

"Can't you free them?" Ros liked Charlie Keys.

"When it's time," RoH said. "I'm hungry; let's go have breakfast."

Fireflies swarmed the farmyard, flitting about. Hundreds had landed on the barren branches of the Lazarus tree, turning it into a dazzling, skeletal Christmas tree. Fireflies were not normal at this time of year.

Greg ignored the light show and hurried to the house. The tree flared and threw Greg's shadow onto the door.

Danny had planned to be in bed when Greg arrived, but the emotion caused by the spectacle in Goderich had killed that plan. He sat glum and introspective in the comfortable rocking chair that occupied the commanding corner of the living area. Danny wore his general's uniform, complete with decorations. He had earned two of these, as a humble lieutenant, under fire, and fighting as a rear guard as his platoon withdrew from an ambush. He would not easily cede the high ground to Greg.

"Well Ringwald, your operation here has turned into a fiasco." Greg ignored formalities. "Where are the prisoners, or did you lose them too?"

"They aren't prisoners." Danny did not rise, claiming symbolic status. "They are here to help us negotiate."

"They're prisoners now," Greg spat, "you have coddled them enough. Those space invaders need to know we are tough. Get them here, now."

Danny sighed. It was an order, but Greg's belief that he had any actual power or bargaining position with Ellie's relatives revealed his deep delusion. Danny issued an order to wake Charlie and Lisa.

"We have babied you enough," Greg sneered at Charlie and Lisa. The sleepy pair sat erect beside each other on the couch. Greg loomed above them, the dominant great ape. Danny rocked gently in the chair.

"General Ringwald has hardly pampered us. It isn't nice being locked in a room and interrogated at random times."

Lisa had guessed the change of who was in charge, and she did not want to betray their friendship with Danny. It would be better to have this new man think Danny was still on his side.

"Poor people," Greg's sarcasm reinforced Lisa's thinking. "Your alien friends haven't gotten the message. They have to talk to us. I'm going to make sure they get the message. If they don't come to us soon, you two won't be around to be rescued."

"They will probably come when you don't expect them, and you won't like it," Charlie said.

Danny finally jumped to his feet but caught himself before he blurted out any opposition.

"How will you let them know?" Danny returned to the chair.

"You," Greg fixed his eyes on the general, "are going to call Siglinde Hilfreich and tell her. She and her bunch can finally be useful. She is near to finding the alien. Hilfreich can tell her, and they will all know."

Greg did not reveal how he knew Siglinde could reach Ellie, and he hid his concern that their operative had not called in at her last appointed time. Still, she had already discovered that Liz Dafoe knew Ellie, and Siglinde had been in touch with the politician. Greg did not know that Siglinde could simply tell Ellie directly.

"I thought you'd shut NAAP down, now that the lid's blown off."

"I thought you were a soldier," Greg sneered. "they are good camo now that everyone is looking at them. They won't think we exist."

"After the spectacle in Goderich, the entire world knows you exist, even if they think you are part of NAAP. Your real problem," Lisa said, "is that they know all about you, up there." She looked at the ceiling.

Danny looked at his watch.

"I'll call Virginia first thing and find out where to reach Siglinde."

"You two... out," Greg snarled. The guard took them upstairs.

"Danny," Greg said, "if the aliens don't cooperate, shoot these two. Let Hilfreich know that." Greg went off in search of a bunk.

"Over my dead body, I will." Danny despaired. He needed a way out.

When the airfield day manager turned onto Airport Road and crested the hill from the highway, he jerked his pickup to a stop on the narrow shoulder, almost ending up in the winter wheat, and stared at a huge grey military transport sitting nose down and blocking his main runway.

"What the..."

He swerved the little truck into the terminal lot, punched 911 on his cell and hurried inside to call Transport Canada.

I guess Old Swede wasn't lying about seeing one of these.

The airport manager raced across the grass between runways to the derelict plane. He did not know why he was carrying a ten-pound fire extinguisher. The grey hulk had died and 5 K of ABC powder would have done nothing against tonnes of blazing kerosene.

The local volunteer fire department arrived first. He discretely threw the puny canister into the grass. If the fire crew saw it, he would be the butt at the Legion and have to buy a round of beer to shut them up.

Although the pumper, rescue, and tanker trucks made a nice show, the firefighters joined the manager in standing around staring at the hulk. Subdued markings confirmed it belonged to the US Air Force. One firefighter found busy work spreading absorbent onto the small puddle of hydraulic oil at the collapsed nose wheel. They put a ladder up to the cockpit and peered through the shattered windscreen. It remained dark, silent, and empty. One firefighter swept up shards of Plexiglas, but the manager stopped him.

"Transport Canada will want to examine all the evidence. Leave it."

The press arrived next; a tumbling herd of city slickers, still in town on their alien hunt, followed a local reporter awoken by his emergency scanner. They thought they were responding to an aircraft disaster and had abandoned the planned stakeout of Charlie Keys' workplace. They would soon decide that the derelict had connections to yesterday's spectacle and the elusive aliens, although no one could decide what those links might be.

Police and curious locals joined the throng, but no one had any idea how to get inside the locked-up plane, short of a cutting torch or crawling through the window. The OPP corporal who took charge of the scene decided that cutting into it would be a bad idea since it was American air force property and no one knew where a fuel line might be.

"Crawling through broken glass is a tactical unit job above my pay grade." The police established a perimeter and waited.

The call to Transport Canada finally yielded results. At mid-morning an RCAF search and rescue Hercules from Trenton, an ancient cousin to the more modern hulk on the runway, made a low pass over the crowd, turned sharply into the wind, and touched down, with screaming reverse props onto the short, general aviation runway. The crew from the SAR plane knew where to find the door handle.

A SAR tech poked her head out of the darkened doorway. "It's empty. No one is in here at all."

"Check all the bars in town," the Canadian pilot quipped to the OPP corporal. "It's always the first thing the Yankees ask for."

Several reporters combined that idea with breakfast.

"So, where the hell are the crew?" The mystery meant a long day for the corporal. "Yesterday it was a mystery appearance; today it's a mysterious disappearance."

***

"Hey, let us out. Where the hell are we?"

Fists pounding on the reinforced metal door attracted the CSIS guard. Two voices puzzled him. He only had one prisoner.

He called for reinforcements. Two men in US Air Force flight coveralls spilled from the cell.

"Who the hell are you? Where did you come from?" The guards levelled Glocks at the confused fliers.

One guard eased into the cell, his weapon levelled and eyes darting everywhere. He wrestled the cot's mattress. There was no sign of prisoner Jimmy Smith.

"Nothing… no trace of Smith… no blood, and the window has its bars twisted out, glass everywhere."

"That's spooky." His partner eyed the two new prisoners. "I never heard a sound. This just happened. I looked in about twenty minutes ago and Smith was asleep."

"How long were you two in there?"

"We just got here," one said. "What time is it?"

"Six in the morning…"

The pair looked at each other.

"It was just after three," they said together.

They herded the newcomers into a windowless interrogation room.

"Where's Cap?" one flier asked the other.

"Who's Cap?" The CSIS man growled.

"Captain Honoree, he's the pilot," one replied. "We were just with him taking off from…" The second man kicked his friend's ankle. He had recovered enough to remember they had been on a clandestine mission in hostile territory, and they did not know who their captors were. This might be an elaborate test of their loyalty.

"So there should be three of you? What was your airplane?"

"Was that what you were doing, just after three, three hours ago?"

"Yes… in a Herc. What have you done with Cap?"

"What happened to the guy in that cell?"

"What guy?"

Jimmy lay on his living room floor, dazed. The open window allowed a chilly breeze inside. He remembered being in the narrow bunk, contemplating food just a moment before. Jimmy sat up and waited until his head cleared. He did not know what had happened, although, considering his chat with Liz, he guessed he had just experienced something alien.

CISIS had ransacked the room. His empty media storage shelves hung on the wall, and the desktop computer had disappeared. The thieves took all of his video work. Jimmy had copied it to the cloud, so that did not matter. What mattered was the government people had his cell.

They will come looking for me… the thought made Jimmy shiver.

Jimmy grabbed his spare keys. He hoped the car would still be at Liz Dafoe's apartment building.

***

Danny Ringwald pushed his breakfast plate aside and sipped the most recent of countless coffees. He had endured the argument with Greg and witnessed the man's browbeating of Lisa and Charlie. The two hours of abuse had affected him more than the captives. One of Greg's loyal minions guarded their rooms. Danny's uniform had rumpled. He contemplated changing, but a commotion drew him outside.

A figure staggered down the grassy lane towards anxious agents. Several had drawn guns and formed a crescent waiting for the newcomer.

The man wore an Air Force uniform. Danny recognized the patch of the Air Mobility Command on the right and the pilot's wings on the left breast. He hurried forward, hoping the armed agents would not shoot. The visitor stopped as he reached Danny. Somehow, the General's uniform caused the pilot to focus. The black man snapped to attention and saluted. A General demanded respect no matter what service.

"Captain Eugene Honoree, USAF…" the thick Louisiana accent seemed strange in this Canadian backwater.

"Danny Ringwald," Danny's hand dropped from his cap, the US Army. "Where did you come from?"

Greg rushed up and recognized his pilot from the night before.

"Captain," Greg snapped, "come with me."

Greg ushered the pilot away without acknowledging Danny.

Danny went to bed.

Chapter Twenty-five

Lady of the Lake, again

"**M**other, why don't we just get them out?"

"Sweet RoH, we want the CIA plot to fall apart on its own. They think that power and force are the only way. We must convince all of humanity that cooperation is the road to the galaxy. If we attack, all the governments will concentrate their power and use propaganda to convince the majority to support them. We don't want to give them an enemy to hate. Their power must collapse internally, and the majority must see it."

"Clavette, and their failure to save the people on Mars, is one of our biggest opportunities, but governments must discredit themselves. Grandmother and grandfather are fine. Cracking their captor's unity will be the way."

RoH pouted into her hot chocolate. She agreed with her mother, but she enjoyed toying with the arrogant people at the farm.

"Don't worry, Âلإنط, you'll get to have more fun before it's all done. I have to go to Ottawa now to visit my friends. They have a key role to play. Everything that has happened in the past two days embarrasses the Canadian government. They want to cover that up, but they are getting angry that the Americans have lied to them. Liz and Dawn will do things to make that situation worse. It will put them into difficulty, but we can't help that. It is necessary."

Ellie patted RoH on the arm and lifted a water bottle to her lips.

***

Jimmy arrived at Liz Dafoe's apartment building in a rainstorm a few minutes after Ellie appeared in the park near Dow's Lake. The only witness to the brief pillar of purple light was a woman high on drugs who enjoyed this latest hallucination. The woman had once been an English teacher, and the ethereal figure emerging from a pillar of light amid lightning flash and thunder roar seemed Shakespearian. As Ellie disappeared into the mist towards Liz's apartment, she glanced over her shoulder at the woman. The addict's mind cleared. She shivered from cold and hunger but felt no effects of withdrawal and had no desire to shoot up.

"You look confused."

Jimmy spun away from staring at the spot where he had left his car.

"They were smart enough to take my car. You're..."

"Ellie, Jimmy, I liked your video of me." Ellie took his hand.

"You put on quite a show, but no one believes it. They say I faked it."

"Denial is their only weapon. The governments can't admit there might be something more powerful than they are. It loses votes. I'm not the power, but a bit."

"Is that why they grabbed me?" Jimmy trembled with fresh fear and desperation. "They're after me. I have to get away."

"They would like to have you back, that's true, but we left them a bigger worry. It's something they really can't figure out."

"I thought my video did that."

"The Americans know the truth in your video, but have kept Canadians in the dark. They learned the Americans hid alien presence. We hope Canadians will get angry enough to split with them."

"I wouldn't hold my breath. We have been ass-kissers too long."

"That's a problem," Ellie agreed, "but cracks form in the ice before it breaks up. We are patient, and in the end, it's a key to solving the riddle."

"What's the riddle?"

"It's how to get humans to save yourselves and travel the stars."

"Let's get out of the rain." Jimmy led the way to Liz's foyer just as another storm cell arrived.

"Why do aliens want to help us?" Jimmy shook the rain from his jacket. "Don't you want to eat us or steal our water or something?"

"You watch too many movies," Ellie laughed. "There's plenty of food, water and everything else available elsewhere. We want your souls."

Jimmy's face flashed in terror, but Ellie laughed.

"I'm sorry I scared you; that was a poor joke. We want to embrace your empathy and mutual bonding."

Thunder pealed, and a flash of lightning lit the landscape.

"We had better get inside. They have alerted the police about you, and we'll be more comfortable."

The door opened untouched and Ellie led the way inside.

Liz found Ellie and Jimmy Smith relaxing on her couch.

"What...?"

"Sorry, we let ourselves in."

Jimmy thought letting themselves in had been alien wizardry. He had seen no light, heard no sound, but the main door to Liz's apartment building, and then her door, had simply opened.

"Anyone but you or Dawn would have me screaming. You had me scared once." Liz chuckled at her panic in London. "Hello, Jimmy."

"Speaking of Dawn, I need to discuss something with all of you."

"She'll be here Monday. There's a party meeting she must attend first; it's probably to kick her out."

"It is that kind of thing that has made us give up on human politics. Events must drive things now. Jimmy and I need to camp out here until then. He's a fugitive, and that's part of what we need to discuss."

"I'm starved." Liz headed to the kitchen. "I have pasta sauce ready."

"Mom used to make veggie pasta in Seattle," Ellie followed Liz.

***

Charlie slathered a plate full of fusilli with a rich meat sauce. Lisa preferred vegetarian, but she was not religious about it. Hunger creates agnostics when food is concerned. Her portion was more modest, and she tried to avoid clumps of ground beef embedded in the garlic-tomato mix.

"It has been an interesting day," Danny tried to sound cheerful. He knew Greg would not hesitate to kill, and he probably was on the list.

Lisa dunked the garlic toast into her sauce. "Greg will not enjoy being here."

"So far, he isn't," Danny smiled. "He's trying to process why the pilot turned up, and how the plane became stranded on the runway. The flier remembers nothing. He was at the controls and then stumbling down our lane. Greg still thinks he has power. That makes him dangerous."

"He'll be more dangerous once he realizes he's defenceless," Charlie frowned. "We saw those types twenty years ago in Texas."

"I know another way he is weak." Danny took a deep swig of beer.

Danny had examined the farm layout and decided that the fence back corner on the side away from the control centre did not have adequate video coverage and was the darkest place in the compound. It had to be soon.

Danny glanced around. The cook and a guard lingered within earshot. He had decided on action, but needed to get Charlie and Lisa alone.

"How about playing some cards later?"

The cook would be off duty, and the guard was bored. It might give Danny the chance to conspire.

"I'm not a card player," Charlie replied.

"I would appreciate the company," Danny said. "I'll introduce you to an interesting game."

Danny winked at Charlie. Lisa caught the signal.

"I'd love that," she said. "It'll be like those times in Texas. Remember the time grandpa came to play?"

Charlie nodded. That was the night that grandpa, the alien who had started all this with the Clarke family, had left in the middle of the night.

Charlie frowned. They had not played cards. The alien patriarch had only allowed Ellie to say goodbye. It was probably when she decided her destiny lay in the stars. Charlie did not like that implication.

Does that mean she and RoH will leave? Charlie desperately wanted his daughter and RoH, this recent addition to his heart, never to leave.

Lisa saw the pain in Charlie's face and relived her memories.

"Let's play a three-handed game, Hearts," Lisa said.

"Maybe we can make the move grandpa did." Lisa glanced at Danny, looking for a hint that she had read the man correctly.

"I'm arranging for a turkey to celebrate Canadian Thanksgiving on Monday," Danny nodded to Lisa.

***

"Are you here to see your lover?"

"Did you meet an alien?"

The reporters' questions flew at Dawn Waasnodae. These journeymen freelancers knew that the sensational sold. The networks would pay for titillation before facts.

Dawn pulled her collar high around her neck. The air was heavy with something between fog and rain, typical for a dreary Ottawa Thanksgiving Monday. She hurried to the doors, her jaw set against the obnoxious badgering. A glance at the little mob revealed one was a cop, *probably a Mountie.* Dawn reached the quiet of the lobby.

At least they are getting wet; Dawn smiled and then regretted taking satisfaction in the suffering of others, even these parasites.

The security guard nodded and returned to watching the horde outside.

Dawn rapped twice on Liz's door and used her key.

"If you go through with what I'm about to ask, I'm afraid you'll suffer more than being watched. You won't have to worry in the long run, but it will be uncomfortable for a while."

Ellie reclined in an overstuffed wing chair and faced the two MPs snuggled together on a luxurious couch. The rain had finally hit, driven on a gale across Liz's balcony and pelting the plate glass behind the couch. The sombre dying of the day fit the mood.

Jimmy had pulled up a less comfortable dining room chair.

"What do you want us to do?"

"We want you to expose the capture of those American airmen we traded for Jimmy by asking some questions in your parliament."

"My Whip will hate me," Liz smiled. She belonged to the government party until the next election, but they allowed no deviation from official positions. A common MP was not supposed to ask a question that the cabinet had not told them to ask. The backroom crowd wrote these questions to allow a minister to spout some line of political propaganda.

"I'll have to rise on a point of personal privilege," Dawn said. "They just kicked me out of our party. They didn't want a lesbian who might have talked to an alien agent," Dawn smiled at Ellie, "if they only knew."

"I thought your party was the progressive one, all-embracing and high ideals." Liz teased.

"That's the lie they tell themselves; it's what I believed when I first ran for election. In reality, votes and seats are more important."

"After this, they'll likely kick me out too." Liz did not sound upset.

"We both have to file the notice of privilege and the questions to the speaker of the house beforehand. They must approve them. I doubt the partisan speaker will allow either of us to do it in the chamber."

"How can we do it?" Ellie did not understand Canadian politics.

"We call a press conference on the steps of parliament." Liz had been in politics for a long time and understood the game. "With our notoriety, reporters will turn up. They might even broadcast it live on cable."

"Question period is two o'clock; we must do it earlier. What we say will be on the minds of reporters and our political colleagues after that."

Their decisions to leave politics had released Liz and Dawn from the need to please the despised party hacks. Both women expected reprisals. The MPs had nothing left to lose, echoing the classic view of freedom.

"Can you do this soon?" Ellie asked.

"It will take a day or two for the Speaker to say no," Liz replied. "The press is desperate to get at us. Thursday will be the best, about ten in the morning, so no one can stop it."

"Here's what we want you to say. Liz, you deal with the fliers. Dawn, I want you to speak about Jimmy's arrest. Jimmy, you must stay here. They want to nab you again."

Chapter Twenty-six

Back to school

Thursday morning, Siglinde and Nancy escorted Bobby Briscoe into Steven Jorgensen's office. This time, Rachel sat nearby. Siglinde frowned. She had not met Rachel, and Rachel looked ready for a fight.

"Can I video?" Bobby asked.

"No," Rachel exclaimed, but Steve motioned for her to relax.

"Let's talk first. Rachel and I are not sure we are ready to go public. Our jobs and reputations are at stake."

"But you have evidence," Siglinde sat. "You met with Ellie and she is indeed part alien."

"Yes, we met her. I may not show evidence, supposing I have any."

Rachel nodded in agreement.

Jorgensen's smile betrayed the truth, but Siglinde ignored it. Bobby desperately wanted to see a tangible object.

"Oh, this is Rachel, my student whom, accidentally or on purpose, Ellie drew into this."

"Maybe the token black woman," Rachel said.

Siglinde thought about Liz, back in Virginia. She had no time for tokens and neither did Ellie.

"I don't think the aliens care about race," Steven said. "Rachel could have been a white Goth, Wiccan with pink hair for all Ellie would care."

"Hey, I'll do the black version of that for Halloween," Rachel giggled.

"We are here to have Mr. Briscoe make a record of this. He promised Ellie that he would not release it until she says so. I trust him, but you can form your own opinion."

"Mr. Briscoe, I knew Ellie over twenty years ago. From my experience, I would not want to violate a promise to her. She and the star people have the power to do whatever they want. That they are involving us convinces me they are not a threat. Quite the opposite, if I read it correctly. I promised Ellie then I would always try to protect her. All of this seems to fit into that promise. She made the same pledge to us."

"She doesn't seem to need protection now, and alien ten-year-olds have come a long way since then." Siglinde thought of RoH.

"She has grown up," Steve thought of the confident and sophisticated Ellie. "What do you want to know, Mr. Briscoe?"

"It's Bobby, and I want your story and why Ellie came back to find you? Start at the beginning."

Steve broke into sudden laughter.

"What's so funny, boss?" Rachel flicked on her cell to record.

"I just realized, Bobby, that Ellie has recruited you, without you knowing, of course. Before I go to the beginning of my story, I must tell you all that the aliens are preparing humanity for the big reveal of their existence. They want to do that publicly and take control of the message away from governments. The recent events creating layers of interest and mystery are part of it. So far, they have manoeuvred governments into telling enormous lies. They hope the irrefutable public knowledge they are here will show governments' dishonesty and destroy their credibility. We are part of the plan."

"I should resent it," Bobby said, "but I met Ellie. I trust her."

"Maybe she tinkered with our brains." Rachel was the raven.

"Maybe," Siglinde said, "but we have been working on the reality of alien existence for over 80 years. I hate to sound defeatist, but even if they are lying, they have the power to do what they want. If they deceive us, it won't matter. If they are honest, they are cracking the door open for us to save our planet."

"Ellie told us our job is to be ready to help interpret when the time comes." Rachel brightened. "They know many humans will oppose them and use fear preventing a peaceful relationship. Steve and I are supposed to lead the effort to translate without depending on aliens speaking Earth languages. One necessity to understand a language is to embrace its culture. Aside from the obvious technical, 'what does this word mean?' they have been sharing their culture."

Steve frowned. "I find their culture to be discomforting. They relate much differently than we do, and I think they realize it. It motivates their desire to learn something from humans. They see the underlying unity in all human cultures, that we are one species and want to be included. Ellie, as a little girl, showed they can tinker with our brains and make us believe in illusions. As Siglinde says, we are helpless either way."

"Okay Bobby, let me start with the invitation and free ticket I got to the Dakotas over two decades ago. I saw Ellie in action, and I saw the American government in action too. The difference is that Ellie hurt no one. For the record," Steve stared into Bobbie's camera, "I'm violating the secrecy agreement I signed back then. Of course, the aliens hurt lots of people from before Roswell to the Dakotas."

"Peter Williams and other abductees," Bobby focused on Steve.

"There were direct deaths and shattered lives," Steve continued, "but I think nothing bad has happened since Ellie turned ten. She can do a lot of things, but her power had limits then."

"Her daughter, RoH, is much stronger," Siglinde added.

"Daughter?" Everyone asked at once.

"You didn't know?" Siglinde smiled. "The little girl we all thought was Ellie a few weeks ago is her daughter, about the same age as Ellie when Steve met her. I've had a long chat with RoH. She's powerful."

"Ááóý..." Steven said. The sound he made was ear-splitting.

"What's that?" Bobby hoped his microphone hadn't broken.

"It's alien speak," Siglinde had heard it before.

"From what Rachel and I have learned and our alien mentors would laugh at my pronunciation, it is the term the star people use for Ellie, and likely this girl you mention. The closest English word is embryo. Both of the hybrids, Ááóý ƚzá," again Steve's voice split the air, "is their phrase for that, is so young in alien terms that they almost do not exist. Aliens measure their lives in millennia."

"We have also learned," Rachel added, "that the aliens, or star people as Ellie calls them, seldom use spoken language. They communicate mentally. Maybe they dislike the sound of it as much as we do."

"Okay, let me tell you about Ellie as a ten-year-old in the Dakotas. They sent me home, and I never went to Texas where she finally fled Earth to keep her supporters from dying fighting the army. The incident in the Dakotas was spectacular enough."

Bobby's video recorder caught it all. He returned to the studio, intending to record a segment to enhance the mystery and anticipation of aliens. Bobby arrived in time to take in a live feed from Ottawa.

Liz swept her gaze over the small crowd of reporters. It threatened rain, but so far only a chill wind. The reporters were freelancers and the networks' B-teams. The parliamentary press gallery saw a news event hosted by a couple of meaningless backbench members to be below their dignity. Besides, it was nearly time for the bar to open in the pressroom. Liz smiled at the one video crew who were live-to-air, making her and Dawn hard to censor. Liz stepped forward at exactly 11 am.

"Thank you all for coming on such short notice. Dawn Waasnodae and I have some questions that the Speaker refused to allow inside the House. We will read our questions with comments and will be happy to answer your questions." I directed my question to the Minister of Justice.

Honourable Minister, last Saturday, October 11th, there was an incident at the CSIS facility at 1941 Ogilvie Road, Ottawa. CSIS apprehended two American airmen, Flight Engineer Ricco Sanchez of El Paso, Texas, and pilot Lieutenant Robert Kowalski of Rhode Island at about six in the morning. Minister, can you explain the circumstances of their arrest, especially at that unusual hour and inside the secure CSIS facility, and why you detained American military members?

"I would likely have follow-up questions for the minister and Minister of Public Safety and Emergency Preparedness, the one responsible for CSIS, but I will not add any more until my associate," a snicker came from a few reporters, "the Honourable Dawn Waasnodae presents her question."

Liz stepped back and noticed that a clerk from the Prime Minister's Office lurked to one side. In the PMO, the live presentation absorbed everyone's attention. The PMO clerk held a portable phone to his ear.

"I also direct my question to the minister. I had asked to rise on a point of personal privilege, related to my party expelling me because I am of two spirits, but that now seems less important."

"Honourable Minister of Public Safety and Emergency Preparedness," Dawn began, "last week I planned to meet with a reporter, James Smith, concerning the strange events he recorded at Dow's Lake, Ottawa. Everyone will have seen the sensational video on television. Minister, Mr. Smith left the home of my colleague, Honourable Member Dafoe, to meet me. He never arrived. I put it down to Mr. Smith, deciding not to meet; however, he did not call to cancel. It remained a mystery until last Monday when I finally met James Smith."

"Honourable Minister, Mr. Smith related a strange story. CSIS agents apprehended him as he left his meeting with Ms. Dafoe, and they threw him into a cell. He claims that this was in CSIS headquarters at 1941 Ogilvie Road, Ottawa. Mr. Smith describes several hours of questioning about the person named Ellie, supposedly an extra-terrestrial. I must add that much of this interrogation involved threats, bullying, and mild torture, such as sleep deprivation. Last Saturday morning, he mysteriously woke up in his apartment at six and discovered that someone had ransacked his home. They took electronics and storage devices storing his life's work."

"Mr. Smith, then fearing for his safety, went to Ms. Dafoe's apartment complex, hoping to retrieve his car. The car was gone, but at that moment, he met Ellie. On Monday, I met with them both with my friend, Liz Dafoe."

"I ask you, Honourable Minister, why was Jimmy Smith arrested? Did CSIS have proper warrants that allowed for the arrest, search of his apartment and seizure of his electronics, videos and car? Could you please tell the house if his disappearance from Ogilvie Road relates to the seemingly simultaneous arrival of the Americans that Ms. Dafoe has asked about? Is the disabled American Air Force transport plane sitting on the Goderich Ontario runway related to these airmen? Is the mysterious appearance of confessed American agents in the town square of Goderich Ontario related to these events? These agents are in the custody of the Ontario Provincial Police."

Dawn looked at the gathered press. The bunch showed more interest.

"These are the questions that we could not ask in the people's parliament. It appears the government has something to hide from us. We will take your questions."

All the excitement about aliens and American agents over the past week had alerted sensation-seeking television to the potential of the story. Questions came from all sides.

Liz, with her long experience with the press, knew that the live television slot might not be open for long, so she answered the questions related to aliens being on Earth. They were not trying to prove anything. Ellie and her associates would do that when the time was right. She aimed at getting the public to talk about it. Liz ended the event during the live broadcast. She had seen several PMO officials gathering, but more threatening were the half-dozen Mounties, accompanied by parliamentary security. Liz and Dawn knew what came next. She arranged for it to happen live on television.

"Ladies," a Mountie sneered, "you have betrayed secrets and violated your oath. Come with us."

The cop accidentally confirmed the MPs' statements. Viewers in waiting rooms and coffee shops across the country saw it live. It filled the morning news in Vancouver. Even in handcuffs, Liz smiled in satisfaction.

Remember, you will always be safe.

It had been a long afternoon of journalists begging for information from the government and the politicians trying to decide what to do next. The Mounties had made vague statements about the MPs revealing national secrets, but they refused to tell reporters what those secrets involved. They refused to confirm or deny the details in the women's statements. The press and the public took the silence as proof.

Government ministers mimicked the police in Parliament with a cascade of denials and claims of ignorance. Their fear and arrogance committed the cardinal political mistake of leaving a vacuum for speculators. Talk of aliens and government cover-ups dominated the media and that of anyone paying attention. Networks replayed blurry videos from American Navy pilots and countless amateurs to embellish the coverage. These all seemed silly when shown beside Jimmy's clear and focused record of Ellie Keys' Star Trek-like ascendance into the sky.

In the late afternoon, Jimmy Smith called one of his contacts among the reporters laying siege to parliament.

"Ellie and I will speak in front of Liz Dafoe's apartment at six."

The man tried to sneak away, hoping for a scoop, but another reporter had overheard Jimmy and soon the rush was on. Precisely at six, Ellie and Jimmy emerged into the gloom in the front lot.

"Hi guys, most of you know me," Jimmy nodded towards a steady cam, "I'm Jimmy Smith, the great alien videographer."

The laughter satisfied him.

"This is Ellie. You may recognize her from my Dow's Lake video."

"Hello, everyone," Ellie's northwestern American accent coloured her words. "I won't be making a statement. Jimmy will do all the talking."

"I want to confirm everything that Liz and Dawn said. CSIS arrested, more like kidnapped me and held me prisoner. I don't know about the American fliers. Ellie gave us that information, but I think it will be easy enough to track down the names and families of the two men. You might even confirm that they were crew on an American C-130 transport that flew from Selfridge Air National Guard Base in Harrison Township, Michigan and landed at Goderich Airport in the middle of the night. That aeroplane sits, marooned on the main runway there with the crew missing. They had me in a cell at headquarters, but that morning I woke up on the floor of my apartment. I only know why because Ellie explained it. CSIS had searched the place, and they took all my videos. I hoped my car was still there and rushed here. They had towed it, but Ellie found me, and I have been here since. I'll try to answer your questions now."

"Are you an alien?" The reporters wanted Ellie, not Jimmy.

"I'm as human as you are, but..."

Before Ellie could finish, a parade of police cars, lights flashing, sped into the driveway.

"We have to leave," Ellie rushed towards the door with Jimmy behind.

They disappeared inside and hurried down the corridor to the elevators. Jimmy hit the up button, but Ellie grabbed his arm. She reached through the open elevator door and punched Liz's floor, and led Jimmy to the back as the elevator went up. The police hammered on the front door and pressed the call button. The security guard tried to respond, but he could not move. In an instant, the fugitives were out the rear exit and made a beeline across the gloomy loading area to the back fence.

At the front door, the guard suddenly felt free and the cops burst through with the reporters in close pursuit. The guard pointed towards the elevators and the mob rushed away. Two cops checked the back door. The rest waited for the lift to return.

"Help me up here." Ellie grasped the top of a large garbage dumpster. Jimmy lifted her by the legs and then reached up as she took his hand and he clambered after her.

The police burst out the back door.

It was a short jump over the fence from the dumpster lid and they thudded into the backyard of an old Victorian house.

In the evening gloom, one cop saw fleeting movement by the fence. They hurried inside to call for help and dogs.

"Follow me," Ellie rushed through the side yard.

An urgent alert went out with a sketchy description of the fugitives. Two constables raced their car into the street to circle behind the building.

"Shhh," Ellie crouched behind a low fieldstone wall as a cruiser slid past with its spotlight searching the streetscape.

"Can't you just do a purple light beam-us-up thing?" Jimmy hoped he would not end up in another cell, but perhaps, if he were awake, what lay at the other end of the purple light held greater horror.

"Not at the moment," Ellie did not react to the science fiction reference. "All of our craft are busy over Africa, Europe and Australia. My half-siblings are finding out about themselves today. I had a hard time when I first realized I was different."

"You didn't send the whole fleet to Earth then." Jimmy laughed despite their situation. "Or is that all you have?"

Ellie turned and stared into Jimmy's eyes.

"Imagine how many ships Earth has on the ocean," Ellie became the patient teacher, "that might give you an idea, but there are only three in our system for now. There are reinforcements on the way. This whole thing has become more complicated than we planned. Clavette has done that. We need more craft to deal with what's coming."

Jimmy had a sudden image of a dark void suddenly coming to life with brilliant specks. They looked like stars until, in an instant, they filled his view, ships of various sizes but all with vaguely circular appearance. He could not imagine the number.

"Our system?" he asked. "I thought you were an alien."

"As I told the reporters, I'm as human as you are, with a bit of star blood, and I care about Earth and all life on it."

"Okay, they're gone," Ellie walked calmly to the street and crossed as a passing car cleared the way. "What's a dark way out of town?"

"Let's follow the river southwest. The city is enormous but there is parkland there. It's about twenty clicks to the farmland."

"Follow me, my Queen."

***

"Queen of Spades makes it twenty," Lisa frowned at another in her series of losing hands.

"Looks like you're going for a point record," Danny deadpanned, as he added up the scores. In this game, the higher the points, the more you lost. "Okay, you're the big loser… game over."

Danny stood and slid the deck into the box. He glanced at the half-dozing guard. The cook had left about eight o'clock and the old Seth

Thomas on the mantle had just chimed eleven. This evening of cards carried on what had become a routine over the past few days.

"Time for bed," he yawned loudly. "I'll escort you upstairs."

The guard led the way. Charlie and Lisa followed. Danny gripped the banister as they climbed. He was going over his long-ago hand-to-hand combat training. A surprise would be the best advantage.

The guard unlocked Lisa's door and pushed it inwards. His body followed, reeling from General Ringwald's well-timed blow to the temple.

Danny stared at the motionless body. The training had been to kill. He hoped he had fallen short of that, but having the man out for a long time would help. He glanced at the camera at the end of the hallway and hoped no one in the ops building monitored it. As planned, the trio rushed to the back stairway that led directly to the kitchen.

"Okay," Danny whispered as the canine robot disappeared around the far corner of the house. "Let's go."

Although lights covered much of the farmyard, there was a shadowed gap at the northwest corner. Tonight, things were better because a light mist washed out detail. They eased towards the corner of the split-rail fence, hoping to avoid motion sensors. So far, they had alerted no one. The thirty meters seemed like a football field.

Lisa and Charlie matched Danny's pace. Lisa remembered when an alien protective aura escorted her home. She glanced skyward in hope. All remained quiet. They closed the gap to five meters and then ran.

The robot dog rounded the southwest corner of the house and turned towards the fugitives. Its motion sensors and the camera zoomed in on the three figures. The inbuilt AI processed the facial data and caused some hesitation. It found Danny Ringwald listed as a friend. The machine only reacted when it processed Charlie and Lisa and analyzed the direction all were taking. As it gave the alert, dozens of fireflies swarmed the device's sensors, effectively blinding it. Danny leapt over the fence and the others followed with surprising ease for a couple of middle-aged non-athletes. They reached the gloom of the scrub.

"Ouch," Lisa whispered as a bare birch twig slapped her face. The darkness now became an enemy and slowed them.

The command controller received the alert, but the robot was not sending new images or data. This cause a delay as she ran the data backwards to find what had triggered the alarm.

A klaxon shrilled. Danny tried to hurry, but he had not thought of a flashlight. The beeper that connected Danny with the robot alerts buzzed in his pocket. The device weighed heavily.

All the robotic guards hurried to the fence. Engines roared from the farmyard, accompanied by shouting.

"Hurry," Danny stumbled forward. They had crossed the overgrown roadway and into the denser trees of the river valley. Danny knew the team at the farm had a search protocol, but he hoped speed would take them further than the agents would expect. Powerful hand lights raised shadows behind them. The well-trained field operatives would find their trail. Vader raced out the farm lane and down the road opposite the point of escape. It turned into the bush, tracing the careless path of the fugitives.

Danny's eyes adjusted to the darkness to reveal a faint light at his feet. A few fireflies flitted back and forth and illuminated fallen branches and rough spots. Several others appeared through the branches at eye level.

This helps, he thought, *but it still doesn't tell us where to go.*

"This way," Lisa whispered, and headed at right angles to the road, "there's a road about a half-mile ahead."

How do I know that?

She headed off, certain of her direction, and the fireflies seemed to agree. Even the general deferred to her lead.

"There shouldn't be fireflies in October," Charlie tried to keep up.

"They aren't fireflies," Lisa said. "I found one on my windowsill. They are mechanical, alien."

"I'm glad you two are at least human and normal," Danny said.

"Well, Charlie's human. I have alien blood in me, but not enough. The combination wasn't right. Charlie's and my genes made Ellie."

The device in Danny's pocket was now a continuous squeal.

Vader stuck to the trail left by the trio. Its sensors received regular infrared signals as breaks in the cover exposed Charlie's back. The jumble of branches prevented a laser lock. Underbrush hindered Vader as much as the fugitives. The humans followed Vader while other robots spread out.

Charlie saw a bright red dot appear to his right on a tree trunk. A 9 mm bullet followed, made a smacking sound, and ricocheted away.

"Hurry, they're shooting." They ducked lower.

"I think they forgot they wanted live hostages," Danny gasped, "though I don't think they care about me." His buzzer howled.

Greg ran in pursuit. They did not close in fast enough. He keyed his communicator. "Com, trigger Ringwald's buzzer."

Danny feared the buzzer was leading the pack to them. He threw it onto the bush on the run. In the command centre, the operator flipped a safety and pushed a blue button.

Trees subdued the bright flash and bang.

A sudden shrill wailing came from behind, uncomfortably close.

"That killer robot has a sonic weapon to scare us. Ignore it." Danny tried to follow his advice as he struggled against the natural barriers.

"Ouch," Lisa cried. Her ankle had twisted on a root. Adrenaline overcame the instant pain, but she slowed slightly with a limp.

"Hurry... faster..." Danny pushed her forward. The wailing closed. More red dots appeared on trees, but no more bullets.

"Maybe we should spread out... give them more tracks." Charlie tried to avoid stumbling into Danny.

"No time," Danny gasped. He had not seen a base gym in a long time.

Lisa burst from the trees onto a maintained roadway. The sounds of pursuit grew louder. Wailing came from close by in the trees.

"What now? We can't outrun them on the road."

"Head that way," Danny pointed up the road to the faint glow from Goderich, but too far away.

They had covered a hundred meters up in a slight grade when the first of the trackers rushed from the woods behind them. A spotlight cast shadows ahead of them. Vader's red dot found Danny, but no shot came.

"Stop, get on the ground..." Danny recognized Greg's voice. He knew bullets would follow and resigned himself to his fate.

Suddenly, just up the hill, a vehicle's lights flared, high beams blinded them, but also blinded the group rushing up behind. The car silently hurtled forward, and the doors swung open.

"Hop in Nana and Papa, you too, General," RoH smiled from the driver's window of Charlie's Martian X.

The doors slammed shut and the self-drive backed the car at high speed up the hill and away from the American agents. The pop of guns filled the night, but the soft-nosed ammunition committed suicide on the front panel of the vanishing car. At the top of the grade, RoH yanked the steering yoke. The Martian X did a reverse skid turn to face away from the danger. A few bright tracer bullets flashed overhead and curved silently into the bush. One of Vader's rockets flashed past. Its infrared sensor could not lock onto the electric vehicle. Fireworks erupted in the forest.

"This is fun," RoH laughed. She deactivated the Hollywood Stunt Mode and they rushed towards the paved county road.

The Martian X sped down the dark road towards the glow from Goderich.

"We can't go to my place," Charlie said. "That's the first place they'll search."

"All planned, Papa," RoH said. "Grandmother and the general are going to stay with our friend Ros from the bookstore. Kerri has agreed to let you stay at her apartment. You desperados will have to lie low for a bit."

RoH had spent some time watching Ros' collection of old movies. She had longed to try out some of the jargon. So far, she had found no one to call a dirty rat. Thanks to her mother, RoH's ability to see people as dandelions in need of loving blinded her for dirty rats.

"How did Ros get involved?"

"One day, Papa, you can ask her. You recruited her," RoH smirked. She had not originally planned it all, but with her grandmother and Danny taking the last space at Ros' house, RoH had thought of the idea of putting her Papa and Kerri close together. RoH knew the woman's heart, but Papa would have to realize that and decide. Kerri had eagerly agreed.

You can't grow a crop if you don't plant a seed, Mother always said.

On a starship, there was little chance truly to experience that. Now on Earth, surrounded by the unfettered frenzy of life, RoH understood the loving wisdom in Ellie's heart.

Oh, Mother, we need to educate both humans and our star family. Father is such a...

Now, now RoH, just say stuck in his ways. RoH, it will be easier to draw him and the people to empathy than to lead humans to the same.

Well, he is, compared to you, Nana and Papa.

Don't pout, dear. Once our star family decides on the rightness of a thing, it spreads through all. Humans are so used to dividing themselves; fighting for survival, that they are afraid of letting their guard down.

Mother, we need to make them feel sure of survival, so they stop fighting.

That's the big step, my love, the big step... good night.

Her mother always gave RoH contentment. The Martian X eased to a stop at Ros' house.

***

"Wait," Jimmy said and peered over a hedge. A desolate but well-lit street crossed their path. "It's deserted, so far, and we need to use the streets. The riverbank is too rough, and that was the last path."

Ellie stared down the roadway towards the promise of the countryside.

"Wait a minute," she said and pulled Jimmy back. A police car crept down the street but did not stop. They watched it turn the next corner and move away.

"It's safe now," Ellie stepped onto the sidewalk. "Hurry..."

A block down, a large dog growled and leapt out of the darkness, teeth bared. Jimmy recoiled. The animal growled again and barked a throaty, menacing sound. It stalked towards them. Ellie stepped forward and extended her hand. The dog abruptly sat, wagged its tail, and whined.

"Nice pooch." Ellie rubbed the dog's ears and then its chest. "Shoo," she said, and the beast scurried into the darkness.

"I'm impressed," Jimmy said.

"I did something similar with an armed man when I was ten years old. Most animals and humans just want a friendly hand."

They hurried on. An hour later, broken several times by urgent scurrying for cover and more barking dogs, Ellie and Jimmy entered a new neighbourhood where the streets had no pedestrian walkways. After midnight, and in a chilling rain, the world became quiet. They stopped in a scrub-covered building lot while Jimmy consulted the map app on his cell.

"Jimmy, what did you plan to be doing before I flipped your life?"

The little screen illuminated Jimmy's face.

"To be the most wanted investigative reporter in Ottawa, and the most un-wanted by politicians," he laughed. "Now, I'm just the most wanted."

"If our plan works," Ellie said, "you will be one of the most wanted reporters around. You and Bobby Briscoe will have the entire story, and hopefully, we will let you tell it."

"What happens if you decide you want to keep it quiet?"

"None of you will remember it," Ellie smiled.

"I don't like that," Jimmy muttered.

"With the Clavette opportunity, I think the chance of that is zero."

"Clavette, is that comet about to wipe out Mars, isn't it?"

"Yes, and no," Ellie said. "We plan to terra form Mars, sort of. Even for us, it's an experiment. The situation out there is rare, and we need more data to understand it. Humans there are an inconvenience but also an opportunity. It will be a spectacular show."

"That'd be something to see."

"I can arrange for you to video it."

Jimmy smiled. "We have to go down the next street to the right to Highway 7 and follow that. It will be more dangerous, and we will do a lot of hiding in the ditch. The advantage is that no important people live in places like this, so there won't be many cops."

When they reached the main road, traffic passed more frequently, but there were no police. Ellie watched Jimmy, shivering but pressing on at a steady pace into the night. They would soon need to rest.

Ellie and Jimmy found an isolated barn with some old straw in the loft in the middle of a field, out of the built-up area. They could rest. Ellie closed her eyes, happy that her mother and father had reached safety.

Chapter Twenty-seven

Down the rabbit hole

Mandy Sternberg stared through the large window at the bleak landscape. A slight swirl of red dust, born on a weak Martian wind, crossed in front of a tracked digger. The robotic machine piled loose dirt and rock on top of an access port. They were sealing these, hoping whatever happened when Clavette hit, it would protect the settlement in their underground tunnels. Jorge DeSantos shared the depressing view. Only a month before, this view had given them joy.

"Mandy, it won't be enough," Jorge's Texas accent added finality.

"I know," she frowned, "but we have to try or we'll all be suicidal."

"Some already are," Jorge said, "but at least they're still alive."

"How is the tunnelling going?" Mandy wanted to focus on doing, not grieving their likely deaths.

"The main boring machine is making about twenty meters a day. It is now on the up angle. Machine 2 has reached the level near the point the two will meet. Once enlarged, that safety bunker will hold about two hundred."

"We moved most vital equipment to deeper levels, but we can't move the oxygen generators." Mandy tried not to sound defeated. Their odds of survival remained about zero.

"The 3-D printer has built about half of the regocrete shroud for the oxygen unit. We aren't sure we can complete it before impact."

The western settlement occupied a complex of surface structures and an expanding network of deeper tunnels on the western edge of Isidis Planitia. In Earth documents, and its radio call sign, it was IP-1. To the inhabitants, because of its mostly underground nature, it was The Warren, although usage had reduced that to simply Warren or "the rabbit hole".

On the surface, Warren resembled a salvage yard populated by gleaming stainless steel spacecraft standing proud. Many ships were one-way units, one serving as the oxygen production component, with the others as storage tanks. Amid the crisis, standing was all that the ships could do. They had not made enough fuel to put over two vessels into low Mars orbit. None could get to a safer altitude. Even if they could, they would only lift a few hundred to safety. No one had planned to have all the settlers leave. Only a handful had intended to leave at all.

Mounds of dirt-covered work structures mingled with various bits of electrified construction equipment. A fleet of wheeled transports, large enough to carry four people in suits and a tonne of material, moved constantly inside the two-kilometre radius of the base. Only two had pressurized cabins for emergency use. They had intended, before Clavette raised its fist, that they would build a satellite community a few kilometres away. The life-support units would carry plants and other sensitive material between the sites until they bored an underground connection.

In its first few years of operation, a council governed a thousand residents, but a team and committee structure ensured input and consensus on everything but emergency decisions. Co-chairs had to be a man and a woman, and neither had absolute authority. At the beginning of the Martian settlement project, the Earth-based patrons of governments and industry designed an elaborate corporate administrative structure. Potential settlers balked at that authoritarian approach and eventually the need to increase recruitment changed it to a series of recommendations. Still, the settlers held a weak position as long as IP-1 depended upon supplies from Earth. Residents saw self-sufficiency as the road to political independence, but that lay in the future. They still had to work within the structured plan, and the earthbound managers' constant interference. Earth control, limited by the speed of light, required flexibility for emergencies. The urgency of survival on this un welcoming planet dictated everything.

"How are the Ruskies and Chinese doing?" Mandy leaned forward to glimpse the oxygen site almost out of view past the port's frame. The bulk of the ship that contained the oxygen generator poked above the rising regolith-printed enclosure and cast a garish shadow onto the red dirt.

The joint Chinese-Russian complex held only vanguard workers, sent to establish an infrastructure for reinforcements due on the next transfer. A joint civilian organization on Earth nominally oversaw the base, but in reality, it ran like a military operation. It had no military capability, but those on the Martian surface had little decision-making authority.

Contrary to Earth politics, every resident of Mars knew they were all in it together. It did not matter if you were on the wrong side of Earthly divides.

Residents applied the term "settlement" for Warren while Earthbound overseers said, "colony". Everyone in the settlement saw each other as a Martian, and although every migrant perhaps had a unique concept of what that meant, all knew that they had to support one another first. It was a rule that humans followed in Earth's polar regions, deserts and oceans. Help at hand was always better than help on its way from a distant place. Because of this, the settlements at Isidis Planitia and Arcadia Planitia had developed back-channel communications eluding Earthbound handlers.

"They are more exposed," Jorge said. "They have no boring equipment and can't get below the surface."

"Could they come here?" Mandy knew the answer.

"Arcadia Planitia sits on the other side of the volcanoes and the ridge. Even on the flat, it's a long way, but they have no way to fly over or drive through the rough stuff."

"They have return fuel capability. Can they get back to Earth?"

"It's the wrong part of the orbital phase. Sandra is in frequent touch with them. They are thinking of getting to Demos, to the site of the international astronomical observatory."

"No one has built that yet. There are several one-ways there with building material and gear waiting for the next Earth transfer."

"The cargo ships have a lot of life support, mainly oxygen and food. The radiation problem makes it unlikely they could survive the ten months until the next orbital opportunity, then the six months for rescue ships to arrive and then another two years before they could return to Earth. They would all likely be dead long before that."

"So will we," Mandy turned towards the window and fought the tears.

The cries of children announced an outing from the crèche. Three youngsters, about six years old, bounced into the viewing lounge. The lower Martian gravity emphasized their excitement. These youngsters held the record for the youngest people to leave Earth. A smiling young woman followed with a baby in her arms.

Two months old, Mandy knew, *our first-born real Martian.*

Some technical types had wanted to name the baby "Primo", but an ex-Canadian Martian said that sounded like a soup brand. In the end, the mother named the wee one "Hope".

"Hi, Sam," Mandy greeted the caregiver. "These guys are cheerful."

"Ignorance is bliss." Samantha frowned, wiped a tear, and forced a smile. "I wanted them to get lots of time here before..."

Her voice trailed off.

"Before we have to stay deep," Jorge added, as if it had always been the plan. "It will be some time before they can come here again after that."

His optimism fell flat.

Jorge swept two of the children into his arms and stepped towards the viewing window. Mandy took the other's hand. The three adults silently stared out at the Martian landscape. The little ones struggled for freedom.

Far away from the drama on Earth and Mars, a fleet of interstellar ships, still past the orbit of Jupiter, arced under the solar pole and headed to the inner planets. While a few of these were of the smaller class that had brought Ellie and RoH home and watched over them, most of the newcomers were massive.

One immense vessel detached and headed to rendezvous with Clavette. The rest of the oversized ships slid into the asteroid belt, where they monitored Mars in relative obscurity. The more agile vessels swarmed towards Earth.

Chapter Twenty-eight

A barn-raising at 'Roswell North'

Greg recalled his forces. He found little comfort that this time everyone returned with him, but their eyes told it all. Morale had hit the bottom. Never, in his experience of victories and defeats, had he seen such despondency. Greg had been angry with Ringwald for losing the agents. Now, he had lost the general and the prisoners.

Greg had not risen to the top by inaction. At daybreak, he dispatched two agents to town to ferret out where the escapees might have gone. Since a car had been waiting for them, Greg assumed locals must be involved. The upsetting reality occurred to him he might have to abandon the farm. Greg still believed in the agency's power and the United States and could not admit that the aliens held all the advantage.

He made one more move. His secretary at Belvoir was an agent, likely a Russian. She had a partner at NAAP. He could deal with that.

Agent Mendez glanced over his shoulder, down the spacious third-floor hallway of the apartment building. His team gripped carbines, short ugly weapons for close fighting in confined spaces. Sasha pressed close behind. Her hand gripped a flash bang, ready if needed.

Mendez signalled. The building manager ducked into the stairwell. Mendez did not want a civilian caught in any crossfire. The CIA had warned that these people might be armed Russian agents. Mendez banged on the door to apartment 312. The door reverberated from the butt of his Glock. He waited. The hallway became deathly quiet. He struck again, but nothing. They had staged the raid early, as usual, to catch suspects sleepy and confused. A neighbour opened their door and then ducked back inside as they saw the hallway filled with gunmen.

In deference to the pleading of the manager, Mendez had changed the raid from a "no-knock" with a battering ram and slipped the manager's key card into the lock slot. He depressed the handle, giving the door a firm push inwards... silence. The lights were off. He extended a small mirror mounted on a pole. Faint morning light from curtained windows, out of sight beyond the foyer, revealed little. Mendez patted his body armour, took a deep breath, and plunged into the gloom. Sasha followed, the pin pulled from her flash-bang and her thumb firmly on the spring trigger. Even if bullets hit her and Mendez, the occupants would suffer a shock. Both agents stayed on their feet, trained to stay low but only to go down if someone fired at them. Like any athlete, being on your feet would leave you with the most options. A third agent hurried, gun levelled, to the right, into the small kitchen space. Mendez and Sasha dashed left into the living area. A short whistle blast brought reinforcements that spilled towards the bedrooms. The occupants were not home.

"Well, where are they?" Mendez holstered his weapon as Sasha stowed the explosive.

"Maybe they are at work. They could have had a gang here," Sasha smiled, justifying by-the-book caution. "We didn't want dead friends."

"Get the manager." As the lead, Mendez would do the investigating. Sasha became his extra eyes and she would make the notes. People videoed and photographed. They documented how it looked before the search.

It might be messy, but not destroyed, Mendez mused. *Investigation and ransack are two different things.*

Not that ransacking did not happen. Often, when raiding some political radicals or other punk types, he and others found satisfaction in a little direct judgement and punishment, especially if they did not intend to pursue charges. Trashing a place and bouncing jerks off walls was fun.

An hour later, Mendez accepted the apartment held no clues; in fact, it held nothing but perfectly arranged furniture. He saw no dust, except now as the team tried to find prints. The refrigerator stored no food, nor did the cupboards. He wondered how a couple of glorified secretaries could afford this place, considering the modest and highly mortgaged small house he and his family enjoyed in Fredericksburg.

The apartment manager stood with Mendez and Sasha in the little kitchen.

"The women leased the place in June, two years ago." The man consulted his notes. "They signed as Elliana Bruna and Daphne DuMaurier, good references and jobs, and they paid the rent on time. I only saw them a few times. Ask the neighbours about them."

Mendez dispatched people to knock on doors. Most residents should be home this early in the morning.

"June, two years ago," Sasha said. She stared at a calendar from a flower shop in Arlington, suggesting it was still June of that year. "I don't think anyone has lived here."

They found no neighbour who had talked to the women.

"The whole thing gives me the creeps," Mendez said to Sasha as they doffed their gear at the tactical van. "It's like they are ghosts, but they always went to work."

"I had the feeling someone watched us all the time we were in there." Sasha tried to laugh it off.

"You watch old episodes of the X-files, don't you?"

When Mendez's report reached Greg, he shared the neck-crawling spookiness that the FBI agent felt.

Why would the Russians be interested in NAAP and the CIA alien projects?

Elliana had not reported for work and that confused Liz and Ted. She had never missed a day and had not called in. To add to the morning's mystery, a car with two occupants lingered in the parking lot opposite the main entrance. The scientists had become cautious since Siglinde's party and the strange vehicle smelled FBI.

"At least we know the Feds don't have her." Ted laughed.

"Why would the FBI want her, or any of us?" Liz peeked out the window. The pair in the car had given her more than a once over as she walked into work. She had felt violated and thought they might be a couple of perverts, or racists, wondering what a black woman would do at a high-tech government facility. Now that Ted had mentioned the FBI, they might have been deciding if she was their target.

Just after 9 AM, a young woman walked through the doorway at FBI headquarters on Pennsylvania Avenue in Washington.

"Good morning, I'm Elliana Bruna. I think you are looking for me."

***

In a barn southwest of Ottawa, Jimmy and Ellie watched a cold mist fall. Jimmy felt depressed and hungry, but Ellie smiled cheerfully.

"Don't worry, Jimmy, we will eat soon." She glanced at the ominous sky as if searching for sunshine. The clouds were a solid grey.

"You always know what's on my mind," Jimmy said. He had not yet admitted to Ellie's abilities. "I guess my stomach rumble tells on me."

"Jimmy," Ellie took his hand, "you and Bobby Briscoe have an important job. Bobby is getting you a camera. You two will not only document it all, but will produce the big show in about two months."

"We have to get out of here and have breakfast first," Jimmy laughed. The stress since his arrest had hit him.

As if to worry Jimmy more, the faint barking of dogs drifted across the field, hurrying closer.

"What the..." Jimmy frowned.

"The police have trailed us," Ellie seemed calm. "They are good and pieced together the odd reports of prowlers and barking dog noise complaints along our path. The dogs guided them the last few kilometres."

Ellie glanced skyward once more, and a smile replaced her frown.

"Jimmy, don't fear what is going to happen next. You'll be in no danger."

"I don't like dogs much," Jimmy stared towards the city and could make out distant dark shadows of people, and the barking grew louder.

"I didn't mean the dogs," Ellie laughed, "but we need to let them get close enough to see the show. Do you remember Dow's Lake that night?"

Jimmy shuddered at the thought of riding the pillar of purple light.

"You did it before, getting out of jail, but you were asleep. Think of it as less scary but as thrilling as a roller-coaster ride, and it will be free. For a human, you'll have collected a lot of frequent flier points."

The dogs and their police handlers left the concession road and headed directly towards the barn following the fugitives' tracks in the grass. Elli and Jimmy retreated into the barn.

The trackers stopped, waiting as a convoy of vehicles arrived and disgorged the tactical squad. Someone had decided that two unarmed fugitives were dangerous. A thin but continuous line of police, rifles ready, encircled the barn. Everything stopped, as if no one wanted to approach.

Ellie closed the door and led Jimmy to the centre of the barn.

"We know you're in there. Come out with your hands up."

"Jeeze," Jimmy's laughter masked nausea, "I've seen that movie."

Ellie held up a hand and Jimmy fell silent.

Outside, a hand signal passed around the circle. The police began a slow advance. Those with riot shields felt they had to bang them. It reverberated through the hollowness of the barn. The circle closed to a hundred meters and stopped. A bullhorn repeated, "Come out with..." The voice trailed off.

Above the barn, the clouds parted with a thunder roll and revealed a large metallic object above the opening. A shaft of purple light shot towards the barn. In an instant, the roof exploded and fountained debris in a wide arc. Large ballistic pieces forced the cops to scatter.

The shaft of purple brightened. Ellie took Jimmy's hand.

"If I didn't know better, I would think my daughter organized this show," Ellie shouted above the cacophony of the falling roof and an undefinable sound from the purple glow. "She has a weakness for fun and drama, but it's her father doing this. Maybe he learned from her."

Jimmy felt nothing, but one instant he saw the dank old barn with a hole in the roof receding below, and the next a luminous grey space embraced him. Ellie still held his hand, comforting.

"Did we just get beamed up?" His calmness surprised Jimmy.

"Not like your science fiction stuff," Ellie said. "That system is unworkable. It's fiction. No, we just use simple anti-gravity. The light beam results from the life support system and the disruption of the atmosphere because of the energy involved. The barn roof had to go to let us out, just like your cell window, to swap the aircrew for you."

"Simple anti-gravity," Jimmy laughed and brushed bits of old straw from his sleeves, "as if you do it all the time."

"We do," Ellie squeezed his hand, "and how we travel the stars. It took many thousands of your years to figure it out. It's all in the head."

Ellie brushed splinters from Jimmy's hair. "You humans will discover it one day, we hope."

When Ellie looked around, she did not see Jimmy's comforting cocoon, but several of the ship's company surrounded them, giving their equivalent of a smile.

Great grandfather, you put on a show.

Softening up the Earthlings, they need to get used to us, so they won't fear. This is nothing compared to the coming show on New Year's Eve.

Do you think blowing up a barn will calm them?

Ellie felt the laugh from her grandfather, and somewhere from RoH's father. It was this un-alien-like sense of humour that helped bond him with Ellie's great-grandmother.

"Can you get Liz and Dawn out?" Jimmy asked.

"They're okay for now. It will happen when the time is right."

Mother?

We are coming now, love.

The grey comfort dissolved into Ros' normal Canadian living room.

In the farm field, body cameras and cell phones had recorded the event. The spectacle confused the police. A neighbour called the fire department. Sirens announced the local volunteer brigade; however, there was no fire. Despite the energy involved in raising the roof, it had not generated enough heat to char the wood or old straw.

"What the hell happened? Where's the fire? Why are you circling that barn?" The fire captain glared at the Mountie in charge of the operation.

"We were told we were chasing Russian spies, not... not..." The cop's voice trailed off.

The firefighter drew his conclusions.

The firefighters were local folks who would not be easy to keep from talking. The neighbour had videoed the affair from the ERT convoy to the exploding barn. They received their minutes of fame by selling the recording. It would become more awkward when the barn's owner filed an insurance claim and threatened to sue the RCMP.

By Halloween, the owner had established a lucrative business catering to the flood of gawkers. A makeshift sign at the gate labelled it "Roswell North". For a fee, tourists could park in the pasture and for another ticket, take a tour through the barn, watch the video and listen to the fire chief or the neighbour tell exaggerated stories of the event. Vendors rented space. In a few weeks, before winter closed in, the damaged barn generated more profit than the field had delivered in the many generations as a family farm.

Chapter Twenty nine

Predator or Prey

Charlie woke to the smell of bacon frying. It did not reassure him. Maybe he had been dreaming. The agents at the farm preferred bacon and eggs every morning. When he raised his head from the couch and opened his eyes; however, he saw unfamiliar surroundings. Charlie had never been to Kerri's apartment.

"Glad to see you awake," Kerri's voice cheered and reassured. Charlie felt safe for the first time in days. Then he remembered the narrow escape.

"Hi," Charlie said, uncertain of the situation, "sorry to be a surprise guest. My granddaughter decided this."

"I'm glad she did," Kerri's voice carried her love, "I've wanted to invite you for years."

"Not for a sleep-over," Charlie laughed.

Kerri said nothing.

The skillet snapped and sizzled and the toaster pop filled the silence.

"Come and get it," Kerri placed the plates onto the counter with mugs of coffee. They sat on high stools on opposite sides. Silence returned.

Charlie ate with relish. Except for the pea-meal bacon, this meal imitated the ones at the farm. Somehow, Charlie felt it tasted better.

Kerri toyed with her food. Her eyes revealed a deeper uncertainty. She spoke, "Everyone but you know how I feel about you, Charlie."

Charlie paused, Canadian bacon suspended between plate and lips.

"I think I know," he said. "I'm a social misfit, but I'm not dead."

He looked into Kerri's eyes. "I feel the same way."

"Why..." she began, but Charlie held up his hand.

"Let me finish. I could never admit it. How could I tell you? You don't know about my part alien daughter. How could I tell you about the part alien woman in Seattle whom the aliens had mated to me? My finding love would mean I had given up hope of Ellie's return."

"Ellie is back," Kerri said, "and I know it all, from RoH and Ellie."

"Ellie is back," Charlie replied and reached across the counter to take Kerri's hand. "Ellie is back."

"... and now..." Kerri asked.

"I love you, Kerri, but let's take it slow," Charlie squeezed her fingers. "I almost don't dare hope. It is uncertain she is staying."

"Slow..." Kerrie agreed. "Oh, look. I have to be at work, but you just asked, didn't you?" Kerri said.

"Yes, I just asked."

"Yes," whispered Kerri, "yes... yes... so eat."

Instead, forgetting the food, Charlie walked around the island and pulled Kerri to him. The intense embrace lingered.

"I'm coming to the plant with you," Charlie held her at arm's length, hands gripping both her shoulders. "I want to get some stuff."

"You can't stay there," Kerri said. "RoH said they will look for you along with Lisa and the General."

"I'll get Francis to drive me back in a work van. Be home on time."

"Don't let Francis know you're staying here. The fewer, the better."

The second kiss was equally intense, neither wanting to break contact.

***

"Ms. Bruna, tell us, who is your Russian contact?"

"I don't work for the Russians; I work for NAAP. The Russians are worse than you guys, if that's possible."

"We both know that isn't true," the FBI interrogator scowled at Elliana. "How can you compare us to the Russians?"

"If there is another truth, it's one you haven't even thought of."

"Ah-ha, so it's the Chinese you are working for." Backing his subject into a corner pleased the agent.

"Wrong again," Elliana smiled, "the Chinese have the American disease. They are more vicious, but they know history better."

"You aren't scoring any points, young lady."

"I don't need points. This isn't a football game."

"Damn right, it's no game."

"So, what is that other truth?" The agent retreated and frowned. They had allowed the subject to control the discussion.

"Who do I work for?" Elliana relaxed in the uncomfortable chair. The handcuffs squeezed her wrists. She eased the discomfort.

"Don't play games." The agent stifled a shout.

"I work for NAAP," Elliana repeated. "That tells you everything."

"You're running around in circles," a folder slapped onto the desk.

"We aren't in the same race," Elliana sighed. "You aren't even on the same track."

"Tell me about Daphne DuMaurier," he tried something different.

"Oh, Daisy is my roommate. We share the expenses."

"You don't even live there," he consulted the file. "You haven't changed the wall calendar from the day you took the place."

"We like the picture," Elliana smirked, despite everything.

"Of flowers," he snapped.

"We like flowers. I know someone who especially likes dandelions."

"You won't be free if you keep this up," he sputtered.

"It isn't time for me to be free," Elliana said, "but when it is, I'll be gone. My purpose is to be here with you nice folks, and I like the food."

The exasperated agent stood, gathered up his papers and ignored his half-eaten doughnut. "I always found you, women, to be mice in these situations. You're different."

"Yes... different... something else..." Elliana flashed a knowing look.

"I think I'll talk to your workmates, if they even tell the truth. Egg-heads aren't trustworthy."

His hand reached for the door handle.

"Liz and Ted are honest workers for the government," Elliana said. "My boss is in Canada and won't be coming back soon."

"We'll order her back,"

"Maybe you can get those CIA agents in Goderich to find her."

He opened the door and left. Elliana handed her handcuffs to the guard, who came to escort her back to the cell.

***

A black SUV nosed into a parking spot in front of the post office. Two agents got out; a man wore a Washington Nationals baseball windbreaker; the woman had a tailored safari jacket with a Yellowstone Park breast patch. Their matching black baseball caps weakened their attempt to blend in. The effect made them appear as off-duty SWAT team members on a date; however, once they spoke, any local would know them as Americans.

"Where do we start?" The man asked.

"The gossips hang out in the coffee shops and bars."

They headed around the ring of the town square and soon arrived at a chic bistro serving designer hot drinks and home-baked pastry. The visitors sat at a table near the middle of the space. Other customers, a rather upscale mix of shopkeepers and legal types from the courthouse in the square, chatted within earshot. While the food satisfied them, they heard nothing useful, although gossip had it that the mayor had a mistress.

After two hours of poking into stores to ask discrete questions, the pair ended up at the Bedford Tap Room. It seemed a good place for lunch and perhaps the early drinkers would have loose tongues.

"I saw Charlie Keys at the factory this morning. I was picking up the garbage dumpster. He usually arrives then, but he was a no-show for a week or more. I bet the aliens had him."

The men's voices struggled through the noise of the bar. A reporter sat with the workers and the CIA agents watched him scribbling notes. They typed their summary on their cells. Even though they waited until the workers left, the men added nothing more that was useful.

The agents left the Bedford and followed the curve of the square to their vehicle. Unnoticed by the pair, an older woman and a little girl, bundled against the October chill, sat on the bench in front of the bank.

"You are sad today, Emily."

"Christmas is coming and I won't see my family. I can barely afford to send them anything."

"Won't they come to visit?"

"I only have a small place, and can't afford dinner. They can't come."

RoH took Emily's hand.

"Invite them for New Year's Eve," RoH stared at Emily. "I will help you do it. Don't worry about money. My grandfather will pay."

"You can't do that. I can't..."

"Shhh," RoH smiled. "You deserve to see your grand kids. There will be excitement here on New Year's Eve."

RoH's eyes narrowed and focused on the agents rounding the corner.

"I must go, Emily. I'll see you soon and we will plan it all."

Emily sighed at losing the joy of being with the girl and this new, confusing longing RoH had raised. She watched RoH rush through the middle of the square, skirting the courthouse towards Hobo Books and Charlie's Martin X.

Mother, the bad guys are trying to capture grandfather at work.

He'll be okay, sweetie. They might kidnap Kerri and Mike.

Just act if necessary. Your father is near if you need help.

"Greg, Charlie Keys is at work. We're going there to stake it out."

The SUV pulled away from the post office.

"Okay, wait there for us. I'm bringing a squad. We'll get him back."

The CIA agents paid no attention to the rental van in the corner of the parking lot. In the same manner, a Hammersmith Inc. van did not attract their attention as it left the facility.

Charlie's appearance in his office had occupied the NAAP agents in the rental. They did not see the dark SUV roll in and park near the gate. Keys had left the office in a company vehicle and the NAAP agents made sure that their video reached Virginia.

A few minutes later, a Martin X drove in and disappeared to the back near the receiving door. They notified Siglinde.

"Don't worry about the car," Siglinde said. "I'm on my way to London. Keep watching Keys' office, record everything."

Siglinde's agents settled in for more boredom. They did not catch the tone in Siglinde's voice, as if she expected something to happen.

Just after Charlie's Martin X arrived, three more black SUVs raced through the gate and to the front entrance. A dozen figures leapt from the vehicles and rushed to the office doors. NAAP binoculars revealed they carried assault rifles, and all wore body armour.

"Who the hell are those guys? Are they Canadian cops?"

"Siglinde, a SWAT team went into Key's building."

"The CIA has been interfering with our work. That is likely them. Just keep recording. They are dangerous, even to us." Siglinde regretted not having briefed her team on the Ringwald conspiracy.

RoH leapt from the car and hurried through the receiving door.

"Who are you, little girl?" The burly receiver blocked her path.

"I have to see Mr. Hammersmith. It's an emergency." RoH tried to step around the man.

"Where is Charlie Keys?" Kerri looked up into the snout of a gun. The agent pushed into Kerri's cubicle and grabbed her arm. She winced in pain but froze beneath the surprise attack.

Two armed intruders seized Mike Hammersmith as he rushed from his office. The armed gang wore masks and black forage caps.

Kerri glanced towards Charlie's office, and Greg saw her.

"In there," he ordered and rushed, his handgun ready, through the doorway marked Keys.

Others dragged Kerri and Mike. They saw no one in the office.

RoH had no time to waste and her obstacle suddenly remembered some urgent paperwork he needed to find on his desk. She raced towards the stairs at the far end of the warehouse.

"Where's Keys?" Greg shouted at Mike.

"I don't know... haven't seen him in days." Mike honestly answered. Greg hit him hard in the stomach.

"Don't lie to me."

When Kerri saw the thug attacking her boss, she twisted away from her captor and grasped the closest weapon at hand, the three-hole punch on Charlie's desk. She swung it at Greg. The painful blow glanced off his right ear and onto his shoulder. Greg twisted and pulled the trigger.

The bullet hit Kerri near the heart, splintering a rib and coming to rest in the rib cage. Her face contorted in surprise and pain as her body twisted and landed heavily in front of Charlie's desk. Greg had just shot the one person who knew where Charlie was.

"No one hits me, bitch."

Mike lashed out in rage, but a glancing blow to the cheek from Greg's pistol barrel stunned him.

The viciousness astonished the NAAP agents in the van. They were technicians and investigators not trained for violence. One of Siglinde's operatives called 911.

RoH reached the top of the stairs, and as she pushed through the door, the intruders disappeared down the main stairway. Mike struggled against the dragging of his captors. RoH raced for the office.

"Oh, RoH," Kerri gasped, her voice weakening. "They wanted Charlie," she sobbed through the trickle of blood from her mouth. "They hit Mike. I... so... sorry..."

RoH sat on the floor and cradled Kerri's head in her lap.

"Shhh," RoH soothed, "Grandpa will be okay. All will be okay."

Kerri smiled, stared into RoH's tearful eyes, and then went limp. Her head twisted sideways. RoH gently stroked Kerri's hair and held her until the sound of people in the main lobby stirred her. The EMS and the OPP found Kerri's body in the abandoned offices.

A constable helped the funeral technician load the gurney with Kerri into the hearse.

"Larry, drop the paperwork in Clinton when you come back from the morgue in London."

The cop returned to the factory through the shipping door. The technician swung the driver's door wide and slipped behind the wheel.

"What..." he exclaimed.

"Drive to the A and W, Larry," RoH said from the passenger side. He obediently rolled the vehicle towards the fast-food restaurant.

"Larry, go have lunch," RoH said. "Take your time."

RoH slid into the driver's seat.

This can't be any harder to drive than that old tractor.

Father...

We have you, Âلإنط

I'm going to the edge of town where no one's around.

Larry spent a leisurely hour with a spicy chicken combo lunch, washed down by three double-doubles. While he ate, Larry watched the good-looking young man behind the counter, a hard worker who seemed to have a friendly, positive attitude. Larry dumped his garbage and felt he had to meet the youngster. Strangely, the image of a dandelion came to him.

"How long have you worked here... Rick?" Larry read the name on the young man's badge.

"About five weeks," Rick replied, and suspicion clouded his face. He constantly worried that his past would catch up to him. "I've only been in town a couple of months."

Larry handed Rick a business card.

"I'm Laurence," Larry said. "We're looking for a good person down at the funeral home, a general helper. I notice you are a decent worker. I bet you don't get enough hours to live on."

Rick grasped the card and stared. "No, but I take extra shifts."

"Drop into the home first thing tomorrow, say nine, and I'll introduce you to the boss. He'll decide. It'll only be minimum wage, but full time."

Larry left through the side door, climbed back into the empty hearse, and sped away. He parked in the funeral home garage and found his boss.

"Wasted my time," he scowled. "EMS took the body to London."

***

The convoy of SUVs sped from the factory. They headed directly out of town, intending to take the back way to the farm; however, the lead driver became confused in the maze of disrupted roads of the river valley and it took an hour to find the way. They finally turned into the dead-end with the late October sun slipping behind the trees. A black Martin X followed them just out of sight.

In the farmyard, Greg climbed from his vehicle and an agent pulled Mike Hammersmith from the opposite rear door. The view that met Greg startled him. All the technical people relaxed outside. One frolicked with a guard robot as if the thing were a real dog. Another robot lay at the feet of one woman. Its head cock up at her as if it had eyes to watch her. No one acted as if the boss and a war party had just arrived. Clouds of small black bugs flitted about the compound.

Instead of anger, Greg suddenly felt happy and relaxed. He wandered over to one tech.

"I see everything is under control," he said. "Carry on."

Five minutes after the raiding party returned, the Martin X quietly rolled down the lane on electric motors. RoH got out and surveyed the quiet scene. An agent wandered over; a cigarette dangled from his mouth.

"Hello, little girl. Shouldn't you be in school?"

"Everyone seems to think I should be in school," RoH laughed. "I'm here to collect Mr. Hammersmith."

Mike sat on the porch, stunned and grieving. He still feared for his own life. These people had murdered Kerri. That they now ignored him had not reduced his anguish. He had not thought of just walking away. Mike recognized RoH. Suddenly motivated, he leapt up and rushed across the yard.

"Get out of here, RoH… run," he shouted. "They murdered Kerri."

She waited for Mike to reach her. His cries had only stirred casual interest from the docile people scattered about the yard.

"Get in the car, Uncle Mike." RoH did not smile. Mike hurried around the Martian X and hopped in. RoH turned to the agent who had greeted her. His cigarette still protruded from his lips. He made no move to stop Mike and everyone seemed to enjoy the show.

"You shouldn't smoke," RoH said.

He looked at the cigarette in disgust and threw it aside. RoH swung the car around and they sped to the road.

"They'll come after us," Mike twisted to look out the back.

"No, they won't." RoH hit the little house icon on the touch screen and the Martin X set a course for Charlie Keys' house. "Greg thinks he's waiting for orders from Fort Belvoir. He told everyone else to relax until those orders arrive. They are waiting for whether they live or die."

Father...?

Not yet, Âﻹنط

The car turned onto the County Road and towards the setting sun.

Good, I couldn't do it, anyway.

Chapter Thirty

Hammer of doom

Jorge DeSantos watched the sunrise as it washed away the cold Martian night. His morning ritual had included standing in the viewing lounge and feeling the hopefulness of a new day. Since the hammer of Clavette had risen over their heads, the dawn signalled a tick towards doom. One less day to survive.

The daylight fought against the floodlights at the oxygen generator. Crews hurried non-stop to complete the protective shell that might keep the unit going. Two months remained until impact. It looked like they would finish the cocoon with time to spare, but The Warren faced a bigger issue than physical protection. The life-giving oxygen plant could not operate long if limited to sharing the power from the mini-reactors, not if all the other vital functions of life support remained functional. No one knew if any solar power would be available. The consensus said no. Jorge scowled at the thought and turned away from the window.

"I thought I would find you here," Mandy Sternberg came to Jorge's side. She held a mug, and from the aroma, Jorge knew it was real coffee from the Earth's supply. He looked longingly at the drink. Mandy noticed.

"No point in hoarding it," she smiled and sipped.

"That sounds defeatist," Jorge muttered with little conviction. He suffered the same feelings. "We have to keep going for the other's sake."

"Everyone but the littles understands the odds. There are a few nearing suicide, but Lammi thinks he can talk them out of it, and they will continue to work. Physical labour seems to help."

"Now that the boring machines have finished, we have lots of work in the shelter area."

"The planning meeting is in thirty ticks. The techs have a proposal on how to survive on ten percent less power."

"Yeah, I heard. I don't think it buys us more than a few months."

"Everyone wants to celebrate Candy Night, as normal. We might as well use up some treats, and we have all been working so hard, stressed, too. It will be good, especially for the kids."

Candy Night replaced the earthbound celebration of Halloween. Martin settlers changed the names of celebrations as a symbol of some independence. The significant holiday was "Arrival Day", on the anniversary of the landing of the first permanent settlers. Individuals were free to call the holidays what they wished and to celebrate as wanted. Settler selection had weeded out religiosity, but not faith. With the coming threat, many reverted to old sources of hope. The leaders knew that if Warren survived Clavette, they might face factionalism because of it. The issue did not worry. It seemed unlikely there would be a future to sort out.

The pair turned to the view port and stood in gloomy silence. Mandy pulled the sunshade over the curved PlastiGlas. In the opposite direction, the dawn light painted the distant hills red. Jorge took Mandy's hand.

Unseen by Earth or Mars, a large star ship settled onto the dust of Phobos, within sensor range of the surface.

In the region outside of Mercury's orbit, Clavette sped on to its rendezvous with destruction and slowing rapidly as it climbed away from the sun. Like a pilot fish following a shark, an alien craft kept pace.

***

"Siglinde, I have news," Ted's image filled her cell screen.

"I'm just sitting down to dinner. Is this going to upset my stomach?"

"Maybe you should swallow some magnesium oxide first," Ted laughed. "Is there any news that isn't a crisis these days?"

"So, what's the news?" Siglinde frowned at the menu.

"Your new notoriety as a flying saucer guru caught the attention of the President. He's pissed they left him out of the loop. He wants you to explain it to him. The media calling him a liar has embarrassed him. His flake got our new woman assistant in tears."

"What new woman?" Siglinde felt a pang of jealousy but was curious.

"Oh, you don't know. Elliana disappeared. We think the FBI has her."

Ted relayed the morning Elliana failed to report for work and the strange car out front that had upset Liz. The watchers had disappeared about ten that morning and there had been no replacement. Liz and Ted had just put the facts together and decided the FBI had arrested Elliana.

"I'll see what I can find out." Siglinde did not panic.

"Maybe you can ask the President," Ted sounded serious. "They have summoned you, the day after tomorrow, ten in the morning."

"If I don't show...?"

"They will shut us down. That would suit me. I'd rather be in Boston."

"Not without me." The words escaped Siglinde's self-censor.

"Sounds good to me," Ted said. "Try hard to annoy the big man."

"Is that the bad news?"

"Only if you think a couple of hours dealing with an idiot are worse than a comet killing a thousand people." Ted's upset came into his voice.

"You know I don't," Siglinde said. "What is the bad news there?"

"They confirmed Clavette's orbit, solid parameters. It's going to sub-orbital just as McCormick predicted. The path is more constrained than her first pass. It might skim the top of Olympus Mons." Siglinde tried to picture the relationships between the volcano and the location of the settlements.

"What do they mean by 'skimmed'?"

"Clavette is over 200 kilometres in diameter. They think they know where its centre of mass will be, but a couple of kilometres difference in radius means the difference between miss and gouge, a bounce or a slide. McCormick should change her first name to Cassandra. She thinks it's going to clip a kilometre or more off the top of the mountain. Planetary experts do not know what that means. The damned mountain might erupt."

"How does that path affect the settlements?"

"The first threat from an impactor in an atmosphere is heat radiation. Even an ice ball like Clavette will heat the surface to lethal temperatures up to a hundred kilometres away. It's going too fast to boil off enough ice to change that. The heat will incinerate everything flammable above the surface if unprotected. And then, even in the thin atmosphere, the shock wave will be huge, kilo if not mega-Pascals at the distance of IP-1."

"Bad..."

"The Martians have burrowed deeper and will probably survive that. No one can predict."

"The Chinese and Russians...?"

"They are on the surface. About 50 of them will be dead."

"The final impact will be on the far side, but likely that won't mean much. Mars is going to have a Clavette winter for some Earth years."

"I'm flying down tomorrow," Siglinde had to end the litany of doom. "Let's get together for dinner."

"Oh, that's good. I missed the original last supper."

"Shut up!"

Siglinde rang off. She made a call, not to Washington, but Ellie. Resolving Elliana's situation was more important. Ellie reassured her.

***

Elliana again sat in the uncomfortable chair in the interview room. As her inquisitors rambled question after question, she had only responded with the request for a lawyer, but knew that these people would not let her anywhere near a courtroom before they thought they had her. The session, like the dozen before this, had droned on with her remaining silent. As always, the interview ended with an outburst of frustrated swearing by the agents and her returning to a cell with only a bed, commode and chair. The video always showed her asleep between meals and the frequent sessions. The jailers called her "Sleeping Beauty".

One thing the FBI knew, Elliana Bruna did not exist. Bruna had a paper trail right back to a birth certificate, school records, and everything else associated with an American adult. However, before Elliana had gone to work for NAAP and rented the apartment, no human could remember her; retired teachers, neighbours or anyone else could not remember seeing Elliana Bruna. The same was true for Daphne DuMaurier. Outside of Fort Belvoir, not a single person could remember meeting her. Of course, the FBI had seen this before, with Soviet agents' ghost identities. These cases differed because, with the two women, the FBI could not accuse one person in any agency of abetting a foreign spy. They found "no small fish to fry".

***

Charlie Keys knew how to cook. The decades of living on his own required that or becoming a processed food casualty. He baked salmon in the oven and scalloped potatoes. Kerri would be home any minute. Tonight would be special. The door opened, and he looked expectantly.

"Hello, Father," Ellie stepped inside and gently closed the door. "I have some news you won't like. Kerri won't be coming home tonight. That smells delicious. Can we eat? Then you must leave here. I'll explain everything."

Ellie avoided mentioning the circumstances of Kerri's demise. She knew her father would not handle it well, and for everyone's sake, he needed to remain functional. Ellie loved him and did not want to break his heart and knew everything would work out well in the end. Unfortunately, she could not share that certainty. It hurt deeply that she could not soothe her father's anguish. The plan was too important.

They finished the meal, washed dishes, and prepared to leave.

"Make sure you leave nothing here for the police. The OPP will be here soon, likely in the morning, as they investigate Kerri. You disappeared when Danny Ringwald had you. You need to remain there."

"Where is there?"

"Our new friend, Siglinde Hilfreich, has rented a room in the hotel, beside the ones that NAAP is using. No one will link it to you."

"The chambermaid will know me. This is a small town."

"Don't worry, Dad. They just hired a new housekeeper named Daisy."

"I don't want to talk with anyone. Won't Hilfreich interrogate me?"

"She knows everything, Father, but you will want to talk with someone sometime. I know the thing with Kerri is hard. She loves you."

***

"Bobby, I have a message for you." Briscoe held his cell as he waited outside the Harmsworth factory for the OPP statement. "Quants Nedmar wants to meet you. He's that CBC Radio guy with the morning show."

"What does he want?" Bobby did not need to baby sit another reporter, and he had no interest in sharing the scoop with anyone but Jimmy.

"He said he wants to do in-depth stuff with the people connected to the alien story. He specifically mentioned Charlie Keys."

Bobby took Nedmar's number. He did not know where Keys might be, but Nedmar enjoyed a lot of respect; he did good person-on-person work. Bobby did not have time to interview everyone, especially minor characters like Keys. He thought Quantz might be useful and television and radio were different media.

The only contact Bobby had in what he had thought of as the "alien group" was Siglinde. He did not know how to connect with Charlie Keys, Ellie, or anyone else. After several attempts, Siglinde answered.

"I can't give you any information," Siglinde replied to his request. "I'll call Ellie and ask her to contact you. She's the focus of all this. If Ellie thinks it is okay, it will happen. Is this Nedmar guy trustworthy?"

"No idea, but he has a good rep."

"Maybe Ellie will scan him before he gets near her father. If the guy is not legitimate, she will know. I'll be in Washington tomorrow, but I hope to be back the day after."

***

Bobby ate while the London news played on the gigantic screen over the bar. Everyone stopped to listen to Bobby's report on Kerri's shooting. The studio had edited a bit out, but the gruesome details survived.

"They transported a deceased female to London for autopsy. We are withholding the name pending notification of next of kin."

Everyone in town knew who had died.

The OPP had shared one new bit of information. An anonymous person had called 911 and reported a gang of armed men rushing the Harmsworth factory. They appealed for the caller to come forward.

The bartender recognized Bobby and asked for an autograph. It took an hour and a free meal and beer before he could politely leave the place. He needed to call this Nedmar reporter.

The usual introductions and professional courtesies took a few minutes. It turned out Quantz had been four years ahead of him in school.

"Quantz, you won't get a room any closer than London. I have a two-bed suite in the Comfort Inn here; you can share the other bed until you find a better arrangement. I'll see you at about nine, room 210. I hope to find out where Charlie Keys is before you get here."

Bobby responded to a knock on his door at 8:30. Ellie smiled and walked in without invitation.

"Who is the man who wants to talk with my father?"

Quantz Nedmar found Bobby and Ellie waiting for him.

"Sorry, I'm late… finding a rental. Who are you?" He looked at Ellie.

"I'm Ellie Keys. I understand you want to interview my father."

Ellie stared at Nedmar for a few seconds and turned to Bobby.

"He's okay," she turned, "Mr. Nedmar, I'm going to discuss it with Father. If he agrees, I'll take you to him."

Ellie would convince Charlie. She wanted to distract him from his grieving, and Nedmar had empathy.

Chapter Thirty-one

Run, baby, run

Siglinde left the executive jet at Andrews Air Force Base. A government car waited on the apron, and soon she sat in a suite in the Coronet Hotel on Pennsylvania Avenue. She would walk to the White House in the morning. They had made the arrangements and had spared no expense. The suite had a formal reception lounge, two bedrooms, and an office. The Comfort Inn at Goderich seemed safer. Siglinde was certain they had bugged it.

Siglinde would call Ted while she ate. It might ensure privacy. A handsome couple left the suite next to hers. They nodded politely as if this woman at the elevator in the dowdy shirt and pants were below their place in society. Siglinde always wore trousers. They had pockets and kept her legs warm in winter. The pair pushed past onto the main floor and hurried around the corner to the lobby. Siglinde sauntered in the same direction, looking for the coffee shop. The couple whispered on the far side of the lobby.

The eatery far exceeded the status of the best restaurant in Goderich. Siglinde picked a table away from the few other patrons. Waiting for her food, she called Ted.

"I'm in Washington to see the big guy. I could find nothing on Elliana, but Ellie told me not to worry. No, we don't have time to meet and don't talk. I have little time." Siglinde watched a fit young man who might have been a lawyer or accountant chatting with the greeter. "We have to postpone our date. I'm going back to Canada as soon as I finish at the White House. You monitor Clavette and look for more reports of alien sightings.”

“Yes, all those lights in the sky in Canada were actual ships. They have moved Ellie around a bit. You won’t have heard of the murder in Goderich, but Greg killed a woman who worked with Ellie’s father. Look at the vid from the team, horrible. It’s in the data bank.”

The man in the suit followed the waiter and, despite the nearly empty room, sat at the next table. Siglinde’s order arrived at the same time.

“I have to go, dear. I love you.”

Siglinde blushed. Even though she wanted to confuse the eves-dropper, Siglinde meant every word. Ted stared at his cell. Despite his long life, he had no answer. Ted thought of Ellie’s great-grandfather.

Siglinde had a ride to see the President. A driver met her just as she prepared to walk. Someone escorted her through the back door of the west wing and to an anteroom outside the President’s office, and they left her to stew as people came and went into the inner sanctum. Then someone paused on the way out with the door partly open and a disembodied hand gripping the edge of the door.

“Why did I have to find out about this from reporters?” The President sounded pissed. “Get that woman in here… now.”

Mary, the woman attached to the hand, opened the door and gave Siglinde a perfunctory wave.

“Stand unless invited to sit. Don’t look him in the eye,” she snapped.

“Good morning, young lady,” the politician stood at the desk and did not bother with phony friendliness. “You put me in a bad spot.”

Siglinde winced at the superficiality, the sexism and the accusation. Here was a man who always had someone to blame for misfortune.

“Tell me what’s going on.”

“Mr. President, aliens are on Earth and they have interbred with humans. They are no threat.” Siglinde sat without invitation. She would kiss no one’s ass. She looked the man full in the face.

The President hesitated, pondering the affront, but the shock of Hilfreich’s revelation stunned him. He sat without comment. He had expected to discover that the media’s sensation was unfounded. In one sentence, his supposedly top scientist examining alien possibilities had confirmed the wildest speculations. To the man’s credit, he wasted no time in trying to argue with someone with superior knowledge. As normal, the

President grasped at a political advantage, and in this case, he saw the possibility of reversing the withering of American global dominance.

"How can we benefit from alien contact?"

"We can't, Mr. President. The aliens are not interested in the USA."

"What, they are going with the Russians or the Chinese?" He saw the world as a contest between the three powers, and in his mid-western down home, folksiness often referred to global politics as "a three-legged milk stool with the rest of the countries the manure covered barn floor".

"None of the empires, they aren't interested in petty human politics."

"I don't think we are an empire, young lady; we are the leader of the democratic free world."

Siglinde ignored the man's obvious denial of reality.

"They think the smaller countries and people should run things."

"So they want to destroy us," he growled. "I thought you said they weren't hostile."

"They have no intention of doing anything like that. They think that the world's industrial powers will destroy life on the planet and make it unsuitable for advanced organisms for several thousand years. Think of the extinction of the dinosaurs. The aliens know they don't have to do anything to wipe out humans, but they would rather we save ourselves. It's lonely in the galaxy or something, and they like our species. World powers are a hindrance to that, but humans will have to figure that out."

"Pastor says that any aliens would be angels of the devil. My faith is my rock. I can't argue with someone delivering the word of God. My spiritual well being and his guidance are more important to me than this bunch of sinners who surround me."

He looked Siglinde in the eye. She tried not to flinch. The President represented the high barrier that Ellie had said they must overcome. Siglinde had seen reports of a growing attack on any potential alien visitors by religious leaders of all faiths. If the evil star people existed, they would be a refutation of human and earthly exceptionality. By necessity, aliens must be visitors from hell. Many preachers, priests, or imams denied there could be aliens. It was all fake news, perhaps a Hollywood stunt. Most political leaders agreed.

The video coverage fought against official reassurances that dishonest journalists had faked evidence of aliens. In reaction, major cable outlets had rounded up what they described as experts to question the visual evidence. These quoted various concepts, such as the outdated Fermi

Paradox, to prove their points. Some guests were colleagues of Siglinde who were not privy to the classified NAAP files. They represented the obsolete thinking before 1947.

Siglinde had made her key points. She knew the President had probably seen all the technical material NAAP had produced. She did not know if he knew of the CIA operation. The man behind the desk projected a mixture of emotions, although anger seemed to dominate.

"We'll show them they can't ignore the United States of America." He slapped the desk.

Siglinde slumped in her chair. She now knew that dealing with American politicians was a waste of time. The aliens had already decided that political leaders were a sideshow globally, but the big three especially. Ordinary people would have to prevail, somehow. She thought of what she knew of world history and recent beliefs revealed by the internet.

It won't be easy; maybe not possible, especially if the President thinks aliens are the devil's angels, she thought.

"Call off the CIA. Some of their armed agents appeared in Canada. The star people can toy with them whenever they want. It shows their goodwill that they have killed none of them. The CIA murdered a woman in Goderich."

"What..." the President cried. "Where the hell is Goderich?"

"In Ontario Canada..." Siglinde was not sure if the man could find Ontario on a map. He probably had a vague idea of Canada.

The President had suffered a crash course about Canada since mysterious forces had stranded the air force plane on a Canadian airfield. The Canadian complaints had become worse after the CIA agents appeared. If agents had killed someone, the Canadians might get unmanageable.

"Can you prove that?"

Siglinde called Ted on her cell.

"Did we send the video of the Goderich killing to the White House?" She hung up and turned to the man.

"We had the office bugged where the murder took place. The video should have been in the material NAAP sent. It is horrific. The Canadian cops have it as well."

The President had not seen the video, and the CIA told him the file was complete. *Someone is lying to me.*

He conveniently hid the fact from Siglinde, but glared into the hidden camera that recorded everything in the Oval Office. He wanted to end this meeting and go tear a strip off his supposed helpers. The operative monitoring the live video made a phone call.

"Thank you, young lady. That is all." An aide escorted Siglinde out to the limousine. A man in the front with the driver turned to her.

"We would like you to stay in the hotel for a few days. It is handier to the President."

"I have a job to do."

He glared at Siglinde and said, "Do not leave town".

When she arrived at the Coronet, she noticed the man from the night before, but he had dressed more casually and sat where he could see the front door and the elevators. These watchers made her nervous, and the person, riding shotgun in the limo, creeped her out. It seemed more likely they were the CIA, not the secret service assigned to protect her. She did not know why she would even need protection, but she had no love for the CIA. Siglinde decide she must escape from what seemed like hotel arrest. That might be difficult.

Siglinde checked for mail at the desk. There would be none, but it gave her a chance to confirm the man in the lobby was bird-dogging her.

She walked towards the elevators and called Andrews.

"I'm sorry, Ms. Hilfreich, they have ordered me to keep your plane here."

"Come on, Bill, I need to get going."

"Sorry, the orders came from the White House."

From the White House, but was it the President? Siglinde wondered.

An ATM stood to the left of the concierge. She withdrew $500. The money went into a pants pocket. They might watch her credit cards. She decided on another route, hopefully, one they would not expect, and she would pay cash. Siglinde went to her suite and retrieved her bag and computer. Assuming they had bugged her suite; she called and asked for more towels. Siglinde closed the heavy drapes and placed her baggage in the entranceway. Infrared video would make her actions useless, but she hoped for the best.

The housekeeper stood at the door with two towels.

"I'd like another," Siglinde saw the service cart. "I'll come and get it."

"Thank you," Siglinde gave the woman a ten. "You are a big help." The worker smiled, as she always did on the rare occasion one of these rich guests treated her nicely. Siglinde trailed her down the hallway and turned to the guest elevators as the cart headed to the service shaft.

Siglinde punched for the third floor and also for the lobby. She got off at the third and took the stairs down. The towels remained in the empty elevator car and arrived at the main level. The stairwell exit gave the option of turning to the lobby or the back exit between housekeeping and the kitchens. She went out to the service delivery ramp, walked down to Constitution Avenue, and flagged a cab.

"The Capitol building," she said.

As a lowly academic, Siglinde had used Amtrak for all trips on the east coast. Boston to Washington had frequent service. She left the taxi outside the Capitol security fence and watched it disappear before walking the few hundred meters to Union Station.

Siglinde bought a ticket for the 11:55 train to New York City and hurried to make the boarding. Siglinde did not want to linger in case they discovered she had left. Once relaxed on the train, Siglinde asked the steward about the Toronto connection from New York City. It dismayed her that the Toronto train left early the next morning. A night in the city would be necessary. She bought a ticket at Penn Station. They accepted cash, but she had to produce her passport to show she would get over the border. She hoped her name would not leave the Amtrak ticket office.

Hotels in the city were beyond her cash reserves. She called a friend at NYU and invited herself for the night.

As Siglinde's train had pulled out of Washington, the agents in the next suit realized there had been no activity in Siglinde's room. The hunt was on. Their prey had left no trace. After an hour of security video, they watched her leave the back door. It took another half hour to see her get into a cab. While they pursued that lead, someone visited NAAP headquarters, but they had no luck. Ted and Liz did not help. The new receptionist had no clue, and the cameras had not seen her.

"I dropped her at the Capitol," the driver told the Washington Police. Siglinde relaxed in her friend's apartment.

"Who was she going to see at the Capitol?"

The Capitol Police were helpful, but after hours of scouring security footage, Siglinde had not appeared.

About 5 am, someone thought of the railway station. By seven, they watched a video of her boarding a train to New York City.

Siglinde tried to relax as the Maple Leaf 7:10 for Toronto left the city. Only crossing the border would make her feel safe. By the time the FBI agent reached Penn Station, the Maple Leaf had travelled well up the Hudson Valley. Even then, it took time to discover she had left for Toronto. Agents alerted the Buffalo office to intercept the train. They would have her before the border crossing at Niagara Falls.

Siglinde felt comfortable in the rocking coach, but the tension overwhelmed her. She would be in Canada soon, and safe.

"Hi," a young girl flopped into the seat beside Siglinde.

Siglinde extended a hand, but the girl stood.

"Siglinde, get off the train and get to Canada another way."

The girl disappeared out the door at the end of the car.

What the hell…?

Siglinde did not know who the girl was, but she felt compelled to get off at Albany. The first bus out went to Burlington, Vermont. There, after a few hours' wait and withdrawing 500 dollars, she took a bus to Montreal.

"Federal agents," the men flashed badges at the train conductor and pushed aboard. "We are looking for this person, Ms. Hilfreich."

Fighting the rocking from the bad track between Buffalo and the border, the conductor leafed through his passenger manifest.

"Car 101, Seat 24…"

"Where are you going, Miss?" The agent looked at her passport. "Hilfreich?"

"Montreal."

"Reason for your visit…?" The French accent softened his tone.

"I'm a scientist. I am meeting a colleague at McGill University."

The agent made a face. Although he had graduated from a cégep, he suspected anyone who went past grade 12. Then he smiled, stamped Siglinde's passport and said, "Bien venue, welcome to Canada."

Chapter Thirty-Two

Free as lovebirds

About the time Siglinde crossed the border, Ellie knocked on her father's door. Quantz Nedmar stood quietly. He was not yet aware that Ellie was part alien, but he felt some power with her he had never experienced. Her self-confidence told of strength, and she gave no hint of uncertainty. Ellie needed someone to distract her father from his grief until New Year's. He had suffered another loss of hope.

"Dad," Ellie hugged Charlie, "I know you are hurting. You can trust Quantz. He has some of what we seek, the good in humans."

"Mr. Nedmar, as you heard, I trust you, but I must warn you, I will not allow you to betray my father or mother. Don't think of doing that."

Charlie stared at his daughter. He had never heard that edge to her voice. Charlie shuddered. Nedmar would not like to meet an angry Ellie.

"So, Quantz, would you like a coffee? It's a long story."

"Good, I want it from the beginning; yes please, coffee, black."

***

Siglinde sipped a tea after a nice breakfast in the Café Éclair in downtown Montreal. Siglinde functioned in three languages and faked it in two more. She relaxed as she read the lead article in a French-language newspaper. The Canadian government did not appreciate American secrecy. The politicians framed everything in diplomatic language, but the paper screamed the headline that the Americans had lied and manipulated Canada. This played well in a country where half of the population harboured an underlying resentment towards their economic masters.

The government would play the game of appearing to stand up to Washington while secretly negotiating a politically acceptable solution. As a show of defiance, the air force plane would remain in Goderich, and without confirming that they had the two Americans, they would detain the aircrew pending a complete investigation and the locating of the missing pilot. Siglinde hoped that the display of independence meant the Canadians would not look for her. She called Bobby Briscoe.

"Can you find Ellie? I'm in Montreal and I need to get to London. I'll need a safe place to stay."

Siglinde looked at her cell. It was October 31st. The Mars settlers had 61 days. That reminded her of Ted. Siglinde called his cell.

Ted had little time to think of Clavette or Mars. The FBI constantly hounded them, even accusing them of hiding Siglinde. A federal agent sat across the table when his phone rang. He smiled at the ID, but then scowled.

"I told you never to call me at work, dear. I'm tempted to quit my job so I could take care of you full time. There is an FBI person with me."

"Don't quit, Ted, and don't let Liz quit. We need to keep NAAP running as long as they let us. Make sure everything is in Bin Six. The President, or more likely the world, might want to see them. You can tell that agent we are hot on the tail of aliens."

"Do we even have a future?" Ted snarled into the device. The FBI agent squirmed. He did not like eves dropping on a family fight.

"Yes, we do, Ted. The star visitors want us to spread the truth. You and I have a future too, I hope." Siglinde blurted out the last. Quantum physics did not include learning to flirt. "We'll talk soon. You may need to come to Canada."

"I love you too," Ted smiled. "I'll get there soon." He blew a kiss on the phone. The agent relaxed.

Siglinde had arranged with Liz, Ted and Elliana that they would copy everything onto several external hard drives. These were code-named "Bin Six". Each of them would have a copy. It had become clear that there might be an effort to hide or destroy the evidence of aliens. Her recent adventures convinced Siglinde of that wisdom.

I wish we had Elliana here to help. Siglinde smiled and went to withdraw more money and buy a train ticket to London.

***

Elliana smiled at her new inquisitor. The woman appeared to be the latest "good cop" sent to interview her. She brought fine coffee and croissants. Elliana could do without, but she drank and ate enthusiastically. Two could play the game of putting the other at ease.

"Your boss saw the President yesterday. We told her to stay in Washington, but she left. Why did she do that and where would she go?"

Elliana noticed the agent thought that she still worked at NAAP. It told her they had not closed NAAP. That possibility had a 40% risk. NAAP had a role to play if things were to succeed.

"I've been in here," Elliana smiled. "I don't know about that."

"Oh, come now, you know we know you know." The agent flashed her warm smile and looked as if she had caught a mouse.

Elliana stared at the woman. The President had directly briefed the FBI. The leader had decided that the CIA was not to be trusted, but he did not have time to decide who the rotten apples might be. Elliana smiled more broadly. Knowledge of the alien presence had spread.

"Do you believe that alien stuff?" Elliana asked.

The agent squirmed. Until an hour before, she would have called alien believers crazy. She accepted that if the President thought they were here, it might be true. Still, the agent could not yet believe that the calm young woman on the opposite side of the table might not be human. The agent might have been more concerned if she had access to the NAAP files and had known about the events since 1947.

The session ended with the usual stalemate; however, the agent decided she liked Elliana, and Elliana felt the beginnings of a possibly useful relationship. This was a change in the attitude of her jailors.

***

In Ottawa, the RCMP had to bring Liz Dafoe and Dawn Waasnodae before a judge. The first attempt had been to have a video appearance, but the obstinate magistrate demanded the women appear in person. The law required a closed courtroom and the women's lawyer could not attend.

"Read the charges," Judge Dallaire glanced at the clerk. The court officer looked up in confusion.

"I have nothing listed, your Honour."

"Ms. Eckhart," Dallaire glared at the crown attorney, "what is going on here?"

"Your Honour, the Crown asks for a detention order to extend our holding Ms. Dafoe and Ms. Waasnodae for security reasons under a public order emergency, as outlined in Section 2 of the Canadian Security Intelligence Service Act."

"Ms. Eckhart, can I see a copy of the cabinet declaration?"

The Crown lawyer sputtered. "There is none. It came from the PMO."

The judge glared down at the Crown Attorney.

"Do you have a statement of evidence? Did the Prime Minister's Office at least give you that?"

The clerk retrieved a folder from Eckhart. Justice Dallaire spent some time leafing through the sparse few pages. His look of annoyance grew.

"We have video evidence as well, Your Honour." Eckhart did not like the look on the judge's face.

"Very well," Dallaire sighed. "Please set that up."

He looked at Liz and Dawn. In a security trial, the accused did not have the right to see the evidence against them. "Clear the court."

In the darkened room, with only the judge, the clerk and Eckhart present, a monitor displayed the media record of the MPs on the steps of Parliament. It also included Jimmy's interview with Liz and the fantastic events with Ellie leaving Liz and Dawn and at Dow's Lake.

"Bring the prisoners back." Judge Dallaire did not sound happy.

"Ms. Eckhart, can I see the warrant for seizure of the Smith video?"

"I have none."

"So that is inadmissible evidence."

"Ms. Eckhart, where is James Smith?"

"We don't know, Your Honour."

"Was he ever in custody?"

"That is an ongoing CSIS security matter."

"Are there two Americans in custody?"

"That is an ongoing CSIS security matter."

"Do you have a witness from CSIS here?"

"No, Your Honour," Sue Eckhart felt as if she were sliding down a steep roof with no handholds.

"Ms. Eckhart, I remind you that this is the designated security court and all matters, including CSIS warrants and charges, would have to be brought before me. I have not had such a hearing regarding either James Smith or two ethereal American fliers. Failure to appear before me violates the law."

Eckhart squirmed in her seat. This had not turned into her best day.

"What you have given me," Dallaire vaguely waved the Crown's folder at Eckhart and the blank video screen, "is a request to imprison two honourable members of the Canadian Parliament for asking questions in public about detentions and events that neither you nor CSIS seems to know about or admit to. I find this curious."

Dallaire slapped the folder onto his desk.

"Why are you here, Ms. Eckhart?"

"The evidence shows the accused consorting with a possible alien agent and their asking security-related questions in public aids that power."

"Someone did not yet accuse them, Ms. Eckhart, since the Crown has not seen fit to lay any specific charge, but that's a quibble."

"What alien government are they supposed to have helped, Russia, China... Wakanda?"

Eckhart winced, and the clerk giggled at the fictional movie reference.

"After reading this," he glanced at the folder, "and watching your television show, perhaps Wakanda is the closest. It seems to me you say that these two are enabling alien space invaders. A comely and innocent-looking young woman seems to lead these invaders, some monster. Indeed, this reads like a movie script. I saw that movie too."

Eckhart turned her palms up, her face crimson.

"Would the detainees please rise?"

"Ms. Dafoe and Ms. Waasnodae, they have brought no specific charges against you; however, the Crown has made serious allegations that they may substantiate, and we might then lay charges. In the meantime, they have given me no compelling reason to hold you in custody." Dallaire glared at Eckhart and returned to the prisoners. "You may go free, but I order you to stay in Canada and be ready to present yourself to the police agency if required. If you violate my order, we will arrest you on a bench warrant."

"Ms. Eckhart, I order you to turn over these documents and videos to the oversight committee for CSIS. It appears they have not followed legal requirements. That is more of their concern than of mine. This is not sixteenth-century England and we do not throw people into the tower on a whim with no charge. You might as well accuse them of witchcraft. Somehow, it seems appropriate that this is Halloween... court adjourned." Dallaire stood and everyone scrambled.

***

Several youngsters scurried up the walkway to a small but elegant house festooned with illuminated goblins, witches, and several lighted pumpkins with garish faces. The structures on this part of Waterloo Street dated from the 1880s. While not as opulent as those of the rich along the river bluff, the structure held a deep connection to the history of Goderich.

The children wore an assortment of costumes, from a princess to a witch. One appeared in an iridescent outfit of grey and blue with a fine-featured mask that seemed alive and could not have come from the dollar store. She appeared to be a movie version of an alien, but without being a monster. The costume clung to its wearer and displayed details perhaps inappropriate for a young girl.

A woman dressed as Cruella watched the youngsters approach.

"What a wonderful costume," she placed a candy bar in the offered pillowcase. "It's the best one I have seen tonight. What's your name?"

"Roberta," the masked moved as if it were a real mouth.

"Where did you get your costume?"

"Mother and Father made it," the eyes in the mask smiled and the mouth broke into a slightly askew grin.

Imp...

Mother!

"They did a great job," Cruella gushed.

"I think so," the little girl giggled.

"Can I please take your picture?"

Roberta nodded, and the woman's cell flashed.

When Cruella glanced at her photo gallery, she saw an image of a girl, about ten years old, with light hair, holding the bulging pillowcase. There were no aliens in sight. The pumpkins suddenly flared up and cast shadows over the street. Cruella looked to the street in shock. The little alien was well down the sidewalk with the others. The bright light from Cruella's pumpkins created shadows from everyone except the alien girl. A giggle came from that direction. The pumpkin light returned to normal.

Imp...

I had fun. She's a dandelion.

Steve Jorgensen enjoyed Halloween. It had been a time when he, as a misfit nerd kid, could blend in with his playmates and not be the only weird one. Now, he enjoyed handing out treats and teasing the young generation.

Siglinde Hilfreich followed several children to Steve's door.

"I'm sorry, you're too old for treats," Steve quipped as the little ones scurried on.

"That's okay, a couch and a blanket will do." Siglinde tried to laugh, but the past two days stressed her. "You don't seem surprised to see me."

"Ellie called me." Steve moved to let Siglinde enter. "You can stay here as long as you need to. Ellie said it will be until New Year's Eve."

"Is this why Ellie led you to me, to give you a safe place to stay?"

"I think so, partly. Nancy and I thought we were cleverly tracking you down, but it seems Ellie plotted it all. They created another safe house in Goderich. The aliens are in control. I should be upset and feel powerless, but I know humans will control the important decision."

"Yes, I feel the same." Steve poured some wine. "Whether our species will thrive or die out. It's our call."

"If we decide to die, no one will be sadder than Ellie and RoH."

"If they decide to withdraw, Ellie will give us all the chance to leave with them." Steve stared at a wall. "What will you do?"

"I don't know. I have a boyfriend. We would have to discuss it. I must admit, as a scientist, it would expose me to things far beyond my current understanding. That would be exciting."

Siglinde paused, contemplating. This was the first time she had ever said she had a person she loved. She wished for better circumstances to savour the feeling.

"A boyfriend, that's good. Rachel would want to chaperone us, otherwise. Ellie measures Earth's future in years, not decades."

"On one hand, it would seem selfish, I admit. Most of us have family ties and many we love. I wonder if the offer would extend to those. Are you and Rachel a couple?"

"No, that would be unethical, and the age difference would require more narcissism than I possess. Rachel is a mother hen. Under normal circumstances, she would go away for a job once she gets her Ph.D. Rachel would have to be offered the chance, but I don't know what she would do. There's an English professor I quite like. We are both tenured and seem to get along. Maybe she would want to write galactic poetry."

"I already know one galactic poet," Steve remembered Ellie's first visit. Then he paused, digesting a thought he should not have.

"Ellie would try to accommodate what everyone needed. I don't think they have any intention of a general evacuation." Siglinde needed a refill of wine. Steve poured.

"They won't even use ray guns on the bad guys," Steve laughed. "Maybe I'll ask them to do that."

"You know Ellie would never allow it, and it would break RoH's heart. She believes even weeds have beauty, and we should find it. I'm going to call my office. One alien objective is that no one gets hurt."

"The CIA didn't receive the memo."

Steve went to answer the door for the last of the trick-or-treaters.

Chapter Thirty-three

Candy night on Mars

On Mars, where the settlement, by its existence, called into question Earthbound rituals and religious celebrations, the marking of Halloween Candy Night, occurred some Mars days after the Earth date. All immigrant communities had lingering attachment to the homeland's traditions.

The design of the settlement with its airlocks and remote living nodes changed the concept of separate dwellings. The few children in Warren did not warrant traditional things. A group party replaced trick-or-treat.

The festivity in the central hub that served as a town square had a distinct adult focus. Similar to most pioneer situations, partying and celebrating broke the boredom and the stress of daily existence. All treats had come from Earth and distributed with reserve. Most local foods came from the still expanding hydroponics and fish farms. Carbohydrates manufactured with artificial anabolic processes barely supplied a basic need, and sugar remained an aspiration. Food production and air supply used the bulk of IP-1's energy generation. Miniature fission reactors produced the vast amount of electricity needed for the oxygen and fuel production for the few ships that would return to Earth. They had laid cables to divert some of this electricity from the bunker to the living tunnels.

"So far, everyone seems stable and is forgetting what's coming," Wendy spoke to Jorge as she sipped a tumbler of distilled water. "We'll be suffering more by Christmas."

"I met with the medical staff today," Jorge sipped a treat, a mug of hot black coffee. He normally could indulge about four times a year. Alcohol did not exist on Mars. "No one is forgetting. They're afraid some may want to commit suicide."

"I understand." Wendy stared at the celebrating crowd. She had even thought about that relief for herself. "Hopefully, we can put them off until after Clavette hits. There will be hope for a time after, if the roof holds."

She glanced upwards. This part of Warren lay buried under ten meters of dirt from the tunnel's boring operations. It provided radiation protection, but no one had engineered it to withstand a comet.

"That's what we discussed today," Jorge touched Wendy's arm, "the look on some medics told me they had considered suicide."

"There's always a chance for a miracle," Wendy clung to hope.

"Sadly, there's no superhero to save us." Jorge wondered why his coffee tasted bitter tonight.

***

RoH carried two steaming paper cups of hot chocolate to the bench. Emily took hers in a mitten-covered hand. The afternoon November sun caught the spot in front of the bank, but it struggled against the first seasonally bitter day of the month.

"I like it when you visit," Emily sipped. The sweet taste and heat warmed her. "It makes me happy."

"You make me happy, Emily."

"Here, let me show you recent pictures." Emily extracted a new cell device and scrolled her gallery. An image of a smiling young man, perhaps twenty years old, brought a big smile.

"That's my grandson, Thomas. He's grown so handsome. He's at college and here is Jaden; she works in Toronto."

Jaden also smiled, but RoH saw something in her expression.

"Jaden needs to come here," RoH smiled at Emily. "She needs you; she needs to be safe."

"They are coming after Christmas," Emily smiled, but RoH's mention of safety bothered her.

"I want to meet her; I need to meet her." RoH sounded sure. "She needs to meet me. That will be just before..."

"That would be nice." Emily stowed the phone and took RoH's hand.

Why does this little girl make me feel safe? Why does she need to meet Jaden, and before what?

RoH sipped and asked Emily about flying. As Emily reminisced, RoH watched a middle-aged woman making her way along the walk.

"Hello, Cruella," RoH waved.

"What...?" The woman stared and then fumbled for the cell in her pocket. She thumbed through her photographs, stopped, held the device so she could look at it and then at RoH.

"I thought so; you're the little alien girl from Halloween. You sure could have been real. There was a great costume."

"I kind of think I'm real," RoH giggled. "I had fun."

"I always have fun on Halloween," Cruella said and sat beside Emily without invitation.

"Dorothy," she put out a gloved hand, "I've seen you here before."

"I'm Emily. I come here to watch people and feel part of things."

"I see you have a little friend," Dorothy smiled at RoH.

"Ah, my weird alien," Emily chuckled. "This is RoH."

"You even have an alien name."

"I'm named after my grandparents' second names, Robert and Heather, Roberta Heather, RoH for short. My weird alien father says RoH is a breeding name, Roberta O'Heather."

"Sounds Irish, suitably alien," Dorothy suggested. "Is your father so weird you think he's an alien? That was a neat trick on Halloween night. How did you do that?"

"Did you see those American agents arrive over there?" RoH nodded towards the stage beside the courthouse. She sipped her chocolate and her eyes penetrated Dorothy.

"Only on television. No one knows how that happened, some say... aliens." She stopped, startled at an impossible connection. A chill ran down her body.

"That was like what happened at your house."

Dorothy looked at RoH, then at Emily, as if appealing to an ally.

"Oh, she won't eat you or steal your mind," Emily laughed. "But I warn you, she will steal your heart."

Emily squeezed RoH's hand.

"I wanted to meet you again, Dorothy. You are thinking in the right direction, but it won't be until New Year's that you know. Do you attend the big bash here on New Year's Eve?"

"Not usually."

"Come this year, right over there," RoH pointed at the stage in the square. "There will be special excitement this time. Please come, and think about all this until then. I'll be there."

"Why...?" Dorothy decided this little girl showed too much maturity.

"I think we can be friends, and the more friends we have, the better. I am just a little girl."

"How did you know what I was thinking?"

"You'll like her as a friend," Emily interrupted. "She always knows what I'm thinking. RoH's special. I'll be here New Year's Eve too, with my grand kids."

"Please stay with Emily. I must go." RoH stood. "She's a pilot and has lots of stories. Maybe she'll even fly again."

RoH wandered off, savouring her addition to the dandelion patch. Dorothy sat with Emily. Their laughter followed RoH around the square.

***

"Siglinde, they are furious that you ran. The President dragged the Director over the coals. He's mad at us. The media made him look silly. The Director promised to feed you to that old lion again, soon."

"That's his pay grade," Siglinde laughed. "It won't be soon if I can help it." Any respect she had for the president had evaporated during the meeting in the White House. Someone had misled the president.

"It was useful, though," Ted smiled into the camera. The Skype call, with the three-dimensional feature, made it seem like they were together. "NAAP is still in business. You are still on the payroll. The President is smart enough to know we are his only honest source of information. We now have to send anything we find directly to him. He believes you have met an alien. Have you?"

"Ellie and I have talked, and her daughter has had her fun with me too, but also told me great things. Ellie is mostly human and RoH is 50-50. Only humans can decide if this doesn't turn out well. We have nothing to fear from the visitors. You have met an actual alien, too."

"Yes, I know, our dear Elliana. I can't understand why she let them take her prisoner."

"They are never really prisoners. Whenever they want to get out or free a human, they can do it at will. You have the video and accounts of the exploding barn near Ottawa. That was Ellie and a human escaping the police. All these incidents, including Elliana's detention, are part of a bigger plan to teach humans humility and deflate our egos."

"The things Ellie's daughter shared with me about physics and how their technology works are mind-blowing. What we know is like touching the paint on a car and then trying to understand from that how the car works. We have a lot to talk about in the future."

"I hope we have a long future together." Ted applied his best physicist's flirting.

"So do I," Siglinde softened. "I would love to have you here."

"Why can't I...?"

"What's up with Clavette?" Siglinde switched subjects.

"It's the same, just more accurate, but the improvements are meaningless for the outcome, except that we know it will hug the surface and almost evaporate before the remnants impact the surface. It's as if we were intentionally adding atmosphere to the place, but it will still be off limits for decades, and that's if Mons doesn't erupt. No one can predict what will happen if it does. McCormack claims to be the best spin-bowler in the solar system."

"What the hell is that?"

"She's an Aussie. That's a cricket joke. The bunch of British- zone planetary boffins have descended into a cricket slang-fest. It's like baseball jokes, including the bean-ball."

"Yes," Siglinde mused, "the whole situation is so horrible I guess laughter is the only way to have hope and prevent insanity. With that velocity fluctuation, it almost seems that a galactic spin-bowler is guiding Clavette."

"Ted..."

"Yes...?"

"We will be together after New Year's."

"Before," Ted said. Siglinde stared at her cell after the call ended. *Ted sounds like he knows something more.*

***

"Mother," Ellie held Lisa's hand as they wandered along the boardwalk at the beach. The bluff protected them from the light, easterly offshore breeze. "How are you holding up?"

"I would like to be in Seattle, sweetie, but I want to be near you."

"Do you want to go now? I would like you here until New Year's Day. I want to spend as much time with you as I can. We may have a few weeks or months before a final decision. We must decide to stay or withdraw. It depends on humans once they know star-travellers exist."

"Will you leave again?" Lisa choked.

"Would you leave with me, Mother? I didn't even want to talk about this, but it may happen, but I have an additional reason to stay."

"You love someone, a human, don't you?" Lisa hugged Ellie.

"Please think about it." Ellie ignored her mother's question. "You don't have to decide soon. The chances of withdrawing are about even. I'm not sure that Father would come. He loves me, but you and I have a stronger bond. There is a new love in his life, but he has suffered a setback. He is smitten with RoH, so perhaps."

"I have a love here, too," Lisa said. "Perhaps he would leave. He already knows about you and is as weird as I am."

"You would get to know what's beyond the sky." Ellie hugged her mother and stared up at the scudding clouds in front of a beckoning, deep, blue infinity. Ellie knew and was at peace with what lay beyond the sky, but she fervently hoped her future lay on this side of the blue.

Chapter Thirty-four

Special delivery; Rural rout

"**H**i, I have the K. Grenier autopsy report for Dr. Takarabe." The pleasant-looking young woman in a pristine PPE gown and with an N-95 mask loose around her neck leaned over the administrator's desk. She held a bright red file folder.

"Oh, that's good; the cops have been asking for it. Kai is through there." She nodded at the double doors. "He's into that murder victim."

The woman behind the desk laid her head on the keyboard and dozed off. Daisy pushed through the doorway.

Dr. Kai Takarabe stood behind an examination table that supported a naked body. Several vials of blood and other excretions sat on a rack to one side. Kai's plastic gown had a few specks of blood on the chest and similar substances smudged his latex-covered hands. Dead bodies only bled a little. His right hand paused, holding a scalpel above the cadaver's abdomen. He looked up as Daisy entered.

"Yes...?" he had never seen this woman before.

"Here's the Grenier report. We just finished up. I know the cops have been hounding you."

Dr. Takarabe was the chief coroner for southwestern Ontario. All the criminal victims came to his facility. He had not heard of any victim named Kerri Grenier but had told the OPP he would sort it out. Unexpectedly, this unfamiliar doctor had the results.

The cops will leave me alone now... I didn't know she worked here.

"Put it on the desk." He pointed with the scalpel.

Daisy watched Kai as he went back to work. His protective equipment could not hide his good looks. Daisy did a quick search. No Asian human had ever been involved in hybrid efforts.

It's time that changed, she thought.

Even in their advanced situation, star people procreating still required the joining of male and female genetic material in the same way, with zygote and sperm. Gender blurred, but star travellers had either male or female gross sexual characteristics, subdued in the advanced evolutionary form the species had reached. Only an alien could differentiate the sexes, and in normal activity, sex did not matter. The breeding banks contained cryogenic material from all individuals, and normally when a reproduction became necessary, it was all in vitro. There was no concept of knowing a father or mother. That had changed with Ellie and RoH, but not without controversy in the community. Most accepted that this human hybrid experiment had importance and perhaps held the key to the advancement of the interstellar community. That exceeded the influence of millennia-old culture. Daisy shared the idea that they had to try new things.

Individual operators such as Daisy took on a human representation of their actual gender, so the human Daisy was a female. In that way, the same as Ellie's great-grandfather, she possessed all functional human physical characteristics, and they worked the same way with hunger, fatigue, interest, and arousal.

Daisy had learned to trust her instincts. Few star travellers trusted anything but science. This deviation was something Ellie had taught her out among the stars. Daisy had been one of those designated to work with Ellie's grandfather and mentor the young Ellie. It had been mutual learning and Daisy had learned as much from Ellie and her alien great grandfather as she had taught. Everyone involved in raising Ellie had developed empathy beyond cold science.

Daisy retreated to the door and stood, staring at Kai. He looked up.

"Yes...?" He said, impatient at the continued interruption.

"You are a handsome man," Daisy said. "We need genetic material."

"Who are we?" Kai stood.

She turned and sealed the door.

***

"This situation has CIA DNA all over it," the Mountie in charge of the operation code-named "Barnyard" aimed his laser pointer at the image projected on the hanger wall. His audience comprised RCMP Emergency Response Team units, OPP Tactical Response Unit team, and commanders from Joint Task Force 2 and the Canadian Special Operations Regiment. Two pilots from 427 Squadron rounded out the compliment.

A short distance from the briefing, the USAF C-130 still sat nose-down on the main runway. Its fate lay entrapped by inter-government bickering, and the derelict had become a tourist attraction. The public stared from the road while several RCAF crews poked inside, discovering features that the older Canadian versions did not have. The LIDAR landing system came as a shock. Today, the plane shared the airport with Canadian transports, including helicopters of the 427 Squadron. A line of army trucks and two LAV IIIs waited near the terminal with a dozen SUVs.

The image on the wall was a high-resolution satellite view of a farmyard. The spy satellite revealed every detail, including vehicles and individuals, some of whom carried long guns.

"As you can see, they are well armed and have a hard perimeter." The red dot danced around the image. "From the last week of ongoing observation, we estimate 20 to 30 people and about half seem to be well-armed fighters. It looks like the rest are support people, cooks, communications types, and that sort of thing. We'll get back to this. I want to show you how we found out about them and what they are capable of."

The photo gave way to a video, the one that the NAAP surveillance team had supplied. Siglinde's motive had been to make sure that the OPP would not accuse Charlie Keys and Mike Hammersmith of the murder of Kerri Grenier. Mike had helped with his voluntary interviews with the OPP. The Canadians neutralizing Greg's operation would be a bonus.

The graphic video upset even the individuals who had seen trauma in their careers. Finding a body always traumatized, but watching a murder unfold in real-time went to a deeper place.

"As you can see," the Mountie frowned, "these guys won't go down easy. We want to take them alive, but no one should take a risk. As in the rules of engagement," several people looked at their notes, "shoot in self-defence. As usual, that means shoot to kill."

"I don't think they could convict that shooter of murder," one cop said, "maybe manslaughter."

"It's up to a court to decide that," a woman's voice with a slight French accent came from the back of the room.

"Ministers," the Mountie looked into the shadows behind the audience, "would you like to say a few words before we get into the plan?" Two figures stepped out of the gloom and joined the lecturer.

"Ladies and gentlemen, Mme Leger, the Solicitor General of Canada, and you are familiar with Mr. Donaldson, Minister of Defence."

"Our being here," Mme Leger began, "should tell you that the Canadian government, at the highest level, takes this incursion against our sovereignty seriously. We have invoked Defence Act provisions so that the military can support your police agencies."

"The President of the United States has assured the Prime Minister that these are rogue units operating without authority. He demanded that the PM allow him to send in his special forces to deal with them. The government has resisted that. We don't need them," she added amid patriotic muttering. "We want to know what's going on. Take them alive. We want their statements."

Mme Leger did not reveal the depth of the government's anger. Cabinet did not accept the American president's excuses. The government felt trapped by the Canadian helplessness as the junior partner in an inescapable military and economic alliance. She nodded to Mr. Donaldson.

"I don't need to say how much confidence we have in our special forces." His eyes swept the military people. "I know you will be professional and successful, as usual. Just remember, this is not a practice operation. There is a probability it will hurt people. Good luck."

"Okay," the Mountie stepped forward, "here's the plan."

The Special Operations Regiment soldiers left first in several three-tonne trucks. They would reach the river on a road above where it passed the farm. Then, they would drift downstream in inflatable boats. The helicopters of 427 Squadron remained at the Goderich Airport, to carry reinforcements when called.

OPP roadblocks closed the County Road several kilometres on each side of the operation. JTF2 and the OPP TRU team established a roadblock on the hill just out of sight of the farm lane.

Behind the old rail fence that ran along the ridge line, three JTF2 sniper teams established firing lines down the slope of the abandoned pasture to cover the farmyard. Spotting scopes followed casual activity in the compound. Everyone below seemed to wait with no urgency.

"There are robot dogs on patrol, and the one they call Vader has a short-range, high-explosive rocket launcher."

The shooter watched several mechanical dogs in the yard.

"Which one is Vader?"

"I'm guessing the black one. It's bigger and Vader wore black."

"Good thinking, Sherlock."

The shooter with the C-15 fifty-calibre sniper weapon squinted through his scope and framed Vader. The other teams had their C-14s at the ready. They had the two most dangerous-looking human targets in their sights.

"Get the man on the buzzer. Ask if they want me to neuter the nasty dog." They snickered.

A minute later the man with the radio said, "He'll give the go to kill the dog as the APCs go down the hill."

The bolt snicked a cartridge into the chamber and the sniper put the black beast in the cross hairs. His finger rested lightly on the guard.

"God, Captain, what a forlorn bit of ditch to paddle down."

"This river is beautiful in the summer," Captain Fontaine dug her paddle into the swirling dark water of the Maitland, "I've kayaked down from Wingham. Try it next year."

The four Zodiac 470s slid downstream on the current. The river ran too shallow and had too many rocks for the outboards, and they did not want the noise. They aimed for an inside corner just above where the farm's dead-end road reached the river. The short distance and calm water allowed ten fighters in full kit into each craft.

"Okay, standard infiltration line, three meters between us," Captain Fontaine slipped her C-7 assault weapon from her shoulder and checked to make sure it was in single-shot mode. "When we reach the fence, come together. The cops will know where we are, and we won't get any friendly fire in the face. We only shoot at a sure target. You saw the murder video. These guys know how to kill. Let's go!"

"River rats in place," Fontaine radioed to the commander once her team had reached the fence.

"Go!"

Two army APCs, driven by soldiers but each carrying a cohort of OPP TRU and RCMP ERT members, charged down the road into the farm lane.

On the ridge, the C-15 belched. Less than a second later, bits of Vader sprayed the yard, lightly wounding an agent. A fragment destroyed a windowpane before landing harmlessly in the farmhouse living room. The rocket grenade in Vader's chest ignited and flew in a beautiful arc into the forest on the opposite side of the road, ending with a brief flash and a muffled boom. The force at the fence crouched lower at the sound, and the fighters near the road bent into a skirmish line facing the blast.

The LAV IIIs smashed through the flimsy cattle gate and swung to a stop so that the bulk of each machine would protect the rear ramps from fire from the house and the steel command centre. SUVs sped past the lane and spilled more heavily armed fighters on a line along the weed-filled roadway and finally joined with the line of special operations soldiers from the river. Up the hill, along the fence line, three scopes watched for any sign of a hostile weapon.

The OPP TRU commander peered around his APC and called out.

"Everyone, down on the ground, spread eagle… no sudden moves or we shoot."

The dozen black-clad figures in the yard complied. While no snow covered the ground, late November made it uncomfortable.

"Everyone in the buildings, come out, hands out, and get on the ground." The commander's voice rang through the compound, amplified through speakers on his APC. The roar of an engine signalled the charge of the CIA fighting vehicle. It flew from the building and the gunner looked for a target. The hostile skidded to a stop when they saw the heavier weapons of the Canadian LAVs pointing directly at them.

"You have five seconds to get out of that tank." It took the crew three. Two dozen people emerged from the buildings and went down.

A blast from the direction of the riverside fence sent everyone for cover. The sound of disintegrating plastic and metal confused them all. A robotic dog had surprised one of the Special Forces fighters, who reacted with a quick round into the breast of the plastic beast. The 9-millimetre load had passed the length of the device before it blew the back end of the machine towards the house.

Soldiers from the river rushed to the rear of the buildings and did a careful search, emerging from the front.

"It's all clear." No one relaxed.

"Who's in charge?" The cop emerged from cover with his handgun ready. Greg stood, hands out, palms down.

"I'm in charge. Greg King is my name."

"Doesn't look like a monarchy," one of the ERT cops quipped.

Small black bugs, which should not have been viable in the cool November air, swarmed from all around the compound and rested in the oak tree. Several of the cops swore they heard laughter.

"This was too damned easy," the commander suggested to no one in particular. "You, King, come here."

Greg did not know why he was so compliant. His unthinking shooting at Kerri reflected his true personality. The oak tree buzzed.

The police zip-tied the captives, and called in the helicopters to transport the prisoners to Goderich Airport. No one had prepared for so many, and it would be a problem deciding where to jail these people.

"What a great battle, Captain," one of the Special Operations fighters jibed. "We blew up two mechanical dogs."

They lounged in front of the farmhouse with open Composite Ration Packs, what the army called a "delicious snack" washed down with water.

"It's modern war, Sanjee. We shoot robots, just like Starship Troopers." Fontaine smirked over her cookie.

"What did you do in the war, daddy?" A corporal quipped. "We took a boat ride, blew up Tonka toys and ate crackers and cheese."

"We hurt no actual dogs in making this war." Sanjee smirked.

"Don't worry, people, I doubt this will be on the regimental battle honours. Officially, none of this happened." Fontaine vainly searched for the delicious part of her snack that the contractor had forgotten to include.

A Mountie in full ERT kit approached the relaxing commandos. From a distance, he appeared to be one of them, but subtle changes in police requirements and military capability made a difference. He pulled out his snack.

"This is the strangest setup I have ever seen." His eyes swept the compound. "What the hell are these people doing here?"

"Beats us," Captain Fontaine said. "We knew nothing until we landed in Goderich. That's how our job works."

"I heard," the cop raised his voice, excited to reveal a rumour to a captured audience, "this has to do with aliens."

"No shit..."

"Not only that," he added, "these guys had some prisoners here who the aliens helped escape. The aliens grabbed ten Yankees and deposited them in Goderich last month."

"We saw that on TV," Sanjee said, "but it looked made up, something on the movie channel, just like that woman disappearing into a glow in Ottawa and a barn blowing up."

"Don't know about the woman," the cop added, "but the barn thing happened, for real. I was there. Spooky as hell, and the people we were after just disappeared. We had them in that barn, poof, the roof, and the suspects were gone."

The soldiers had gathered tighter. If nothing else, it was a good story, and they waited for the punch line. It never came. The cop looked around.

"This place gives me the creeps," he said. "Something is wrong here. These Yankees looked vicious, but we found pussies. Yes, something is wrong here... glad I'm shipping back to Ottawa."

He looked at the oak tree and wandered away.

"Captain Fontaine," a man in camouflage but with the insignia of a Major General, feet apart, and hands behind his back, loomed above Fontaine. She jumped to her feet and saluted her boss. He beckoned her away. The Special Ops units were small, with an easy casualness among the officers when in private.

"Ghislaine, we want you to lead a unit to occupy this place, you, and about ten members. The cops are in charge, but they only investigate the legal stuff. We want this place secured until we figure out what is going on. Why in the name of hell were the Yanks here? The Yanks will want their toys back, but we will tell them we are guarding them until we do the paperwork."

"Rumour says aliens, Mack," Fontaine laughed. She only half-believed the alien story. "Maybe this damned thing is a Spielberg movie." Captain Fontaine thought, *maybe I do commanded starship troopers.*

The general did not laugh, as if he knew more, but could not say.

"Just hold the place. We'll send in logistics. Their pantry has lots of grub. You'll be comfortable." He touched the small of Ghislaine's back. She pulled away in reflex. Ghislaine had experienced Mack's familiarity before. She hated the misogyny from the upper ranks.

"We have it, General." Fontaine reverted to defensive formality.

"Report anything strange, you see or hear." Mack glanced at the sky, frowned, and then turned abruptly to visit with his JTF2 units.

Ghislaine selected Sanjee because she liked her and then added nine others. None had family commitments, and Fontaine thought this detail might last more than the four weeks until Christmas. Those with family back at base or other responsibilities would go home.

What the hell did the General mean by 'anything strange'?

Chapter Thirty-five

Meeting strangers, making friends

Quantz, you don't know how good it has been, having you here for these weeks. I suppose you'll be leaving for Christmas.

Oh, you're single and the family is in Egypt. Glad you're staying. If my daughter is right, big things are about to happen. Like you, I don't know when or what. Ellie told me she would be away for a few days, until the New Year celebration, and she sounded mysterious.

I don't know where my granddaughter will be.

Captain Ghislaine Fontaine waited patiently in the checkout line at the butcher's shop on Goderich square. Christmas Eve had reminded her that the Yankees had lots of steak and pork in the stores at the farm, but they had no seasonal food. It seemed they had not planned to be in Canada for Christmas. They were still in detention with suspicion of murder charges and terrorism. They had sent the C-130 pilot to detention with his crew in an Ottawa hotel.

The butcher offered the only fresh turkey in town, and this was the last stop before heading back to the farm with supplies for a feast. Fontaine knew how to cook, but she had chosen a man who had a reputation for being the best. Ghislaine's on-the-ground experience overseas had taught her that, whatever else, the food had better be good. There was no such thing as a "tasty" CRP. The troops called them CRAPs.

Ghislaine put the turkey into the back of the American SUV and slid behind the wheel.

"Tap... tap... tap..." A smiling face of a little girl in the passenger window caught the kaleidoscope light from a Christmas display. Ghislaine released the door lock.

"Hello, Captain, I'm RoH." She slid in and deposited a bright shopping bag with a snowman between her legs. "I have presents for you and your people. Can we go now?"

"Go where?"

"To the farm."

"What do you know about the farm?"

"I've been there several times. The last time I watched you arrive in those neat boats. I'm glad you got those evil men. I used to think everyone could become good, but I don't think their leader can, that Greg guy."

Ghislaine sucked a deep breath. "Who are you?" Ghislaine checked to see if she could get out the door.

"I'm RoH. Don't worry, I'm a friend. You don't have to jump out. Just drive us back there."

RoH melted Fontaine with her smile. She circled the square onto East Street, not sure why she followed the instructions of this little girl.

"What's going on?" The SUV swung onto Victoria Street.

"Everything is going on. Ghislaine, you want to know and why you didn't complain when the general gave you this assignment."

"How do you know about the general?"

"I was there. Well, I had eyes there, and they told me. You believed the Mountie who saw the barn explode near Ottawa. That was my mother leaving town, and she thinks I'm the imp." RoH laughed.

"The TV show was spectacular." Ghislaine turned onto the farm road.

"The media more or less had it accurately. It scares the government. They don't know what's going on and they can't control it. The Americans have known about star visitors for many decades, but have kept it secret. They hope to exploit us for their benefit."

"Us...?" Captain Fontaine shuddered at the obvious answer.

"Look at me," RoH said. In an instant, Fontaine knew the entire story, but she would need hours to sort it out. Initially, she felt surprised that her first alien would be a young human girl.

Either the aliens are not a threat, or they are cleverly evil.

"We aren't evil, Ghislaine. You won't have any targets to shoot at. There will be no need for starship troopers."

The SUV topped the hill and headed down slope. Its headlight revealed the road, which then disappeared into the darkness of the river valley. Suddenly, the invisible farmstead burst into brilliant light. Varying coloured lines of Christmas lights outlined every eve and gable. The oak tree burst into a pulsating rainbow of colour. RoH's face glowed in the reflection. Ghislaine almost drove off the road, captivated by the little girl's look of satisfaction. She headed down the lane and stopped in front of the house. Her squad stood, awed by the fantasy of light.

RoH leapt from the vehicle, clutching her overstuffed gift bag. Several dozen lights flew from the tree and formed a cascading vortex over her head, as if they were following a magnetic field with RoH as the iron core. The light show followed her as she walked around to help the stunned Ghislaine from the SUV. It seemed they watched royalty.

Imp, get on with your job. You'll scare everyone.

Yes, Mother RoH sighed aloud.

She waved her hand, and the lights sped back to their places on the tree. Unintentionally, this reinforced her regal appearance.

"Sorry," she held the Captain's hand, "I like to have fun."

"You looked like some Disney Princess arriving."

"Perhaps I made a mistake," RoH smiled and squeezed Ghislaine's hand, "I'm just a little girl."

"Yeah, right..." Ghislaine digested the revelation from up the road.

Most of the squad had been in harm's way in their careers, but they all stood in astonished paralysis, their training forgotten. They could just as well have been bank clerks from Toronto.

Ghislaine led RoH into the house, followed by the stunned troops.

Once they had deposited the food in the kitchen, the band sat around the living room sipping eggnog laced with Yankee brandy. RoH enjoyed her usual hot chocolate. She lifted her gift bag and pulled out woollen knitted scarves in red and white, one for each of the soldiers.

"Sorry I missed Diwali, Sanjee." RoH handed her a silken scarf.

"I want you all to have a delightful holiday," RoH extracted two kilograms of dark fruitcake. "The genuine excitement will be New Year's Eve."

"Why? We'll be stuck here watching TV."

"You'll get two visitors," RoH said. "Ghislaine, you know one of them."

"Who's that? When are they getting here?" Ghislaine finished an elaborate knot in her scarf.

"You'll find out on New Year's Eve. It will be spectacular." RoH set her empty mug on the coffee table. "I have to go."

"I'll drive you back to town."

"No need, grandpa's car has come for me."

The mob followed RoH into the yard. RoH hopped into the Martin X and they sped away in a cloud of dusty snow.

"Captain, should we call for reinforcements?"

Fontaine glanced around at the light display pulsating over the yard.

"Would it do any good? Besides, I think she likes us."

Yes, you'll be fine.

Several lights flew from the tree and one landed on each of the fighters' shoulders.

***

"You know," Steve Jorgensen handed Rachel the alien tablet, "analyzing this language and what we have learned of star culture would be a fitting next step in your research."

"You want to kill my career before I start?" Rachel smirked at her mentor. "Are you afraid of competition?"

Steve laughed and tried to get used to the idea that Rachel, his star pupil, had now qualified as a colleague. She had defended her thesis two weeks before the holiday. The paper had the arcane title "Mutually reinforcing feedbacks between language and perception of reality."

It was two days after Christmas. Rachel had not yet received the decision of the adjudicators, but Steve had received several effusive phone calls. It was not his to pass on the good news. Steve could only smile.

"I think you will have a career in it, and the world will beat a path to your door. Now check my note about this last bit."

"Hi, Steven," Ellie walked in and claimed her place on the funeral chapel relic. "I hear you're making progress. You are teaching them too, you know." She glanced upward. "I'm going to take Siglinde off your hands for a few days. We are going to take a trip."

"Where...?"

"… to an experiment in inertia, momentum and terra-forming."

"Are you going to fix Earth?" Rachel sounded serious.

"That's humanity's job," Ellie smiled. "This is smaller scale and may mean nothing in the long run."

"I won't ask." Steve stood in front of Ellie. She beamed up at him and he blushed.

Why did Ellie look at me like that?

"I like you Steve, a lot and hope we have a future together... working together. Be ready for a bit of work after New Year's Eve. I'll let you know. You will put some of this work into practice."

Ellie jumped up, gave Steve a lingering hug and a peck on the cheek, smiled at Rachel, and disappeared.

"She likes you." Rachel smiled.

"You've been working with this book too long." Steve waved the now-tattered copy of "A Stranger's Heart." "Besides, I'm too old."

"Did you tear your shirt off in the Dakotas?" Rachel smirked.

"Jimmy," Ellie sipped her water. She and Siglinde had appeared at Ros' house unannounced. "I have a scoop for you, but you'll be away for a few days. Bring your camera."

Chapter Thirty-six

From the jaws of death

"**J**orge," Mandy and her fellow coordinator occupied the viewing cupola for the last time before they shielded it for the Clavette impact. They had about six hours. "We have a puzzle. There is one too many on the headcount."

The reddish glow of sunrise on the last day coloured her cheeks. Mandy briefly wondered if she had just this last day to live. She handed her tablet to Jorge. He stared at the real-time display of computer output. The field for the population count flashed red.

"Someone just miscounted..."

"No, we did it twice, manually. The computer caught it first. The sensors track us by our RF tags, so we know locations in case of a breached air seal. A day ago, it flagged an unknown on the habitat levels. That's why we did a census. The computer insists, but can't show us the location of the anomaly. The individual has explored all of Warren."

Mandy watched the robots hurrying to complete the outside work before they returned to their storm shelters. AI configured robots performed four-fifths of the outside activity. They used an astounding variety of machines, crawlers, some on wheels or two to eight legs and a flier. If they could not re-activate the machines after the event, it would doom IP-1 for sure. She eyed the control to start the cupola covers.

A shadow cut off the morning glow that darkened into deep gloom. "What...?"

A shrill klaxon rang. The airlock had activated.

"No one is supposed to..." Jorge could not finish his sentence. A tall figure in a serviceable yellow tunic with an almost familiar insignia on the breast strode into the space.

"I'm James Thomas Church..."

RoH's impishness had influenced a few of her stodgy star family. Ellie had brought many human cultural references and more creativity.

With a ten-minute delay, images from the Mars orbiting surface observer reaching Earth showed what appeared to be large circular storms on the Martian surface approaching IP-1 and the Chinese-Russian base. Two minutes later, the data stream froze.

Siglinde tried to decide how long they had been in space. Being there had jolted her, but curiosity replaced the disquiet. They had lifted from Charlie Keys' front yard inside a glowing column, and instantly were in a cozy, Earth-like apartment. Ellie had ushered each into a separate sleep space and to a comfortable cot. Sometime later, the smell of frying bacon and chatter drew her into what looked like a farm kitchen, complete with an old couple preparing breakfast. The crew had a lack of imagination for alien-human interaction on a starship. Jimmy had already dug into his food.

Ellie came through a doorway. Behind her, Siglinde thought she saw a human that looked like Ted, but another glance only showed an alien form, not too unlike the one RoH had showed many weeks before.

Is Ted here? Maybe I'm dreaming.

The incident had upset her, but hunger won out. Ellie seemed to have borrowed RoH's impish grin.

After they ate, Ellie led them through a maze to the skin of the ship.

"There's Clavette," Ellie pointed through the large view port. They had created the opening to accommodate the needs of humans. The clarity made Siglinde wonder if a physical barrier separated them from the vacuum. A large, grey, almost spherical object hung in the void beyond Ellie's finger.

Jimmy shouldered his video equipment and focused on the visitor. The ship kept pace with the object, and he could not tell the amount of separation. Siglinde knew Clavette was big and had a high velocity, but there was no frame of reference. The scientist longed for data.

"Ted will receive all the data. We will follow it down," Ellie said, "and then we will meet another ship to take on guests going to Goderich."

Their view slowly moved until they took up a station behind the object. In the distance lay Mars as a bright red point.

"We are five Earth hours from atmospheric entry." Ellie smiled as if unconcerned with the humans on the target. "You can start shooting about ten minutes before. Even the approach will be spectacular."

The red spot became a definite disc. Siglinde had seen similar things in graphic computer output. It seemed as if she stood inside a model run.

"We are going to evacuate you."

"Who the hell are you? What if we don't want to go?" Jorge flared. He never enjoyed following orders.

James Thomas Church did not take "no" for an answer.

"We are friends and have a stake in your survival. Even if you resist, we are taking you. If you stay here, you will die within three months. If we wanted to save you and leave you here, we would have diverted Clavette, as you call it. You would never have met me."

"Clavette will almost double Mar's atmosphere, and it will clip two kilometres from the top of the rise you call Olympus Mons. The mountain will then continuously erupt for about twenty Earth years and add billions of tonnes of water and gasses to the atmosphere. Mars will be a better place for humans, but for three decades you won't be able to visit."

"Thirty years is a long time," Mandy said. "I enjoy being here." She edged away from the intruder.

"Humans have less time than that to stop destroying life on Earth, two or three years and no more. If you don't do that, resupply missions will stop and you'd be dead in ten years, even if we diverted Clavette."

"It's too late for that anyway, even for us. It's too close now."

Bright purple light burst through the view port. A glowing pillar had engulfed the only airlock viewable from the cupola. Mandy watched a stream of settlers emerge from the open port. She gasped. They did not have excursion suits on. They just vanished into the glow.

"Come," Church said, "it's time to go."

Chapter Thirty-seven

The line in the sky

Ghislaine Fontaine stood in the farmyard, her hands on hips, feet planted in a solid stance. The rumbling in the sky had drawn her squad outside. They had been watching the television coverage of the impending disaster on Mars. A strengthening glow came from beyond the hill. The Christmas lighting danced and shimmered. The sound, a cross between a large armoured vehicle and a thunderstorm, grew louder. A sharp edge crept over the brow, glowing brightly against the midnight sky.

"Put that damned rifle away," Fontaine growled at Guy, who had run out with his weapon ready. "What the hell do you think that will do?"

As Captain Fontaine watched up the snowy hill in Huron County, early morning walkers and New Year's revellers still on Nevskiy Avenue and the Palace Embankment in St. Petersburg, Russia, saw their shadow cast by a growing brightness moving upstream along the Reka Neva. The sun had not yet risen on this first day of the New Year. In a few seconds, a large disc hung a kilometre above what was, ironically, the Field of Mars. A few sober people hid, but the majority, including those still celebrating New Year's, hurried to the park. Some believed the light show came from the holiday celebration; others thought a plane had crashed.

A pillar of purple light shot down from the hovering craft, and twenty-eight figures appeared between the high snowbanks beside the Monument to the Fighters of the Revolution. The pillar shot skyward, and the arrivals, dressed in Mars-base surface suits, clumped together in confusion.

Another pillar of light streamed to the square, and a diminutive figure, bipedal and shimmering grey with humanoid features, walked towards the new arrivals. The crowd of spectators pressed closer, instantly sober. The grey figure turned to the mob and smiled; at least later, everyone would testify that it smiled. The entity's mouth released a string of sound that witnesses described as a building collapse.

"Говорить по-русски" one of the drunks shouted back.

"Or English," another shouted.

The grey figure turned to the original shout and pointed at the drunk.

Whether from curiosity, fear, or compulsion, the man shuffled towards the stranger. The alien focused on the approaching Russian, and with each step, the man appeared to overcome his alcoholic confusion. He towered about thirty centimetres above the grey alien, who did not seem intimidated but reached up to place a hand on the man's temple.

In an instant, the visitor spoke in working-class Russian. Its voice rose to address the rapidly expanding crowd. An English woman who witnessed it sarcastically reported that Russian still sounded like a house collapse. The police siren grew and then faded at the gate.

"Humans, here are your brave space travellers," it gestured to the bunch behind, "we have returned them safely from Mars, where their base will shortly be in ruins and they would have been dead. It is a small gift of life to show good faith. Several of these are from this city. They are home. We will visit again."

Two uniformed police charged into the square, batons drawn as if expecting a brawl. They came to a sudden stop at the edge of the crowd.

The stranger waved skyward, and the pillar of purple light returned. In an instant, the light and the visitor had gone, leaving a stunned crowd and equally confused Russian cosmonauts. The brilliance from the hovering disc snuffed out as the craft shot high into the sky.

The police attempted to apprehend the arrivals, but before they could begin, the laughing and singing crowd surged around the group. The apparent deliverance had replaced the months of public grieving for what everyone had thought was certain death for the cosmonauts who had been brave or foolish, depending upon which drinking establishment one frequented. Within half an hour, the mob had dragged their heroes to Nevskiy Avenue and entertained them in many coffee shops. All wanted to hear the story directly from their Martians.

An instant after the ship had left St. Petersburg, the brilliant, mid-day sunshine lighting Chang'an Street, Beijing became even brighter. Hundreds scattered as a brilliant purple glow engulfed a spot in front of

The Great Hall of the People. Thirty-one figures appeared, and as in St. Petersburg, a shimmering grey figure followed.

Unlike St. Petersburg, the police almost outnumbered the sizeable crowd. Well-armed officers in green uniforms swarmed from their stations, guarding the centre of the Chinese government. Officers advanced, guns levelled and shouting at the confused pangunauts. The alien moved between them. The police froze in uncertainty.

As in Russia, the alien spoke. Here, with such a large audience, its voice amplified through the many speakers around the public space.

"Da Yu... Da Yu", the people in the square chanted the unofficial popular name for the Chinese pangunauts on Mars. Da Yu was the legendary figure who had made the Earth habitable.

An officer rushed from the People's Hall and ordered his force to take the alien and the pangunauts as prisoners. The alien raised its arm, and in an instant disappeared in the purple light. Police rushed the pangunauts into the building and dispersed the stupefied crowd. By nightfall, the story of the incident had spread beyond Beijing via the internet.

Liz Dafoe and Dawn Waasnodae hurried. A taxi waited at Liz's apartment building's front door. The press and police had cornered the women there since the court hearing. Ellie had asked them, through the un-alien-like method of a cell call, to go to the New Year's celebration on Parliament Hill and to be there by ten in the evening. Neither woman knew why, but Ellie warned them to prepare to be the most sought-after politicians in Ottawa. Liz thought they already were that.

A single pool reporter and a cop watched them leave from the comfort of their cars. The reporter alerted the news media and followed the women's cab. The cop tailed them both.

"Aren't you the ladies who met an alien?" The cabby's eyes flicked between the rear-view mirror and the road.

"That's us," Liz laughed.

"Did you? The media claims it was a hoax."

"Yes, we did," Dawn did not smile.

"Wow," he sounded sincere. "Can you arrange a trip to Mars for me?"

"No one wants to go to Mars," Liz frowned. "It's about to be blown up; how about an orbit of the moon?"

The taxi led a parade of three police vehicles and several press cars to the Elgin and Wellington intersection. The women hurried towards the sizeable crowd in front of the parliament building.

"I wish Ellie had told us why are here," Dawn shouted above the amplified music that vainly tried to enliven a tragic New Year's Eve.

The set ended and a parade of political leaders, headed by the Prime Minister strode onto the stage. Savvy politicians would never pass up such a large, nationally televised photo opportunity, and the PM had a few minutes to speak. He stepped towards the microphone.

"Mesdames et Messieurs, ladies and gentlemen, before I go on, I call for a minute's silence for the people on Mars, who in just over an hour will suffer an appalling disaster. Several of the settlers are Canadians."

The crowd fell silent, some shed tears, and the politicians dutifully laid their hands on their hearts. High above, a glow penetrated the overcast. As the minute ended, the clouds parted in a burst of brilliance. Upturned faces glowed and the hole in the overcast framed a large disc. No one knew how high it hovered, so its size had no reference. Screams came from everywhere. Liz and Dawn wormed their way to the front, where iron barricades and Mounties blocked their way. The politicians retreated to the back of the stage.

A purple shaft shot down. Four figures appeared… three Canadian Martians, and Ellie Keys. The stunned Mounties reached for their guns.

"I am Ellie," her voice rang and hushed the crowd. "Most of you thought I was an actress or fiction. I'm as real as you all, and almost as human. My star family rescued these Canadians from certain death."

The crowd's cheers echoed from the parliament wall.

"We want to talk with you," the Prime Minister shouted to Ellie. He had mustered the courage to reach the front of the platform. Ellie looked up at the man, but turned back to the crowd.

"I cannot stay tonight. I have other work to do. My representatives, Liz Dafoe and Dawn Waasnodae, will be here for you." Ellie swept the crowd and glanced at the politicians. She beckoned the two women forward. The steel barrier in their path rose and rattled onto its side a few meters distant. The women embraced Ellie.

"Liz and Dawn know the simple message that the star travellers have for humans: save yourselves and you too can travel the galaxy. Humans are in no danger from my people. We have saved the people on Mars as a gesture of goodwill. The worst we will do is to leave and never return, except to examine the remnants of our planet."

She whispered to Liz and Dawn, "You both know the path humans must take. Keep advocating that, and make sure the government understands that there is nothing to negotiate. We want nothing except human success and offer nothing to help. You will always be safe."

Ellie pointed to the sky. A smaller vessel had joined the massive one.

"You won't always see them, but they will watch over you."

The Prime Minister waved at the Mounties. He wanted the women and the Martian refugees apprehended. The police advanced, guns drawn; a pillar of light wrapped around Ellie and she disappeared skyward. As the police tried to take the women MPs into custody, a purple glow dropped around Liz and Dawn.

On the fringe of Ottawa, the balcony door flew open in the hotel suite where CSIS held three American fliers. The startled prisoners disappeared in a flash as their guard burst through the doorway.

"Please stop that nonsense," Liz glared at the Prime Minister.

The three stupefied returnees gave no resistance and followed the Mounties into the building. One cop pushed his weapon into the glow, and the pistol suddenly shot skyward, breaking a finger. Everyone retreated, but Liz and Dawn, in the light's embrace, strode up to the stage and stood, feet apart and confident, in front of the stunned and silent PM.

These are lowly backbenchers who should know their place, he thought.

"The star travellers have asked us to talk to you," Liz commanded.

The politician nodded, and the light disappeared. The stage lights turned the women into a beacon in the dark coolness of the Ottawa night.

***

"Montgomery... 0423 Zulu... inbound unknown 27.6, -90.18... heading 45 dot six..."

The USAF major on duty at the Joint Air Defence Operations Centre, Joint Base Anacostia-Bolling, Washington DC, touched a screen and magnified the airspace covering the southeast into the Gulf of Mexico.

"What are altitude and speed?" Demanded a voice from somewhere in the NORAD network.

"Montgomery... unknown… God... it's high and fast... 27.1, -88.7... heading 45 dot three... it's too fast for us to calibrate... might be sub-orbital ballistic... can Space Force get a fix?"

The major called the colonel in command. The man was at a New Year's party and took a minute to answer. This began the most spectacular New Year's Eve in Washington's history.

At JADOC, the major pushed the panic button, summoning others into the command centre. They had all been watching the events on Mars, now live with the normal delay since the orbiters had come back online. He grabbed his scramble phone, activating the NASAMS defence system at Langley Air Force Base. The 113th F-16s lifted off from Andrews with orders to climb to the operational ceiling and head southwest.

Did the Russians make their hypersonic to be operational? The major flipped to a map showing the known locations of Russian strategic assets. They had nothing in the Caribbean or the Gulf of Mexico.

Where did these damned things come from?

"JADOC... Montgomery... is it an actual target?"

"Montgomery... 0426 Zulu affirmative... now 36.5, 80.3... descending fast, Angels 60... heading 45.2."

The F-16s turned, hoping to intercept east of Charlottesville, Virginia. *Too close,* the major thought.

"Montgomery... 0428 Zulu... we have lost contact."

"I see it. I see it."

"My God," a voice from an F-16 shouted, "what the hell passed us?"

"What the hell...?" The security person inside the front door of the FBI headquarters jumped to their feet as the doors snapped their hinges and flew into the street. A purple-blue light shot through the atrium and blew through the next set of armoured doors, which joined the outer ones in the street. A fire door, a vending machine, and a chair added to the growing pile in the middle of Pennsylvania Avenue.

The guard drew his gun and approached the gently pulsating tunnel of light, and extended his hand. He recoiled at a growing tingle in his fingers. The lack of any sound except ripping fixtures made the thing seem more threatening. Neither his radio nor the telephone worked.

The light snaked its way to its target. One last door escaped its frame, and Elliana walked from her cell, into the light, and followed it down the hallway. The glow contracted behind her as she reached the street. A sizeable crowd had gathered, along with police and FBI agents. They followed Elliana as she turned down 10th Street.

One agent fired his pistol at her. The bullet simply disappeared, but the gun leapt from his hand and flew out of sight into the dark sky. The agent ended up sitting on the debris from the FBI building.

Elliana reached the area surrounding the Lincoln Reflecting Pool. The space held thousands of people. The government had called a vigil for the imminent doom of the Martian settlers, and the flood of people pushed to the steps of the Memorial. A huge portable LED display played the live feed from the Martian orbiting cameras.

An array of NASA, military and religious VIPs occupied a platform built above the steps. According to NASA, Clavette would hit in twenty minutes and the crowd had become subdued. Newsrooms tried to confirm growing reports of strange happenings in Russia, China and Canada.

Elliana made her way to the front and up the steps, all the while bathed and protected by the purple barrier that came from some invisible spot high above. The tingling glow thwarted security attempts to intercept her. Elliana stopped beside the platform. The astonished dignitaries had retreated in fear. The crowd roared and surged towards the spectacle, and then retreated in terror as a gigantic disc glided from behind the memorial and hovered overhead. A huge pillar of light joined the shaft, protecting Elliana.

A steady stream of people dressed in the everyday coveralls of IP-1 stumbled from the light and soon filled the space between the crowd and the platform. Elliana approached the abandoned microphone.

"People of Earth," her voice echoed through the park and from far buildings, "here are the Mars settlers we have rescued from death."

The over 500 returnees milled about, confused by their unexpected salvation. The crowd roared.

"Look," Elliana half-turned and waved their attention to the huge mobile screen they had fixed across the pillars of the vast temple to American history, obscuring the stone man's stoic gaze. The clock counting down to Clavette's first contact with the Martian atmosphere reached zero, about ten minutes after the few minutes of terror had occurred on Mars. "This is what the fate of our friends would have looked like."

The feed from an orbiting Mars observatory showed a growing glow from the left and quickly arching to the centre of the image. In a few seconds, the glow flared to obscure the screen with light and then reduced to the image of the fiery streak disappearing over the horizon to the right. The image rotated and then tumble as the effects of Clavette's death hit the satellite.

***

Jimmy held Clavette in the centre of his frame as the craft kept pace with the intruder, and then he panned the camera to show the surface of

Mars rushing towards them. The illusion reversed the reality that they were speeding towards Mars.

A glow began at Clavette's lower limb and then grew in brightness, washing back over the surface. The alien craft kept pace, further out, above the Earth-made orbiters. Jimmy struggled to control the exposure.

Chunks of debris flew from the object and twisted away into the glowing wake. It reminded Jimmy of lava bombs from a volcano caught in a high wind. The bombs exploded into clouds of glowing gas. In seconds, the elevation vanished and Clavette seemed about to crash. The ship jerked further away as the leading edge of the boiling mass scoured Olympus Mons. The mountain exploded in a fantastic bow wave, and the reverse spin of Clavette slowed dramatically, but not quite stopping. Chunks of the Mars' mountain arched upwards, close to the view port, and then curved back towards the surface. Other pieces shot sideways, into nearby mountains and then skidded over flatter surfaces in a swath that extended thousands of kilometres. Jimmy felt the burst of heat on his face, and then it vanished as the window no longer allowed infrared through.

Dying Clavette shone in a searing brightness that would incinerate anything in the line of sight within thousands of kilometres. The individual chunks changed into iridescent streamers. They could have been looking into a blast furnace.

They followed Clavette, now free of Olympus Mons and curving over the horizon. The glare made it uncertain, but it seemed the ball shrank rapidly, raising a rooster tail high into space. These feathers arched and then began a majestic curving trajectory back towards the Martian surface. Within minutes, on the opposite side of Mars from Isidis Planitia, the remnants suddenly burst into a spectacular shower of super-heated fragments and gas with a small core smearing onto the surface in a thousand-kilometre skid before becoming nothingness. The path remained as a glowing girdle of super-heated gas and surface rock turned to molten glass in a path half of the circumference of Mars. Mars's atmosphere shimmered on both sides of the line. The glow expanded rapidly. Behind it all, Olympus Mons cleared its throat in a massive blast and fountains of magma erupted, accompanied by tens of thousands of tonnes of sulphur dioxide and carbon dioxide. Jimmy lowered his recorder as the ship beneath his feet shot past the carnage on the surface and flitted into dark space on a curving trajectory for Earth.

I guess Mary McCormick took the wicket.

"What, who said that?" Siglinde, standing mesmerized beside Jimmy, could not tell if she thought it or heard it. She searched the viewing space.

Ted stood in the doorway, smiling.

"Hello, Siglinde, would you consider an inter-stellar romance?" Ted wrapped his arms around the stunned woman.

"You're...?"

"Yes..."

Liz made her way from Constitution Avenue towards the turmoil at the memorial. She struggled through the tightly packed mob until she reached the barrier that now separated the refugees and the stage from the press of the crowd. A cop moved to stop her there, but a shaft of purple dropped around her. This time, having learned from Elliana's arrival, the cop simply opened the steel fence and let Liz through. She examined the faces of the rescued Martians. Up to now, they had been a number to her. Liz reached the podium and Elliana hugged her.

"Sorry, you had to take a taxi," Elliana smiled, "but everyone is busy."

They turned towards the gathering.

"People, I am what you call an alien, a star traveller, but this is Liz, and she is human. Liz has been part of the most recent generation of a secret government project that has been studying our presence on Earth since 1947. That was when they found the first proof of our existence at Roswell, New Mexico."

"That was a weather balloon," a man in the uniform of an American army full colonel stepped from the crowd of dignitaries.

"That was the line to hide the truth. Here's what happened."

Elliana pointed to the screen and an image of a grounded saucer, several grey alien-looking forms on stretchers, and then a large blimp carried the saucer away. The next image showed a hangar at Groom Lake and a brief sequence of a grey figure moving about in a cell. There was a brief image of an alien in front of a Texas farmhouse, and then the screen went blank.

"I saw that movie," the colonel snarled.

"Who do you think did the special effects?" Elliana laughed. The soldier shut up. She turned to the gathering.

"Liz and the people of the National Agency for Aerial Phenomenon will be our representatives in the United States. They will not be diplomats, but supply information and answer questions. Neither this country nor any of what you think of as world powers can be lead humans hope to survive. These people," she pointed at the dignitaries, "are irrelevant. They represent the danger to life on Earth. We will ignore them. It is you," Elliana waved her hand over the masses, "who must decide to join the effort to restore Earth. If you do that, you might learn how to travel the stars. In the loop of life, the current self-appointed leadership and their greed are the problem, not the solution."

Gasps, angry shouts and a growl rose from the crowd. Arguments broke out. Elliana hated conflict, but the star travellers had realized that humans deciding the future would not come easily. Humans had to resolve the issue and decide on their future. Elliana had one last task.

"Come here, Colonel." The man cautiously left the safety of his peers. As a desk thumper, he had always mouthed the bravado of the smug, but had never been in any combat danger of confronting the enemy.

Elliana looked at the man but spoke into the microphone. "We will not intervene, but there is one thing we will do immediately. By tomorrow morning, we will have disabled all weapons of war. We have already done that to the global nuclear forces. Warships not sailing towards the nearest port, and combat aircraft, even if they are in the air, will cease to function. We are disabling munitions factories. Try to move forward without the threat of killing. We have debated for a long time if and how we should intervene in human affairs. We tend not to interact with planetary ecosystems, letting you thrive or die on your own, but in the end, partly because of Ellie Keys, a name you may not know now but soon will, we gave you a more level playing field besides this most recent token of our concern."

Elliana waved her hand over the group of Mars returnees.

"Mars is now uninhabitable for at least a generation. There may come a time when we decide to leave Earth to its fate. That decision will depend upon you humans abandoning the idea of flags and borders but embracing each other as part of the living Earth. It is a decision our species and other interstellar beings had to make. If you choose repression, you will have preferred your doom. By your own doing, you will draw a line in the sky that will trap you here, and forever make the stars beyond your reach. I love this planet, and hope you can choose wisely."

"None of the major countries will host our official presence. Accidentally, we had the location for what you might call an embassy selected for us over twenty years ago. It is a little town in Canada none of you have heard of."

Chapter thirty-eight

Goderich

The bright disc rose above the hill. Its light ran down the snow-dusted pasture, giving the impression of a sunrise at midnight. Captain Fontaine checked her watch. Unlike daybreak, this rising sun held a mixture of the sinister mixed in with promise. The farmyard shone in day-like warmth as the impressive craft stopped directly above. In the brightness, a purple glow descended in front of Fontaine, and a man and a woman shambled from the centre. They struggled in the unfamiliar gravity of Earth.

"Where are we?" the man asked and then stared at the Captain.

"Fontaine," he exclaimed in recognition, "where the hell are we?"

"You're back in Canada, Armand, on Earth, home."

"An alien told me you were coming." Ghislaine grasped his arm. "It had hurt knowing a friend on Mars who might die."

The alien craft began a slow rotation and shot skyward, leaving the yard in the muted glow of the elusive firefly lights.

"Damned aliens," Armand exclaimed, "I don't know what was worse, being scared we were about to die, or an hour later being in space, in an oversized living room with our friends, sitting in comfortable stuffed chairs and listening to awful elevator music."

"Now, my love," the woman spoke for the first time, and laughed. "They tried to make us feel better. I liked the fruit juice and cookies."

"Who's this, Armand?" Ghislaine smiled at the woman.

"This is my wife," Armand softened, "the love of my life. She calls herself Beta Nine, a Trekkie thing, but she is Elizabeth Nicole. We met and fell in love in the hydroponics gardens."

"It was the oxygen generator, dear, with all that ugly LED lighting and the hum from the compressors. You had to put your ear to me to hear, and I kissed you. I had my eye on you since we arrived."

"I thought you just wanted the perks of a couple getting a private sleeper instead of the dorms."

"Mandy married us the next day. Where is Mandy? Can we sit somewhere?" Roberta said. "This gravity is killing me."

"Maybe they were on another ship. Where did they take the others that were with us on the ship?" Armand gazed at the dark sky.

Peter Williams and Ros made their way towards Goderich Courthouse Square. RoH walked between them, holding their hands. Flashing lights and the loud music of New Year's celebrations greeted them. This small corner of the universe seemed far from the ongoing Martian tragedy, but it would change in a dramatic spectacle.

The star ship bearing Jimmy, Siglinde, Ted and the others made a sweeping arc over the North Pole and down the longitude line to the eastern shore of Lake Huron. The vast fleet of alien craft neutralizing nuclear weapons had overwhelmed global radar systems. One more blip made no impact. Several ships converged on Goderich, including the one carrying Ellie from Ottawa.

The black sky above Goderich burst into light as four alien craft converged above the courthouse. While not as spectacular as the recent appearance in Washington, DC, this would be the most important of the Mars return missions.

Around the world, several small but locally impactful visits happened in Nairobi Kenya, Cape Town, South Africa and a teasing appearance above the Sydney Opera House in Australia. Overall, these returned dozens more Mars refugees. In Goderich, almost 400 Martian settlers appeared in the inevitable purple glow. Ellie, Jimmy, Siglinde, and Ted appeared, but on the raised stage in front of the courthouse.

Bobby Briscoe recorded it all.

RoH stood near the back of the crowd, holding Emily's hand. Emily's granddaughter Jaden stood on the other side, gripping her grandmother's hand in terrified fascination. RoH's Halloween friend stood nearby with her children gasping in awe.

"It's just like the movies, Mommy."

RoH smiled. While adults felt terror before anything else, children could embrace the glory without fear.

That's fascinating, Mother. The children are so accepting. RoH watched her mother confidently standing on the distant stage.

It helped to be a child all those years ago, My Sweet. It helped me survive those first confusing days on Grandfather's ship.

Maybe that's why I find Earth so comfortable, as if I was home.

None of the refugees was Canadian. All but three had originated in the U.S.A. The exceptions were a Chinese couple who had fallen in love on Mars, and a Russian army colonel whose strength of character and ability to stay sane in this ordeal had earned the aliens' notice. Another thing that made the three eligible was their ability to speak English to counter the inevitable propaganda. The aliens understood that the USA, China and Russia were the largest threats of mischief. Anything that weakened that would increase the chance of human survival on Earth. While the star travellers would not stop these people from going home, the alien strategy wanted the world to come to them in this little, previously unimportant town. That all countries, including the poorest, could not wage war, at least as long as the aliens would choose to stay, made it likely everyone would come. Goderich would not be a diplomatic post but more of an observatory. The locals might not even notice much of the alien presence. The Chinese and Russian would stay at the farm.

Ellie's un amplified voice filled the square as she repeated the message that Elliana had spoken in Washington.

"Goderich," she added to end her speech, "must prepare to be the centre for most of the interactions with my star family. Unfortunately, even though we will try to be unobtrusive, life will never be the same here as you once found it. We hope it works out for the better."

"Aliens are from the devil," the shout came from near the street. A man with a long black frock and a scruffy beard stood on a small stepladder and waved over a crowd of similar men, and women dressed in ankle-length dresses and black bonnets. They had come to the Mars vigil, and many carried signs that summed up their purpose: "Mars is being punished by God." and "IP-1 is Gomorrah".

The group of zealots had been prepared to condemn the Martian settlers to death, their God's punishment for daring to leave Earth and creating a modern Babylon. The appearance of survivors, along with their alien rescuers, had forced a change in message.

"Only two things can come from the sky, God's angels, and the devil's incubi and succuba." Pastor George continued with many shouts of "Amen," and "Praise the Lord!"

"That thing on stage is one of them and we should put her to death under God's Law. She is a mongrel aberration with supernatural powers... a succubus, a witch. These," his finger swept over the stunned group of returnees from Mars, "have submitted to the evil. They should have accepted God's judgment for leaving Eden. They are cowards."

"Death to the witch, death to the mongrel, death to the cowards," chanted the knot of adherents.

To be fair to the eager believers, no one moved to carry out this death sentence. None was sure that taking on a power that could appear from the sky and fling people between planetary orbits would be a good idea. Divine protection only went so far.

"We must raise a mighty army," the man cried to justify the inaction, "and confront the hordes from Hell." He had a knack for saying some words as if he had capitalized them. In her speech, Ellie repeated the information that all military-style weapons would be useless. The preacher ignored her. His mighty army would be ill-equipped. National armies had wielded strength; now all languished in impotency.

Someone in the group began a credible a cappella version of Onward Christian Soldiers, and soon everyone had joined her. Their fervour attracted people from the crowd. The preacher smiled in anticipation of accepting tithing recruits. The death threats finally goaded the police into action, and they isolated the frenzied congregation.

Pastor George made no move to act. He chanted in an unintelligible language that one might mistake for a drunk alien in a pub.

The ominous sideshow in the square was part of a huge crisis for world faiths. Most Christians spent a good part of their lives trying to prove the truth in the old Hebrew history and its story of creation. The most important part of that required that God had chosen humans as unique in the universe. The appearance of a species that lived among the stars did not fit. Branding them as Satan's agents returned star people to their rightful place in Abrahamic condemnation. "They are not aliens at all, but devils", had become the dominant orthodoxy of preachers, priests, rabbis, and imams worldwide. This message had grown since Jimmy Smith's sensational video of Ellie leaving Ottawa. It fed on the movie monster image of aliens. It required little thought or understanding.

A televangelist from Houston had been the first to take advantage, marketing a bottle of blessed oil for twenty dollars plus shipping and handling. He spent one complete episode of his television show in an elaborate ceremony that blessed cases of the protective elixir. He promised buyers that this would protect them from Satan's angels from the sky. A company in Sioux City, Iowa converted twenty cents' worth of soy oil and lavender into vials of gold. They could not keep up with the demand.

Others rushed to fill the gap, and from many holy places in North America and Australia, the faithful could source everything, from a book of anti-alien prayers and "kill-songs", to a copper bracelet that generated a force field against cosmic weapons and cured arthritis. By the time the aliens rescued the Martian settlers, millions of dollars had changed hands. The appearance of actual aliens would lead to exponential growth.

Church services roused the believers into frenzy with the thundering message from pulpits being "death to aliens". "Death to scientists" also joined the chants. In the USA, these services inevitably ended with hundreds or thousands of throats singing The Battle Hymn of the Republic.

The roar of hostility drowned out the voices of the moderate leaders of all religions advocating acceptance and understanding.

Ellie watched the preacher and frowned. She had believed that the more powerful governments would be the biggest threat, but she, and those on the ships above, now saw that the mass solidarity they hoped for would not be easy and perhaps impossible. An intense debate occupied the minds living on the thousands of vessels that swarmed the inner solar system: to stay or immediately abandon this bright Earth to human destruction.

RoH had been wandering Jaden's mind, sensing the disquiet and hopelessness. The young woman had not suffered the trauma that Rick had revealed at Charlie's house, but Jaden had been on the brink of suicide. RoH saw a new light in the young woman's eyes; a spark that she knew meant Jaden felt a fresh purpose, a hope. RoH had not tinkered. The feeling came from within Jaden, her reaction to this new reality of something larger than her previous life.

Is there enough time, RoH contemplated Jaden, *to connect with humans one at a time?*

Emily noticed the change as well, and her smile grew wide.

"Emily," RoH gripped her hand, "you are one of my first friends on Earth. As long as I am here, I want you to remain my friend. I hope that's forever. I want Jaden to be my guide. Can she stay with me? We will be at a farm near town and will visit often."

Chapter thirty-nine

Fliers in the cockpit; a farmer in the dell and the voice from hell

The sudden arrival of hundreds of Martian refugees created an instant crisis for local authorities. Goderich could not absorb so many needing housing and food, especially since the media onslaught of the past months had taken up most motel rooms.

"What can we do?" The mayor, still in semi-shock, had cornered the OPP commander. "Those aliens didn't think this through, dumping all these folks on us."

The mayor had been happy with the off-season business that the alien frenzy had brought. It no longer seemed a free ride, now that the aliens were real. The star people had deliberately created this local crisis, both to reinforce Goderich as their point of contact, but also to show that they did not intend to foster, be caregivers or spoon-feed solutions to humans.

"Ah, be happy, Jack," the OPP corporal put a hand on the mayor's shoulder, "that Wiarton woodchuck won't be able to compete with Goderich Grey Men."

His laughter hid worry. The mayor did not want to laugh. He had made urgent calls to Toronto, but so far, no response. Mustering busses to transport four-hundred people to London appeared to be almost as impossible as providing rescue ships for Mars. As a temporary solution, they moved the arrivals to the YMCA in a school bus commandeered from Pastor George. As the night passed and word spread, townspeople arrived at the Y with food, blankets, and clothes. When people discovered a refugee had a baby, the only real Martian-born human, toys and other supplies poured in. By nightfall on New Year's Day, a mound of surplus gifts provided a windfall for various charities.

Bobby Briscoe and the rest of the reporters swarmed the few refugees who were stable enough to talk. Life on a starship had not been exciting. They had jumped from a few months of fearing death to breathe good Earth air and labouring against higher gravity. It overwhelmed them.

As the town struggled to accommodate the refugees, a bright light over the airport went un remarked, except by the police and soldiers guarding the C-130. Engineers from Trenton had restored the front landing gear and windscreen and brought the craft to what they thought was flight-ready; however, despite their best efforts, the electrical systems remained dead. New batteries had died in seconds. The plane had languished and captive to the argument between Canada and the USA.

A purple light startled the Mountie sheltering from the cold in an SUV idling beside the craft. He slammed the vehicle into drive and blindly shot into the snowbank at the edge of the runway. Brilliance bathed the C-130 and the cargo door dropped to the ground. Navigation and cockpit lights blazed into life. The rest of the guards rushed from the terminal and saw the pilot at the controls.

A stunned Captain Eugene Honoree sat in the left seat of the C-130. It seemed he had just been watching aliens on television, and now he sat in his old seat. His civilian clothes reminded him of his ordeal.

"Bob, what the hell is going on?" Honoree looked to his right.

Lieutenant Robert Kowalski appeared equally confused in the adjacent seat. Before he could reply, Flight Engineer Sanchez appeared from the cargo bay. He had slipped on Air Force coveralls. The plane shuddered as the rear cargo ramp closed on its own.

"Captain, can we get out of here before anything worse happens?" Sanchez dropped into the third seat.

Sanchez's voice stirred Honoree to action. He ignored the checklist and acted as if they were under fire. For all he knew, they might be. Engine number three spun up on the battery and stabilized, then four, two and finally, one. Out of the corner of his eye, Honoree saw flashing lights from a police car.

"We have company," Kowalski muttered, "flaps 50, no time for checks and warm-up."

The captain pulled full-throttle and released the brakes. They still pointed for take-off over the lake. He held the yoke centre and the empty plane hurtled down the runway. The cop car faded behind.

"98", Kowalski called out.

Honoree pulled back on the yoke just as the runway disappeared into the black abyss of Lake Huron. They were going home.

"Bob, call Selfridge and tell them not to shoot us down."

To be safe, Honoree flew low, trusting his sensors. He kept all the navigation lights on and turned on the transponder. Selfridge would not think they were trying a sneak attack. Honoree did not know that all the larger weapons at the base had ceased functioning.

The actual sun rose above the hill on New Year's Day morning, bathing the farm in light, but even the bright sun could not offset the bitter cold that had come overnight on a strong north wind. It had blown the overcast away with arctic breath. A massive snow squall lay to the north.

Captain Fontaine had just settled in after a night of emotional partying with Armand and Beta-Nine. Ghislaine drifted into sleep with a smile, thinking of the woman's sci-fi name. Despite her fatigue, slamming truck doors startled Fontaine awake. When the guard arrived to wake her, the captain had boots on and gun belt secured.

"We have company," the guard seemed serious but had a strange smirk, as if the situation were a joke. "An old farm couple just drove in."

Before Fontaine could move, the door swung wide and a middle-aged couple strode in. He wore insulated coveralls and green and yellow farm boots. She had dressed in a long quilted overcoat with a bright red wool cap. Ghislaine thought the woman looked like a blue penguin.

The woman extended her hand, before realizing her lack of courtesy, and removed her woollen mitten. Fontaine took the offered shake and raised her eyebrow in question.

"They gave us the job," the woman spoke, "to be in charge of the farm. We decided looking human male and female would be less upsetting."

"I..." Fontaine struggled to frame a question.

"You and your people will provide security here," the female continued. "Goderich will be our point of contact with Earth."

"I have no orders," Ghislaine finally blurted out.

"Your government has already agreed. They will inform you soon. We want you here because RoH likes you and says you are a good person." The woman stared at Fontaine for a few seconds. "I agree, but then she knows humans more than I could."

Fontaine sat, stunned at no longer being the boss.

"Don't worry, the male added. We will consult with you on everything operational, your comfort, and all the other things important to you. For anything else, we won't surprise you. Call us Jake and Elsie."

Ghislaine giggled. These seemed like characters from some ancient television show.

"We have archived every electromagnetic broadcast from Earth since your year 1898. Any of us preparing for stationing in your solar system must absorb it all. Our names came from those transmissions. We don't always understand the nuances."

Fontaine found this admission of imperfection to be reassuring.

"We brought your friends from Mars last night to prepare you for our presence. Expect a Chinese couple and a Russian officer this afternoon. We do not intend to harm anyone. But you are tired," Elsie looked at Ghislaine, "go back to sleep, and we can work out the details this afternoon. Jake and I have things to do."

Bobby Briscoe and Jimmy Smith had not slept since the event in Goderich. After a night of viewing their raw video and comparing notes, they sketched out a rough script for a blockbuster television presentation and convinced Bobby's boss with the information that they had a video of Clavette hitting Mars, shot from an alien spacecraft. At daybreak, New Year's Day, they were in Bobby's car, on their way to the editing room in London. Ellie and General Danny Ringwald rode in the back seat with Siglinde. The network would carry the presentation of the video story plus a live interview with the two from the NAAP team and Ellie. They had syndicated the event to every network around the world.

By the morning of January 1st, all the major religions of the world had split into two opposite views of the aliens. One side claimed that their god sent angels in answer to a variety of prayer requests, from the salvation of the Mars settlers to world peace. The majority camp claimed the aliens were "the devil's angels" and "how dare they interfere with the military" of whatever country the preachers and holy men belonged.

A rare few religious leaders renounced their beliefs, saying it had founded them on ignorant myth. A harder-to-find minority said that aliens were children of God and they should bring the lambs into the fold.

The television preachers led the charge from early morning, and most congregations heeded the call to special services during the day to pray for salvation from the proclaimed alien threat.

As the spectacle began from the London studio, a robust mob of chanting picketers had gathered outside. Nervous London cops and a security guard were all that stood between the restless mob and the doors.

The presentation began on time. A half-circle of stuffed leather-covered chairs supported the five participants. The network had provided video of the spectacular arrivals in Ottawa and Washington, with cell phone video from Russia, China, Kenya and Australia. The opening ended with Jimmy's visuals of Ellie leaving Ottawa at Dow's Lake and the barn exploding as he and Ellie escaped the police.

Bobby introduced Jimmy. The visual shifted to a starry black void with a small disc rushing towards the camera.

"That is Clavette," Jimmy said. "I shot this from a view port on an alien ship. I won't say anything, just watch."

Clavette spent several minutes committing suicide on-screen. Then the scene jumped to a view of the crowd that Jimmy had videoed from the raised platform at the courthouse in Goderich. He had panned over hundreds of new arrivals in Martian jump suits and then to Siglinde, Ted and Ellie on the stage. The view cut to what Bobby had shot from the audience, showing a huge alien disc in glorious detail. The purple column suddenly lifted to the ship, and it disappeared so rapidly one could wonder if it had ever been there.

"I guess people can say we are lying and this is a hoax," Jimmy said, "because we all were there and that's too convenient." It was a pre-written cue for Danny Ringwald, who sat in uniform.

"I'm Daniel Ringwald, an American general, or at least I was. I worked for some years with a semi-secret organization called the National Agency for Aerial Phenomena, NAAP. We were carrying on the investigative work that began in Roswell, New Mexico, in 1947. Yes, a so-called flying saucer crashed, although they displayed the debris of a real weather balloon. It just had nothing to do with the alien ship. It's a long story, and hopefully, we will make the NAAP files public."

"We have copies," Siglinde again spoke up, "and I will release them. They matter less now that we have met aliens." She reached out and squeezed Ellie's hand.

"Now you all have seen aliens," Bobby looked into the camera. "Carry on, General."

"Although I worked with NAAP, I was a spy, employed by the CIA anti-alien operation based in Fort Belvoir, Virginia. NAAP was to find aliens, and we were supposed to capture them, or something. You can see how arrogant are we to think we can go toe to toe with such power? Now they have taken away our toys so we can't even hurt each other unless we look each other in the eye. As a soldier, I tell you that is a hard thing to do."

"The CIA imprisoned Ellie's mother and father at a farm near Goderich. They planned it years ago when they discovered that Ellie's father had moved there after she left on a ship. The aliens captured some of those agents and dropped them into Goderich a few weeks ago. I was in charge of the Goderich operation, but realized the situation and helped Lisa and Charlie escape, under fire, I might add."

"Canada has the rest of the CIA agents locked up. I'm sure Washington is throwing a tantrum to get them back. Thanks to our friends," he looked at Ellie, "they can't invade."

"Now we all know about the aliens," Ringwald stared directly into the camera, "what do we do? They tell us we must get together and cooperate, not exploit each other if humans are to survive. Can we?" Danny stopped.

"The question is larger," Siglinde jumped into the pause. "Ellie's daughter, RoH, told me that if we can survive and tap into the potential of everyone, we could be able, one day, to travel the stars. There is an idea, what we thought was just a hypothesis called the great filter. It suggested that an intelligent species like humans had to pass many gates and most would fail and die. RoH showed me that many species on countless planets have reached where we are and died. Just by existing, the aliens show us that success can happen. She mentioned at least one other star species." Siglinde might have been a trained actor as she turned to the camera. "Can we make it three?"

Bobby hoped the eyes of the global viewers had not glazed over at Siglinde's lecture.

"I hope so," said Ellie. "You must treat each other with equity and care. Empathy and caring are basic human traits that have disappeared from the star travellers. I hope we can find it again from you. That is the only thing my star family hopes to take from Earth, to learn to have empathy and love like most humans."

"Do not forget, you are brothers and sisters on one fragile planet. Your artificial borders and divisive beliefs are irrelevant when you look at earth from space. One aspect of that great filter ensures that conquest and power do not motivate any star travelling species. There has never been and never will be a galactic war. Species that do not learn to behave on their planet never live to fight among the stars. This is hope for Earth and the galaxy."

Bobby then told his story, and Jimmy added his experiences from when the rumours of flying saucers broke in September. Almost two hours passed with no throat cutting from the producer to end it. The story captivated and stunned the studio crew and there were no sponsors. The global syndication money reflected more than a year's advertising revenue.

Along with all the other feeds, the programme played live on the gigantic screen outside the front of the studio. It enraged the gathered fanatics.

The chants from outside grew more frenzied and loud enough to penetrate the studio.

"Death to the alien, she is the voice of hell. Death to the alien Jezebel."

A few of the rabble dropped their signs in the snow and walked away.

"I understand you have a daughter," Bobby hurried to finish the interview. The hostile chants made him nervous. Ellie calmly smiled and appeared to be peering through the walls.

"Yes, I have a daughter named Â طنإلإ," Bobby glanced around, relieved that the sound of Ellie saying the alien name had not exploded every light in the studio.

"I won't talk about her. She will be available on her terms if she decides. She is more powerful than I am, and she is more loving."

"I can vouch for that," Siglinde added.

"You must understand," Ellie continued, "I am human and love the Earth and want to love everyone here. My daughter loves Earth. She has more than half star genes and was born out around a star system that is invisible from Earth. Mother, Father, and I call her RoH, short for Roberta Heather. RoH represents the next step in sentient evolution in the galaxy."

"Many of us might blow roofs off barns," Ellie giggled, "but if RoH did that, she likely would go back and restore it. That being said, she can blow up barns."

After the presentation, they gathered in the front lobby of the station. They could see the mob through the glass doors. Bobby and Jimmy stood to one side chatting with station people. Many seemed afraid of Ellie and snuck furtive glances. Siglinde and Danny flanked Ellie as if to protect her. Bobby finally came to them.

"I'll go bring my car around back. The mob isn't there."

"No," Ellie firmly said, "we'll go out the front. Bring your car to the end of the driveway on the road."

The doors opened and the snarling mob surged forward but stopped so abruptly that the following herd knocked some at the front onto the ice and snow. Ellie led the way, surrounded by a glow. Somehow, the colour had deepened to a royal purple.

The facade reflected cries of: "Blood of Jesus save us." Some expected to die on the spot. Many of the flock had what looked like blood smeared on their foreheads, as if asking God for protection in some grotesque mimicry of the Hebrew pass-over.

Ellie advanced towards the wall of stunned demonstrators. The glow extended to cover Siglinde, Danny and Jimmy. They turned down the driveway, and the crowd parted to let them pass. One preacher leading the frenzy likened it to the parting of the Red Sea.

The light around Ellie turned to a faint golden. A few stunned onlookers later claimed that she was the light-haired Mary the Mother that Roman churches depicted. The crowd went deathly quiet and watched them climb into Bobby's car and speed away.

"I've arranged for police to guard the hotel," Bobby said.

"That's good for appearances." Ellie reached over and squeezed his hand. "It won't be necessary for us, but we want humans to be in control as much as possible. We will only intervene to prevent anyone getting hurt, the mob," she glanced back, "or us and our friends."

"What if that mob attitude is the majority?" Siglinde sighed.

"I hope it isn't," Ellie twisted to look at her friend in the back seat. "It is a thing humans need to solve. Ignorance and superstition will be the largest hurdle for humans to clear. If you can't, I'm selling tickets to Z263-A. It's a nice Earth-like planet with sentient beings who would love alien company. Humans would be alien enough for them. I like Earth better."

"I don't think we will defeat superstition," Danny muttered.

"If we withdraw," Ellie said, "you will have another religion, like your cargo cults in primitive, isolated tribes. You will see lots of icons of our ships and some grotesque statues of me and the others." Ellie giggled. "I detected some of that mob reconsidering. I have hope."

"Actually," she added, "perhaps those old Greek gods were based on a visiting star species. There is the one that visited Earth about that time. The native stories document some of it, with their mythic overlay. Maybe the Greeks did too. Perhaps the Greek myths gave them grotesque behaviours that the species did not have. We don't know if they act like Greek gods since they have isolated themselves. Maybe, when they saw what the Greeks said about them, they left in disgust. However, any star travelling species would have seen some strange behaviour from primitive, sentient species like humans, so I think nothing could be disgusting, just scientifically curious."

"You sound like Spock," Danny laughed.

"He was an alien," Ellie smiled.

The car arrived at the hotel. The four disappeared inside and Bobby drove off, leaving the police to deal with the cavalcade of pursuing vehicles. Many zealots would spend a long, chilly night chanting and sermonizing in front of the hotel.

In the morning, as the chaos developed in Goderich, a woman in the uniform of a service worker walked out the front doors of the hotel in London. The early hour had subdued the crowd, and she passed easily and went down the street. At the first block, Ellie turned the corner and hurried along. Steve Jorgensen kept early hours, and she knew he had a lecture at ten. That would give her enough time. Her face flushed with excitement.

"A coffee...?" Steve moved to the pot, always hot on the cupboard near his desk.

They eyed each other over the rims of mugs. Steve became uneasy.

"Why are you here?" Steve sipped his coffee. "I hope you don't look at us as just some sort of cosmic coffee shop."

"Take me to your Tim Horton." Ellie laughed. "You know what we want and speaking of coffee shops, togetherness."

"I thought the aliens might just be looking for busy work."

"My star friends didn't run out of things to do," Ellie said. "They lost sight of why they should do them. In 1947, that accident stirred up many new questions. If they could show excitement, they would have been excited. They hope humans will force them to hold on to that new desire."

"No," Steve leaned towards Ellie, "why are you, Ellie Keys, here talking to lowly Steven Jorgensen? I don't think you need a linguist, but thanks for asking."

Ellie flushed slightly and leaned close to Steve.

"Because I love you," the words seemed inadequate to match the feelings that had grown in a little girl in the Dakotas, warmed her through the loneliness of the stars, and now brought her back to the one human, other than her parents, her heart could completely embrace.

"I'm 18 years older than you." Steve's shocked voice whispered.

"Oh, Steven," Ellie said, "love isn't sexual, it's deeper. Sex, from what I have learned from Liz and Dawn, is simply the icing on the cake. Maybe we will eat a lot of cake." She winked. "Up there, 18 years is nothing."

"We need you as a linguist. Having Rachel thrown in is a bonus. She is smart and open. I have cared for you since your kindness when I was little. I had thought I was just on a technical mission when I recruited you, but Liz Dafoe woke me to my genuine feelings."

Steve remained stunned.

"I had not considered... would never have guessed... I'm not sure I have those same feelings." Tears and smiles competed on Steve's face.

"I had to let you know how I feel and expect nothing in return. You bring the same happiness you gave me in the Dakotas so long ago. I don't know if we can ever be a couple in the human physical or cultural sense," Ellie said, "but I hope we can spend lots of time together. You reaffirm my human essence."

Ellie hugged Steve.

Chapter Forty

Departures, arrivals and dreams

Quantz, I often think this has been a dream, sometimes a nightmare. I wanted my daughter back so much. The reality of it is almost too much to believe.

On January 2nd, 10 buses idled in front of the Y loading the refugees for the trip to London. Tractors and pickup trucks rushed down Suncoast Blvd, blocking it and keeping the busses in the parking lot. The blockage overwhelmed the OPP. Honking and chanting, along with several impromptu hymn-sings, disrupted the area. Many farmers and others held fundamentalist religious beliefs and had organized this to support the bigoted messages from their pastor. Some simply hated all governments. When the OPP asked them to move, one belligerent pickup driver, sporting a huge Canadian flag, said, "Make us."

Goderich authorities were eager to send the refugees on their way, and the refugees now wanted to reunite with families and friends. Sanitary and sleeping conditions had deteriorated.

Just after lunch, a little girl walked off Bayfield Road onto the blocked street. She stopped and placed her hands on her hips. Despite the bitter cold, she wore no coat. The loud rabble paused. One woman rushed towards the girl with a blanket, fearing the little one would freeze.

"Move your vehicles away." RoH shouted. "Let my friends leave."

The little girl suddenly transformed from a vulnerable child to a hated enemy. The woman with the blanket threw curses at RoH.

RoH gave the woman a sad look.

"In the name of God, die!" The bearded pastor from the night at the square advanced, fists balled. A posse followed.

RoH raised both arms and brought her hands in front of her face. The attackers took that as her trying for futile protection and charged. RoH waved her hands to the sides. The charging mob froze, unable to move.

RoH walked forward and passed through the helpless line, and repeated her arm motions. Vehicles slid sideways and came to rest beyond the snow banks as she advanced. Their drivers and onlookers followed them in fear. She progressed along the street until the main road out of town. She then returned at a leisurely pace and reached the driveway to the Y. She had left the two heavy tractors in place, blocking the way. The mammoth machines suddenly flew into the nearby field and rested upside down. RoH walked to the mayor.

"We did not want to intervene," RoH said, "but these people have suffered enough. Get the buses out now. We do not want to do this any longer than needed."

"I think you've riled them up even more."

"We have calculated," RoH looked towards the street and frowned, "that an extreme believer in myths and traditions will seldom change. Most of these won't." She nodded towards the street. "But some will," she added hope.

The mayor winced. He attended church and the faith community respected him. His beliefs had already changed.

"I hear you can alter minds," the mayor said. "Why don't you do that to these folks, to all of us?"

"We have no desire for puppets. You humans must work out what you will do in this new reality. You now know you are not alone in the universe, and that removes the concept of specialness. Religions that believe they are God's chosen will always find a reason to reject reality. It is how they justified slavery by defining others as outside their god's grace. They will preach that against my star family."

RoH stared deeply into the mayor's eyes.

"Those of you who believe in a god will have to work that out."

The mayor shrugged and went off to make sure the buses moved.

After the buses had left, RoH walked back along the street, restoring each vehicle to where it had been before she had acted.

Charlie and Quantz watched the latest alien coverage on television. Live-action had given way to replay of the past few days, especially the happening on Suncoast Boulevard in Goderich. With sunset at about 5

PM, things had quieted down. RoH had disappeared and the parking lot of the Y sat empty.

"That's RoH," Charlie had pride in the actions of his granddaughter.

"I hope I can talk with her too," Quantz made a note on his cell.

A loud rapping on the door interrupted.

"Grandfather," RoH's voice came through, "can we come in?"

Charlie hurried to the door, eager to embrace the girl and hoping Ellie was with her. He yanked the door open.

"Hi, Rob," Kerri smiled. Charlie slumped against the wall. "How...?"

"Can we come in?" RoH stepped from behind Kerri and strode past Charlie and towards Quantz, leaving her grandfather to Kerri.

"I'm RoH. I hear you want to talk." She took Quantz's hand.

Behind her, Kerri embraced Charlie, gently at first, but with a sudden urgency that woke him from his stupor. He returned the hug. They kissed.

"They have skilled doctors up there," Kerri smiled. "They can even bring you back from death."

She and Charlie snuggled on the couch. RoH sat in a large chair sipping a hot chocolate. It had been chilly on Suncoast Boulevard. Quantz was busy gathering up his possessions, intending to vacate the hotel.

"You weren't dead." RoH seemed nonchalant. "I kept you from actually dying, but we had to fool everyone. We had to expose that nasty bunch of men. The cops had to think you were dead for that to happen."

"Well, thanks, but did it have to happen at all? Could you not have stopped them before they shot me?"

"The CIA surprised us. We didn't consider the emotions of that Greg guy. He acted out of anger and made it unpredictable. By the time I realized, I couldn't get there in time."

"What, no fancy alien transporter stuff?" Charlie laughed.

"They weren't close enough, Grandpa, and it's not transporter stuff, but gravity manipulation... takes less energy and at least is possible. They know I can take care of most situations. Once it happened, I had to call father to take Kerri for help."

"I found it nice on that ship," Kerri said, "but I wished you were there, too."

I know, Dad, but you will love someone one day now that your heart has healed. Charlie remembered Ellie's words the first day she had returned.

"Maybe, one day, my granddaughter will give us a joy ride."

"One day, Grandpa, but your ride might be because we have no choice. I hope not."

"Quantz," Charlie finally realized what his friend was doing; "you don't need to move out. Kerri and I are going to stay at my place if it's safe... RoH?"

"It's safe, Grandpa; it will always be safe for you, from now on."

"I'll stay here to chat with this nice man." She looked at Quantz.

Charlie held the door and Kerri slipped into the passenger seat of the Martian X. His house was just ten minutes away on the far side of the river.

The Martian X descended the long grade and sped deftly over the Maitland River at Donnybrook Bridge and up the steeper south side of the valley. Charlie dozed and dreamed as the autopilot took him through the night. He had been in Orangeville, training the factory people there, and looked forward to home and bed. He would go into the Goderich factory and check in with Kerri later tomorrow.

About one in the morning, the black car came to a gentle stop in his driveway. Soon he sat on his couch and sipped a drink, thinking of his bed. Idly, he flipped on the television cable news from the CBC.

"This just in," a voice overlaid a shaky image of a brilliant burst in the sky, "we have seen strange bright lights over parts of southwestern Ontario."

His cell jingled, and a text popped up. Maybe Lisa had finally replied after her strange message early yesterday. Charlie frowned. The usual sender handle was missing, replaced with a star symbol.

"Are you awake, Dad?"

The doorbell chimed.